Praise for the Band of Four

"Greenwood continues to give his audience exactly what they want—(a) fast, furious read." —*Publishers Weekly*

"Amazing and indescribable . . . thrilling action . . . fantastic magic . . . fast paced with an enormous barrage of pyrotechnics . . . all the genius of Greenwood action with all the genius of Greenwood characterization . . . " —*Dragon*

"A new series, a new land, and a band of adventurers we can root for—it's got everything a fantasy fan could ask for and more. Much more." —*SF Site*

"*The Kingless Land* . . . supercharged action and attention to detail that will undoubtedly satisfy Greenwood's core audience. There's more than enough arcane magic, pumped-up swordplay, and gory injury for the most dedicated gamer." —*Quill & Quire*

"A new world of magic and bold deeds . . . a graceful tale of high fantasy." —*Library Journal*

"Agreeably entertaining all the way." —*Booklist*

"Energetic." —*Kirkus Reviews*

"Creating fantasy requires imagination and a deft, but subtle, and which Ed Greenwood has long showed himself capable of in his creation of the *Forgotten Realms* world. Ed's skill lies in his ability to make the ordinary magical, and integrating magic and legends so thoroughly in his work. His sense of humor and drama combine in wondrous adventure tales with depth and pacing that makes his books single sitting treasures." —Mike Stackpole

A DRAGON'S ASCENSION

A Tale of the Band of Four

——◆——

ED GREENWOOD

A TOM DOHERTY ASSOCIATES BOOK
NEW YORK

A DRAGON'S ASCENSION: A TALE OF THE BAND OF FOUR

Copyright © 2002 by Ed Greenwood

Maps by Miguel Roces

A Tor Book
Published by Tom Doherty Associates, LLC
175 Fifth Avenue
New York, NY 10010

www.tor.com

Tor® is a registered trademark of Tom Doherty Associates, LLC.

ISBN 0-765-34144-1
Library of Congress Catalog Card Number: 2001054052

First edition: March 2002
First mass market edition: February 2003

Printed in the United States of America

0 9 8 7 6 5 4 3 2 1

To Shaiyena

Let Your Road Be Bright
Your Heart Happy
Your Friends Many
And Your Chest of Memories Shine

The foe of the Serpent
Is the Dragon.

No true crawling viper
But a black-robed mage
Heart darker than garb of night
Hands adrip with blood
His spells so deep
Crawl and creep
Beyond death and passing years
Kings falling, towers crumbling
Always watching,
Lurking in shadows
Slithering in dark dreams
The Serpent Who Shall Rise Again.

Whispers he to princes
Steals he into minds by night
Men of malice chant his name
Grasping fools fill his fane
Crowns tumble before his fangs
Men mutter of him, and cower
True crawling viper, after all
Yet stand against him not in vain
Keep sword sharp to be his bane
Stray not to peaks snow-cloaked deep
Ruins forgot, nor echoing grot
Hunt no wyrms, gold aseeking

For the foe of the Serpent
Is the Dragon.

from *The Way of Valor*
by the Bard Haelithe of Ranshree
penned in the days of King Gaur
(Too long ago.)

From the Chronicles of Aglirta:
A History

*N*ow in the Time of Many Wizards, when all Darsar sought the Dwaerindim and realms rose and fell with each passing season, there arose in Aglirta four heroes, who were destined to give the Kingless Land a king once more—though to many it seemed not the salvation and peace for all Asmarand that had been foretold.

This Band of Four arose in desperation, in the time after Baron Blackgult sought to gain an edge in his long feud with the rival house of Silvertree, and made war upon the rich Isles of Ieirembor, seeking to make their tall timber and trade-metals his own, but was vanquished, and hurled back with great loss of armsmen and armaragors, Blackgult himself being thought lost in the fray.

Then did the cruel Faerod Silvertree, the fell magic of his Dark Three wizards his main weapon, seize the barony of Blackgult, and he made war on the other baronies nigh his own holdings, and flourished. So great was the rise of his power that it seemed that he would soon be King in Aglirta, whose king had slept for years beyond the memories of living men.

Then did two desperate warriors of Aglirta—the great armaragor Hawkril Anharu, most trusted of Blackgult's blades, though he refused all rank; and his closest friend, the barb-tongued and nimble procurer Craer Delnbone— return as outlaws to Aglirta, and made so bold as to try to steal gowns from the Lady of Jewels—Faerod Silvertree's own daughter—from her very palace bedchamber. She being skilled in sorcery, her father's Dark Three had trained but also enslaved her, making Silvertree Castle her prison, and planning someday that she'd be bound into its very stones, to serve them as a living fortress. Thus Embra Silvertree, who could have slain the two thieves, instead made pact with them to carry her away.

Pursued by her father's forces, the three fled to the Silent House, the cursed and long-abandoned mansion of House Silvertree, and there did meet with an aging healer, Sarasper Codelmer, who could take the shape of a long-fangs—called by some a "wolf-spider"—among other forms. Sarasper was friend unto Craer from long before, but was in hiding from all men to escape being enslaved, as barons chained all healers for their usefulness.

So the Band of Four were born, as merry a band of rogues as ever enlivened bards' ballads, and in their strivings Faerod Silvertree and his Dark Three were thrown down, and the Sleeping King awakened, to rule from Flowfoam once more.

King Kelgrael Snowsar rewarded them for their deeds with the titles of Overdukes of Aglirta, in the same wise as he made the returned Baron Blackgult Regent of Aglirta, ere returning to his spellbound Slumber—for only when Kelgrael slept could his age-old foe, the fell and most mighty archwizard remembered by men only as the Serpent, be held also asleep, and away from the world he so desired to rule.

Yet in all this strife of ambitious barons and wizards, of folk everywhere seeking the four powerful Dwaer-Stones, the folk of Aglirta were grown tired indeed of misrule. And they turned to the worship of the Serpent, whose scaled priests—who were not priests at all, but wizards who as they grew in power took on more and more of the shapes of snakes—led them into intrigues that sought the Crown of Aglirta. They turned also to various barons, who hungered after the same thing, hoping each one would become the great king that Aglirta had lacked for so long, who would restore peace and justice to the Kingless Land, so folk could rest easy and the land flourish at last.

And all the while outlander mages eyed the rich Vale of Aglirta and thrust their own hands into the fray, and the fabled Faceless lurked behind all, and the Band of Four rushed hither and thither, seeking to set wrongs aright.

Yet the slaughters and Dwaer-seekings continued apace, and none of all those hard-riding folk foresaw the Great Doom rushing to meet them.

Or rather, the apocalypse that their own deeds were bringing down swift and hard upon their beloved Aglirta—and all Darsar around it.

A
DRAGON'S
ASCENSION

Prologue

*L*amplight flickered back from the bright-polished rims of a dozen Delcamper shields. A young man in a magnificent silk shirt stared past rich blue tapestries into that dazzle, and murmured, "For if all the world my love forsake . . . her life like a flame the wind doth take . . . doth take . . ."

He sighed heavily, tossed his parchment down, and speared an innocent quace-fruit with his quill. "Oh, to be the bard they think I am!" he quoted darkly, glowering out his open window at the stars.

Flaeros Delcamper brought his boots up onto the gleaming top of his best bedchamber table with a crash, and leaned back in his chair.

Fighting dragons was easy—now, composing ballads, *that* was hard.

The shore breeze rose, bringing the familiar tang of the sea to him. Restlessly, Flaeros swung his feet back down and sprang upright, striding across the room in an idle parody of a gliding, courtly dance. Slapping his palms down on the sill, he stared out over Ragalar Bay, its waters shimmering under the light of the rising moon and the familiar vault of stars.

He'd stood here on early evenings for years, looking out at a little slice of Darsar—a slice that rolled or blew past uncaring how haughty or coin-bright the Delcampers might be, or noisy and bustling the gray city of Ragalar might become. His great-great-grandsire had stood in this room when as young as he was now, and undoubtedly stared out at these same stars. This castle, Varandaur, seat of the Delcampers, had stood here like a grim, weary fang of stone for five centuries at least, looming over this corner of Ragalar Bay—the tower he was standing in, all nine floors of it, actually overhung the waters, jutting up and out above the spray like the prow of a great stone ship, and—

A chime sounded musically behind him. Flaeros whirled around. *What could befall at this time of night?*

It sounded again, like a discreet servant's cough. The Bard of the Delcampers smiled thinly, and called, "Enter!" Then he raised an eyebrow. "Janthlin?"

"Of *course*, Lord Flaeros," came the dignified reply.

The bard turned back to the window, so that only the stars saw his smile flash into a broad grin. *Janthlin always sounded so world-weary, so pained to humor the nobles he served.* Face composed, Flaeros turned his head. "What brings you up here after moonrise?" he asked the row of shields. "Is someone in need of a song?"

"Nay, m'Lord. We are well supplied with music, downhall. A minstrel of the road is harping in return for candle-feast and a bed. He's come from Aglirta, he says, an—"

Flaeros whirled around and strode past the servant like a rising storm. "*Yes,* Janthlin, you've done well. My thanks! Aye, my thanks!"

The last words echoed back up the stair in his wake. The old servant turned, tottering slightly, to watch the young lord's shadow race down the wall, and grew a slow smile of his own.

So like his father, this one. Flits like a bird, leaps like a flame . . . Janthlin's smile died as his thought came inevitably to the next line of that old ballad.

Dies cry unheard, naught left but his name.

That was the thing about ballads. All too often, they went where you didn't want them to. Like love. Like life. Hmmph. Janthlin reached into the breast of his tunic, drew forth the flask of liquid fire he kept ready to wash away such morose, increasingly frequent thoughts—and used it.

The high, lacy harping died away into a few last, aching tones as Flaeros bounded down the Urdragon Stair and paused on the landing overlooking the High Hall.

Under the lamps below, a great crowd of servants jostled with Delcamper uncles in their crimson and gold, goblets dangling empty in many hands. And no wonder, with nary a maid hastening to refill them. Everyone was speaking at once, hurling questions at the sad-eyed man in worn leather, who sat on a stool perched atop the long feast table nearest the great open sea window, his harp still thrumming in his hands.

News from Aglirta was always worth hearing—and here was a taleteller who could be asked things, not the usual few paltry, suspect whispers heard seventh hand . . .

The minstrel looked up at Flaeros and seemed to nod slightly, though his drooping moustache made the gesture hard to read. "I came to *this* happy house," he said abruptly, his words hewing a sudden stillness out of the clamor of voices, "because amid all the latest tidings of barons' boasts and lost lasses and trade shortages, there's real news for one here: the Regent of Aglirta has put out an urgent call to parley with one Flaeros Delcamper!"

Heads turned, brows lifted, and murmurs rose. "Flaeros?" more than one uncle asked, in astonishment that might have pained the young bard had he not been hastening down the last flight of stairs so eagerly, spilling out the words, "I am he!"

The minstrel—*Three bless him!*—waved his free hand out from his harp in the flourish with which folk of music salute bards. "Lord Flaeros, I am Taercever Redcloak, harp of the road, and honored to meet you. Before you ask: I know nothing more than the bald proclamation I've just imparted. The regent hopes to see you at Flowfoam soon, for parley."

Flaeros drew himself up, feeling all eyes in Varandaur on him, and made his voice as deep and mellifluous as he knew how. "I thank you, Master of the Harp. Your music honors our house, and I'll ask no more, save what all here would know: what news rides high in Aglirta?"

The bard Taercever smiled, something akin to mockery in the twist of his lips. "The usual chaos of barons clawing for power. The waiting hands of hireswords are filling with coin in plenty again, as brigandry is so sharply on the rise."

"And is it?" the nearest uncle of Flaeros growled, waving a gleaming goblet as large as two servants' heads like a disapproving finger.

The minstrel shrugged.

"When armed men at loose ends wander so rich a realm, Lord," he told the glossy curves of his harp, "trouble always awakens, and with a sharp edge. Yet so much swift and unforeseen trouble that only dozens of lancers and scores of bowmen can quell it?"

"Aye," another uncle rumbled, "I take thy point. 'Tis a tune we've all heard a time or two too often before. So it's war again, sooner or later. Anything else?"

"A talking cow shown at market in Ibryn," the minstrel said lightly, pausing for the expected—and enthusiastically given—snorts and dismissive growls. "Oh, and something more: word hisses over all Aglirta like shaken bedsilks that the regent is looking for—*this!*"

From the folds of the weathercloak bundled beside him the minstrel plucked up something bright, that caught and flashed back hearthfire like a hand mirror. It was a scepter of massy gold swept into the likeness of a dragon's head, jaws slightly agape, atop the proud curve of a many-scaled neck.

The minstrel moved his arm slowly, so that all gathered

around him could see its magnificence. The eyes—amber-hued gems?—seemed to glitter, as if the wyrm could truly see them.

There were gasps, and some drew back. "The foe of the Serpent," someone in the crowd muttered, before Flaeros could.

And then from among the servants crowded to the fore a figure darted. A handsome steward, who thrust aside the plucking arm of a Delcamper uncle with a hand whose fingers were suddenly hissing, snapping snake-heads.

Amid the gasps and shrieks the steward never slowed, racing forward to spring up onto the feast table where the minstrel had bent to wrap his cloak around his harp.

Taercever glanced up, saw his peril, and flung the scepter in his hand—not at the rushing steward, but towards Flaeros at the foot of the stair.

The bard grabbed for it, but tried to keep his gaze on the steward's charge; the heavy scepter dealt his arm a numbing blow and clattered on the steps beside him.

A knife flashed.

Serving maids shrieked.

The minstrel sprang back.

An uncle vainly hurled a goblet and another bellowed for guards as Taercever caught his heel on his stool. It tumbled under the diving steward as his gleaming blade stabbed down, rose again—and Snake-worshipper and minstrel plunged out the window together.

There was a thunderous splash below—and everyone started running.

"Fetch the snake-head!" Uncle Hulgor shouted, his hoarse bellow cleaving the uproar like a trumpet. "I'll deal with him!"

"Three look down," Uncle Sarth snarled to Hulgor, giving his young kinsman a glare as the bard snatched up the scepter and stared at it in wonder, "but young Flaeros seems to wear drawn swords and danger like an always-flapping cloak!"

"Aye," Hulgor said with some satisfaction, as they both

drew their slender, ornamented swords and watched guards trotting into the room with halberds in their hands. "The lad's become someone of importance—in Aglirta, at least."

"Aye, Aglirta," Sarth said sourly. "Where all the troubles always are."

Yet even as Hulgor waved his blade at the window and snapped orders about boats, lanterns, nets, and hooks, Sarth stood guard over the wonder-struck bard, who was still hefting the scepter in his hand, turning it round and around as he felt something stirring within it, some magic that made his arm thrum and tingle.

"The regent must have this, and my presence, too," Flaeros murmured. "At once."

The bard sprang up the stair in a sudden charge of his own, heading back up to his chambers to prepare.

Sarth shook his head and ran after him, gasping and growling after a few flights of steps, his sword gleaming in his hand as Varandaur erupted into shouting tumult around him. He was getting too old for this. . . .

"As we all do," he grunted, slashing a particularly ugly display of crownflowers out of its urn as he passed. They fell before his blade without a fight, scattering petals in a golden rain, and Sarth raced on, his legs feeling heavier and heavier. Aye, too old by half.

Something rose dripping out of the night-dark sea, glistening wet in the moonlight as a fin grew fingers, and then a human arm. That arm took firm hold of a wet rock, and a faceless snout rose to join it.

The snout rose, thickened, and became a head that watched a second creature rise from the waters, sinuous tail curling, and grew arms of its own, its faceless head split in a great vertical mouth to spit forth onto the rock a damp cloak, wrapped around a harp.

The other shapechanger's head grew a similar gash. It

spat the steward's knife onto the stone beside the cloak, and then twisted into a jagged smile.

"Nice harping."

"I try, Indle. I try."

The Koglaur who usually went by the name of Oblarma heaved herself out onto the rocks, fins and tail melting away in the moonlight to reveal the curves of a shapely human woman. Beside her, the Koglaur often called Indle rode the gently lapping waves a little longer, tarrying to gaze back across Ragalar Bay.

Many lanterns were bobbing back and forth along the shores nigh the dark mountain of Varandaur's turrets, and torches flared and sputtered on boats cleaving the waters like an aroused swarm of fireflies.

A real firefly darted past Indle's head. A tentacle flashed out, curled, and swung over Oblarma's head. When it withdrew to become one of Indle's new fingers again, the firefly winked amid Oblarma's newly formed lustrous tresses.

"Hmm," Indle said, regarding it critically as he held out the bundle of clothing they'd hidden here earlier. "Why didn't I think of that before?"

One of Oblarma's eyes bulged from her face, thrusting forth on a finger of flesh—a stalk that curled up and back until she could gaze at the top of her own head, and see the firefly's silent blue-green flashes.

"Like a little jewel," she murmured approvingly, settling a vest around a pair of magnificent—and quite dry— breasts that hadn't been there a few moments earlier. "I rather—"

Indle hissed sharply, chopping with his hand for silence.

Oblarma gave it.

In the stillness, they heard the splash of oars, voices grumbling to each other on the boats, the thud of someone's boot against old and sodden planks—and the thunder of hooves. It sounded very like Flaeros Delcamper, riding hard with two house armaragors right behind him, and took but a few moments to die away into distant darkness. They *were* in a hurry.

"Adventure comes late to some," Indle said in satisfied tones, heaving himself onto the rocks in a flurry of spray that made Oblarma roll hastily aside to keep her clothes more or less dry. "It seems our little deception worked as well as—"

"A typical day at Flowfoam," the other Koglaur replied in dry tones. "And just like a courtier caught at treachery unawares, the real steward will be strolling home from his little Serpent-worshipping moot right about now—straight into the arms of all those hard-eyed Delcamper armaragors, and roaring-rage Delcamper uncles."

Indle gave her a little bow. "And I even managed not to stab you."

Oblarma chuckled. "Just as well. I *like* being Taercever."

"As long as you don't come boot to boot with his creditors, hmm?" Indle said, plucking up his clothes from the tall grass above the rocks.

"He died alone in the backlands six summers ago, now," Oblarma replied. "As successful as minstrels of the road ever get to be. You think he owed much coin to anyone?"

Indle shrugged. "All it takes is one debt to see a man dead—if it's the wrong one."

Oblarma's answering smile was thin. "A lesson too many folk of Aglirta seem never to learn. Who shall pay the final price next, I wonder?"

1

Gracious Hosts of Aglirta

The breeze was all too steady.

The leaves of the trees around the four riders rustled ceaselessly.

Craer frowned and hunched a little lower in his high-cantled saddle.

Hundreds of archers could be crouching within easy bowshot in this sun-dappled forest—Three take us, every second bowman could be felling trees for firewood, with the rest shouting encouragement!—and in all this hissing and roaring of foliage, riders on the road wouldn't know of the danger until 'twas too late, and they were all wearing rather too many arrows to ignore.

These four riders in particular: the Band of Four, Aglirta's only Overdukes. Four folk Craer suspected the barons of the realm—loyal, good, and otherwise—were already heartily sick of. He glanced back, collected Hawkril's calm nod, and muttered to the placid gray beneath him, "Horns of the Lady! I've lost track of where we're headed! Why can't we call on the nearest baron and then the next, in some sane sequence, instead of riding forth and back and up and down the whole blessed Vale?"

Embra's chuckle sang in the air beside him, making his horse's ears twitch.

Craer sighed; he'd forgotten her chatter spell. The Four could whisper and murmur and yet be heard by each other as clearly as if sitting in a quiet chamber with heads bent together, not riding through this windy forest spread out to deny archers an easy, massed target.

"This way," the Lady Silvertree explained with infuriating sweetness, "my fellow barons will find it just that trifle harder to play gracious hosts by thoughtfully preparing 'accidents' for us . . . or stealing away the prize we seek."

Ah, yes, the prize: the fourth magical Dwaer-Stone. Present whereabouts unknown, but held—at least on the day when they'd been made Overdukes and Embra's father Blackgult named Regent—in secret by one of Aglirta's barons.

Finding it was why the overdukes had spent far too many days riding the roads that flanked the Silverflow, crisscrossing Aglirta to visit baron after baron.

Not that Craer Delnbone had the worst task of the Four during visits. Here in the forest, as front-riding target, now . . .

"*Thank* you, Embra," he said in the most silky tones he could manage. "Now if you knew a spell to repel lurking archers instead of eavesdropping . . ."

"Gently," Sarasper's rasping voice reproved him, as if Craer were a disobedient but indulged dog. "*Gent*ly!" Treated like an unwelcome wyrm? Be then an unwelcome wyrm.

Craer growled like one of the yipping perfumed and beribboned lapdogs the Baroness Rildra so doted on, of ankle-shredding acquaintance three baronial castles back. At least he'd had the satisfaction of shaking one persistent boot-gnawing creature out a window into the moat below, under the carefully unseeing gazes of two smirking guards. What attraction even silly baronesses saw in such—

"Anything amiss, Swiftfingers?" Hawkril murmured.

Craer snorted. "An army could be tramping along beside us, hewing down trees to clear a road for their passage, and I'd hear them not." He peered ahead all the harder, as if his eyes were torches that could sear through ever-dancing leaves.

"Pray silence for the eminent Overduke Delnbone," Sarasper intoned. "Trees, attend! Winds, bow down!"

A wordless but decidedly rude sound was Craer's only reply. They were at least another day's ride away from the next baron—where once again Embra would work Dwaerindim-seeking magic from the privacy of whatever chambers they were given, whilst Hawkril stood watchful guard over her, Craer made oh-so-clever talk with stewards and guardcaptains and seneschals, and Sarasper used his spells to ward away the harm of all poisons and venoms offered to the Four in their food and flagons.

So far, they'd failed to find the missing Dwaer—and survived two poisonings, choosing to smilingly ignore the attempts to slay rather than confront their hosts.

"We're not managing much more than to make ourselves more widely disliked and offer ourselves as ready targets, are we?" Sarasper's voice came suddenly out of the breeze nigh Craer's left ear.

"Now, don't forget the chance to see Aglirta's beautiful countryside," Hawkril rumbled. "I've been a target in worse places."

"Far too much of Aglirta's beautiful countryside, I'd say," Craer grunted.

"So we spent an extra day riding the back lanes, lost and testy-tempered. A wandering that befell when one Craer Delnbone was scouting our way, if you *must* remind us," Embra told the backs of her fingernails idly.

Sarasper chuckled. "Aye, some blundering heroes we are."

"Nay, my good fellow Lord of Flowfoam, we *were* blundering heroes—now we're pushy Overdukes," Craer told the old healer triumphantly. "Try to remember that, and the necessary pomposity will flow *far* more smoothly."

Something hummed past his cheek then, so closely that it burned. Craer's horse reared with a startled sound that was almost a shriek, and the smallest of the Overdukes kicked clear of his stirrups with an alacrity that seemed suddenly far more necessary than any pomposity.

The long-anticipated arrows came leaping out of the trees in a hissing storm, flaring with enchanted fire and slowing noticeably as they reached Embra's waiting shielding spell.

"Brigands again!" Craer snarled, clawing at reins as he snatched out a dagger and tried to see exactly where the shafts were coming from and how many bows must be sending them forth. "Clear the rats from one forest, and they scurry to another!"

Embra's shielding flared into a visible glow around them as she called on her Dwaer for more strength. The arrows seeking them now hung in her spellglow by the dozens, sliding very slowly on through the air. Craer struck one aside with the edge of his dagger, freeing it from the magic—it shot away to crack and shiver among roadside stones in an instant—and ducked around the wicked point of another.

"A dozen?" he called, peering into the trees as he wrestled his snorting gray under control.

"More this side," Hawkril replied calmly. "A score, at least."

"Brigands whelm in armies these days, it seems," Sarasper grunted. "Do we try to outride them?"

As if their unseen attackers had been listening, grim-faced men in leathers sprang from the trees, leaping out from between dark trunks and twisted shrubs to block the road before the Four . . . and behind.

"Twoscore, and more," Hawkril corrected himself grimly. "Fast-breeding brigands!"

The armaragor bent low over his saddle to better reach the hilt of the great warsword slung across his shoulders— and then found himself wrestling the reins of his mount as the horse danced sideways in alarm. More men burst out of the trees close at hand, and a fresh volley of arrows sped out of those rustling leaves.

Embra gasped in pain, and her Dwaer flared into sharp brilliance. Hawkril cursed and wheeled his horse, furiously slashing aside arrows with his warsword as he went. If his lady was hurt—

The Lady Silvertree was reeling in her saddle, her face twisted, though the charging armaragor could see no arrow that had bitten to cause her that pain. Sarasper, too, was clutching his head and groaning. Unseen spell-arrows, then, that struck at those who could work magic? So—wizards in the trees, too?

No matter; the Four had to get out of this, or they *would* be slain. The real arrows were gliding ever closer, a tightening net of glowing points drawing in around Sarasper and Embra. Hawkril growled out his rising anger and plucked at the shield bouncing behind him. It was too small to cover them all, but if he could win a few moments for Embra to hurl some mighty fire, or to snatch them out of the closing jaws of this trap, it just might befall that th—

Craer abandoned his own saddle an instant before no fewer than six shafts lanced home in the flanks of his doomed gray, sweeping aside a seventh arrow as he threw himself into the road dust and rolled enthusiastically out of the gods-blessed way. In another instant his horse would come crashing down right here, rolling and screaming and kicking, and Craer did not want to be observing its painful death from right underneath it.

The procurer didn't want to be observing its painful death *anywhere*, but the Three seemed to demand that a certain foursome of overdukes provide them with frequent and violent entertainment, and. . . .

"The day does draw on," Craer told the dagger in his hand, as he sent it spinning into the face of a shouting archer who'd drawn a wickedly curved sword of his own, "and we seem to have fallen behind on our bloodletting. All of this peaceful riding about and feasting and polite over-goblets chatter must be to blame! Die, horseslaying *dog*!"

The archer gurgled, tried to reach for the dagger that sprouted in his eye, and then toppled forward without offering further reply.

Arrows were striking the ground and each other, now. Thus freed from Embra's slow-shield, they shivered along the stones underfoot or thrummed away with new vigor. Craer vaulted over one shaft, snatched another dagger from a handy sheath, and then flung himself flat to avoid another arrow as he raced back towards the hooves of Hawk's charger. Choked-off cries and oaths around him told him that some of their attackers lacked his agility.

"Ah, I suppose they're just not fit stock to be overdukes," he muttered, racing on.

"Craer," Embra snarled, something that sounded horribly like a sob in her voice, "*will* you be *silent*?"

Her next word might have been a scream, if she'd still had breath enough for screaming. It came out as a sort of horrid dry gasping, instead—that was promptly drowned out by Hawkril's roar: "Embra! *Embra!* Lass, speak t—"

It was his turn to groan and gurgle, and Craer risked a look up from his own deadly game of rolling and sprinting and flicking arrow-sighting glances right and left.

He was in time to see his oldest friend topple from the high dragon saddle, one armored shoulder bristling with arrows—as the huge horse under Hawkril twisted and lashed out its hooves at empty air in agony, its right flank a forest of quivering shafts.

Embra's shielding was melting away. They were going to die here on this sun-dappled road amid the beautiful and be-damned-rustling trees, beset by this army out of nowhere, and with noth—

Sudden purple lightings snarled and spat across the road, half-blinding him. Craer flung himself flat in a place he hoped no arrows would find, and wondered what magic was seeking their lives *now. Gods, but Aglirta seemed to hold an overabundance of folk eager to deal death. Couldn't they cleave to baronial style and provide a good feast laced with a little poison? Did their murthering attempts always have to involve road dust and searing spells and Three-be-damned arrows?*

"I can only conclude," the strained tones of Sarasper rasped next to his ear, "that you wish to proclaim to the listening land once more your usual complaint, procurer? Too much magic, wallowing in the dust, and arrows—have I captured the list rightly?"

"Fancy yourself a herald?" Craer murmured back. "So I started shouting, eh? Pray pardon . . . Embra must be still aware for the farhearing to work. I'm flat on my face, still seeing purple-and-white fire whenever I try to stare at anything—care to enlighten me as to what happened?"

"Later," the healer told him grimly. "For now, be silent, and lie still."

"Eh?"

"*Silence*, procurer!"

Something in the steely fury of Sarasper's tone made Craer obey, for once. Through slitted eyes he stared at the curling dust—just visible as lazy shadows beyond the white-and-purple fire that still danced before his mazed eyes—and waited until his sight returned enough to show him something more of what had so scared Sarasper.

Whatever it was must have slain or stunned the archers with those lightnings; the only sound was the muffled thudding of a downed horse twisting in its last throes. Craer waited tensely, dagger in hand, hoping he'd be able to see a foe before a sword or spear was driven through him.

A boot crunched on road stones very close to his head, and he heard Embra gasp. Should he fling himself wildly away, or—?

Not all that far from the roiling dust and many sprawled bodies in the road, a cautious hand closed around a knob

where once a branch had sprouted, so its owner could lean
around the curve of a dark, old tree trunk and peer through
the rustling leaves at the few figures still moving where
battle had raged moments before.

Not an arrow sang, nor did any bowman stand ready to
shoot more—yet the Overdukes of Aglirta had, it seemed,
fallen far short of victorious. The thief among them lay in
the road, motionless. But for a betraying ripple of tense,
quivering shoulders, he might have been dead.

Wincing in a half crouch on the road not far away, his
arm dark and wet with blood and transfixed by many arrows, Overduke Hawkril Anharu grimaced at a lone figure
walking slowly up the road towards him. Twice the hulking
armaragor tried to pick up his warsword in the trembling,
blood-dripping fingers of his stricken arm . . . and twice he
failed.

Beyond the armored warrior, against the ferny bank that
bounded the far side of the road, the healer and the sorceress lay huddled, the old man trying to shield the slumped,
white-faced body of the woman with his own. He, too,
glared his defiance at the lone approaching figure.

The watcher in the trees drew back, crouching low and
pressing close against the concealing trunk, yet watching
still.

Red mists of pain curled at the corners of Hawkril's vision. Spitting blood, he fought to hold them at bay, to keep
clear sight of the man now walking towards him. Tall, slender, dark, and young. Handsome, too . . . a small tattoo like
a vertical drawn dagger on his left cheek, and sharp—nay,
smouldering—dark eyes above. A few rings on long, slender fingers, those hands not marked by work. A dagger at
belt, black hose, high boots, and a dark tunic above, richly
made but bearing no device nor noble colors. Someone,
Hawk knew, he'd never laid eyes on before.

The newcomer stopped just out of reach of any desperate lunge a man of the armaragor's size might make, and

stared down at the pain-wracked warrior. His hands hung empty at his sides, but cupped slightly. Wisps of purple smoke studded with winking white sparks still rose from his palms—sparks that crackled menacingly as he raised his hands to point at Hawkril and Sarasper.

"Should I slay you all, Overdukes of Aglirta?" this unfamiliar wizard asked, his voice barely more than a whisper. "Or can you give me good reason why I should let you live?"

"Lord Baron," the old seneschal said nervously, "there's a man come to see you. In full armor, with sword ready and a dozen war-ready fighting men at his back. He gives as name only 'Little Flower.'"

Baron Nesmor Glarond smiled thinly and lifted one hand in a signal that stirred his guards into a brief flurry of drawing swords and stiffening into new positions, here and there about the throne room of Glarondar.

Their master cast a glance up at the gilded balcony and made another sign. His pages saw, turned, and snapped low-voiced but coldly firm orders. Many faces of courtiers who spent hours every day along that opulently carved rail, peering down at Baron Glarond, awaiting his smallest slip—or slightest sign of favor—abruptly vanished, amid unfriendly murmur.

Glarond lost his smile. Let them wonder at why they'd been swept away. Ambitious rabble, all, best kept distant from the bargaining ahead. Only those who mattered need, or would be allowed to, stay. His "Little Flower" was a dangerous man, and would undoubtedly drive a hard bargain; if things went poorly for the Pride of Glarond, the fewer folk who were watching, the better. Baron Glarond was well aware he was not a deeply loved man.

In a matter of moments the seneschal stood forth, near the doors, and bowed to his lord; the populace of the hall was now as the Pride of Glarond had desired it. The man on the throne nodded back, lifting his hand almost idly to indicate the doors. The seneschal turned, flung them wide, and stood back without announcing who was entering.

A near shout would have been necessary to do that heralding above the sudden, rhythmic clanking that arose then: the sound of men in full coat of plate marching swiftly in step. Into the throne room of Glarondar they came, bareheaded and empty-handed, but striding as if they were masters in this hall. They ascended the dais before the throne, and there stopped as smoothly as any formal guard on parade.

The baron's guards stiffened, eyeing the new arrivals nervously. It did not take a veteran eye to judge that they were outnumbered—and probably overmatched. Most of them failed to notice brief scuffles on the balcony stairs and along the back of the hall, as procurers in leather harness, hand crossbows held ready but pointed at the ceiling, wormed their way past courtiers and pages alike, to certain vantage points. Unfamiliar men, who stared about the hall with hard, eager eyes, seeking targets.

"Be welcome, Lord Bloodblade," Glarond said calmly, rising from his throne. "Your fame precedes you."

The man at the head of the armored throng acquired a ghostly flicker of a smile that stopped far short of his eyes, and said, "No *lord* am I yet, Glarond, though some have called me 'warlord.' Sendrith Duthjack, at your service—*if* we can come to agreement."

Baron Glarond inclined his head. "I am not an unreasonable man."

Some who stood listening in that hall might have disagreed with that statement, but no one in all that tensely frozen assembly chose to do so audibly just then. The baron was also not held to be a swiftly forgiving man.

"And I," Duthjack said clearly, "honor the pacts I make. I believe you know that."

Glarond inclined his head. "I do. I am also in the habit

of honoring pacts, as it happens. Shall we begin by my stating what I desire to hire you and the swords you command for?"

"Do so. No task is unacceptable to me, if we can agree on price—and mine shall be my first answer," Duthjack replied. His men turned in perfect unison, though no order or sign had been given, to face the courtiers on both sides—and their gauntleted hands clapped firmly to the hilts of their weapons.

The silence, when it came, sang as tightly as a drawn bowstring. More than one man in that hall swallowed—and found his throat dry in doing so.

"I desire," Baron Glarond said calmly, "to be King of Aglirta. Before first snowfall, I would sit upon the River Throne, undisputed master of all the Vale, all barons sworn to me or dead. Plain enough?"

Duthjack nodded. "Have you wizards to fight for you?"

The baron shook his head. "None," he said, in a tone that suggested he was about to say more. Instead, he fell silent. A sheen of sweat had appeared from somewhere to gleam on his brow, but he lifted his chin and stared at his armored visitors as if he already was king.

Duthjack said flatly, "Others will. Our losses will be heavy. Two thousand gold coins—sundars of Ragalar or Carraglan zostarrs, not Aglirtan minting—for every swordsman I bring to the fray. A written roster of my command, copies held by us both. Half paid out before blades are drawn; survivors only to collect the balance, by midwinter at the latest."

Glarond nodded slowly. "And your share?"

"One hundred Ragalan sundars, and a downriver barony. Brightpennant, I think."

"Loushoond," the baron countered firmly.

Silence fell, softly at first but then, as it stretched, rising in tension. The courtiers who remained in the hall glanced at each other, then swiftly looked away. No one dared gaze for long upon the two men facing each other at the heart of the hall.

Slowly, Duthjack nodded, his face thoughtful and withdrawn.

Scarcely believing it could be this easy, the baron leaned forward on his throne. Sweat was streaming down his face as he asked eagerly, "So—have we a deal?"

The man often called Bloodblade smiled. Drawing off his gauntlets and handing them to one of his men behind him, whom he did not look at, he stepped forward and held out his hand.

The baron rose from his throne, descended the single step to the dais where the mercenaries stood, and reached out to clasp Duthjack's offered grasp.

Their hands met, gripped, and a look of pain crossed Glarond's face. Before he could utter even a gasp of protest, the warlord's other hand took the baron by the throat.

Fingers of iron tightened, and the Pride of Glarond made a thin, startled, throaty sound.

Duthjack's smile was as cold as his voice. "No, my Lord of Glarond, we do not. I've taken counsel with others in the Vale besides barons, and heard other views as to the best future for the realm. Why should I settle for being a baron—among so many fat, decadent, arrogant fools of barons—when *I* can sit on the throne of Aglirta? You need me, dear Glarond . . . but I don't need you."

He drew his fingers together with sudden, quivering strength, a throat crumpled into bonelessness, and the strangled noises coming from the baron ceased. Deftly Duthjack plucked the golden coronet from the brows of the sagging Pride of Glarond—and then his shoulders tightened, muscles rippled, and the mercenary infamous as Bloodblade in a hundred bloody tales *threw* the corpse away from him. Limply it tumbled down the steps of the dais.

The baron's guards surged forward, hands on sword-hilts, snarls rising in their throats . . . and then paused uncertainly as those little crossbows rose to menace their throats and faces, all over the hall—and the Pride of Glarond came to a stop, his lolling head staring glassily and purple-faced at the ceiling in frozen, eternal startlement.

From out of the shocked group of courtiers nearest the throne a grandly dressed man stood forth in ruby silks. Clearing his throat, he gestured with one heavily ring-adorned hand, essayed a brittle smile, and called, "All hail Baron Duthjack!"

The warlord smiled, strode forward to meet the man, and said coldly, "No. I think not."

With smooth, unhurried grace he drew his sword—and ran the courtier through. As bloody steel burst out of the man's trembling back, slicing through ruby silk with the briefest of whispers, crossbows twanged all over the hall, and courtiers groaned, screamed, gasped, or gurgled—and started to fall, dying.

"Barons have been Aglirta's curse for too long," Duthjack told an old guard who stood stiffly at attention a sword's reach away, gray-white moustache trembling in fear. "It's high time, and past time, that someone should have gone baron-hunting. Not quite as good sport as chasing stags, but hopefully more profitable. Your name, old blade?"

"Th-tharim, Lord Bloodblade," the guardsman stammered, going to his knees and presenting his sword-hilt to Duthjack.

"You're wise, Tharim," the warlord said with a cold smile, "and prudent. You may live, if you serve me diligently in one small service: tell the armaragors of Glarond I'm their lord now. Baron of Glarond, if you must. Oh, and tell them one more thing: their warlord bids them arm, make ready for war, and report here two nightfalls hence, ready to ride."

"Aye, Lord Bloodblade. Ready to ride." The old warrior rose, then hesitated, waiting.

Duthjack's wintry smile widened. "No, I'm not going to tell you where. Just say: we ride to war."

The guardsman nodded. "Hunting barons along the

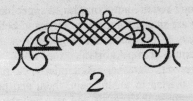

2

Saddle Deep in Adventure

The figure behind the tree leaned closer, trying not to miss a single murmur or indrawn breath of the doings in the road below. Flies were already buzzing above the heaped, ragdoll bodies of the bowmen—and the lightning that had slain them still curled around the hands of the wizard who stood in the road.

"You should let us live if you care for Aglirta," Sarasper rasped, no trace of fear in his face as he squinted at the wizard. "Too long has this land been not only kingless, but lawless, unless one holds as 'law' the ever-changing whims of unscrupulous barons and tersepts. We strive for an Aglirta where all may walk unafraid, laws are strong, and peace unbroken allows folk to harvest and craft and make coin without living always in fear of cruel barons and their . . ."

"Wizards?" the handsome young man sneered. "I think we all want peace and good rulership, healer. And bows were always better bent to take deer for the table, not men's lives." Nudging the nearest dead archer with his foot, he added, "Yet mayhap these would also claim, if they lived, that they stood to keep the peace, under the orders of a wise and just ruler—and what is there to choose between you? You are but four who swagger like brigands, while they are many, someone's command belike . . . and in these days of overdukes and regents, I cannot believe that rebel armies tramp Aglirta!"

"Who are you," Sarasper asked quietly, "to mock us?"

Hawkril snarled in urgent pain, then, and both wizard and healer turned their heads and watched the armaragor wrench an arrow forth. A gush of dark blood followed, and Hawk slumped over onto his side in the road, rocking back and forth and groaning.

Sarasper settled Embra gently back amid the ferns, rose, and went to Hawkril.

"Stay where you are!" the wizard snapped, raising a spark-spitting hand.

Sarasper knelt by his stricken friend, and said calmly, "Healing is what I do, Sir Mage. The many folk I've aided down the years, and the many more I may live to heal in years ahead, can all only hope that blasting all who don't obey you isn't the only thing *you* do."

With fingers drenched in Hawkril's blood, he fumbled for the straps and buckles of the armaragor's shoulder-plate.

"Attend me, healer!" The wizard's voice was sharp with anger. "I am Jhavarr Bowdragon, and—"

Sarasper lifted his head to look into the mage's eyes, and nodded. "You've come to Aglirta to avenge the murder of your sister," he said softly. "At the hands of a wizard, I might add."

Bright lightnings raged briefly around two clenched fists, and faded. The mage drew in a deep, shuddering breath, then said calmly, as if discussing the unremarkable weather of some days back, "You see things rightly, healer. Cathaleira Bowdragon was the most able living mage of all our family, and we two were—close. We farspoke often, and I know well that she came to love her master here in Aglirta. Yet so far as my magic can learn, she was butchered by his hands, and her sentience made part of a monster of his making. This I can scarce believe, and yet . . ."

Jhavarr's voice gathered strength again as he snapped, "Yet I've also learned that you Four helped slay that beast, sending my sister into the cold, endless sleep that none return from!"

Sarasper sighed.

"Someone has told you false: we did not," the healer explained. "Those who hacked it down also sought our deaths that night. Tharlorn of the Thunders betrayed your sister, yes—growing jealous and over-wary of her growing skill at sorcery, I doubt not. Forgive the blunt saying of this, but he cut open her body like a Sirl fishmonger gutting the biggest fish in his catch. One of his lesser apprentices, who was there and saw, confided in a friend, hoping to work a measure of revenge on Tharlorn if his master served him the same fate."

"And the famous and much-feared Tharlorn is dead," Jhavarr said grimly. "I wish I could be sure of that."

Trembling as he worked healing on Hawkril, and the armaragor shuddered beneath his hands, Sarasper looked up sharply. "You've cause to doubt it?"

Jhavarr Bowdragon drew himself up, and said slowly and coldly, "I doubt nothing because as yet I know too little. I can trust in nothing for the same reason. Yet hear this: I shall slay anyone who had any hand in Cathaleira's death. No matter where they hide or how they defend themselves. *This I swear.*"

The mage paced forward between sprawled bowmen, sighed as his gaze fell upon flies crawling on skyward-staring eyeballs, and added in gentler tones, "I know something of the ways of wizards, Sarasper. I seek the Thunder's apprentices, to make sure Tharlorn is truly dead and didn't send someone else into battle in his guise . . . and to learn if anyone else helped craft the mage-slayer."

Whirling around, he added in a whisper that was almost a sob, "All shall pay—and they'll die in pain and knowing why I take their lives. Darsar is the poorer for the loss of her—but I shall beggar it deep and proper before I'm finished!"

Hawkril winced, wrenched out another bloody arrow, and shook anew.

Sarasper nodded wearily at the wizard as the healing continued. "Usually a vain undertaking," he murmured, "and all too often one that comes to ride the avenger like a slavemaster—but none of that makes your cause less noble. I hope you find what you seek, young Bowdragon . . . and peace, besides."

They stared into each other's eyes for a long time before Jhavarr replied, in a voice that was calm again, "Thanks for those words, healer, but hear fair warning: if I learn that any of you overdukes, or Regent Blackgult, or anyone else yet living in Aglirta had anything to do with my sister's death, I'll destroy the guilty—as cruelly and painfully as I know how."

Embra swayed into a sitting position, murmuring, "H-hawk? Srass—?"

Bowdragon stared at her, then smiled suddenly, lifted ready hands, and gave them lightning.

It was not a nice smile.

Blinding-bright bolts of purple and white snarled across the road and back, washing over the folk huddled there. Sarasper reeled, Embra fell back among the ferns . . . and then Bowdragon beckoned, and his lightnings flowed back to him.

Borne within crackling coils of his magic, something came with them, snatched from Embra's breast: a mottled brown-and-gray stone.

Bowdragon took the Dwaer into his hands, trailing the last sparks of his spell, and hefted it. It was lighter than it should be for its size, but it was a Worldstone right enough. Power surged up his arm, and his smile became wide and real.

"This will be useful to me—and less of a danger to Aglirta than it is in your lax keeping, oh-so-mighty over-dukes. No Dwaerindim are toys suitable for anyone but a wizard . . . and a responsible, calm mage at that."

Hawkril struggled to rise, face twisted in pain, using his warsword as a crutch to help him totter to his feet and reach for the wizard standing so near . . .

Bowdragon smiled and made the Dwaer call up light-nings this time. 'Twould be fun to hurl a man as far as the eye could see while roasting him, now that it cost nothing to call on such power! Over yon hilltop, there . . .

It took some few moments to feel how to make the Stone do his bidding, and in the process, Jhavarr inadvertently lofted it into the air above his palm, where it spun, spitting eager sparks. Bowdragon raised his other hand casually to slay the staggering armaragor—and something silvery-bright and as cold as ice flashed through his fingers, leav-ing him gasping in pain as he shook them . . . and saw blood. Wincing, he glanced hastily whence the silver thing had come.

A slender figure had sprung up from amid the corpses on the road. Another hurled dagger was whirling right at Jhavarr, and a third dagger was already in Craer's hand. Bowdragon ducked hastily away from the thrown blade, snatched the Dwaer out of the air—and took himself else-where, leaving only a few sparks whirling around in the air where he'd been. Craer's third dagger flashed through that space just an instant too late.

It was suddenly very silent in the road.

Craer sprinted after his daggers, in case the mage had fartraveled just a few trees away and decided to hurl light-ning at where the procurer had been standing. Scooping them both up, Craer whirled, crouched, and froze to lis-ten . . . hearing nothing but the rustling leaves.

Cautiously, the overduke peered here and there into the trees, seeking anyone—bowmen, as well as murderous young wizards. The leaves rustled as cheerfully as ever,

sun dapple danced in the tree gloom, and—he could see
no menacing figure amid all the large, dark tree trunks
around him.

Cursing silently but fervently, Craer ran back to the
road. Hawkril had fallen on his face with the sort of sob
that he only made when his wounds were very bad, and
wasn't moving. Neither were Sass or Embra, and with the
Dwaer gone, there wasn't much a procurer dared try, if
they were dying . . . nothing much beyond prayer . . .

"Forefather Oak and Lady of Grace," Craer began un-
steadily, clambering hastily over dead bowmen and through
whizzing flies to where Hawk lay fallen, "hear now my—"

"Tanth the road! Overdukes, I come in peace!"

Craer's head jerked up. The voice was male and sounded
young, uncertain, and different from Jhavarr Bowdragon,
and "tanth" in backlands speech meant "I'm hailing you
but in peace, and don't want an arrow in reply"—but anyone who wanted to get close enough to strike true could
cry such a thing!

With a single angry bound, Craer crashed through ferns
and into the trees whence the call had come, daggers
gleaming ready in each hand.

"Why," Aglirta's newest baron asked the armaragors gently, "do you want to ride with me? Tell me truth, now."

The younger knight flushed and cast a quick glance at
the older armaragor beside him, who frowned, fixed
Bloodblade with a level gray gaze, and said, "I've heard of
you, Duthjack—good an' bad, but more victories than not.
No turning away from your men, either. That's good—an'
that's what I want in a king. So, to tell you true, that's why
we're here: to find a new road to glory for Aglirta. We want
to grow old in a strong realm, an' a just one, not this kingless land of barons stabbing endlessly at each other an' hiring wizards to try out their newest and cruelest spells on
Vale folk."

Bloodblade nodded thoughtfully. "A new road to glory for Aglirta." He looked up and grinned fiercely. "Handy, that—because that's what I want, too." He bounded up from his seat and held out his hand.

"Let's build that road together."

The Regent of Aglirta strode to the map on the wall, gazed at it for perhaps the thirdscore time that day, and sighed. Neither the Sleeping King nor any of his crowned predecessors had thought a map of Aglirta was necessary—and now he wished he had three of them, to mark out with stones and wood tokens all the whelmings and journeyings of his ambitious barons and their forces. Aye, they and the Sirl wizards had grown so arrogant as to regard Aglirta as a vineyard ripe for their private plucking—to say nothing of Aglirta's homebred mages, and the mysterious Koglaur, and the fell priests of the Serpent. Aye, the Snake-lovers were active in every hamlet and trailmoot, from one end of the Kingless Land to the other.

Ezendor Blackgult sighed. When he'd been the Golden Griffon, a warrior baron, chief rival to the fell Faerod Silvertree, the "Noble Baron" many hated and others hailed but all respected, he could ride and swing sword and dispense justice as he liked, with the occasional oath hurled at the absent king and many more snarled at his rivals. Now, striding the echoing vaulted chambers and gleaming marble of Flowfoam, ever watched by the ambitious eyes of a hundred glib-tongued courtiers, his hands itched to swing a sword in battle.

Yet he dared not leave the seat of power, lest another seize it or urgent messages fail to reach him, leaving him ignorant of what this map showed and loose tongues told. Three Above, had not men in Aglirta anything better to do than scheme and sharpen daggers and use them by night?

"We could be so *great* a land!" he roared suddenly, startling the nearest dutiful page, standing by the door beside an impassive guard. "Peace, and a few good harvests, and we'd be awash in coins and folk eager to better their lot . . ."

His voice trailed off as he strode angrily over to the map again. *And I could go hunting*, he added silently, his eyes wandering over the painted likenesses of the Windfangs and thinking on how poorly the map showed all the little hidden dells and back trails, and that he'd have to do something about that soon . . . if peace permitted. *Hunting traitors and outlaws and rogue mages, who are all become an overnumerous curse on this fair land.*

Blackgult's lips curled as he turned away from the map. As if *that* was anything new.

"I understand," the warlord in full, gleaming armor said from the towering height of his high-cantled saddle, "that a veteran warrior by the name of Belth Ardurgan dwells here. Do I understand correctly?"

The slack-jawed boy stared up at him, eyes dark and wide, then stammered something inarticulate but affirmative.

Bloodblade smiled encouragingly, and said, "Will you take me to him, please?"

Vigorous nods were added to the incoherency. Bloodblade smiled again and swung himself down from the saddle, landing with a clank. He looked even taller when standing on the ground, somehow. His guide, now mute with excitement, beckoned him in through a dark doorway.

He ducked his head, peered within—and found himself looking into the calm eyes of a scarred man who held a bent bow in his hands, the arrow pointing straight at Bloodblade's throat.

"Fair day," the warlord told the bowman without pause. "I come in peace, desiring to do business with Belth Ardurgan. Have I found him?"

"You have," was the calm reply. "Your business, Goodman Nameless?"

The tall man in armor smiled.

"My name is Sendrith Duthjack; men call me Blood-blade. I have for years been a hiresword of some success."

Belth Ardurgan nodded. "I, too, once rode to war for coins. Once. When I was younger."

Bloodblade nodded. "I also grow old—and I find myself increasingly hungry for peace. Peace for all Aglirta."

The bowman snorted. "Those are words I've heard be-fore." He lowered his bow and turned the arrow aside, just a trifle. "And so?"

"And so I need swordcaptains, and I'm told you're one of the best. I need swordcaptains because I find myself now Baron of Glarond—and have no desire to be one more baron among the endlessly squabbling barons of Aglirta, with their raids and their wizards and their knifings in Sirl alleys. I want peace. I want a *new* king for this Kingless Land—a real king, who'll keep order and justice through-out the land . . . for *all* Aglirtans, not just those with coins and castles."

"A new king," Ardurgan said slowly, as if tasting the words. "And this 'real king' would be you, I take it?"

Bloodblade bowed his head. "If the Three Above grant so."

The old warrior lifted his bow again. "I'm tired of swords and blood and hard riding. Very tired. I could end all your dreams right now, you know—just by letting go of this bowstring."

Duthjack nodded. "So you could." He spread his hands, showing that his fingers were nowhere near his own weapons, and asked quietly, "Is that what you want for Aglirta?"

"No," Belth Ardurgan said slowly. "No, it's not." He lowered his bow and cleared his throat. "Hiring swordcap-tains, you said?"

"At twice the usual coin," Bloodblade said flatly. "I want good officers everywhere in the realm after I'm on the throne—not just men to die valiantly getting me there."

" 'Just.' " Ardurgan said, shook his head—and then grinned suddenly, stepped forward, and held out his hand. "I believe, Lord Baron and king soon to be, we have a deal. For Aglirta!"

"For Aglirta," Bloodblade replied, clasping forearms with the old bowman, as warriors do. "For a True King at last!"

"A True King at last!" several voices echoed, from behind Duthjack. He whirled around, and found himself facing several carters, a farmhand, and the miller, all crowded together at the door. Gods, but they'd come quietly. Some of them had knives in their hands—but they were raising them, under his gaze, in hasty salute.

"Aye?" Bloodblade asked mildly.

The miller licked his lips. "Well . . . Lord . . . we're not much in a fight, but . . . you'll be needing armsmen, won't ye?"

"And carters, to haul food and ale," one of the carters said.

"Coins are few, these days?" the warlord asked lightly.

The miller spat to one side. "Coins I have in plenty," he said bluntly. "It's kings, and good law, and feeling safe, that I'm in short supply of. If you'll be a good king for Aglirta, we're for you."

Bloodblade smiled. "Then I'm for you. All who desire to ride with me—and get honest pay for it—come to my camp at Blackhelm Ford this evening." He looked back at Ardurgan, and added, "Come ready to ride, armor and all, Swordcaptain."

Ardurgan grinned and nodded. "By your order, Lord."

"Awww," said the small boy, from down below Bloodblade's belt. "Does this mean you're not gonna fight him? No one's gonna die?"

"I'm afraid not," Bloodblade said solemnly, bending over. "Not here, gods willing."

The boy looked disgusted. "What good's being king, then, if you can't kill people?"

There were embarrassed chuckles from the men standing around, but Bloodblade drew himself up, and asked quietly, "How can the lad know any better, if that's all he's ever seen and heard done? *This* is why it's time, and past time, for a new King for Aglirta!"

"A new King for Aglirta!" someone cried, and they all joined in. Bloodblade waved to Ardurgan, turned, and strode back to his horse, amid much excited chatter. Many woman stood watching, and they did not look happy.

"Taking our men off to be killed?" one of them cried.

Bloodblade swung himself up, and turned in his saddle. "No. I ride to make peace—and a new King for Aglirta!"

"Huh," one of the women said bitterly. "That's what they've all said."

But as Bloodblade smiled, shrugged, and turned his horse away, cries arose behind him of "A new king!" and "A True King!" and "Bloodblade! For Bloodblade, and victory!"

He grinned, and spurred his mount into a gallop. For Bloodblade and victory . . . *that* had a ring to it. He'd use that.

He urged the horse still faster; he needed a lot of warriors yet and had to see a lot of Ardurgans. "What good's being king, then, if you can't kill people?" he murmured aloud. "How right you are, lad. How terribly right you are."

Meanwhile

Over Shaunsel Rise a lone horseman came riding.

His cloak flapped behind him, the road was clear, sunbright, and nigh deserted, and he'd left his escorting armaragors—full-armored and riding two horses that had been weary when they'd begun, a night ago—far behind.

Flaeros Delcamper laughed aloud at the blue skies above for sheer pleasure. He was saddle deep in adventure once more, the Regent wanted to see him, and minstrels saluted him like one of the great grand bards of old!

"Aha!" he roared aloud. "Delcamper *High*!"

He'd never dared bellow that battle cry before—not in all his years of being too slender, too weak, and too clumsy with a blade to so much as draw a dagger in defense of the family honor . . . and strictly speaking, he wasn't in battle now, only galloping hard along the coast road far too fast to ensure his own safety. But there was no one to hear him, and—look, all watching Darsar—he was someone important, by the Three!

This ride to Teln would hasten his journey a good dozen days, or more. He could board one of Malavar Obalar's swift spice-and-silks traders, and sail right up the Silverflow to Flowfoam! Yes! "Delcamper High!" he cried again, and laughed wildly.

"Three Above, what a racket!" a roadside mound of hay snarled, rising suddenly man-high and hauling hard on the waxed cord bent around an old fence post at its feet.

"Aye! 'Twill be a pleasure, taking *this* fine young idiot down!" another pile of hay agreed from the far side of the road, pulling on the cord's other end—as the racing Delcamper horse struck it, tripped, and crashed to earth with a scream and a heavy tumult of thudding hooves, dust, and dazedly rolling rider.

Trailing hay, Suskar laughed and lumbered forward, long knife in hand. The horse had broken its neck, and lay still but for one feebly kicking back leg. There were no saddlebags—but the rider, now, all silken finery . . . and was that the gleam of *gold*?

"In at him, Baerm—don't let him flee!" he roared, as the lad on the ground ceased spitting and retching to scramble wild-eyed to his feet, and whirl away.

Whirl and limp, badly, stumping comically through the hayfield, arms windmilling for balance, with Baerm leaping after him.

One long and dirty arm caught the stumbling lad by a shoulder, spun him around into a kicking fall—and Baerm drove both his fists into the lad's gut, with the expected result.

"Beef and carrots," Suskar said disgustedly, as he stopped above the twisting, spewing silk-clad tangle that a grinning Baerm was standing guard over. "Why is it always beef and carrots? Does all Aglirta dine on nothing else?"

"Well," someone growled from just behind him, "you could try a meal of—cold steel!"

Suskar stiffened as something cold and sharp slid into his back, bringing a numbness that burned, and then burst out of his belly, dark and wet and pointed.

Baerm gaped at it, aghast, for what seemed a very long time before his gaze rose, almost reluctantly, to look up over Suskar's shoulder. And then he screamed.

"Ah," that gruff voice greeted him, "you *are* pleased to see me. I like that."

Baerm hadn't taken more than two running strides after whirling to flee when a heavy, hard-thrown mace struck the base of his skull and brought him red oblivion.

Suskar's groaning body struck the ground close by, and bounced. Flaeros winced, shaking his head to try to rid himself of the agony raging in it, and gasped, "W-who—?"

"My parents, whose tongues must have been nimble, named me Glarsimber Belklarravus," the gruff voice said from above him, as strong fingers caught up a fistful of fine silk, and hauled.

Flaeros blinked, suddenly upright and staring into a face he knew . . . from that magnificent whelming in Flowfoam, where the Smiling Wolf of Sart had been named—"B-Baron Brightpennant!" he gasped.

"Aye, that would be my newer name," the jowly, fierce-sideburned face agreed, as its owner sheathed his sword and strode a few steps to pluck up a mace. "So bright-born that I'm not used to it, yet. You, of course, are the bard Flaeros Delcamper."

"Y-yes! By the Three, my thanks, Lord! I'd've—you—you saved my life!"

The baron shrugged, smiled, and clapped an arm around

the bard's shoulders that almost sent him wobbling
groundward again.

"Come, lad, back to the road," Glarsimber said briskly.
"You were in some haste, as I recall."

"Yes," Flaeros agreed, stumbling. His head was still
ringing—it had all been so *sudden*, and—

He frowned. "My Lord Baron," he said, "the Three must
surely be smiling upon me, to have brought you so far from
Aglirta to rescue me!"

At his elbow, the baron chuckled, and muttered something that sounded like, "No fool here."

They walked on together a few hay-trampling paces before Flaeros dared to look up at his rescuer and prompt,
"Baron?"

Glarsimber grinned crookedly—and then looked away
towards the sea. "Well, lad," he told the air in front of him,
"I was sent here, to—do a thing."

Flaeros gasped. "You must be on a mission commanded
by Blackgult!"

The baron shrugged, grinned even more lopsidedly, and
said only, "Perhaps."

The deep blue smoke writhed a little higher, and the wizard
standing beneath it held up the Dwaer in his hand and
chuckled.

"Think of it, think how to do it, and—'tis done. No
dozens of spells and days of hunting up rare powders and
words of binding. No wonder the Lady of Jewels defeated
the Spellmaster, and strolled so languidly through a dozen
spell-duels since."

Jhavarr Bowdragon's smile widened. "And Blackgult has
another two of these, doesn't he? I'm almost forced to conclude he had something to do with Cath's death. Oh, yes."

The smoke spun more swiftly, and out of its coils something came undulating, something long and dark and
smooth-scaled: a Vale viper!

Yet no Vale viper had ever boasted small, fluttering wings behind its head, and more down its length, gently beating amid the smoke.

"Little flying serpent," the wizard muttered, "bound as I decree—fly forth now, and spy for me!"

He brought his hand forward as if hurling a stone into a pool—and the blue smoke roared around in a spiral, racing away in howling fury to an otherwhere lost in the shadows beyond his study door—and taking his flying snake with it.

"A clumsy incantation," he told his reflection in the oval glass by the door, "but it's spellbound to me nonetheless."

He turned back to the last whirling wisp of blue smoke, as it spun, sinking and fading, above the clutter of his casting. "Lurk, and trail after the Band of Four," he murmured. "Spy on every last overducal deed, so that I may see, and know. For guilty or not, they are like prowling hunting cats in Aglirta. Trouble follows them, and they bring it to others in their blundering . . . and somewhere out there is the fourth of the Dwaerindim. Yes."

He went to a certain gem that lay on a tabletop, its lower side smooth and flat, its uppermost surface curved and glossy, oval, and as long as his hand. He polished it with his fingers, and blue smokes rose from where he touched it.

Staring into them, he beheld a road strewn with bodies. A familiar road. He shrugged and turned away, letting the smoke trail away again.

His lurker would spy tirelessly, and would remember for him whatever he saw not through its eyes. And if these four buffoons of overdukes should notice it and lash out with blade or spell, the snake would grow when struck. Blow by blow it would grow, to do battle as a turret-tall flying behemoth, if need be. Jhavarr Bowdragon smiled; *that* would be worth watching.

Idle entertainment, aye—but then, what were "heroes" for?

3

Wizards Dropping Out of the Trees

The wide-eyed, white face was one Craer knew.

He'd not expected to find it here in this Three-cursed forest of rustling leaves and deadly arrows, but here it was nonetheless, above a nervously swallowing throat his dagger was a whisker away from slitting open.

"Raulin Castlecloaks," Craer snapped, in a voice soft but hardly gentle, "what by all the holy dancing gods are you doing *here*?"

"I—I—" A slender hand rose to push Craer's blade aside. Raulin looked a little surprised when the procurer let him move the steel instead of working swift surgery on fingers or throat with it. He cleared his throat, fixed Craer with very steady eyes, and said, "I've been watching and following you Four."

"Why? D'you want your clothes back?"

Raulin flushed. "Lord Delnbone, *please*. I—I've been watching you in hopes of another chance. I want to be like you, and ride with you to make Aglirta strong, and—and help you when you've need of—"

There was a thunderous snort from behind Craer.

Hawkril Anharu was on his feet, pale, bloodstained, and

trembling—but clear-eyed and holding his warsword in firm hands.

"You've found your chance, lad, and welcome. Aglirta has few enough friends, and every hand that helps her has a place beside ours. Craer, put that fang away and come down here. Em looks bad."

With something akin to disgust, Overduke Delnbone whirled away from the boy who'd fought alongside them through an inn and—despite a certain procurer striking him senseless and borrowing most of his clothes—a great battle in the Silent House, and led the way down through the ferns to the corpse-strewn road.

Raulin gazed around at all the spilled blood and bodies sprawled amid the flies and dust, went pale, and swallowed several times. Craer gave him a glare and then a wave across the fallen bowmen to the far roadside bank, where Sarasper and Embra lay slumped side by side, mute, white, and motionless. Their garments were scorched, and a strong burnt smell hung in the air around them.

"So, lad," Craer asked bitterly, "know you any healing magic?"

Raulin opened his mouth to make a reply that was not going to be a "yes," but left it hanging open without uttering a word as the air several corpse-strewn paces away suddenly shimmered, danced with brief silver shadows—and was as suddenly filled with four women.

They stood together, dark-gowned, slender, and tall—taller still because their booted feet stood on air a handspan or so off the ground. They seemed sisters, sharing the same beautiful features and large, gray-green eyes, and in their hands were wands crowned with glossy gems that crackled with magic. They regarded the folk standing in—and lying on—the road, and their faces looked neither impressed nor friendly.

Craer's manner matched their cold, wordless sneers. "What *is* this? A magemoot? Or have we blundered into the trail that every last wizard and sorceress of Darsar trots down, to draw spells from the same well every morning?"

A wand lifted almost lazily to point at the procurer's chest—and then a sneer widened, and it was turned to menace Hawkril instead.

"We follow Jhavarr Bowdragon," the sorceress who held that wand said coldly, stepping to the fore on empty air, "and know he's been here. Who are you, and what's your business with him?"

Craer glowered at her, but Hawkril rumbled their names and titles, identifying Raulin as "the Bard Castlecloaks, son of a famous father," which left the lad red-faced but beaming. Then the armaragor added, "None of us had ever seen this Bowdragon before. His business with us, it seems, was to attack us."

"Your turn," Craer said bluntly to the four women. "*We* are the ranking nobles here; unburden your names to us."

"Ariathe, Dacele, Olone, and Tshamarra," was Olone's prompt, proud reply, indicating who was who with one finger—while her leveled wand never wavered from Hawkril's armored breast. "Sisters all, and not so less noble than some. Talasorn is our name."

Craer stiffened. "Any relation to Raevur Talasorn, of Sirlptar?"

"We are his daughters," Olone told him coldly, "and we seek revenge for his death. The Risen King and his Regent must die, among others."

"Talasorn fell in battle against the Baron Cardassa," Hawkril rumbled thoughtfully. "Many died that day, the Old Cro—Cardassa standing for the king, and the rest seeking the Throne o'erthrown." His brows drew together in a frown. "Which makes those who attacked Cardassa in his own castle enemies of Aglirta."

"Our father was courteous, and diplomatic; he stood among the foremost wizards of Sirlptar," Ariathe said, sounding nettled. "He allied with the Baron Adeln against the Risen King not in some crown-seeking conspiracy, but because he sought a strong, united Aglirta wherein increased trade and wealth would mean more patrons seeking to hire wizards—by which our father sought to provide lives of wealth and importance for us."

Craer's brow wrinkled. "Pray pardon?" he asked, incredulity warring with bafflement. "Wealth and importance as—?"

Raulin Castlecloaks put a hand on Craer's arm and cleared his throat. Then, holding up a finger for silence, he strode forward until he was almost touching the four sisters. As many wands shifted to point right into his face.

Ignoring them, Raulin looked up at the sky and started to chant, as if recalling something learned long ago and not thought on again until this moment: "The spellcraft of Raevur Talasorn's four daughters outstripped his. His wife Iyrinda long dead, he doted on Olone, the eldest; Ariathe of the mighty spells; Dacele; and Tshamarra, deeming them too clever and beautiful to be wedded off—and, thus 'brutalized by some warrior-baron,' denied any chance to use their magic or follow their own wills."

Craer's eyebrows lifted, but the four sorceresses smiled. "They teach bards well these days," Dacele remarked. "Not a word of untruth."

"Enough of this," Ariathe snapped. "These overdukes serve the Risen King—blast them and let's begone!"

"*Nay,*" Tshamarra said flatly. "Hurling spells too quickly got Father into trouble time and again; we'd do better to follow Bowdragon and learn who is who first."

"Well said," Olone agreed. "There'll be time enough and chances aplenty to blast castles to dust later."

"Let it be soon," Ariathe snapped, glaring balefully at Craer.

The procurer stuck out his tongue at her in reply—an instant before Olone's upswept hand took the four sisters away into shimmering nothingness again.

No bolt from a wand crashed into the thief, and nothing

remained to show that the sudden apparitions had been there; flies buzzed through otherwise empty air.

Craer looked at Hawk, and Hawk looked at Craer. Their sighs came more or less in unison.

The procurer took a dancing step forward, then wheeled to face Raulin and Hawkril. Spreading his hands, Craer said in sudden exasperation, "What *is* it about Aglirta? We ride along on a nice bright day dealing with one nice, tidy little mystery—and suddenly wizards are dropping out of the trees and the sky and the Three know where else, and lads want to join us, and doom bids fair to fall on us all in moments—"

Raulin held up a hand again for silence. Glowering, Craer granted it with a "pray proceed" gesture.

The lad held out a small, ornate metal flask to the procurer. "One of them—Tshamarra—put this into my hand," he explained, "and then pointed at Sarasper. She didn't want the other ladies to see."

Craer held the flask up and stared at it, his face a battlefield between bewilderment and suspicion.

Hawkril smiled and echoed: "What *is* it about Aglirta?"

Silently, the procurer looked at Sarasper and Embra, turned his gaze back to Hawkril, and gave a helpless shrug.

Hawkril shrugged back. "What choice have we?"

Craer nodded, unstoppered the flask, sniffed its contents suspiciously, stoppered its mouth with a finger, and tipped it just enough so as to leave that finger wet, sniffed and licked the residue—and then, as they'd all known he'd have to, slid the mouth of the flask between Sarasper's jaws, and imparted a small dose.

The old healer coughed, gave a great shiver as an expression of bitter distaste flashed across his face, embarked on another deep, racking cough, and started sputtering like an indignant drunkard. His eyes remained firmly closed throughout. Craer frowned down at him, then sighed and turned to Embra.

A clawlike hand tugged at the procurer's elbow from be-

hind before he could apply the flask to her mouth, accom-
panied by a raw, rattling shout of: "Wait!"

Craer turned. "Save it," Sarasper croaked. "Any of us
can drink it. Let me heal her."

Waving one hand in a florid gesture to indicate that the
healer should proceed to work on Embra, the procurer
restoppered the flask, hooked it onto his belt, and shook his
head. "I wish—just for once—I knew what was going on,"
he told the trees above him. "Back when we were warriors
of Blackgult, or even starving outlaws, things were much
simpler. One knew where one stood—"

"Aye, a running stride ahead of the hangman's noose,
usually," Hawkril growled, "thanks to your urge to steal
things large, florid, and useless."

Craer spread eloquent hands. "Large you are, aye, I'll
grant, and useless, too—but florid, now—"

"Right," Sarasper agreed, a twinkle kindling deep in his
weary eyes. "*I'd* not go around saying a man was 'florid,'
by the Three."

"We're mad, boy," Hawkril explained to Raulin. "Run
fast and far, while you still can."

The young bard grinned at him. "In truth, Lord Anharu,
I've been missing this. There's a shortage of good buffoons
elsewhere in Aglirta."

Craer stiffened.

Sarasper looked up, then slowly drew the dagger at his
belt, squinting hard at Raulin. Like the side of a ponderous,
armored mountain, Hawkril slowly turned to face the
young bard squarely.

Large-eyed and beginning to tremble, Raulin met the armaragor's gaze steadily. Eyes as sharp and fearless as a
swordblade stared into—and *through*—Raulin Castlecloaks . . .

And then Hawkril's face split into a gigantic grin. Roaring out sudden laughter, he swept the bard into a bruising,
dust- and blood-spattered embrace.

Grinning in wild relief, Raulin laughed right back, and

they waltzed briefly past a smirking Craer, to where
Sarasper was shaking his head.

The old healer did not, however, lower the fine dagger. It
had been a gift from Regent Blackgult, Raulin recalled,
watching Sarasper's lips tighten.

The bard gasped as a blue glow began along the edge of
its gleaming blade, kindling swiftly to blue-white fire.
Sarasper turned it slowly, murmuring, "So may all slaying
magic pass."

The old healer's hands trembled . . . as the blue-white
glow crept slowly down from the blade to his wrinkled
hands, his arm, across his chest to his other arm . . . and then
down the spread fingers of his other hand, to Embra's throat.

As Raulin watched, entranced, he saw that beautiful
flesh rise in a deep breath. Sarasper held his hand steady,
the raised blade now dark and lifeless, and Embra swallowed under the healer's touch. Slowly, those wrinkled fingers trailed up to her chin and touched her lips.

Her eyelids fluttered immediately, she moaned softly—
and opened her eyes and blinked at him. "Again, Sass?"
she asked quietly. "How many times have you put me back
together again, now?"

"Less than I have these two gown-stealing dolts of
yours," the old man growled loudly. "They've even
arranged a replacement for you."

He jerked his head towards Raulin, who smiled nervously at Embra, bowed, and said formally, "My day is
brightened by our meeting, fair Lady Overduke—uh, Lady
Baron Silvertree."

As his formal words stumbled in confusion over what
Embra was now properly called, the Lady of Jewels
grinned remarkably like Hawkril, and replied, "I am honored by your regard, Bard Castlecloaks. Call me Embra—
only please, *not* 'Em.'" She cast glances at the rest of the
Four, and added, "Listening, gentlesirs? A little courtesy
never comes amiss."

Craer launched himself into a fluted parody of a deep,

elaborate court bow, and lisped in affected tones, "*Good my radiant* Lady, I deeply regret my past and utterly misguided attempt to lighten thy wardrobe, but am forever grateful that the Watching Gods above saw to it that this my dastardly failing brought us two into close harmony and the *courteous* bindings of friendship!" Straightening, he added in his normal voice, "To which I can't help but add that in my professional opinion, it will be brilliant policy if we move on from this place before any *more* wizards—or archers—make an appearance."

"Aye," Hawkril agreed quickly. "We should move, if only to give the wolves and wild dogs more sport in trailing us."

"Sport? They'll have to drag themselves along our trail on their bellies if they devour all of these bowmen first," Sarasper commented.

Craer and Hawkril shook their heads in unison. "Nay," the armaragor explained grimly, "to the fanged foragers of the Vale, battle dead are sure meals, and lures to bring curious creatures hence, to be slain and made yet more fare. Our tracks, away from this place, will be followed first."

"Always expand the larder," Craer added. "We must get moving!"

"Where?" Embra asked, rising from the crushed ferns to stretch—and promptly wince, sway, and let Sarasper steady her. Pale, she sat gracefully down again, waved away Hawkril's anxious hand, and added, "Men in Aglirta seem to set great stock in rushing places, waving swords and yelling as they go—but I, being a lazy, pampered noble thing, always like to know where I'm bound, and for what reason such haste is necessary, before *I* commence shouting and hastening."

"A destination stands ready in your mind, I can see," Hawkril said quietly, staring at her. "Where and why?"

Embra shrugged. "My Dwaer is gone. I'm sure you'll tell me how and who took it, but leave that for later. The echoes of recently spun spells are so strong around us here that it's like having men shouting different battle cries into my ears whilst standing shoulder-to-shoulder in some small robing room. Let's get ourselves to Flowfoam. There, bolstered by Bla—by my father's two Dwaer, and by more of my precious family dancing inkwells and singing jewel boxes, I can try some elaborate magics to trace my Dwaer-Stone."

She rose again, took two careful paces along the road, turned, stepped delicately over a sprawled body, and blurted, "I feel—naked without it. As if it's a part of me, something I was meant to have. Any wizard aches to have a Dwaer, yes, but . . . it's mine, now, as if the Three intended it for my hand."

Sarasper glared at her, then sheathed the dagger he'd drained all magic from to heal her with an angry flourish.

"It's not that simple, Embra," he snapped. " 'The gods meant me to do this, so I will.' D'you know how *dangerous* such words are? How crazed those who spout them become, and the damage they do? The gods don't announce neat little destinies for us, lass. It's never that simple."

"Easy, Sass, easy," Craer murmured. "Yet your point is a good one. Bard, let the telling stand that Embra *feels* she needs her Dwaer back—and the rest of us are ice-cold certain that we'll all be dead in short order without it . . . at about the time we encounter our next unfriendly wizard."

Ere Raulin could reply, the procurer turned to look at him directly, and added, "Well, here's where we'd best part w—"

"Nay," Hawkril said firmly. "Even if it was not truly throwing the lad to the wolves, to leave him go his own way from here, I say he bides with us. I said before: every hand that strikes for Aglirta must be made welcome—or how shall the land ever be more than self-interested, warring families and cabals and handfuls of swordbrothers? What if there were a hand-count *more* foursomes of angry sorceresses flitting about the realm seeking to work avenging murder on real—or imagined—foes?"

Sarasper sighed. "Raulin Castlecloaks. Valiant, willing, of good character—and one more body for me to try to heal," he told his hands, looking down at the dried blood all over them. Most of it was Hawkril's, but a little was Embra's and some his own. "One more life for us to throw away in our little adventures."

The healer looked up sharply, and added, "Lad, if you come with us, you're a fool. Swift death is your most likely fate, and the gods will probably bestow it sooner rather than later—with our blundering help."

"I say Raulin has proved his usefulness to us and to Aglirta before, and has every right to stand in danger with us—or be more prudent, and go elsewhere—if he chooses," Embra said. "We're not speaking of someone who hasn't ridden with us before, and doesn't know the danger, or hasn't already shown he can handle it. The choice should be his."

Craer looked at Sarasper, and they exchanged shrugs.

"Lady," the procurer said, turning back to the sorceress, "we abide by your counsel—if only to spare our ears all the things you're sure to say, and say again, many times over in the days ahead, if we do not."

Embra smiled sweetly. "Ah, we understand each other clearly at last." She glanced at Raulin. "Still want to journey with us? We play tongues-as-daggers all the time."

"I do," the young bard said firmly.

"Well enough," Craer told Raulin briskly. Pointing at the bodies all around, he added, "Daggers. Fetch me a score—bundle 'em in a cloak someone doesn't need anymore. Use another cloak to carry any decent boots you see; they're worth good coin. Then—"

"Craer!" Embra snorted. "We've gained an ally, not a pack-mule!"

The procurer turned to her with wide eyes and spread hands. "What, Lady Baron Overduke? Is this collecting not exactly what I'd be doing, were Raulin not with us? Hmm?"

*   *   *

Despite the high sun beating upon the road where an increasingly white-faced youth gingerly plucked daggers from sheaths—and then collected those sheaths, and the belts that went with them, too, under the harsh tongue and helping hands of Overduke Delnbone—two bats clung, awake and aware, to the same tree limb.

Intently they watched and listened to the humans below. When at last those five set off along the road, still trading jests and barbed comments, the bats looked at each other and rose into flight. One swooped after the departing humans, and the other flapped purposefully in another direction, flitting low amid the trees.

Craer was wont to suddenly turn and look back when out walking—several times—but the bat following the Four-plus-Raulin took care to duck behind leaves and follow unseen.

Nor did the alert and suspicious procurer notice a whorl of silent sparks and strange colors suddenly boiling in midair between two thaerul trees a little way behind the bat. Out of that whirling, in a puff of blue smoke, spun a viper with many tiny wings beating along its length. It reared up for a moment and glided forward, following the five humans trudging along the road. It, too, took care to keep hidden—both from the procurer whirling from time to time to look back and from the fluttering bat ahead of it.

If the bat saw what was behind it, it gave no sign—but then, bats seldom do.

The lonely figure in the dark, warm cavern stiffened above the drift spell, and then bent to peer closely at it. "Strong," he said, in a surprised voice. "*Very* strong—but slumbrous. Not a Dwaer, but what?"

Then he shrugged, and told the empty darkness, "No matter. Whatever it may be, I shall have it! With warlords whelming iron-heads to march on the throne and Snake-lovers everywhere, no magic is too much."

The darkness answered not, but that had long since ceased to bother the lonely wizard. He talked to the darkness a lot.

Right now, he was smiling rather unpleasantly. Moving a safe distance away from the glowing fog of the drift spell, he cast another magic. "Go forth, my Melted. Go and snatch this thing of magic for me."

Then he sighed, and added, "Even if your fellows haven't yet managed to slay four bumbling overdukes for me. Corloun, your creations leave something to be desired."

Corloun, of course, was far too dead to answer.

"Desired," the wizard murmured to the darkness—and, as always, thought of Embra Silvertree. Bare and beautiful, as she'd been so often when he'd spied on her, that first summer while binding her to the castle. Furious . . . and helpless . . .

He sighed again, and told the darkness, "Embra, you'd have made a lovely slave."

Then he smiled again. "And you still might."

If one believed the faded signboard out front, the Glory of Aglirta was some sort of gold two-headed dragon with an impossibly long, looped, and knotted tail. But then again, perhaps too many tankards of dark ale do the same dark work on the vision of artists as to more common folk, and the real dragon had but one head and a more modest tail. Or then again, perhaps the artist had been blessed by the gods with the opportunity to see a nightwyrm and live to remember the experience . . . and had merely gotten the color wrong.

Dragons, nightwyrms, and glory of any sort were all sights so rare as to be legendary in this upland corner of the Vale, hard by the foothills that became the Windfangs, north and west of Tselgara.

Off-color converse was the norm in the dim, dirty interior of the Glory, where rats scuttled among the rushes, the dirt floor was none too even, and weary men in worn smocks and many-patch cloaks nursed more drink than stew. Grumblings about gold-drenched merchants in distant, thieving Sirlptar and the fool heads of Flowfoam were even more common than mutterings about the wolves, the weather, outlaws, and strange beasts of the mountains. Folk everywhere snarl about their kings and the doings of kings, from taxes to heavy-handed soldiery to threatened war.

Yet there was a grimness in the Glory this afternoon, a darkness of heart and hope that had lurked at the bottoms of its large tankards for nigh a season, growing steadily stronger and heavier.

"Chaos grips Aglirta like a strangler's hand on throats, he said," Old Adbert said, propping the stump of his left leg on the bench beside him with a grunt of pain. "I heard him—and him a bard, too, up and down the Vale like sea wind, seeing all and hearing Three near all, too!"

"Chaos has been choking Aglirta since I was born, and before," Thaeker Blackcloak responded, spitting onto a passing rat. "Aglirta takes a long time dying, y'must admit."

"Admit nothing," one of the Luroan brothers called, from his corner table. "Always safer that way!"

"Ye've found it so, hey, Guruld?" Thaeker flung back, swirling his tankard. "Look at it as entertainment, sent to us by the gods! This baron defies the regent here, and that one defies him there, in this small way or this larger way— so the Sleeping King awoke and named one baron his regent, what then? Blackgult's the same rogue we've always known, wizards spellslay as much as they ever did, our precious king took himself off into dreams again, and— what? This is *still* the Kingless Land, that's what!"

"Aye, that's truth," another man said. "Barons have been snatching at power and making war on other barons since my grandsire's day, and probably before that, too. Nothing changes."

"And what of these precious overdukes?" Guruld Luroan snarled. "What good are they? Just *more* barons, I say!"

He spat on the rushes and banged his tankard down, but Old Adbert turned around in his chair so swiftly he almost toppled over. "Now you heed!" he barked angrily, startling men all over the dim taproom of the Glory. "I saw the Band of Four on the last wagon run I ever did, and took my measure of them—which is more than any of the rest of you've ever done!" He waved his tankard so wildly that ale slopped out and down it—and that shocked the others in the room more than any words could have done. Old Adbert, spilling a drop of ale?

"I heard about their big battle at Flowfoam with Silvertree's wizards, too," the one-legged man added. "Oh, you all did, I know, but I talked with men who were *there*, swords out and fearing to die, any moment—and let me tell you something: we should all thank the Three every night on our knees for the Band of Four. They're all that's holding back the barons, right now!"

"Well said!" a traveling peddler spoke up. "I, too, have seen and heard, up and down the Vale. They at least keep barons from swording or hanging everyone whose face they don't like, or lands and daughters they *do* like! If the Band of Four falls, who'll stop the barons?"

"Aye," Thaeker Blackcloak added gloomily, "and the Serpent-priests?"

The oldest man in the room, Saurn Belrastor, raised his own tankard and rapped on it to show the tavernmaster that it needed refilling. It was so rare for Saurn to do this that men's heads turned at the sound. Saurn looked at them all, and said sourly, "If the fate of Aglirta rests on the shoulders of four wandering adventurers, we are doomed indeed. Four to save us, against armies?"

"We are doomed indeed," Old Adbert agreed quietly, staring into the depths of his tankard. He didn't seem to fancy whatever he saw there.

"I'm taking my kin all the way around the Windfangs,

into Dalondblas, brigands or no," Tarsam Faurolk told the taproom grimly, causing many jaws to drop. Leave four hills and all the sheep on them, and run away to—nothing?

As if in answer to their amazement, he added darkly, "There's nothing but death and doom riding Aglirta's roads, these days. Better coinless and alive than a wealthy corpse when war sears up and down the Vale again. All the barons are arming. Get out while you can, if you've any sense."

Old Adbert's laugh was a short, bitter bark. "Any sense? Lad, I'm Aglirtan—of course I've got no sense!"

Scattered chuckles agreed with Adbert, but none of them held much mirth. Even the tavernmaster, refilling more tankards than he'd been called on to do for many a month, found it hard to smile.

He couldn't stop seeing dead men lying in the upland fields, awaiting the wolves.

There'd be time for smiling then.

Skulls grin easily.

4

Riding to War

The guard at the bridge tilted his helm back against the heat of the bright morning sun, ran a disgusted hand through his sweat-soaked hair, and looked longingly at the shade of the old shieldwood tree. *When these next few folk are past . . . yes, b'yr Lady! A little shade, a little cool water followed by a swallow from my boot flask to take the foul taste of river mud away, and . . . yes . . .*

Sammarthe's herb cart creaked by, and he gave the straining woman and her two daughters a nod and smile. The youngest child, skipping along barefoot with a spray of tansel in her hand, was the only one who smiled back.

Kuldin shrugged, and thought again of the waiting coolness yonder. Ah, to be out of this *sun!*

He didn't bother to lower his spear or helm when the next arrivals into Sart came onto the bridge. The foremost man was dirty and wild-eyed, his clothes torn and his mouth ababble with strange phrases, nonsense words, and half-sung snatches of rhyme. Leather straps encircled his forehead, each arm in three places, his thighs and ankles, and were also clipped to a stout belt. The other ends of those straps were held by two guards who looked as weary as Kuldin felt. They trudged along behind their captive—

and each of them held a loaded hand crossbow—what was called a dart gun in Carraglas—ready in his free hand.

"Madman," the nearest guard explained, nodding at the drooling, gabbling man in his care. "Going to the trade fair, for the right soothing potions."

"*Rich* madman," the other guard commented, "or you'd not catch me out walking a man like a dog in this heat."

"Aye to *that*!" Kuldin agreed, his feelings heartfelt. He waved them on into Sart—and so it was that his arm was still raised and his mind abrim with friendly thoughts as the guards turned in unison and fired their crossbows.

One dart found a home deep in Kuldin's nose, but the other went right through one of his eyes. The madman had already whirled to spring at the guard, a dagger flashing in his hand.

Kuldin toppled back against the bridge rail, sagged, and half rolled along it. The dagger rose and fell, and then an enthusiastic hand went under the guard's knee and heaved. The bridge guard pitched up and over the rail, finding coolness at last, with a splash.

The madman turned to the two warriors who'd been shepherding him and held up Kuldin's signal horn with a grin. "Got it!" he announced, and then turned and ran back down the road whence they'd come.

The two guards exchanged glances as they sought cover on either side of the road, on the Sart bank of the bridge.

"Enjoys this just a bit much, doesn't he?" one of them muttered, readying another dart for his bow. "I sometimes think he *is* a little mad."

"Ah, actors are all like that," the other replied, ducking behind a wyvernthorn. "He's just crazed at the thought of earning some coin for a change."

"We're not supposed to kill him until everyone's across the bridge, right?" The words came from behind a suddenly trembling sroanberry bush. "You don't suppose we could hasten the process just a trifle?"

"Bend a direct order from Bloodblade? Not dragon-dung likely! Looking for an early grave yourself, perhaps?"

"All right, all right!" the sroanberry bush said sourly. "'Twas just an idle thought."

"It's best if loyal warriors refrain from having 'idle thoughts,'" a new voice said flatly, from very close at hand.

There was a moment of frozen silence, and then one of the bushes asked hesitantly, "L-Lord Bloodblade?"

"Of course. Point those bows at the ground or die."

"Yes, Lord!" two voices agreed hastily, as the thud of hooves and the creak of saddle leather grew steadily louder along the road. Around the bend whence the herb cart and the escorted madman had come, out of the trees of Sirl Forest (no one used the name on the new maps; "Bright Forest" just seemed *wrong* for a place so dark, thorny, and tangled, somehow), came a knot of mounted armaragors . . . followed by several dozen crossbowmen, a long column of spearmen, and more mounted knights. At the head of this host rode a tall man in magnificent fluted armor, astride a taller horse in full barding.

"But—who—" the sroanberry bush said in confusion.

"A false-me, of course, in case any of Sart's defenders are seized by bravery or desperation, and decide that a headless army is a beaten one," Bloodblade said coldly. "I didn't order you not to think, Lornelth, I suggested that my most loyal warriors refrain from idle thoughts when in battle."

"Y-you know my name?" The bowman, until recently the youngest and least-regarded of Glarond's house guard, was dumbfounded.

"Of course. A baron who knows not his sworn men? That man would be an idiot."

Across the road, the wyvernthorn chuckled uneasily— and then the tramping and hoof falls and dust passed between the two bushes, ending all easy converse, as the forces of Sendrith Duthjack, Baron of Glarond and better known as Bloodblade the warlord, entered Sart.

* * *

"Calm yourself, Craer," Sarasper said mockingly. "There are only three hundred or so miles of back roads betwixt here and the Silverflow alone—to say nothing of what lies in the *next* barony, or yet the next. And the royal writ of safe passage can be shredded on each and every one of them, scores of times each day."

Puffing and sweating as he trotted past, the procurer flung Sarasper a furious, wordless glare as he hastened towards the next blind corner, where the road dipped into deep forest and made a sharp turn around a jagged shoulder of wet, vine-and-creeper-cloaked rock as tall as six men. Craer peered into that deep shade for a long time before he made the hand signal for them to join him.

"I heard something, I tell you," he scowled, as Raulin and his fellow overdukes sauntered up to him, Sarasper and Embra wearing bright smiles for his benefit. "We're being followed, or watched as we move into a waiting trap-of-swords, ahead. I can feel it."

"Oh? Do you have such feelings often?" the old healer asked innocently, as they stood together in the tree gloom. "Before or after you empty flagons?"

Craer gave him a dark look, and murmured, "Be still. Please. I—there 'tis again!"

They all froze obediently, straining to hear what had alarmed Craer.

Silence . . . silence . . . a distant birdcall, and the whir of wings as an alarmed forest-fall took wing, much closer by.

"There," Craer breathed. "No birdcalls close, but a bird—probably a pinecock, by the sound, and they fly up at the last moment, right when your boot's about to come down on them—disturbed right close by. In against the rock, quick and quiet, and then everyone be still again!"

Everyone obeyed, and when they had shoulders to stone, watched Craer's upraised hand. It urged silence, and silence they gave.

It seemed a long time before they heard the deep, faint sound of a stone turned over by a heavy tread. It seemed to be coming from everywhere, from back behind, from—

Craer pointed straight up, at the top of the rock face above. Then he put his finger to his lips and made the downward, clawlike motion that meant "freeze, keep still."

Raulin and the four overdukes pressed themselves against the rough stone for what seemed a very long time before small stones started to shower down; something was climbing down the rock face.

At about the same time, a warrior strode suddenly out of the ferns and underbrush, into the road ahead . . . followed by another.

Raulin peered at them, and then gasped.

The warriors stared sightlessly as they came, and their flesh was sagged and twisted, like old candle wax frozen in middrip. They strode steadily but clumsily, as if not quite alive, and—

"Melted," Embra whispered to him. "Beware! If you touch them, they can burst into flames!"

As she spoke, Hawkril unslung his great warsword and stepped away from the wall to face the oncoming warriors. There were seven or eight Melted on the road now, and probably more in the trees. "Behind?" the armaragor asked calmly.

Craer ducked his head out from the stones. "None, but"— he twisted himself around to peer—"four coming down the rocks, and more above."

Embra looked up and took a step away from the rock face, but Sarasper caught at the arm she was raising, and said, "Save your spells—for now, at least. We may need them to get clear of this."

"W-what should I do?" Raulin asked uncertainly.

"Watch out back the way we came, lad," Craer snapped, pointing, "and yell out if you see anyone or any beast coming—what, how many, and how close."

With a sudden rush Hawkril slashed the ankles out from

under a Melted. It fell heavily on its side in uncanny, un-
breathing silence, and the Melted behind it fell over it. The
warsword beheaded that second Melted even before the
first warrior rolled to its hands and knees and started crawling towards Hawkril.

He hacked at it once, and then ducked back as the next
three Melted came striding swiftly forward, in a group.

"Which mage, d'you think?" Sarasper asked Embra.

The Lady of Jewels shrugged. "It could be anyone; who
knows how many wizards may have seen Corloun's notes?
They must be meant for us, mind, and that explains Craer's
watched feeling—someone is farscrying us right now."
She crossed the road swiftly, knelt beside a dead sapling,
and murmured forth fingerflames. Holding her hand like
an axe blade, she seared through the base of the sapling,
caught it as it started to topple, and handed it to Craer.

With a wordless nod the procurer turned, summoning
Sarasper with a jerk of his head, and thrust the wooden
pole up the rock face, at the lowest of the Melted.

It was just out of reach, and Craer swung the pole hastily
down and around to catch the shoulder of one of the Melted
in the road and smash him sideways into his two fellows, as
they stood slashing at Hawkril's parrying warsword.

In a flash Hawkril bent and chopped low at the other
side of the stumbling trio—and they went over together
like a collapsing haystack. Craer leaped into the pile with
his dagger in one hand and the pole in the other, hacking
like a madman.

There was a sudden great roar of flame from the
writhing heap of bodies, and the procurer tumbled hastily
back out of the sudden inferno by vaulting with his pole—
scorched and smiling fiercely.

"So a watching mage wants us cooked, hey?" He thrust
the blackened, flaming end of the pole up the cliff again,
and this time managed to deal the legs of the lowest Melted
a solid blow.

It slipped, clawing vines and rock, and fell—and the

procurer and Sarasper pounced on it, caught hold of a boot and an elbow, and threw as hard as they could.

In the same dead silence the Melted whirled past Hawkril like a rag doll, and crashed into the blazing heap of its fellows. Two more Melted were trying to push past this small conflagration, but were being held back by great swings of Hawkril's warsword, which threatened to sweep them into the flames even if they parried it to avoid losing limbs.

Craer glanced back up at the rock face and the Melted still standing above it, and then at those stiffly striding around the blazing heap in the road, seeking to outflank Hawkril, and called, "Raulin—still clear?"

"Yes!" the young bard shouted. Craer nodded and cried, "Fall back, everyone! Hawk, draw back beyond the rock face!"

The armaragor growled his dislike of butchering walking dead men, but stepped back a reluctant pace—and as he did, the Melted poured forward, coming out of the trees in numbers, now.

Craer was still looking up, smoldering pole in hand, as he waved the others back along the road. What he'd been awaiting befell almost immediately: a Melted sprang from the rocks, seeking to land atop Sarasper.

With a brittle smile the procurer darted to just the right place, planted himself—and held firm as the plunging warrior impaled himself on the sapling. It shivered, splintered, and then collapsed in the process, and Craer sprang back just before the Melted burst into flame.

Another Melted jumped or fell from the rock face, and the panting procurer sprinted to Hawkril's side to guard the retreating armaragor's flank, and then to turn suddenly, and call, "Embra! *Now!*"

The Lady Overduke raised both hands over her head, snarled something intricate and hissing, and then flung her arms forward as if she was hurling a flour sack down to someone waiting below. Craer and Hawkril threw themselves off the road into the trees as Embra's shapely hands came down.

Flames roiled forth from the empty air in front of the sorceress, a great snarling flood of fire that plucked Melted from the rock face, caused two more to fall from the trees above the rocks, and swept over everything on the road.

There were sudden bursts of fire here and there as who-ever was controlling the staggering dead men caused them to burst apart in flame, hoping to catch one of the Four.

Embra smiled grimly, and tugged at her fire as if she was clawing at an invisible quilt or fishnet in the air, seeking to drag it back and—

Sweep the last Melted from atop the rocks, scorching the leaves there with a loud crackling, to plunge in that same dead silence down into the flames below.

Raulin and the Four watched the conflagration and the forest on either side closely, but saw no foe beyond a lone, blazing Melted that lurched forward at least ten paces out of the flames, trying to reach them even as it crumbled to ash.

"Feast, anyone?" Craer asked, waving a hand at the dy-ing flames.

"I fear the meat is a bit crisped," Hawkril replied, "but my thanks for your kind invitation." He squinted at the crumbling bones in the thick of the angry red flames, then pointed.

"That one, yonder, is less scorched than most. Is there any way to tell what mage sent it, love lass?"

Embra smiled and shrugged. "I doubt it, but it won't hurt to have a look."

Gingerly, she picked her way between the heaps of ash and guttering flames, heading for a Melted that had es-caped the flames from its thighs upward—or rather out-ward, for thanks to Hawkril's warsword, it lay in a sprawl of severed limbs to one side of the road.

Embra cast wary glances all around, then bent to peer at it, frowning. After a long moment she sighed, shook her head, and rose again—only to tread on a hot ember and leap swiftly aside, to an ungraceful landing on her knees nearby.

In midleap, something whipped past her—flashing by her shoulder to bury itself in a tree.

"Sargh!" Craer snarled, and launched himself into the trees in a furious, crashing sprint, leaping deadfalls and racing through tangles at breakneck speed, not even taking the time to snatch out a dagger—wherefore it took him an instant to do so, and throw, when he came out into a little clearing and saw a robed man, running ahead of him, plunge into an inky, upright whorl in the air.

The man vanished into the rotating oval of darkness and it promptly spun faster, spiralling into nothingness at his heels. It swallowed Craer's flashing blade just before it grew too small to see—but if his steel struck something, it left no sign behind.

Snarling, Craer rushed forward to slash through where the whorl had been with another dagger, cutting the empty air repeatedly. He'd known it was futile when he started, but . . . 'twas always best to be sure.

Panting, Craer retraced his steps through the deep forest and found his companions staring grimly at the arrow that had sought Embra's life.

It was no arrow at all, but a snake stretched out straight and rigid, fangs agape and buried deep in the tree bark. Its slitted eyes swiveled to better see the procurer as he bent to scowl at it. The scaled body must be held rigid by a spell . . .

"It'll stay that way until its fangs touch flesh," Embra murmured. Craer quirked an eyebrow, and slowly reached out to take hold of the serpent.

"No," the Lady Overduke snapped. "It can be used as a focus for magic, against us. Leave it be."

Craer hesitated, moved his hand a little closer to the snake—which turned its eye still more, to look at him— and then, reluctantly, drew his hand back. He grimaced a little; it never sits well with a procurer, to be able to reach something interesting, but know he shouldn't.

"Well," Sarasper grunted from behind him, "at least we've achieved *some*thing this day. Craer Delnbone learned a touch of prudence. His first, I believe."

Craer turned his head very slowly to give the old healer an unloving look. In the process, his gaze swung across Raulin—who kept himself carefully expressionless—and both Embra and Hawkril, who both suppressed smiles rather poorly.

The face of the swordlord who sat on a splendid chestnut war steed at the head of the hastily assembled garrison was rather pale. As white as Windfangs snow, in fact.

The big man in the fluted armor smiled as he raised his open hand in greeting. "Hail, Swordlord of Sart! Where's the Baron Brightpennant? I've business with him!"

The swordlord licked his lips. "N-not here," he said reluctantly. "Gone on a mission for the Crown, we know not where." He eyed the ready-armed host behind the big armored man, and asked, "Who are you, sir—and what business have you in Brightpennant that needs an army to accomplish it?"

"Your eyes behold the new Baron of Glarond," the man at the head of the host replied, "but men more often call me—Bloodblade."

A swift murmur arose amid the guards of Sart Castle, and someone among the line of them that barred the way through its gate gasped aloud.

"My fame precedes me, it seems," Bloodblade said pleasantly, "which should make our business together much easier."

"Ah—our business?"

"Well, since Baron Brightpennant is so careless of the safety and rule of his barony that he leaves it open and undefended to invading armies—such as this one, that whelmed in the very streets of Gilth without a blade raised to stop us, and has come hither with similar lack of challenge or scrutiny—I deem Glarsimber Belklarravus unfit to hold such office, and declare these lands forfeit to me. In short, *I* am now Baron Brightpennant, and—"

"You *dare*?" the swordlord shouted, snatching out his sword and hurling it, in one snake-swift motion. "Men—resist this outlaw rabble!"

The swordlord's throw was as sure as it was unexpected, and the huge man in fluted armor toppled silently from his saddle, his open-faced helm sprouting a sword-hilt and spraying blood in all directions.

With a roar the men of Brightpennant surged forward—only to come to a confused halt before a line of suddenly leveled spearpoints.

Another, deeper voice snapped, "Bowmen!" and the spearmen suddenly flung themselves to the ground, to reveal a line of stone-faced crossbowmen. The crash of their volley of bolts was deafening in the castle foreyard—and before its echoes had died away into the mad whirring of half a hundred windlasses as the bowmen readied their bows again, the swordlord and his steed had both crashed to the cobbles, so transfixed by arrows that they resembled many-branched trees. Very dead trees.

The order had come from a second, slightly smaller man in nondescript, much scarred armor, seated on a horse behind the now-riderless mount of the giant in fluted armor. As the men of Brightpennant watched—and the spearmen rose to menace them once more—this man could be seen to smile, in the few moments before he swung the visor of his helm firmly down.

"As it happens, *I* am Bloodblade," his voice came hollowly to them, sounding almost lazily casual, as he raised one gauntleted hand in greeting, "and I offer you a choice: surrender or death. Gilth is mine, and Sart shall be mine by nightfall, one way or another. I am your new baron; will you serve me, or not? Choose, men of Brightpennant, for neither patience nor mercy runs strong in me."

A few moments of tumult followed under the castle

arch, as Brightpennant armsmen traded glances, jostled, and cursed. Some flung down their arms, and stepped back. Others stood their ground defiantly, one of them swinging his blade at a fellow who'd surrendered his steel. No one moved to stop the brief, brutal thrusts that followed.

Bloodblade's spearmen watched impassively . . . and ere long, silence fell like a tense cloak over the scene, and it could be seen that perhaps a score of the armsmen of Brightpennant stood defiantly in the arch, swords and shields raised ready for the fray. Almost as many stood uncertainly aside, openhanded and looking rather foolish.

"Those who've surrendered," Bloodblade said flatly, "get you down on the stones, *now*—facedown, and move not until I say so."

After a moment of uncertain hesitation, the unarmed men clattered their ways onto their bellies, leaving the few defiant armsmen alone in the arch. "Such loyalty should be rewarded," Bloodblade declaimed grandly, looking up and around at frightened faces peering out of house windows and castle balconies. And his open hand swept down.

The line of spears was flung, and Bloodblade's spearmen hurled themselves to the cobbles in the same movement. The Brightpennant armsmen were still staggering and reeling when half a hundred crossbows fired again, the crash and thrumming as loud as ever.

When that hail of heavy quarrels was done, only three men still stood in the arch. Bloodblade's horse danced restlessly, snorting at the smell of blood, but he sat in his saddle as easily as if it was a solid, immobile throne, and asked gently, "You three brave men—do you reconsider? Will you fight for me, or still stand against me? I pay well, but coin is brighter payment than the waiting grave."

One armsman threw down his sword and shield—but the Brightpennant guard beside him turned and drove his blade through the side lacings of the man's armor, and he fell. Grim-faced, the two surviving armsmen looked at each other, then straightened their shoulders and stood ready against Bloodblade's army.

"Halduth," the warlord said calmly, and the ranks of his host parted before a man even larger than the false Bloodblade in the fluted armor—a man who drew back his arm and hurled a war spear as large as a tree without salute or delay.

It struck one of the two remaining defenders in the chest, plucking the man off his feet and bearing him some twenty paces into the castle courtyard. When the spear slid to a stop, the bleeding, broken thing wrapped around it no longer looked like a man, let alone clung to life.

The last man wept, flung down his shield—and then with a wild roar, raced forward into the ranks of Bloodblade's men, hacking frantically. For an amazingly long time he slashed, thrust, kicked, and spat, loudly crying, "Brightpennant!" thrice . . . but in the end he was overwhelmed, and men turned from him to raise bloody blades in salute to Sendrith Duthjack.

Bloodblade gestured wordlessly to the castle, and with a roar they surged inside, waving blades and bellowing triumph. Their orders were clear: no breakage or burning, no harrying of horseflesh, no savaging of any clergy, cook, or kitchen maid—but all armsmen, swordcaptains, courtiers, and other women were theirs to sport with.

As the screaming began, Bloodblade turned in his saddle to look down into certain waiting faces, and said, "Lorthkul, stand guard around me with all your command. Darag, go and secure what I've ordered."

Darag saluted him impassively and led his men off at a trot.

Bloodblade watched men hooting and running this way and that across the castle yard for a time, and was seen to smile. Then he turned again, and said to Lorthkul, "Find me the trade fair. We'll buy herbs there and enjoy fair Sart town, until Darag sends word that the feast is ready. Castles are such noisy, bloody places."

5

A Storm of Serpents

The faces of the commoners were white with terror;
clearly they expected to die here this night, as they
shuffled into the feasting hall of Sart Castle under the gentle but firm hands of Bloodblade's armsmen.

When the seats were filled—fourscore full-armed warriors, still in their reeking and blood-smirched armor,
seated across from as many frightened commoners—and
swordcaptains at each table had rapped for silence and received it, the tapestries behind the baronial high seat
parted, and a large man in a plain tunic came into view,
bearing the baron's great goblet in his hand.

"Welcome!" he said pleasantly. "I am your baron—
Lord of Brightpennant and Glarond both. I'm sure you're
all well aware of the unpleasantness that befell earlier this
day, and my men have shown you several chambers full of
carrion we scoured out of these halls: courtiers who
should have been dead years ago, or doing honest work as
you do, rather than simpering over feasts here while you
sweated."

He smiled around at them. "No, friends, there are no
tricks. Unless one of you is so foolish as to draw blade and
try to harm any warrior here, none of you will die this

night. Eat and drink heartily! Be merry, for this is a bright new beginning for Sart and for Brightpennant!"

He raised his goblet in salute. "This is your feast now, and your castle. In Bloodblade's Aglirta—yes, the rumors are true, may we always meet in pleasant peace—there'll be no more such bejewelled parasites bleeding you white with taxes. You will find my hand light and merciful, and my rule fair—so long as you but spare some food and drink for my army, as I march on Flowfoam, to take the River Throne and become your rightful king."

The faint echoes of distant, drunken singing came to him. The man who called himself Bloodblade smiled faintly, and went to find the errant open window.

When he found it, amid all the fine paneling, tapestries, and gleaming statuettes, he drew it firmly down to shut out the sounds of revelry, murmured, "The feast is well advanced, indeed," and retrieved his goblet of wine.

Three Above, but these barons treated themselves well! This rich, cherry-red Best Aluith from the Sheiryn uplands was like nuts and fire, warming the belly as much as it pleased the tongue.

Bloodblade swirled the goblet to watch it flash back reflections of the candlelight as he padded barefoot across what had been until recently Glarsimber the Wolf's study. His men had installed two terrified but still attractive chambermaids in the bed he'd sleep in this night, but the warlord was in no hurry to seek that particular door. Darag had gagged the wenches to keep them silent, and bound them to the bedposts to keep them unharmed and where they should be; they would keep until it suited him to go visiting.

He wandered about the study. Books, many books, some of them too old and dusty to have known Glarsimber's touch. Idly he drew one forth, flipped it open to a random page, and read aloud, "The blessed text begins, aye, so it doth, calling forth trumpet-clear o'er hills and turrets, bat-

tlements and spires, to smite the ears of foolish men and
their hearts besides, and leave no life untouched, no soul
unguided . . ."

Smirking, Bloodblade slammed the book, rearing his
head back from the inevitable cloud of dust, and slid it
back into place, shaking his head. Why did otherwise
clear-witted men waste their time with such airy frip-
peries—such utter dross?

There was a restlessness in him, this night. Sart had
fallen too easily; the task seemed unfinished, somehow.
The Baron of Glarond and Brightpennant lingered by Glarsimber's map of Aglirta, staring thoughtfully at the twists
and turns of the Silverflow. "Where to conquer next?" he
asked the empty air lightly. "Ah, decisions, decisions . . ."

The voice from the darkness behind him was as unexpected as it was soft. "Nay, Bloodblade, don't alter what
we've agreed to. We can't shield you with magic if you
turn willful tyrant on us and ride where we don't expect."

Sendrith Duthjack's face was suddenly as hard as stone,
his eyes two glittering gems as his hand closed like a claw
around the baronial goblet—but he took care to relax his
features into a calm mask ere he turned to face the speaker.
He did not, however, smile.

*Red-gold it was, bright against the darkness of his dreams,
looming up bright and fierce to stare right at him.*

*He stared back into the dragon's golden, knowing gaze,
caught and held by its regard as if he was transfixed on a
sword. He could not move, could not speak, too terrified to
even weep as the great wyrm turned lazily, so smooth on its
vast wings.*

*As large as a castle it dived at him, racing down, its
great jaws and claws opening . . .*

And then, as always, he woke up.

Meanwhile

Flaeros paused for breath, wiping sweat from his brow with his sleeve. "Baron," he gasped, "could we rest, perhaps?"

The Baron of Brightpennant turned and gave him a quizzical glare. "Why, lad? It's been but half a day, at none so brisk a walk! Have you stepped on something? D'you nurse some hidden wound or other?"

The Bard of the Delcampers drew himself up, breathing heavily, and then gave Glarsimber the Wolf a miserable smile. "No," he panted, "I'm just not used—to this—"

The baron snorted. "How can you be a bard, and sing of long pursuits and hunts, if you've never even walked in the woods for a day? Wet with sweat, and not even wearing armor! What do Delcampers have for backbones, anyway? Broken straws?"

Flaeros winced, but Glarsimber put a heavy hand on his shoulder and practically forced him down into a sitting position on a wayside stone. "Sit, lad, and rest," he growled. "It's not like Aglirta hasn't needed saving for several centuries or so! What boots another day or two?"

And he lowered his own substantial backside onto an adjacent stone.

They'd been sitting thus, breathing in heavy unison, for quite some time when the baron stiffened, turned his head a little, and listened intently, holding up a hand for silence.

Flaeros bent his head and leaned in that direction, too. It wasn't long before he heard what had caught the baron's attention—and that even now made Glarsimber put a finger to lips for silence and gesture that they should both rise. The old warrior promptly drew his blade with exaggerated care and slowness, so that it made not a sound, and put a hand on the bard's wrist before Flaeros could attempt the same thing.

Transferring his grip up to a handy Delcamper forearm,

he led Flaeros back away from the rocks, to where there was a little open space around the road where a tree had fallen long ago. Then the baron turned again to face the direction from which those soft sounds—of footfalls, boots planted heavily and clumsily on soft ground—had come, and crouched with his sword hilt low before him, its tip up and foremost like the prow of a ship.

And then the shambling Melted came.

Dead they were, or looked it, and yet moved. Stiff and clumsy, striding ahead with unseeing eyes and blades in their hands, their flesh melted and sagging hideously away from skulls and lesser bones.

"Oak and Lady both be with me," the baron swore, eyes narrowing. Melted! Hadn't they all fallen with Corloun? Or—gods, yes!—didn't every damned wizard write everything down so he could boast about it? And those scrolls fell into the hands of other mages, and so on . . . but of course: every wizard in all the Vale probably knew how to make these shamblers now!

"Run, lad," he said shortly. "You can't stand up to these—try, and let them get a grip on you, and they'll explode into flames and take you with 'em!"

"But—I can't leave you!" Flaeros protested, dancing in fearful indecision, torn between fleeing and not daring to leave the reassuring safety of the Smiling Wolf's blade.

"Ah, got to stay and see the heroic baronial fall, and write the ballad about it, hey?" Glarsimber said, eyes never leaving the advancing cadavers. "Can't you see it from a distance, lad? Or perhaps work some useful magic with that scepter you've been so clumsy at trying to keep hidden from me?"

"I—uh—"

The silver-tongued bard Flaeros was still struggling for words when the first Melted reached Glarsimber—and swung its blade with a vicious speed that was astonishing for something that tottered along with such faltering, stumbling strides.

But the Smiling Wolf wasn't there. A quick sidestep, a lunge around and to the right—and the slashing blade missed an armored thigh by inches, while Glarsimber brought his own stout blade around in a chop that half severed the Melted's head. It flopped loosely atop the bloodless neck, but seemed not to slow or confuse the shuffling cadaver at all. The Melted turned with a lurch and struck out vigorously again, striking sparks from the baron's parrying blade—and this time Glarsimber backed hastily away from it, as three other Melted came within reach and chopped at him in unison, heedless of each other's blades or the intervening arm of the first Melted.

That arm dangled from a few strips of flesh when they were done, and one Melted had been knocked over by the backswing of a fellow, but none of the lurching corpses seemed to feel pain or even to notice what wounds they took or what happened to their fellows. They stumbled forward, and Glarsimber cast a quick look back over his other shoulder, swore, and lunged with his blade right under a Delcamper armpit. "Gods, lad, don't you ever look behind you?"

Flaeros gulped, ran a few steps and turned in time to see the Baron of Brightpennant slash open the face of a Melted with a flurry of swordblows, duck forward to trip the corpse over backwards, then spin away to rush back to where he'd first been fighting, and parry the thrusting blade of *another* Melted before it ran Flaeros through.

"Would this be the hearty exercise you were saving your strength for earlier, lad?" Glarsimber panted, as he pounded past. "I'd appreciate it if you jumped about a bit, even if you don't want to swing a blade—just to give these corpses a little sport, that's all!"

Flaeros shot him a shocked look, then realized the baron was jesting and ducked frantically away from the blade of a Melted—only to feel the icy sting of another blade, its tip just slicing flesh after cutting through a stout cloak and fine Delcamper clothing. Glarsimber shouted and hacked that

Melted furiously away, sending it staggering back on its heels with its forearms cut off, and then it seemed to the panting, stumbling bard that they were ringed all around by dark blades, closing in slowly as the Melted holding them advanced impassively, and that despite the baron's raging, they were doomed . . .

Suddenly there was a coldness in the air around them that shouldn't have been there, and a blue mist or smoke, and then strange shadowy trees that didn't match the trees around them—and the blue radiance shaped a ring or arch around them, through which the thrusting blades of the Melted were forcing them, as Glarsimber cursed and stamped and slashed . . .

. . . And then, suddenly, they were somewhere else, in a forest that looked Aglirtan: Flaeros, Baron Belklarravus, and a dozen or more Melted.

"We were herded, lad! Watch sharp!" Glarsimber roared, hacking and parrying like a madman. Flaeros ducked away from one Melted, rolled away from the thrusting blade of another—and suddenly found himself with no foe standing in his way, amid long-dead branches in the undergrowth of a deep forest. Sun reached down to light up small pools of the forest floor in the distance—glades choked with green leaves blazing bright in the sunlight—and in the far, rolling distance, the green gloom brightened where there must be an edge to the trees, with open land beyond.

The bard found his feet and ran like he'd never run before, crashing through brittle dead branches and plunging down slippery slopes choked in deep leaves and moss, whooping for breath and just running, running, all thoughts of brave barons and dragon scepters and regent's summons forgotten in his frantic flight to be away from silent, lurching corpses that reached for him with drooping, dripping flesh.

*   *   *

"For Brightpennant! For Sart! Ah, Lady take you—for *me*, damn it!"

Baron Glarsimber hacked through what must have been his fortieth severed Melted arm. *None of these had caught flame, thank the watching gods—why, I wonder?*

That had been a spell-gate, and they'd been herded through it, he and the lad—why? And where by the Claws of the Dark One *was* Flaeros, anyway?

The Smiling Wolf chopped aside a Melted blade and then an elbow, beyond, spinning the cadaver around. Then he hacked viciously at its knees from behind, pitching it over on its back, forever.

That was the last. He was done.

Wearily, Glarsimber leaned on his sword, panted for breath, and bellowed the lad's name. No reply.

He peered about, under the trees, fearing the worst, and shouted for the bard again. Nothing but Melted and their pieces, lying where they'd fallen. Not even a trail of blood.

The Baron of Brightpennant panted out a fervent curse on all bards, hacked aside a sapling that was in his way, and grimly started searching.

"Along the towpaths, Lord, all day and night," the man gasped, before he fell on his face on the polished marble of Flowfoam.

Blackgult knelt beside him, ignoring courtiers' shocked looks, and said to that battered, exhausted face, "Blood-blade claimed to be Baron of Glarond, ere his men carried Sart Castle?"

"Aye, Lord Regent," the man said in a dull, fading voice. "Glarond and Brightpennant both, he said—and our army to join his." His next word trailed off into an unintelligible moan, and his eyes closed.

"My thanks, loyal sir," the regent said, clasping the man's shoulder.

He rose and snapped at the nearest courtier, "Temple healers! Here, at once, to see to this brave man!"

"L-lord?"

Blackgult caught the disbelieving courtier by the shoulder, pointed at the unconscious and travel-stained body sprawled on the marble before the River Throne, and snarled, "*This* is what a courtier should be! Remember well true loyalty, and its reward—and by the Horns of the Lady, get those healers! *Run!*"

This last bellow nearly deafened the courtier, and made him stumble backwards down the steps to a hard and painful landing on his behind—but he scrambled up and promptly trotted away, painfully but at a respectable speed.

Blackgult whirled around to point at another courtier. "You! To the barracks, forthwith! Tell the swordcaptains full provisions—ready for war!" He pointed at another courtier. "You! To the South Tower; tell Halvan to be ready. Then drop all else and submit to Garzhar's orders. He'll be in charge here."

The courtier gaped at him. "Old Garzhar of the Guards? In charge? But—but Lord, where will you—?"

"I'll be riding to war," the regent told him with a savage smile, "at least one last time. For Aglirta, and a future for us all!"

His smile twisted wryly. "As the bards say."

The attack was a complete surprise. Thinking themselves safe with the hastily whelmed forces of Brostos massed between them and the brigand army of Bloodblade, the red-cloaked knights of Maerlin were still fetching out their best blades and brightest armor when barges grated against their docks and the warriors of Bloodblade stormed ashore, spitting everything that moved on their spears—and greeting the indignantly charging knights with volleys of heavy crossbow quarrels, whistling storms of death that slew hundreds in the space of a few breaths.

Then it was just a matter of seizing riderless horses and riding through the barony, swording half-armored, magnificently moustached men as they tried to hide or gather their best treasures before fleeing.

Brostos would keep, an all-too-sparse line of armaragors and farmhands hastily made armsmen waiting in grim fear along the borders of the barony. They'd not move a stride onto lands not their own—so why break blades against them, when they'd surrender like the grateful cowards they were, once summoned to Flowfoam by the new king?

Castle Maerlin was scoured out by nightfall, its dungeons crowded with terrified baronial heirs, wives, consorts, and courtiers who had—or claimed to have—hidden wealth with which to buy their freedom, if taken under escort to reclaim it.

Bloodblade was already hard at work on the list of those his men were to make sure "accidents" befell after their treasure was safely in hand and of those who were harmless enough to be let go.

There were *three* fair lasses waiting in chains in his bedchamber this night, but they would have to wait until another feast was done, whereat another dumbfounded, fearful crowd of commoners would be told that there'd be no more "bejewelled parasites" of courtiers overtaxing them in Bloodblade's Aglirta—if they but spared some food and drink for his armies, as he marched on Flowfoam to take the Throne.

It was so close now that Bloodblade could taste it.

"I've a bad feeling about this," Craer grunted, as they trudged along the road together.

"What, walking? Try to remember all the years before you became an overduke, and your feet should recall their familiar aches," Sarasper told him with mock tenderness and sympathy.

"No, you old dolt, not my feet—the road. 'Tis too quiet,"

Craer snapped. "Where're all the peddlers? The carters? By the Three, not even a wagon, let alone a caravan! Just locals, like those woodcutters—no one who's travelled far!"

"That's true enough," Hawkril rumbled, looking thoughtful. "Aye, these roads'd have to be busier than this."

Raulin and Embra both looked at Craer with wide, fearful eyes.

The procurer nodded slowly, and voiced the fear rising in all of their minds. "So *what* has been happening in Aglirta while we trudge along the backlands of nowhere? What *now*?"

"Ready, Halvan?" Blackgult called, reining in his huge black warhorse and ignoring its dragonlike snorts of outrage.

"Ho, Regent!" the fat armored man on the bay mount almost as large roared back. "My Sirl Swords can o'ermatch anything Bloodblade can send against us!"

Blackgult grinned. "For the coin you cost, that's the least I'd expect! What, no dancing girls, too?"

Halvan threw back his head and roared with laughter.

They understood each other, the Regent of Aglirta and the Sirl mercenary captain. Blackgult had whelmed a few hundred men from the fragments of his own old baronial forces—but if the news that Bloodblade had taken Maerlin was true, that meant the Regent of Aglirta commanded just enough men to guard the stables of Castle Maerlin, and keep safe the horses of the would-be usurper.

Halvan's troops numbered nigh a thousand, but a fifth of those were untrained younglings eager to bloody their blades for the first time—and apt to be reckless wildheads in the field, a danger to friend and foe alike.

Yet Halvan could be trusted, his loyalty guaranteed by the spells of three Sirl wizards, who could dash his head to bloody gobbets from afar if he betrayed Blackgult. That was the best thing about hiring Sirl mercenaries, and made them worth three times any muster of other hireswords.

And if they were all fated to die at the hands of Blood-blade—well, at least he'd have to be a strong warcaptain to take them down, perhaps strong enough to hold the Throne against fell wizards and sneaking Serpent-priests, and make Aglirta strong again.

The Golden Griffon had enjoyed a long run and a good one, and the gods gather us all in the end.

Not that it wasn't more fun to send *others* into the ever-lasting embrace of the Three first, cheating the Sirl odds-makers one more time . . .

The breeze gathered force, setting the leaves of the trees ahead to rustling—and Blackgult grinned again, like a carefree lad let out to play. He was riding to war in his old armor once more, free of chattering courtiers, scuttling scribes, and endless papers, papers, and more papers to read and sign.

There was a brief confusion of jostling horses and good-naturedly cursing riders as the Royal Host of Aglirta narrowed to a point, like a gigantic spear, to pour down the dark, narrow road ahead.

When things were sorted out, the riders gathered speed. "Lances down," Blackgult and Halvan ordered the ar-maragors ahead, in unplanned unison, and then traded grins again as the thunder of hooves grew loud in the dim-shaded corridor around them. From the farms nigh the docks, the main road through southbank Silvertree ran through these tangled woods to the open meadows of Sarth Fields.

There, with the sleepy hamlet of Sarth hard by, they'd meet Bloodblade's army, with room enough to swing swords. If the day went against them, they could always fall back into this wood and fight in the shade, sword to sword—but if that befell, it was likely Bloodblade would send barges past them, seize Flowfoam, and proclaim himself king.

Similar forests—and bogs to the south, so treacherous and stinging with insects that no man dwelt there—trammeled Duthjack's way east from Maerlin. Unless he made all his armsmen swim, or built a hundred new barges overnight, the usurper would have to come to Sarth.

If Blackgult could only get there first, he could use the old ditches and cart bridges and hedgerows as his shields, and make Bloodblade pay dearly for daring the snatch at the Crown. If only . . .

There was a shout of triumph from his foremost riders as they spurred out of the trees and found the rolling fields empty of banners and waiting, glittering steel. They were in time! They were—

Pitching from their saddles in startled silence, to be trampled underhoof and lost, man after man of Blackgult's best. What, by all the gods?—there!

"Lances to the side—strike at will! Visors *down*!" Blackgult roared, standing in his stirrups to make his voice carry back.

Serpent-priests were standing among the last few trees, hurling tiny javelins overhand at the riders pounding past.

Javelins that trailed fleeting glows of magic, and found targets with unerring aim: the unprotected faces and throats of men who hadn't laced gorgets up and clasped visors down. No, not javelins, but arrows . . . arrows with strange heads, like the gaping fangs of—

"Serpents!" Halvan swore. "They're throwing *snakes* at us!"

The priests threw snake after snake, little rigid darts that struck down all too many warriors, tumbling them dying out of their saddles. Those that missed hissed and slithered underfoot, though many were crushed by the plunging hooves. Blackgult saw one priest throw his last snake and then race forward with knife in hand, screaming with rage, eyes fearless, to slash at stirrups and girth straps and the flanks of warhorses. He was kicked aside by several horsemen, but always rose again.

Fearless—they were all fearless. Drunk on some potion or perhaps a spell of their wizard god.

Blackgult leaned down from his saddle to slash one dagger-wielding priest across the face, met the glare of glittering, hate-filled eyes for a moment, then swept on. That man had not bled! His sword had laid open flesh to grate along bone beneath, right across jaw and nose and forehead—yet no blood!

"*More* magic!" he cursed, and felt for the Dwaer in their pouch slung under his left armpit. Well, if sorcery was the favored sword this day . . .

That thought took him as far as the first cart bridge in Sarth Fields, where the road crossed winding Crommor's Creek— and the realization, as armaragors cursed and wrestled with their reins ahead of him, that the bridge was missing. To avoid a breakneck plunge into the narrow, deep creek bed, riders were turning right and left along the banks—and there were shouts and the clang of weapons making war.

Blackgult turned one way, and Halvan the other—and both found themselves staring at an army now scrambling on foot up the slopes of the creek to attack them with an uneven line of dark, dung-smeared pikes and bills and man-forks.

Mercenaries! A ragtag, motley host of tattooed and strange-armored hireswords from seemingly every port and town in Darsar—thousands of them!

Blackgult gaped in utter disbelief. He could see red-sashed pirates out of Jarrada, running shoulder-to-shoulder with grim, spire-helmed knights of Pelaerth! Even as the Royal Host crashed to a halt in a welter of shouting, hacking men, there came a sudden thunder of hooves from beyond the barns of Sarth—and into view around an orchard came a long line of horsemen, riding hard. Pennants of bright silk— oranges, golds, and vivid lime greens, colors never seen in Aglirta—streamed from the tips of their long lances.

"Flame Riders!" Halvan shouted, sounding every bit as disbelieving as Blackgult. The fearsome warriors of the hot South, not seen on a Vale battlefield before . . . dusky-skinned and straw-haired men of far Sarinda beyond Carraglas, who fought in silks with streamers of silk whirling from bracers at their wrists, with no armor but glassy plates down their arms, and wielded swords of hardened glass!

The coffers of the Scaly Ones must be deep indeed to reach so far, and bring so many here unseen! There was no sign of Bloodblade—this must be the Snake-lovers' own doom for Aglirta!

A hurled spear clanged harmlessly off his shoulder-plates, and fell away. Blackgult snarled a curse and snatched at the horn that hung at his belt, to blow the call to form a lance ring. Barely onto the field, and the Royal Host would be making its last stand!

Halvan was watching for the horn already. Blackgult held it up so the Sirl warcaptain could see it clearly, but turned his head south again as he blew it, to look towards the river. Was the disaster complete, and Bloodblade sliding past this fray on barges?

No—the Three had granted him that small mercy, at least. Well, 'twas time to die gloriously, for Aglirta and the Rightful King!

He roared that battle cry as he wheeled his mount, heading for the highest nearby hill, and heard the men around him—his own loyal men of Blackgult—take it up, raggedly and then proudly, as the hooves of their war mounts trampled barley, and the hilltop seemed to leap towards them.

Behind them the galloping Flame Riders gathered speed, lances lowered, seeking to overrun the Royal Host before the lance ring could be formed.

Serpent-priests were running fearlessly alongside the Aglirtan armaragors, hurling daggers. Blackgult glared at more who rose out of the barley to meet them, with more serpent-arrows—no, they'd been whisked here by spells.

No matter. He looked into their eyes, and they looked back—looks that promised death.

The Serpent-priests, smiling coldly, had also come to play at Throne-snatching.

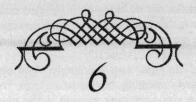

6

A King Shall Arise

The road ahead wound through overgrown, abandoned farm fields—Craer growled; the tall grasses were the best sort of cover for lurking brigands—and plunged into a shady hollow, crossing a small stream and vanishing into trees. Peering along it, they could just see a few bright patches of sundapple in the distance.

"Raulin?" Craer asked quietly, from the head of the weary procession of walkers.

"Nothing but stray flies and fluttercloaks," the bard replied, from his post at the back, looking ever behind him.

Craer looked at Hawkril. "This is eerie. Unless there's a plague we've not heard about, or a dozen hungry dragons came foraging last night, the countryside shouldn't be nearly this empty."

The hulking armaragor spread his gauntlets in a helpless shrug. "Mayhap they saw you coming, and decided to hide what they hold most valuable."

Craer snorted. "In backcountry farms, that'd be a cow."

Sarasper shook his head. "Nay, Lord Overduke—when times are hard, the only valuable possession left to the farmer is himself."

The procurer made a rude, derisive sound. "So they all

dragged trunks out of hidey-holes, leaped inside, locked the lids down, bumped themselves back into the holes, and caused the ready-heaped earth and turf to fall neatly back into place atop them, is that it?"

"Gently," Sarasper said soothingly, "and eyes front: I thought I saw something moving in the trees, yonder."

"*I'll* give you something moving in the trees yonder," Craer snarled, "in a breath or . . ."

His sour promise trailed away as they all saw it: a heavy-set man in armor, stalking along through the forest with a drawn sword in hand. Lurching along, the warrior seemed to be alone . . . and that jowly, long-sideburned face looked familiar, somehow . . .

"Brightpennant!" Craer called. "Smiling Wolf!"

The man's head jerked up, and he peered through the trees at them. He'd obviously been following the line of the road without getting too close to it, or paying it overmuch attention. Now he came crashing down through the ferns and manythorn canes towards them, wearing a frown.

"Fair day, Overdukes," he greeted them. "Have you seen a young fool of a bard running this way?"

Four heads turned to look at Raulin, who stared at Glarsimber of Sart in puzzlement.

The baron lifted an eyebrow and spoke directly to the lad. "Well, have you?"

"This one's a bard," Sarasper explained, jerking a thumb in Raulin's direction.

Glarsimber's brows drew together. "Nay, nay—'tis Flaeros Delcamper I'm looking for! This lad's a bard, too?"

"Well—my father was," Raulin said quietly. "What befalls, Lord Baron?"

Glarsimber looked quickly from the young lad to the overdukes; Embra smiled and murmured, "Pray speak freely. We've no secrets between us—or betwixt us and the regent, for that matter. What befalls?"

The Baron of Brightpennant frowned. "A lot of things,

but one over all: the hiresword men call Bloodblade has whelmed an army, and marches on Flowfoam as we speak, to crown himself King of Aglirta—over the bodies of all who stand against him."

Several jaws dropped. "Pardon, Glarsimber," Craer said sharply, "but—you've seen the warlord with your own eyes?"

The baron shook his head. "No, and I can scarce believe it myself. Yet I trust the one I heard it from."

"Who was?" Sarasper asked promptly.

Glarsimber of Sart looked uncomfortable. "King Kelgrael himself," he replied, leaning close to them and lowering his voice. "Like a ghost, mind—flickering like a candle-flame, and I could see through him all the while."

"That would be the king, aye," Hawkril said slowly, shaking his head in disbelief—and dismay. How could so much have gone wrong in the Vale so swiftly? What was so amiss about this realm he loved, and called home, and now served? An usurper—seen by the Risen King and yet not by us? How could this be?

He and the rest of the overdukes traded frowns, and there were several other headshakings.

"Pardon, Lords," Raulin ventured, "but why look you so puzzled? You believe the Lord Baron, and yet believe not his news?"

Craer's answering grin was entirely empty of humor. "Right, lad—exactly."

Sarasper added, "You see, mercenaries don't act this way. Why stick your head into the noose of rulership, when you can collect endless coins by fostering small skirmishes and avoid all the work and danger of actually sitting on a throne. So what in truth is going on?"

"A king shall arise . . ." Sarasper quoted an old ballad— and it was Raulin's turn to frown, as he found he couldn't remember the words to the rest of it.

And that was not a good sign.

* * *

"A king shall arise," a soft voice purred in a room suddenly a little less dark—as the glow rising from a large, tilted mirror shaped itself into vivid, moving hues, and then spun suddenly into clarity: a scene of the towering walls of Flowfoam Isle, and a surging in the river water that became scores of slow-moving, purposeful warriors climbing up the stones. "And about time, too . . ."

The man in the splendid tunic looped with glittering chains of gold wore a thoroughly bored expression as he strolled down the hall. Whistling more tunelessly than he thought he was, he idly regarded the gilding of his fingernails— yes, chipped, just as he'd feared—and stopped to gaze at his reflection in one of the oval mirrors flanking the statue of King Olaurim, who'd ruled Aglirta so long ago that there'd been no baronies then.

"In the days when the Three walked the land and trees were all rooted in the air, floating freely and blowing hither and thither with the storms," the courtier quoted grandly, waving his hands like a great orator, "then was Aglirta born, king and all, and great was the war and wrack of its founding. Beasts were hurled back and roads laid down, and deeds actually *mattered* . . . instead of this endless, *yawning* boredom . . ."

"If it's not too much trouble, Saraedrin," the impassive guard standing at the doors at the end of the hall said suddenly, "could you stir your bored legs a trifle and get yourself to the throne room? Ranking Sword Garzhar's *waiting* for your report."

Thelmert Saraedrin's head snapped up. "And if he is? I'm not in the habit of taking orders from old fools in ill-fitting armor—or doorguards, for that matter!"

"We can all learn good habits before we die, Saraedrin," the guard said ominously. "Even if our death's not all that far off . . ." He put a hand to his sword-hilt and drew forth his sword a meaningful three fingers' worth.

"Threats, threats," the courtier sneered. "That's all you steel heads know, isn't it? All dozen of you broken-down old men, swaggering around the palace like strutting roosters now, with the regent gone to war!"

"Aye," the guard agreed, "*to war*. Which is why your oath of loyalty to the Throne binds you to obey Garzhar as you would the regent—and him as you would the king himself! Now *jump*, or war will come to Flowfoam even swifter than Bloodblade can ride!"

Saraedrin snapped his fingers insolently. "I tremble, I tremble," he taunted the guard, as he reached the doors. "See?"

The doors swung wide under a practiced hand, the courtier drew himself up with a last sneer in the guard's direction—and a boot connected solidly with Saraedrin's backside, sending him sprawling forward onto the gleaming marble of the throne chamber.

"Why, you—" the courtier sputtered, voice rising into inarticulate rage.

Before he could think of a suitable string of oaths or even get to his feet, an old and dry voice above him commented, "Your haste is commendable, Saraedrin. Have you those figures for me at last? They won't wait forever; I'm not a young man, you know."

The courtier picked himself up, face dark with anger, and snapped, "Who cares how many barrels of salted fish and wheels of cheese we have, anyway? The regent rides to war and all we fuss over is—"

"Preparations to withstand a siege, if need be," Ranking Sword Garzhar said in a voice of cold iron. "On the morrow, Thelmert Saraedrin, you'll be fitted for armor and taught to hold a sword. By the day after that, I'll expect you to swing it without falling over."

"What?" the courtier almost howled. He met Garzhar's cold stare, choked back what he'd been going to say, and instead asked sarcastically, "And what will you expect me to do on the day after that?"

"I don't expect there will be a day after that," Garzhar said quietly, "for any of us."

The courtier stared at him in disbelief. The bent old man in armor ran an unsteady, callused hand through his few remaining strands of white hair, and said grimly, "There's no way I can hold this island against any attack, with twelve old men in arms, three dozen fat, lazy, and utterly untrained courtiers, twenty chambermaids, and as many cooks. Even if we're attacked at only one spot, and we all happen by the great blessing of the Three to be standing right there, ready to fight—instead of having to run across the Isle from somewhere *else*—we're doomed. A few moments of sport for a handful of good armsmen, and we'll be feeding the flies forever."

"*What*?" Saraedrin cried again, getting good volume this time, so that his voice echoed across the throne chamber and made other courtiers look up and start to drift over from the various pillars they'd been leaning against. "Then—then—why do we stay here?"

"I and the guardsmen under my command stay here because we were ordered to," Garzhar said slowly and coldly, "and that's what loyalty and a Crown Oath *mean*." He turned away. "As for you pretty-boy dandies who don't understand the oaths you swear or intend to keep them, I've never understood why you stay here, loudly lamenting your boredom. The free food, I suppose."

"I resent that," another courtier said in his customary grand, deep voice. "Why, in all the years I—"

"Sword Garzhar!" the guard from the doors shouted. "Melted! Scores of them! They came over the wall by Northlook Tower, and are at the Garden Gate already! Daeruth's calling for aid!"

"My thanks, Ilibar! You guard the throne!" Ranking Sword Garzhar was already limping across the polished marble, drawing his sword as he went. "Tarth!"

"Here, Lord!" The young page was already at Garzhar's side. He put the old man's helm into his hands—then handed him a flask of wine.

The old man's eyes widened, and he clapped the boy on the arm, and said, "My thanks for this. Get the cooks and maids away, *now*." He strode on.

"What?" the deep-voiced courtier snapped. "You still have boats? I thought the regent took them all! Where are they?"

"Get to your post, Nilvarr!" Garzhar roared in disgust, not slowing in his march to the far doors.

The courtier ignored him. "Boy—*boy*! I demand that you—"

"Tarth!" The ranking sword called back. "Follow the order I gave you last night!"

"With *pleasure*, Lord!" the page cried, darting for another door. Saraedrin and Nilvarr raced after him, shouting at him to stop.

Saraedrin was swifter, but Nilvarr was much closer. His heavy hand fell upon the page's shoulder when they were a little more than halfway across the nigh-deserted throne chamber. "Stop, you disobedient little *dog*!" Nilvarr snarled, spinning Tarth around. "I'm a lord of the court, and I gave you a direct order! You're in a lot of trouble, and you'll be in a lot more if—"

"—I do *this*!" Tarth shouted suddenly, clawing aside Nilvarr's ornamental silver filigree codpiece with one swipe of his hand—and lifting his leg in a full-strength kick that met Nilvarr's best hose at precisely the spot where the courtier's legs joined his torso.

The tall, florid Nilvarr made a high-pitched, birdlike chirping sound as he rose a few inches into the air, attempted some futile clutching, clawing motions—and fell on his face, senseless, right at Saraedrin's rushing feet.

Helplessly, Thelmert Saraedrin tripped and went sprawling—and by the time he'd scrambled to his feet again and joined a few other courtiers at that door, the guard, Ilibar Quelver, was standing in their path with his back to the door Tarth had vanished through, his sword in his hand, and a cold grin on his face.

"I will have no choice," he said in a voice soft with eager promise, "but to regard any man who tries to get past me as a traitor to the Crown and an agent of the would-be usurper Bloodblade—and be warned: I'll treat such a man fittingly." The tip of his sword lifted a little, meaningfully.

The courtiers hesitated, not wanting to turn away or to look at each other—and in that uncertain moment, they heard a wrenching cry of agony from somewhere distant in the palace, followed by the faint clash of arms.

There was a sudden, scrambling rush, and Ilibar Quelver was alone again, shaking his head at the retreating backs of men busily scampering up staircases and along balconies, each heading for his favorite bower or back closet.

"They'll all be lonely in their various hiding places," he murmured, as he swung his sword at empty air a few times and prepared himself to die, "lacking their usual chambermaid companionship. I hope they won't all be *bored*."

The skirl and clang of swords grew louder. Ilibar swallowed. *By the Three, but we're giving ground fast!*

Only the eldest and most infirm guards had stayed on Flowfoam, he well knew—and this handful of fussing courtiers who truly had no welcome elsewhere. Everyone else had taken horse to ride with Blackgult, and hurl back Bloodblade . . . if they could. Even with the Sirl hireswords, it probably wouldn't be enough. Not if the warlord truly was rolling over baronies like a boy tumbling down a riverbank, and all their surviving soldiery was now marching under his banners.

Well, at least he'd die somewhere important, doing something that mattered. Hurriedly, Ilibar took up a stance in front of the empty throne, bared blade in hand, and said aloud to the empty, echoing chamber, "Horned Lady, bring us victory from beyond hope; Forefather Oak, keep me standing; Dark One, guide my biting blade. Be with me, you Three, if you love Aglirta half as much as I do!"

His last words had been almost a whisper, but they rang clear in the empty room—and as their last echoes died, he heard a desperate shout from outside the room, followed by a crash, some cursing, and then a louder boom as the doors he was wont to guard burst open.

Ranking Sword Garzhar—his helm gone and one shoulder-plate dangling uselessly—and two other guards reeled back into the room, grunting and gasping with every weary swing of their swords. Slow, weak, and reeling with weariness, they'd have been dead long ago, Ilibar saw, if they'd faced young, fresh foes.

Yet in some ways, the Melted were worse. Unseeing, inexorable, staggering forward heedless of pain, they kept coming—

Ilibar winced as two blades slashed from different directions. Old Garzhar flung up his sword in a desperate parry, tilting his head away, and sparks flew from the fury of that meeting of war steel.

Unscathed by any swordblade, the old man in armor staggered back and almost fell—and Ilibar could take no more.

"Garzhar!" he cried. "To me! To the throne! Rest you, and let me sport a while!"

The old, weathered face turned towards him, in surprise, and then grew a slow grin. The ranking sword waved his blade in a weary gesture as the two Melted pressed forward. "Be my—guest, good Ilibar," he gasped, his words almost drowned out in the scream of one of the other guards dying with two swords through him. "I'm—about done—"

Ilibar launched himself forward in a rush, almost losing his footing on the slick marble. As it was, he came sliding into the fray faster than he'd intended, lost his balance ducking back from the slashing sword of a Melted—they were blind, yet they always knew where living foes stood!—and sat down hard on his behind, crashing into the dead legs of one of the cadavers.

It crashed over past him, and he hacked at its head and arm and leg as he rose—dancing back as the next Melted came at him. He stepped aside so that two couldn't catch him between them—and then looked down the hall at a legion of stiffly marching Melted, coming towards him, and knew just how soon his doom would come.

"Three be with me!" he snarled, and lashed out recklessly at the nearest Melted. By luck his blade caught its throat, spinning it around with its head lolling at a horrible angle—but it swung back at him as if he'd done nothing to it.

"Fall back!" Garzhar shouted, his voice cracked and breathless. "Back to the throne, lads!"

The other guard—Keldert, perhaps, though Ilibar never had time to look properly and be sure of who it was—groaned as he took a blade in his stomach, and never even had time to try to obey. Ilibar saw the Melted hack him down with brutal efficiency as he ran back across the slick marble, to where Old Garzhar stood facing the foremost Melted.

"We're the last," the ranking sword panted, as Ilibar joined him. They backed around behind the throne, so that it guarded one flank, and stood back to back. "I hope you're at peace with the Three."

Ilibar nodded. "That I am. You?"

Garzhar grinned. "There's this girl I always meant to marry, but never did," he panted, between thrusts and hackings, "but it doesn't seem to matter now . . . so I suppose I am." He beheaded a Melted with a wild whirl of his blade, and shouted, "For Aglirta!"

"For Aglirta!" Ilibar took up the cry, and they hacked and chopped like angry butchers for a long time before Old Garzhar went down silently. Then Ilibar did something he'd never dared try before—he leaped up onto the throne itself, and fought from its height, shouting his defiance at the seemingly endless waves of walking dead.

Above a glowing mirror, there was a soft hiss of disgust, and then a few muttered words. The mirror flashed blinding bright.

* * *

The Melted around him suddenly burst into flames, and Ilibar screamed at the pain—screamed and sprang forward, howling, hacking blindly in the inferno as dead men crumbled all around him. More of the cadavers were tottering in by the doors he was charged to guard, he knew—unburned dead men, coming to hack him down.

Unseeing, he swung his blade, lurching towards where he knew the doors must be, the stink of his own burning hair and sizzling flesh overwhelming him, choking him—

Something hard and heavy took him in the ribs, and he reeled, losing his sword somewhere in the raging flames before another blow ended it all, and drove Ilibar Quelver down, down, into the waiting, cool darkness . . .

Soft laughter rose above the flickering mirror. It displayed dying flames in the Throne Chamber of Flowfoam, then dozens of Melted converging on the Throne of Aglirta, and then empty halls and feast chambers, followed by deserted kitchens, and more scenes of marching corpses, lurching into every room of Flowfoam Palace while even the bats flapped hastily away above their heads.

"I wonder," that soft voice said then. "The Master of Bats? Lives he yet?"

And then it snorted dismissively and passed a hand over the mirror—which went dark in an instant.

Robes whirred as their owner hurried out, to stride along a corridor—and through a whorl of sorcery spinning lazily at its end.

That same soft laughter rose again, echoing around the Throne Chamber of Flowfoam. An almost casual hand gestured, and in silent obedience the Melted shuffled back to leave clear a path to the high seat.

Shadows cloaked the robed man who stood facing the throne down that open way—the shadows of protective spells, writhing in a ready mantle. Their owner raised his hands and carefully cast a new magic. From the shadows cloaking him a new, brighter radiance stole forth, drifting along the marble to ascend the throne dais, and slowly encircle the seat. It was bare of crown or scepter, and the radiance seemed to prowl around it, searching for something, before slowly dying away.

Silence followed, and the man cloaked in shadows cast the spell a second time. Another wave of seeking radiance toured the dais, the ceiling above, and the throne itself— but no lurking magics could he find. Magic was bound about the seat, deep and many-layered, yes, but no triggers were to be found, and nothing that was awake in its power.

With a chuckle of relief the robed figure strode forward—and sat on the throne.

His mantle of shadows billowed away into nothingness in an instant, and Ingryl Ambelter, Spellmaster of Flowfoam, threw back his head and laughed aloud. The crown itself might yet be adorning the head of that fool Blackgult, but the River Throne held even stronger enchantments, and could be used to power mighty spells indeed. King or not, know it or not, Aglirta now had a new ruler.

He bent his will, and nigh a hundred corpses went to their knees in unison around him.

With a soft, eager smile Ingryl looked around at his Melted, curled his hands around the armrests of the throne, and drew on its power to weave a spell he'd been waiting a long time to unleash.

In but a few moments and a whirl of sparks, it was done. The Spellmaster crowed in triumph—and far away, in the thick of battle, the Regent of Aglirta reeled in his saddle and clutched at his head in sudden agony as a spell that seared like fire took hold in his brain.

7

Scepters, Bats, and Playing Vultures

*I*t was cool in the shady hollow, and the stream slid past dark and wet and inviting. Raulin looked at the peaceful forest all around and could scarcely believe armies were thundering into battle in Aglirta right now, screaming and shouting and dying. He shook his head, a movement unnoticed by the five grim folk standing around him.

Craer was speaking, as usual. "For the nonce, at least, we must leave off Dwaer-hunting! Bloodblade must be dealt with first—after all, if he goes on killing barons, it won't matter which of them was hiding it; it'll either be lost, or the warlord'll have it in his fist when he comes calling, with his army at his back!"

"And how do you propose to 'deal with' Bloodblade?" Embra asked quietly. "Overdukes, a baron, and a bard we may be, but that's just six against his army—or *armies* by now, for all we know."

The procurer smiled and bowed, indicating her with a flourish. "Why, Lady Silvertree, I propose to deal with Bloodblade by assiduously following whatever brilliant stratagem you unfold to us now!"

"I *thought* so," Embra said sourly, amid a few chuckles.

All four men—Raulin and Glarsimber included—leaned forward eagerly to hear the next words from her lips.

She sighed. *Three Above, why me?*

And then Embra heard herself speaking, swift and sure, for all Darsar as if she knew what she was talking about. Perhaps the gods had heard her, after all!

"We must get to Flowfoam as swiftly as we can. If I can call on the power of Bla—of my father's Dwaer, perhaps we can find Bloodblade. Then we use the Dwaer to give Hawk the warlord's likeness, spelljump to him, slay him—and Hawkril pretends to be him. With the right commands, Hawk can turn Bloodblade's troops to fighting among themselves, and so blunt this sword-thrust at the Throne."

There was a roar of approval, and even Sarasper grinned and shook his head. "Impossible," he said. "So crazily impossible that it just might work."

"Right, we do it!" Craer snapped eagerly. "Enough of this wandering back roads—there's a realm to save, barons to twit, and fell wizards to knock on their backsides!"

"An engaging philosophy of life," the Baron of Bright-pennant agreed. "You *are* going to take me with you, aren't you?"

A little silence fell, in which the overdukes traded swift, grim glances. "We have a problem," Embra said carefully. "Right now I can't even take myself to Flowfoam, let alone anyone else. Too little magic."

Glarsimber's eyes narrowed. "What sort of magic is needed?"

The Lady Silvertree sighed. "Anything that bears an enchantment of sufficient power that can be sacrificed—for my spells will drain it to crumbling dust."

The Smiling Wolf grinned at her and tugged aside his gorget. Fishing out a neckchain, he triumphantly produced something small and gleaming, and held it out to her on his palm.

"My little keepsake from the battle in the Silent House,

where Ornentar grew into the Serpent-thing, and Bla—the Lord Regent revealed himself to be Stormharp."

The overdukes bumped heads trying to get a good look at what the baron held. Even Raulin peered at it: a small pendant-charm such as highborn ladies wore ere they took husbands or lovers, and adopted lockets with hair and limned likenesses of their beloved. It was delicately sculpted, and looked almost new: a bright-burnished copper hand.

Brightpennant did off his chain and held it out to Embra. "One of the barons was wearing it—the one who turned out to be a Serpent-priest. Touch it to metal, and it sings; the tone tells if the metal's true."

"Serpent magic—and you carried it?" Craer snapped suspiciously, but Sarasper shook his head.

"Older, lad, and better work. This is *old*."

Embra nodded and sighed, holding the copper hand up high in front of her to begin weaving a jump spell. "It does more than taste if gold's gold," she murmured, studying it critically. "Yes, something I'd love to study and keep safe . . . but"—she grimaced, and closed her hand around it—" 'twill do, burnt-out in an instant, to answer our need."

Raulin gaped in astonishment at what Craer did next. As Embra muttered an incantation and raised her free hand to cut certain exacting gestures out of the empty air, the procurer calmly plucked the tail of her tunic up out of her breeches to lay bare her midriff, planted a firm hand as high on her back as he could reach, to hold it the garment aloft— and all of the men leaned in to put their hands on her skin.

Glarsimber grinned, shook his head, and added his hairy hand to the crowded group, whereupon Raulin gingerly and hesitantly did so, too. Her skin was velvet-soft, gently warm, and smooth.

Blue radiance curled at the edges of their vision; Raulin turned his head to get a better look at it, but could see only the trees. He could feel something stirring, under the Lady Silvertree's skin, tingling in his own fingers . . .

The enchantment ended with a clearly enunciated couplet wherein Embra repeated her earlier comment: "By this magic spilled to work our deed, burnt-out in an instant, to answer our need."

"As Aglirta burns so many things, lass," Sarasper grunted. "Precious magics, dreams, illusions, trusts . . . and people."

Raulin found himself suddenly on the verge of tears. He blinked at the homely old healer.

"Stop cheering me up," Glarsimber growled, close by his shoulder. "It's time to go kill someone."

"Isn't it always?" Embra murmured, as she closed her eyes and brought both of her hands together high over her head, feeling the magic roiling up around them. "Isn't it always?"

Meanwhile

The scepter felt reassuringly smooth and heavy in his hand. Flaeros Delcamper hadn't the faintest idea how to awaken or wield the magic that must slumber inside it—else why would the regent need it, dragon scepter or not?—but holding it made him feel better, even with the Melted far, far behind.

He was clutching it now, as he knelt amid the damp, rotting leaves and fallen branches and fungus of the deep forest, peering out through ferns at mounted warriors galloping along the road.

"A king shall arise," he murmured, seeing the banners of barons flashing past in gauntleted hands. Loushoond, Ornentar, and Tarlagar, bright-fluttering from lancetips, as rider after rider spurred past, the ground shaking with the thunder of their hooves.

War was come to Aglirta, without a doubt, for these armaragors of three baronies were galloping in haste along the road that led to the Silvertree docks—and ready passage to Flowfoam Isle.

Abruptly there was a flash of light, shouting, and the tumult of rearing horses and hooves thudding to halts, swift gaits broken. Flaeros blinked, and dared to lean forward and hold aside a fern, straining to see with eyes still mazed with brightness.

A man had appeared, standing on empty air several feet off the ground. A wizard, it must be—tall and slender and angry-looking, with blue-green flames swirling around his arms.

"Jhavarr Bowdragon am I!" he shouted. "Let none be so foolish as to bend bow against me! I seek but one man!"

A veteran armaragor, who was still wrestling with the reins of his wild-eyed mount, snapped, "Who, then?"

"Is Blackgult the Regent among you? I found him not on Flowfoam."

"He is not," another knight replied. "We hear he's taken the field against the warlord Bloodblade, in southbank Silvertree."

The wizard snarled in anger, threw up his hands, and vanished in a swirl of his flames.

"And kings shall fall," Flaeros murmured, letting the fern dance back into place, his eyes better.

Peering under it, he beheld warriors pointing this way and that, and shouting—save for an old armaragor, closest to the edge of the road, who merely growled, "Wizards!" in a tone of deep disgust.

A man in bright-gleaming armor with the arms of Tarlagar resplendent on a never-worn-before overtunic rode into view, flanked by two bodyguards in matched harness. "Ornentar!" he called, in a deep, self-important voice, "the foreguard must be almost at the docks by now. Shall we ride?"

"Aye," an almost-as-grand shout came back. "We must press on, crazed wizards or no! We'll never have a better chance to—nor Aglirta a greater need for us to—seize the Throne!" An unseen hand must have given a signal, for in the next instant they were all agallop again, thundering on amid the rising dust.

"And which of you will rule it, when you do?" Flaeros muttered, as he sprang to his feet in the wake of the last riders and trotted along after them, just inside the concealing edge of the forest.

"The old, old problem, my Lords," he told the empty air reprovingly, as sticks snapped under his boots, "and not settling such things beforehand is the old, old disaster that goes with it."

And with that wise judgement Flaeros Delcamper stumbled over a tree root and toppled, crashing right onto his face in the dead leaves.

Something hissed over his head, and struck a tree trunk a few paces head. Flaeros gaped at it—an arrow? No, gods, a rigid snake, its spread fangs sunk into the bark, and its eyes turning to look at him!

Flaeros whirled around to see whence the deadly thing had come—and found himself gaping past half a dozen trees, to where a single man in robes stood sneering at him. A Serpent-priest!

That sneer broadened, and from his sleeve the priest drew another snake, straight as a stick, and hefted it, overhand, to throw.

Flaeros gulped and snatched out the only thing he had that might serve to bat aside the serpent-dart—the dragon scepter.

At the sight of it the sneer fell away into a look of terror, and the priest whirled around and fled headlong through the trees, sprinting as swiftly and as desperately as Flaeros had ever run in his most terrified flights.

The Bard of the Delcampers stared in bewilderment at the place where the Serpent-priest disappeared from view, and then looked down at the scepter, shrugged, and whirled around to resume his pursuit of the baronial force. This time, he missed the first few tree roots.

* * *

In a tower remote indeed from the Silverflow, hard-galloping knights, and armies crashing together in fields, a man stood by an open, arched window.

Bats by the pairs, trios, and dozens were flapping out of the sky to swoop into that window, but the man never glanced at them—even when they settled on his shoulders like perching birds, in a silent but increasingly heavy living black cloak.

The Master of Bats had eyes only for a gently drifting array of upright, glowing ovals of radiance that almost filled the room around him.

One showed a chuckling man sitting on a throne, surrounded by silent, dead-looking warriors whose flesh sagged and drooped like the wax of old candles. Another showed hard-riding knights bearing the banners of three baronies, and another a furious battle raging between hundreds of screaming, thrusting, hacking men—who struggled to find footing on ground cloaked with hundreds more men, and horses, too, dead and fallen.

There were other scenes, also, of tense audience chambers and women brooding alone and young magelings crowding around scrying glasses.

The Master of Bats shook his head grimly as his gaze roved from scene to scene.

"Too many players in the game," he murmured, rubbing his cheek against a bat that was chittering softly by his ear.

No, he was not going to enter the coming fray between Ingryl Ambelter, Blackgult and his pet heroes, Bloodblade who sought to be king, and the Serpent-folk. It was just too dangerous.

Far better to bide his time and wait. Two years ago, he could not have held back—he would have rushed in and been burned. He'd done just that.

Yet sometimes—slowly and reluctantly—even mighty wizards can learn lessons. He would lie low here in his tower, and just watch.

Of course, any magic let fall by someone slain in this fight—and anyone sufficiently wounded in the fray who could be caught alone by a properly prepared wizard—would be fair game.

But for now, it was time to just play vulture.

Ezendor Blackgult was dimly aware of his mount rearing under him, and men who'd served him for years hacking aside blades that sought his life, raising shields to protect him and leaving their own throats and joints endangered.

He cared not, nor could muster wits enough to do anything except wrestle against this gnawing worm in his head, this red, clawing *thing* of agony that savaged him and raged through his brain and clawed ever farther.

He was weeping, he knew, and roaring nonsense—when he wasn't spewing vomit, shuddering, and railing against the wizard's spell-lash.

He knew who it was. Oh, yes, he knew Ingryl Ambelter was gloating at the other end of the spell clawing at him . . . he could *feel* the Spellmaster grinning and enjoying his wails and retchings, peering at whatever memories he could see as they fought across his mind—the regent ever retreating, and the wizard striking at will.

Three Above, what did it take to kill a wizard? This one should have been dead several times over—and deserved to die a hundred times over—yet here he was, grinning and plunging mindworm spells into anyone he pleased to torment, using the—

Horns of the Lady! He was sitting on the throne and drawing on its power for his damned spell!

With a roar of sheer rage Blackgult called upon the throne himself, by the linking enchantment Kelgrael had laid upon him. It was a feeble thread, doomed to fail against any strong-willed creature sitting on the throne, let alone an archmage—but his furious effort shook the Spell-master's gnawing, just for a moment.

And that was long enough.

He snatched the Dwaer forth and flung them into the air above him, calling on their power as he did so—and power roared into him, like a white-hot flame, storm lightning come calling to crackle right through him, shocking him with its pain and cleansing him of mindworm and Ingryl's gloating both.

With a grin that clenched his jaw white, Blackgult rode that roiling power right back along Ambelter's spell, leaping across the miles between Sarth Fields and the Throne Chamber of Flowfoam in an instant. Ruthlessly, he smashed into the Spellmaster's mind, searing and scouring in a mind-blast as brutal as the spell Ingryl had used on him.

"Die, bebolten wizard!" he roared. "Graul you—*graul* you!"

Ambelter would survive even this, somehow; he knew it even as he bellowed his heartfelt desire. Wizards always did. Grimly he lashed about in the cringing, shuddering mind, not knowing quite what he was doing but trying to work harm nonetheless.

All too soon—perhaps only moments after his first triumphant lance into that dark and gloating mind; he knew he could never tell—he felt the raging power of the Dwaer turned aside, deflected like a swordblade parried in the fray.

Dimly aware of screaming around him and the Dwaer whirling above his head, in a sky where lances thrust and quarrels hummed, Blackgult snatched back his power, and was abruptly back on a hilltop overlooking Sarth, with Flame Riders washing over the last of his men around him, pressing forward with fierce grins to slay.

The Regent of Aglirta gave them a fierce grin of his own, and his eyes flashed dark and terrible. Someone moaned in sudden fear—even before Ezendor Blackgult rose in his stirrups and gave them all good cause to fear.

"For Blackgult!" he roared, in a voice that rolled and echoed across all that battlefield. *"For Aglirtaaaaaaa!"*

And a white flame arose on that hilltop so bright that it outshone the sun. Men cried out, blinded—even before the flame leaped forth among them, two Dwaer almost singing as they spun hungrily around each other in the air, and they died in their thousands.

Sarindan silk sighed into nothingness in an instant—and Sarindan flesh boiled and was gone an instant later. Black-gult roared out his rage in a voice of thunder, and men died wherever he looked, as a trembling built within him that told him he must stop soon, or be torn apart by the very Dwaer he was harnessing . . .

Only Ingryl's scrying shield saved him. A trifling defense, thrown up out of habit to cloak himself from the prying eyes of distant wizards—and thrown up poorly, he saw now, with two great holes in its working that meant it concealed him from no one.

Yet it saved his life. In the moments before his awareness would have boiled away forever, Ingryl managed to bow before the regent's mind-bolt, let it roll over him—hugging the throne as a spell-anchor, in all the raging—and deflect it into the scrying shield.

Like a fireball caught in a net, he could hope to hold it there only a fleeting time—but as it blazed up brightly, spilling energies in all directions, Ingryl used that energy to transform his faulty scrying web into a better warding.

For the space of a few breaths, Flowfoam was girded about with a shield that blocked all magic—forcing the regent's strike back whence it came and preventing any lurking foe or opportunistic hedge-wizard from striking at him in his spasming weakness.

Not for nothing was he called the Spellmaster.

Smiling grimly—for he knew just how close to death he'd come, this time, and how fortunate he'd been to cheat it—Ingryl Ambelter reached behind his ear and broke the dragonfang he wore hidden in his hair there, on a dainty coif net wrenched long ago from some cringing noble lass or other.

It was the only one he'd ever seen, and the enchantment he'd sourced in its power had taken a long time to oh-so-carefully cast. He'd known that if he ever had to use it, the time would be desperate.

The fang broke, sighing away into nothingness as legend insisted they always did—and his spell awakened immediately. Until he slept or worked magic again, he was "not there" to all magic, hidden and unreachable.

A guard's blade could still slay him, but no spell could see or touch him—no matter what it was. Or so the enchantment claimed.

Gasping in relief and pain, Ingryl Ambelter slid bonelessly forward off the throne and ended up on one hip on the cold, smooth marble. The Melted stood like silent statues all around him, and he gathered himself against the shuddering pain and started crawling slowly through them, on his hands and knees, seeking the back passage and the stair to the north that would take him down, down into the dark ways of Flowfoam, where Gadaster awaited.

Freed from his control, the Melted started to wander, stumbling aimlessly about, truly staggering at random. Wincing—if one fell on him now, he might be pinned helplessly, or even slain outright—the Spellmaster crawled on, weeping softly from the pain of shattered fingers. Other things were broken within him, too, not least his mind, which persisted in presenting him with sudden, blinding-bright images of events long ago, and folk long dead . . . most of them slain by him.

Groaning, he clawed his way out of the throne chamber. He'd slain Gadaster, for one—Gadaster Mulkyn, his master and perhaps the most coldly cruel archwizard Ingryl had ever met.

Now he had to reach Gadaster's bones, and embrace

them, drinking in the vitality he'd spelltrapped there, and bound for his use in dark moments like this. He'd done it before . . . in similar times of dark defeat.

He didn't like to think about those times, now or ever, but they had taught him one timely lesson: Aglirta would keep until he had strength to contemplate ruling it again. Oh, yes . . .

He lay slumped against the door to the stair for a long time, shivering, too weak to go on. Thankfully, there were no prying courtiers or watchful guards still alive to find him. He had Flowfoam all to himself—just as he'd wanted, for so many years.

All his, the Great Isle, every tomb and crypt and turret of it, every forgotten spellbook and enchanted bauble, all the magics grasping Silvertrees had crafted, stolen, or stored since they'd fled the curse of the Silent House. All his, now—except for the wench, Embra, who'd slipped through his fingers. She should be his bound lover, his Living Castle, part of Flowfoam Palace, another Gadaster to drink from at will . . . but she'd escaped him.

Never again. When he was whole again, he must hunt for her. The Lady of Jewels first—not her Worldstones, nor the Throne of Aglirta. They could keep, clawed at by barons and the Snake-priests alike, and would be his in due time.

Embra Silvertree must come first, and surrender to him utterly.

Yes . . .

Blue radiance swirled, flashed, and was gone, washing away behind their eyes—and suddenly six figures were standing a little dazedly on the Silvertree docks.

"Embra," Craer complained, his voice as sharp as any tutor's, "Flowfoam is over *there*. Why did you bring us here?"

Embra held her forehead, and said softly, "Ingryl Ambelter. He touched my mind just now. He wanted me. Oh, how he wanted me."

She swayed, there on the silver-weathered wood amid the bobbing moored barges, and Hawkril's long arms snapped out to cradle her, hold her close, and soothe her. She settled into them with a sigh, and said to Craer, "Some sort of barrier—magic of more force than I've ever felt before—blocks magic into and out of Flowfoam. This is where it threw us, when my jump spell struck it."

"What she's saying, Clevertongue," Sarasper observed wearily, "is be thankful you aren't dead."

"So what does a spell-barrier mean to our ah, grand scheme?" the Baron Brightpennant asked, squinting at Embra. "Is your father in there, with his Dwaer, or somewhere else? And what do we do now?"

Embra spread helpless hands, feeling Hawkril's ire growing around her. She patted his hand soothingly, and asked brightly, "Raulin, what do bards generally do, when everything goes utterly wrong?"

Raulin Castlecloaks looked back from gazing wonderingly at Flowfoam Isle to give her a sudden grin. "Why, Lady, we generally stroll along, whistling nonchalantly, and pretending that everything is unfolding just as we planned it. Whereby we fool surprising numbers of folk."

"Just so long as it's the right ones, lad," Glarsimber of Sart grunted at him. "Just so long as it's the right ones."

8

Magic Hath Two Sharp Edges

The Lady of Jewels closed her eyes, and her companions saw the color drain out of her face in an instant. She started to tremble in Hawkril's arms, sagging like an empty cloak.

"Lady Embra!" the Baron Brightpennant snapped. "What ails you?"

"The Spellmaster," she replied with a wince, looking down at her empty hands a little wonderingly, as if she'd never seen them before.

"I'm right sick of him, too," Craer said meaningfully, "but *how* does that wizard 'ail you,' just now?"

"He set a trap for me," Embra replied, lifting her head to gaze out across the sparkling Silverflow to the battlements of Flowfoam Isle.

Raulin peered at her a little warily; she wore a strange expression that was part anger, part sadness, part weary wisdom—and part hunger.

"A weird to bind me to him," she added, after staring across the river in silence for a breath or two more. "Part of the Living Castle spells he spun to enslave me." She shook her head. "So much power, surging . . ."

There was a thudding of fast-fleeing boots and a clatter

of boat boards. The Four and their two companions whirled around on the docks—in time to see a few frightened boys in ill-fitting leather harness running for the nearest trees. One bore a fluttering crown-and-river banner of Aglirta in his hand. Evidently talk of magic was enough to frighten away the few boys Blackgult had been able to spare to garrison the Silvertree docks and its small muster of boats and barges.

Craer, Glarsimber, and Sarasper exchanged swift glances, but then shrugged and watched the youths go. Raulin frowned and shook his head as he saw them plunge into the trees. Craven weakreeds . . .

Then he remembered what had seemed so all-important a few moments before, and whirled around to look again at the Lady Silvertree.

Her gaze was on Flowfoam no longer; now she was regarding Baron Brightpennant. "Your magic saved me, Glarsimber," she said slowly. "My thanks."

"*My* magic? I have no sorcery, nor . . . oh: the copper hand?"

Embra nodded. "Some of its other enchantments. I think." She curled her lip in a mirthless smile. "Whatever the reason, Ambelter got almost as nasty a surprise as I did." Then she looked again across the river to Flowfoam, and her mouth tightened into a thin line.

Shaking her way free of Hawkril's arms, she strode to the edge of the dock beneath her boots, and peered again at something unseen that seemed to shimmer above the water between the shore and the royal island. Then she whirled around to face them all, flung up a slender arm to point at Flowfoam, and burst out, "We *have* to get there!"

As if in reply, before Hawkril could even bend to the moorings of a single boat, angry shouts rang out from the shore road. With them came the drumming of hooves—and suddenly mounted armaragors were racing towards the docks, lances lowered and pennants fluttering.

"What treachery is this?" Raulin gasped, staring at the

onrushing knights and the rising dust fast-curling in their
wake. "Do they not recognize you? Overdukes of Aglirta?"

Sarasper gave him a wry, weary grin. "Oh, they know
who we are, lad. Yon's the livery of Loushoond, and Tarlagar . . . and Ornentar. We've seen two of their masters quite
recently. Aye, they know quite well who we are."

With a sudden grunt and heave Hawkril swung the
smallest moored boat up out of the water, whirling it dripping over his head, and roared, "Glarsimber! Craer! A
hand, here!"

They sprang to catch hold of the craft as the hulking armaragor staggered under it and almost fell into the water—
but with their aid, he caught his balance in time. Together,
as oars and rudders clattered and tumbled in all directions,
they ran the boat forward to where they could wedge its
transom against two pilings and perch its crossbraces atop
a third, so it jutted up from the weathered boards of the
docks like a gigantic lancetip, pointing at the onrushing
riders.

"Can't we just take a boat and get out on the river?"
Raulin shouted, waving at the many bobbing craft around
them.

"Can't!" Craer snapped. "They always have bows!"

"Or worse," Sarasper said gloomily, clambering past the
stoutly wedged boat onto a bare finger of dock beyond.

"Lass!" Hawkril roared, panting from his effort.
"Raulin! Get back here, behind! Hurry!"

He waved his hand to beckon them after the scrambling
Sarasper, out onto the longest dock in the lee of his impro-
vised shelter.

Raulin hastened to obey, but before anyone could do
more than launch themselves into a run, a dark figure
among the fast-approaching horsemen stood up in his stirrups, waved one hand in a gesture Embra knew all too
well—and the world exploded.

Bright fire . . .

. . . blazing . . .

Jagged shards and splinters of wood burst everywhere, stabbing and tumbling in the blinding, dancing inferno. Craer shouted something excited and probably clever as he cartwheeled helplessly through the air, blade in hand, heading for the waiting water.

Hawkril flung up a warding hand in front of his face—in time to save his eyes, but not before a handlike spray of joined splinters sliced open his cheek and ear. As the pinwheel of slivers sliced past, the planks beneath the armaragor's great boots erupted, and he was plucked into the air, up and back, into a sky filled with a hail of splintered wood. Shattered and torn boats and docks were tumbling everywhere . . .

Raulin's fingers found a piling, and he clawed at it frantically, his rush to reach Hawkril turned into a crazy spin around the old wooden posts. The young bard could hear nothing, though he knew the groans of rending wood must be louder than any human scream. The boat Hawkril had wedged to blunt the charging knights leaped through the air and flew like a war hammer, smashing three knights from their saddles with a brutal force that shattered horses, men, and armor with equal disdain. Raulin, watching with his mouth open in awe, knew there must be screaming going on. Lots of screaming.

Then the young bard's hearing came back with a ringing, echoing rush. There were sharp tearings and snappings of wood striking earth far behind him and tumbling away through brush and shrubs; the thunderous crashes of many, many things striking water, and the wet thuds of spears of broken wood impaling armaragors.

There were evil bubbling sounds from behind him, too—either the fabled lurking monsters of the river come foraging, or more likely boats sinking in the mucky shallows; Raulin dared not spare a moment to glance back and learn which—and then the tumbling timbers of a dock fell away from the air in front of him, and he could see the bloody chaos that moments before had been the eager foremost ranks of the foreguard of three baronies.

Fountaining blood, huge lumps of meat studded with horse heads, hooves, and protruding bones sagged and fell aside—and through their ruin galloped snarling men in armor, lances lowered. Raulin saw one of them swing viciously with his mace at another mounted man he was passing—and the wizard who'd wrought such ruin spewed blood and brains as he pitched forward out of his saddle, the back of his head missing.

"Bastard *idiot*!" the armaragor screamed at the falling mage. It wasn't the sort of battle cry Raulin had heard before—but then, he'd never been in a battle like this before!

Boats were drifting away from the shattered docks now, plucked by the river—some of them overturned or full of water already, soon to sink or fetch up on the rocks a little way downstream—and then Raulin had no more time to snatch glances at anything, as a glittering forest of lancetips reached for him.

A stocky figure in torn and jangling armor sprang past him, smiling wolfishly. "*Well* now," Glarsimber Belklarravus cried jovially, sword flashing in his hand. "Well now!"

The baron ran along the heaved and shattered dock to meet the lances, even as his would-be slayers reined in sharply, horses reared—and one overeager armaragor and his mount slid helplessly along the muddy, board-strewn bank and plunged into the water.

"Stand and hold, men of Aglirta! *Hold!*" Glarsimber roared, in a voice that must have carried clearly to the far-off north bank of the Aglirta. "As a Baron of Aglirta, I command you! Get you *back*!"

His answer was a chorus of sneering laughter—and two viciously thrusting lances. He chopped one aside and ran a few paces along the other ere grasping it and tugging, hard.

Its wielder pitched from his saddle to crash heavily down onto a broken tangle of timbers. Bloody points of wood jutted up through twisted armor—and that armaragor flopped and arched twice or thrice, like a fish landed on the bank, then fell limp and still.

More lances thrust at the baron, but he danced back onto the ruined dock with that same wolfish smile on his lips, and said, "Treason, is it? Men of Loushoond, and Tarlagar, and Ornentar, I charge thee with treason against the River Throne! For that, the penalty is *death*!"

"Hah! As to that, we'll feed you death soon enough!" one of the knights snarled, urging his mount forward. Its hooves slipped on wet planks, and he drew it hastily to a halt, lance wavering, as he saw Overduke Delnbone advancing along a lone dock timber to his left with a cluster of knives protruding from between the fingers of one hand, Brightpennant smiling bleakly at him to his right—and straight ahead of him, beyond a twisted ruin of splintered spars and oars, the old man of the overdukes slowly changing shape into something large, and hairy, and spider-legged. . . .

There was a sudden growl from the water beyond, and a large, gauntleted hand came into view. It closed over the end of a piling, fingers tightening like talons, trailing a grunt—almost a growl—of effort in its wake, and then the familiar hulking shoulder-plates of Hawkril Anharu rose into view, trailing river water, and through a wet and tousled forest of hair Raulin saw the armaragor's eyes blazing like two coals. The cause of his rage hung like a rag in the fold of one of Hawkril's mighty arms—a slender and shapely rag. Embra Silvertree's eyes were closed and her mouth hung open, limp and slack.

"I believe," Hawkril said, with terrible care and gentleness, "that it's time—and past time—I did some killing. Of men who richly deserve it."

He took two swift, ponderous strides forward and thrust

Embra's body at Raulin. "Here, lad," he said curtly. "Don't let her fall, see that she breathes, and keep her shielded from arrows behind *this*." He waved a hand at the tangles of smashed and heaved dock boards all around, watched Raulin stagger back under his heavy burden— and then strode past, his warsword appearing as if by magic in his hand.

A glittering array of lances awaited him, wavering in the air a little way onto the dock where the overdukes stood. Hawkril strode determinedly forward to meet them.

One of the armaragors who'd dismounted well back behind the line of lancers readied a crossbow—and Craer threw a dagger. It flashed through the air, catching sunlight for an instant like a silver fish leaping from the river . . . and sprouted in one of the archer's eyes. He stiffened and toppled over without a sound, as the procurer called casually, "Anyone *else* foolish enough to try to use a bow?" and waved his cluster of daggers meaningfully.

There were murmurs of wariness and fear from the armaragors of the three baronies as they saw the wolf-spider that Sarasper had become creeping forward in Hawkril's wake, plucking up a shattered cross of timbers as a crude shield as it came. Raulin stared at it and found himself shivering. Embra moved slightly in his arms, and hastily he bent his head to peer at her, sitting down hard and swiftly in the lee of a tangle of timbers.

"Hawk? . . . Who?" the Lady Silvertree murmured, and Raulin held her as gingerly as if he was cradling precious crystal.

"Uh, Raulin, great Lady," he blurted, "and—uh—are you well?"

Lips twisted into a wry grin even before her eyes focused on him. "As eloquent as an overduke, I see, Master Bard," she said almost fondly. "My pendant, here—pluck it off, will you? I'm loath to lose it, but I fear we're going to need some magic soon, or . . ."

She did not finish the sentence, but Raulin knew very

well what she meant. Cautiously, he reached to her throat and closed his fingers around the little thing. A glossy-smooth black stone, enwrapt in fine chain. "This?" he asked.

"Aye. Tug it off. Swift and hard, but don't lose hold of it. My arms are still . . . untrustworthy."

Raulin winced—and tugged.

"You'll never lure them," Craer murmured, close by his head. Putting the stone carefully into Embra's hands and helping her close her fingers around it, Raulin glanced up. The procurer was speaking to Glarsimber. "Fools they may be, but even they can see these docks'll never hold their mounts."

The baron snorted. "They wasted more than enough good horses learning that," he replied—and then launched himself into a sudden, sword-waving charge.

"For the regent and the Risen King!" he cried, hacking aside lances. "For Aglirta!"

Long, cruel lancetips stabbed at him, but Hawkril stepped in to chop them aside—and then two armored men were trotting in under the lance shafts, staggering as the alarmed knights tried to strike them down or aside. There was a brief, crowded confusion of snorting horses and men cursing as they kicked with their spurs and wrenched at their reins—and then Hawkril reached the nearest of the horsemen, and the clang of steel arose.

A man pitched helplessly from his saddle with a shout, to disappear under the dancing hooves—and then there was a groan and a splintering crash as a piling gave way and dock boards collapsed under a dapple gray; its yelling rider went over its head in an unintended dive into the Silverflow.

"Waste of good horses!" Glarsimber snarled, hacking with his sword as hard and as fast as he knew how. "Call yourself armaragors?"

The rest of the knights had crowded forward to try to join the fray, but officers among them were roaring curses and orders at them to pull back as the dock boards groaned warningly and horses stumbled and reared.

"Lances!" one of the officers cried. "Take up lances and force them back! Then *get* those horses *away* fr—"

Hawkril's warsword slid through his throat then, and the rest of the swordcaptain's rage was lost forever in a gurgling of blood.

Lances were being snatched down from the horsemen, however, and another horse sprang from the dock into a shrieking fall against the bank, onto the ribs of a smashed boat. For a moment there was a clear path ashore, and both Hawkril and the longfangs that was Sarasper sprang for it.

Bright blue-edged flame kindled before their faces, hurling armaragors and their mounts aside like toys. Tall and terrible, it loomed like a wagon where there'd been nothing moments before. The force of its presence struck Hawkril to his knees, and the baronial foreguard shouted in alarm and scrambled back, abandoned lances bouncing and clattering, as the flames grew vivid blue, with a white, searing heart.

Searing, yet cold. Icy cold. Hawkril scrambled back, shaking numbed hands, as two horses fled, on the bank beyond, in a wild thudding of hooves. Out of that whiteness stepped four tall, slender dark-gowned figures he'd seen before. The Talasorn sister-sorceresses. His heart sank as he saw hostility on their faces.

"We know, now, just who serves our father's killers," Olone Talasorn said coldly, "*and* who seems to always be eager to hack down wizards, wherever you ride in Aglirta. Die, meddling fools!"

Four wands aimed—and spat dazzling fire along the dock at the overdukes and the two who stood with them.

His arms felt like battered clubs, too heavy to lift—and his head seemed like the scorched aftermath of a cookfire,

black and ravaged and smoldering. Weak, numbed emptiness rode in him as he sat in his saddle atop a hilltop in
Sarth Fields strewn deep with the dead, and amid the flies,
high-wheeling vultures, and men too weary to smile in victory, the Regent of Aglirta struggled to keep from swaying
and falling right out of his saddle.

He wanted to lie down and rest. Three Above, speak
truth: no, he wanted to lie down and *die*.

The Dwaer spun silently above him, and with a cold
ruthlessness he jerked his hand in a beckoning gesture. Two
burly but pale-faced armsmen of the Royal Host of Aglirta
brought forward the next struggling Serpent-priest, turning
their heads aside for fear that his spittings were poisonous.
More than one had been, and men kicked their heels and
arched in shuddering agony right now as they died, not far
off, with their swordbrothers powerless to help them.

He'd let the Dwaer ravage him, using them too long—
but being Regent of Aglirta meant doing such things. If the
Vale needed him to be a taloned monster, the Golden Griffon in truth, then a taloned monster he would be.

But he was damned if he was going to let his frightened
but still-loyal warriors think he was enjoying the murders
he was doing now.

Blackgult stared into the hate-filled eyes of the Snake-
priest and said grimly, raising his hand like priests did in
benediction, "I do this for Aglirta. For justice and for the
need of our fair land. Die, traitor, that Aglirta may live!"

And then he bent his gaze on the man's eyes, and called
on the Dwaer for their darkest fire.

Not to sear and melt flesh, as he'd done earlier, but to
drink life, stealing it into him as the man gasped. Glittering
eyes slowly went dark above whispered prayers and curses
as the priest sagged in the fearful grasp of the armaragors,
and died.

Ezendor Blackgult drew in a deep breath as the stolen
life force surged through him, soothing and strengthening

all at once. Ignoring the grim gaze of the warcaptain Halvan, he said quietly, "Bring the next one."

He didn't want to meet Halvan's eyes, and see the carefully shielded disgust lurking there, amid the fear—and more: the growing resolve that, personal death sentence or not, it might be best for all Darsar if the Sirl Swords were commanded to hew down the Regent of Aglirta before he stole more lives with the fell Dwaerindim.

Deliberately, he dismounted and turned his back to the stout Sirl warcaptain, standing within easy reach. Best to let Halvan see his chance, and decide for himself not to take it. Even a Blackgult gone magic-mad and deadly with power was preferable to bullying barons snatching at the Throne, and Serpent-priests smirking at the resulting ruination and slyly provoking fray after fray, until all the Vale was an emptied, death-choked battlefield. . . .

There were stirrings, all around the hilltop. Blackgult ignored them, too: the sounds of good men of Aglirta remembering old tales, as they saw for themselves why some legends cursed the Dwaer, and called them the Warstones.

Aglirta had won a victory this day, and there were still a grim handful of armaragors of Aglirta alive to know it. Halvan's Sirl Swords had taken the brunt of the losses, as desperate Jarradar pirates and a few tall knights of Pelaerth had tried to hew their way free of the slaughter. Of the proud and haughty Flame Riders, not a man still lived; Blackgult and the Dwaer had seen to that.

The Dwaer had won the battle for him. Without them, the fray would have ended with the Sirl Swords dying one by one, hacking defiantly at wave after wave of gutter scrapings from across Darsar, five or six for each man of the Royal Host of Aglirta. Instead, this unforeseen viper had been crushed into the grass.

Aye, the Serpent-worshippers were Aglirta's real foes. Their honeyed tongues and merciless murders and ready coins had wrought all of this. He hoped none of them had escaped. Halvan and his men had ruthlessly ridden down all seen trying to flee the field, but the right magic can snatch a man far in an instant, and in all the shouting and swordwork . . .

Blackgult allowed himself neither a sigh nor a grimace. Six Snake-robes had been captured, and only one was left, now. Not as fearless as the rest, this last priest screamed and struggled as they dragged him forward, and Blackgult fought to keep a sudden, fierce satisfaction off his face as he strode to meet the man.

The Dwaer above him were already aflame, he knew, and the priest stared at his doom in horror, sobbing out curses that one of the soldiers ended with a backhanded slap of his gauntlet. As swift as a real snake, the priest sank his teeth into—unyielding metal plates. More of the same knuckle-plates smashed his face red and left his ears ringing as the other guard dealt him a brutal blow that left the priest reeling on his heels.

By then Blackgult had hold of his shoulders and was staring into the depths of that fear-filled gaze, deeper . . . and deeper . . .

The life flooded out of the man in a rush, making the regent shudder, and he turned away abruptly as the now-familiar warm surge spread through him, making him feel strong, alert—and hungry for more. Damn Ambelter for inadvertently showing him how to use the Dwaer thus . . . and yet thanks to him, too, by the Three, or there'd be no grim victory for Aglirta this day. Blackgult shook his head. All this, and Bloodblade still to come.

"Post sentinels on this hilltop, and yonder one, too," he ordered. "Halvan, set some of your men to fetching every last snake-arrow, and snake, too—scales, pieces, fangs, and all. We'll make a fire here and burn it, all of it! The rest of you, back to the trees whence we came; this open land is deadly."

He lifted his head to gaze across the Sarth Fields once more; was that a plume of dust, away west? Was the usurper's army that close?

A faint, familiar thunder arose from the earth beneath him, and Halvan cursed. They all knew what it was: the sound of hooves, many hooves. An army, riding against them.

A Sirl man cried out, pointing south. Aye, riders, and in plenty. Blackgult strode a few paces in that direction, to get a better look. Halvan cursed and wheeled around. "They're coming from the west, too," he snapped. "More than a thousand, for sure."

"And the north!" another man cried, pointing.

Men peered. "Many," one of them said grimly. "I can't tell their number, but . . . many."

Blackgult shook his head and smiled. Well, now, this was more what he was used to. Perhaps the Three were truly sick of Aglirta, and wanted to see it all swept away . . .

"No sentinels nor snake-hunts, then," he shouted, "but everyone to the trees! East, back towards the docks—and once in among them, there we turn, stand, and fight! Let the forest be our shield. Take up all bows and shafts you find, but tarry not in searching!"

"No fear of my doing that," a hiresword growled, as everyone started to hasten. "Look yon!"

Few warriors bothered to turn and peer west, where the man was pointing, but on the way to their weary horses, Halvan and Blackgult did look. A forest of moving glitterings and gleams met their eyes; two thousand armsmen at least, hastening forward on horseback.

"Trying to catch us right here, before we can reach shelter," Halvan grunted, swinging up onto the saddle of his big bay. It snorted and stamped in complaint, sore and weary.

Blackgult looked at the scarred and bleeding flank of his own warhorse, then turned and lifted his voice in a merry shout: "Farewell, loyal men of Aglirta! I'm proud to have fought at your side! If Sarth be our doom, let it be one the bards sing of with awe, a hundred summers hence! This night, I'll see you again around the deadfires, where the Three wait for us all!"

He raised his sword, but few of the armsmen of Aglirta looking back at him saluted him in return, or even managed a bitter or weary smile. It's hard to find mirth when you know you're doomed.

9

Skulls Grin Easily

Magic flashed as bright as lightning, snarling along the shattered wharf.

Sarasper hunched as low as he could in wolf-spider form, Craer hurled himself behind a tangle of boat timbers and splayed boards—and, on her knees beside Raulin, Embra murmured, "Let it be enough. Oh, Lady Above, let it be enough!"

As delicately as a mother's caress, a bolt of searing sorcery stabbed out at the Lady of Jewels as it passed. Raulin yelled in fear as his hair tingled and he felt the flesh on his face creep, cringing back before the slaying force surging so close—surging into Embra's cupped hands, and the tiny pendant there.

That jewel had been too paltry to bring them all hence in her spelljump, or she'd never have sacrificed the baron's copper hand . . . and Raulin thought he knew the sort of enchantment it held: a little glow, such as many high ladies could call forth from their gems, to light them in soft evening-gloom as if with soft candles, and make their jewels sparkle. That was all—just a spellglow, to be turned on and off by the wearer's will. What help could it possibly be against *this*?

In the next roaring instant, Raulin's despairing question found an answer. Though the Lady Embra bit her lip and threw her head back in obvious, trembling pain, the magic shocking into her didn't hurl her dying out over the waters, or melt away her hands to bony stumps in a flash. Instead, it plunged into her cupped hands, trailing fire, and roiled there, impossibly held and caught—only to spill out from between her fingers as a bright, leaping net of spell-strands.

Two of those strands arced out, almost as if by accident, to snare a bolt that had scorched a line of upthrust timbers into flame and driven a groaning Baron Brightpennant reeling out from behind one of them, clutching his shoulder in staggering agony.

The strands whirled around that bright lance of slaying sorcery—and then plucked it and hurled it out across the Silverflow, straight and true, towards Flowfoam. "Lady!" Raulin gasped, as Embra shuddered again, her face wet with tears. "What befalls? How can I—?"

"Help me?" Embra panted. "Touch me not! Just . . . leave me be . . . an instant longer . . ."

Something snapped back from Flowfoam with a bright flash that made the armaragors on the bank shout in pain and dismay, and clutch at their blinded eyes.

Raulin's own gaze swam, but through his tears he saw Embra smile in grim satisfaction—as a flood of ravening magical fire thrice as great as the bolt she'd snared came howling back from the distant island, to crash into the blue Talasorn fire with a crash that sounded as if every bell in all Darsar had been shattered with one brutal blow.

Raulin spun around, in time to see a fallen, tumbling wand blaze into ash in the wake of four sorceresses, as they were hurled end over end over the dead horses and sprawled armaragors into the trees, trailing screams.

Four blue flames blossomed there—and vanished abruptly, one after another, as the Talasorn sisters snatched themselves elsewhere.

Embra gave Raulin a weary smile. "A spell net—one of the few useful enchantments of all the Living Castle restraints and lashes laid on me. Given power by their magic, it sent their bolts to smite the barrier that kept us from Flowfoam—and the barrier struck them the same blow it would have used on me, if I'd had foolishness and spells enough to try to smite it down."

Her gaze shifted wearily to the trees. "It does every young sorceress good to be astonished by magic a time or two." Her smile twisted. "I should know."

And still wearing that wry smile, she toppled sideways, crashing into Raulin's startled arms like a dead thing.

She felt just as heavy and still as she'd been earlier, when a furious Hawkril had put her in Raulin's care. The young bard looked wildly up and down the blazing dock. "Hawkril?" he called. "Lord Hawkril?"

"Here, lad!" came a low growl, from somewhere on the other side of a plume of smoke. "What befalls?"

A scorched and bedraggled Craer was suddenly bending over Raulin, peering at Embra.

Sarasper lurched towards them, too, two or more of his spiderlike legs curled uselessly under him. Somewhere on the shore, armaragors were groaning and cursing. At least one was weeping.

"Don't you just love magic?" the procurer murmured, putting his hand gently against Embra's chin. "Flash, boom, and another dozen lives made dust! If Em here wasn't so beautiful—and so gods-cursed useful in keeping us all alive, grant you—I'd start strangling all wizards right here and now!"

"And if you do that," Glarsimber said in a raw, wheezing, pain-filled voice from somewhere nearby, "it'll be back to brute-force barons and their armies swording each other up and down all the Vale again! A vast improvement, don't you agree?"

Craer crooked an eyebrow. "What an odd thing for a baron to say," he commented, patting Embra's shoulder gently. "Well, she's alive, but probably kitten-weak again. I think I need to steal us one of Blackgult's Dwaer, if we're going to go on battling here-in-a-flash sorceresses . . ."

"No," Hawkril said grimly, as something that sounded like ragged but approaching thunder came to them, from along the shore road, "I think we're in for an unhealthily large dose of brute-force barons and their armies, about now. Swords out, all!"

As Raulin stared, Craer cursed softly, and Glarsimber lumbered past them drenched in blood, the thunder from the road grew.

The young bard hadn't known that wolf-spiders could sigh, but the beast that was Sarasper did so quite loudly as it limped past, joining Hawkril and Glarsimber on the shore.

More armaragors were galloping down to the docks, lances and pennants fluttering above them in a bright forest. Raulin stared—if those standards told truth, all three barons—Loushoond, Ornentar, and Tarlagar—were among the sinister-helmed, hard-riding men.

"My, but Aglirta spawns an overabundance of greedy, greedy men," Craer observed in a mocking voice. "A pity we haven't enough crowns to go around."

He cast glances in all directions as swiftly and as sharply as if he was hurling spears, and then snapped, "Raulin! Those boats, there—cut them clear, so none can follow you! Then get down into this one, and get Embra clear!"

The procurer slapped a gleaming dagger into Raulin's hand, and set off down the dock to join Hawkril without a backward glance.

The young bard stared after him. "Uh, ah—what'll you be . . . doing?"

"Bards usually refer to it as a 'doomed, defiant last stand,' I believe," Craer called back. "It's what nobles of Aglirta do best."

The Baron of Brightpennant turned and waved at Raulin almost jauntily, as the foremost armaragors lowered their lances and someone snapped, "Stand aside, or die!"

"As an Overduke of Aglirta," Hawkril rumbled calmly, "I believe *I* give the orders here. Where among you are the barons whose banners you bear?"

There was a little silence, ere someone in the press of men in armor said in bored, dismissive tones, "Kill them."

Armaragors surged forward—and with a roar, Hawkril and Glarsimber rushed to meet them, hacking aside lancetips, seeking only to bear the weapons down. The wolf-spider sprang over the struggling men, to land on the riders wielding those lances. In an instant, the first rank of horsemen became a chaos of cursing men, flashing daggers, and death—even before a slender man in leather sprang into its midst.

Craer launched himself into one armaragor and sent the man sprawling from his saddle. Alighting on its cantle doubled up like a frog, he leaped to the next horse, catching its rider by the neck. They struggled for a moment ere Craer's dagger found a way under a helm and into the throat beneath—and then the procurer was scrambling to his feet for another leap.

Lances stabbed at him from horsemen beyond, so he spun around and jumped at the back of the first rank of battling armaragors—specifically, onto the back of a shouting knight who was trying to carve up the longfangs perched on the head of his screaming, bucking horse.

The last Raulin saw of the procurer was two daggers rising and falling in a vicious whirlwind, and Craer's face appearing momentarily above them to snarl, "Are you deaf, Castlecloaks? *Get Embra clear!*"

"They certainly *enjoy* their butchery," the man with no face commented, as he rose smoothly from in front of the glowing whorl of magic.

The man still crouched over the whorl looked up sharply. "An Aglirtan failing, but not one exclusive to the folk of the Vale. You're off to—?"

"Find and follow Flaeros Delcamper, and see that the dragon scepter is kept safe. It's worth a thousand dead Aglirtans."

"Or more," the Koglaur who'd cast the scying whorl agreed, looking back at the bright scene at its heart, wherein battle was raging at the burning Silvertree docks. "Fare you well."

A fierce, beaklike nose and a high forehead grew smoothly on the smooth, blank flesh of the departing Koglaur's face. "Fare you better," he replied, still eyeless. He did something with one of his hands to a ring he wore on his other hand—and vanished.

The Koglaur above the whorl curved his lips in a smile that held no mirth and bent his will upon his scrying magic. Obediently the spinning wheel of flickering light grew larger, and the scene within it swam closer—reaching out to dwell upon one shouting, sweating man.

Glarsimber Belklarravus, the Baron of Brightpennant, wore an expression of fierce joy as he staggered and hacked, limping badly and covered with blood that was mostly his own. Lances stabbed and tore at him, clenched jaw and corded neck betrayed his pain, and he reeled in weariness—but he laughed betimes, amid the clang of arms, and his eyes danced with excitement, like a young boy at play.

"He's going to die," a new voice murmured, from above the whorl-caster's shoulder, "and yet he seems to . . . enjoy it."

"Aglirtans are like that," the scrying Koglaur replied. "I would find some of the customs of Sarinda strange, I'm sure. This, you'll get used to. It's one of the reasons I love this land."

The Koglaur from Sarinda leaned closer to the whorl. "Might I know some of the others?"

The whorl-caster's smile was real, this time. "So much old magic, waiting to be snatched up and used. Endlessly scheming barons, all of the doings of the Serpent-priests as they grow restless to get their hands on both magic and the Throne . . . and the folk of the Vale dream so fiercely, too. Right now, they've hunger for a strong king, and turn to this Bloodblade in hopes he'll become such."

"And will he?"

"Too early to say, yet. Warlords are seldom good kings—brutal, efficient kings, yes, but farsighted and caring for their realm, except as a prize to clutch tight and defend against the thieves, no." The whorl-caster shrugged. "Perhaps he'll be different."

The Koglaur from Sarinda gestured at the bright scene of battle, where Baron Glarsimber was still staggering and hacking happily, shouting defiance at the armaragors he was hewing down. "Yet for Bloodblade to crown himself, this man we watch must soon die."

The whorl-caster looked up. "We love this land, and admire some of its folk—but in our meddlings, we dare not favor a few." He waved a hand at the battling baron. "We needed him to do a thing, and he did it. His time is done; Thuulor goes now to guard the scepter."

"Ah, this one was your tool to blunt the claws of the Spellmaster? Yet he knows not of us, or why he was sent to guard the young Delcamper fool?"

The whorl-caster nodded. "This man, long called the Smiling Wolf—rough, yet swift-witted, an able fighting man capable of staunch loyalty when he found lords he could believe in—was told privately—and separately—by both those lords, to guard the bard and his scepter."

"Those lords being?"

"Regent Blackgult and the King of Aglirta—or rather, the flickering phantom of King Kelgrael, who warned this Glarsimber that keeping the scepter safe was his true task. Kelgrael led him to a spell-gate that took him to the coastal road nigh Ragalar without the need for a long ship voyage. Of course, those lords—or at least, the Blackgult and the Kelgrael who appeared to this baron—were two of us."

He smiled again. "I particularly enjoy being Blackgult. All dark, grim swagger, hints of great intrigues and high missions, and enemies everywhere; richly earned, too."

The Koglaur from Sarinda nodded. "So while this naive dolt of a Delcamper remains necessary, we guard him closely, of course. Given that we're counting on the Band of Four to do so much actual work against various evil wizards and would-be Kings of Aglirta, why aren't we guarding them with the same diligence?"

The whorl-caster smiled. "We watch the Four, but guard them only lightly, because we want them—and Aglirta needs them—to be tempered like fine weapons, in battles large and small, to be good defenders of Aglirta in the years ahead."

The Koglaur from Sarinda smiled wryly. "I see." He waved at the scrying whorl. "I also see that the forge fires are raging. The Band of Four can't be enjoying themselves, about now."

"Ho, Tall Post! How fare you?"

"Passably well," Hawkril grunted, swinging his warsword in a great roundhouse blow that struck sparks off the swords raised against it, and sent two armaragors staggering back with numbed hands. "I don't seem to be hewing my way any closer to any real barons, mind you."

"That's because," Craer panted, "these craven upstarts believe in cowering behind heavy guard, ordering their swordsworn to die for them—a task, I might add, that in the main they accomplish remarkably well."

"Your tally?" Hawkril shouted back, hewing an armaragor to the ground and springing back before the man could trip him—and other blades reach in to stab him from several sides.

"Four and ten, I make it!"

"Five and ten," Glarsimber corrected, shoving a dying knight away and reeling back against an upthrust dock piling. "That one you kicked off his horse spitted himself on someone else's lance."

"Well, well," Craer called, snatching up a dagger from the belt of a dead armaragor and hurling it into the face of a rushing armsman, "we may soon leave them with no one to hide behind!"

"And then, no doubt," Hawkril rumbled, parrying two swordcuts and leaning over on his backswing to slice through the back of a knight's knee, "we'll be treated to the sight of three belted barons of the realm running away!"

"Ah, but will it be fast enough?" Baron Brightpennant cried, lurching forward to hew down the swordarm of an armaragor who was trying to stab Sarasper before the long-fangs bit out his throat. "I've a hunger to cut the heels off the slowest one!"

Sarasper bit down, blood spurted, and the knight fell with a wet, wordless sound. Glarsimber snatched a dagger from the corpse and tossed it to Craer's feet. "You seem to be collecting these, so . . ."

"Kill them!" Baron Tarlagar howled at his men, brandishing a bright, unused sword from some distance back behind the fray. "What does it take to kill *three men* and a spider?"

"More armaragors than you remembered to bring, evidently," Craer called back. "Why don't you show them, Tarlagar? Or should I call you 'Baron Coward'?"

"Now, now," Glarsimber gasped, as he parried a knight's blade a handwidth in front of his face, "if you do that, I'll grow confused, and I might start hitting things! After all, there are three of them! *Which* Baron Coward do you mean, exactly?"

"Slay them!" Baron Loushoond snarled, as Craer threw another dagger, an armaragor spun around and fell on his face—and Glarsimber charged forward through the gap, to swing his notched blade at a "real baron" at last. "Slay them now!"

Loushoond's next words were lost in a yelp as the staggering, bleeding Baron Brightpennant smashed through his guard and sent a gem-adorned baronial sword spinning away. Loushoond stumbled back, moaning in fear. *"Slay them!"* he shrieked wildly.

"Best ask Ornentar to do that," Craer called, leaping over a blade to roll and spring up under a man's guard and drive a dagger into a throat from inches away. "Tarlagar doesn't know what it takes, remember?"

Three knights leaped forward, blades flashing. Steel clashed and rang—and Glarsimber Belklarravus groaned, reeled back with a blade in his side, and fell.

The wolf-spider sprang forward over him, but six or seven armaragors surged to meet it, shouting eagerly to each other, and Sarasper was forced to dart away again.

"Hawk!" Craer snapped. "Brightpennant's down!"

"On my way," Hawkril growled, parrying with such force that his foe staggered away, cursing. *"On my way!"*

With a roar the hulking armaragor hewed down a man, kicked another in the codpiece hard enough to lift the man right off the ground, and ducked past a third knight.

"Aid!" the man he'd kicked gasped, writhing on the corpse-strewn ground. "Aid!"

"Now, *Hawk!*" Craer called reprovingly, as his sword-brother reached Glarsimber and took up a stance over the fallen, groaning baron. "You kicked Tarlagar himself, and forgot to use the boot with the toe-blade! Again! That must make a dozen barons you've forgotten to slay this year alone!"

"Fall back!" Baron Ornentar snapped, striding forward to stand by Tarlagar and gesturing to his men to help the stumbling Loushoond to his side. "Shield ring, around us three—now!"

Hawkril roared again and slashed so hard at a knight that the man reeled back, slipped—and then fell, his neck broken by Sarasper's pounce. The wolf-spider scuttled away again before any other armaragor could reach him with a blade—through renewed roars from Ornentar for his men to form a shield ring.

Craer shot a glance over his shoulder, shook his head, and called, "Hawk! Embra!"

His friend was large and heavy-armored, but not stupid. "Carry to the boat?"

"Precisely," the procurer agreed, snatching up belt-daggers from dead knights like a madman. "Glarsimber first, hey?"

"And who'll entertain our ambitious barons?"

"Sarasper and the most handsome overduke, of course."

"Ah, that would be Embra," Hawkril growled, snatching up Brightpennant and lumbering over bodies at what might, given good footing and distance enough, become a run. "I suppose you meant to say the most clever-tongued overduke."

"Ah, yes," Craer agreed, as the armaragors rushed forward and he was forced to hurl half a dozen daggers with snake-swift speed. "I suppose I did."

Sarasper pounced on one knight, rolled, and sprang away again, leaving the man bleeding from a huge bite on his neck. The other armaragors lost their sudden enthusiasm, and—under the lash of a steady stream of curses from Ornentar—returned to their defensive ring.

Hawkril skidded to a halt at the splintered edge of the dock, and almost fell. "That's the best boat left, lad?"

"Y-yes," Raulin panted, paddling clumsily in the water with an oar. "It has the Lady Embra in it, see, and—"

"That would make it the best craft, yes," Hawkril agreed gravely, shooting a glance back down the dock to see if anyone was charging towards him, as he knelt to lower Glarsimber's heavy body into Raulin's anxious grasp.

No one was coming, and Craer's stream of brightly mocking comments hadn't abated, so Hawkril tucked the blood-dripping baron under one arm and swung himself down into the water, wrestling Brightpennant aboard the boat and heaving himself towards another, larger boat in a desperate, wallowing splash.

The new boat tipped alarmingly as he forced its rail

down and rolled over it into the bottom, seeing the sky for a few alarming moments ere the craft righted itself, and Hawkril found himself bobbing not far away from Raulin's leaking boat.

Someone had left behind a shield with broken straps in the vessel; Hawk dug into the water with it as if he was stirring gruel, and drove his boat up against Raulin in a few furious strokes.

"Roll them in, lad," he growled, clamping the boats together with his huge hands. "Gently."

Raulin grunted and banged and even muttered a curse before it was done, but Hawkril hadn't had time to do more than look around, see that there were only three other boats still afloat—all of them adrift, and well downriver already—ere the bard said, "Uh, Overduke Hawk . . . Hawkril! Uh, sir!"

Hawkril turned his head, saw that Brightpennant, Embra, and Raulin were all now in his boat, and roared, "Craer! Sarasper! *To me!*"

Swords clashed, beyond the smoke, and there came no answer. For a moment Hawkril wondered if his friends had fallen—and then the wolfspider came scrambling into view, someone threw a lance far too feebly after it, and Craer vaulted into sight over the heaved and splintered wreckage of a boat that had been driven partway through the dock, and came sprinting past the still-quivering lance. "About time!" he called. "I was almost out of daggers!"

"Behind you!" Hawkril roared. *"Right behind you!"*

Craer dodged abruptly sideways, leaping into the water—and the armaragor racing after him hacked desperately at empty air, overbalanced, and pitched into a tangle of timbers, face-first, with a grunt and a very meaty thud.

The second armaragor tried to slow and turn, skidded, and finally managed to lurch to a stop—in time to see the wolf-spider, on the very end of the dock, dwindle into a bony old man who lowered himself clumsily over the edge, and was gone.

"After them!" Baron Ornentar bellowed, waving his sword in reckless flourishes. *"After them!"*

"Up and in, old Longfangs," Craer said, coming up beside Sarasper in the water and boosting him towards the boat. "We're bound for Flowfoam."

"Ah, yes," Sarasper agreed sourly, "where we'll be sure to find restful peace in plenty. Thankee."

With a splash and tumble, he was aboard, Hawkril's iron strength holding him until he could catch hold of the nearest thwart. Craer surged after him, up and in, as smoothly as a river otter—and Hawkril leaned out with his warsword in his hand, and drove it solidly into the bottom of Raulin's leaking boat. Water welled up in a rush, and Hawkril snatched back his sword and shoved down, enthusiastically.

The boat was half-full as it slid astern, and they watched pursuing armaragors run out of dock and discover there were no usable boats handy, at about the same moment. Ornentar pointed downriver at the few fast-dwindling boats in the distance and shouted something, and as Hawkril tugged oars out from under Embra's slumped body and handed his shield down the boat to Craer, they saw the armaragors begin to run the other way, back along the ruined dock towards shore.

"Well, at least there're no bowmen left!" Raulin said brightly.

"Still your tongue, lad," Sarasper snapped. "We're not out of bowshot yet—give them no ideas!"

The old healer was already clambering awkwardly along the boat towards Brightpennant, who still wore someone else's sword in his side. "Have any of them started swimming yet?"

"In that armor?" Craer looked back. "No, they're idiots, but not complete fools. I think."

"No," Sarasper agreed, *"we're* the complete fools—on our way to we-know-not-what, in yonder castle, with our Dwaer gone and our sorceress stricken." He glanced up at Craer, and added gravely, "We fight well, though."

"A score and seven," Craer replied promptly. "One more if the one who was chasing me just now broke his neck."

Sarasper shook his head. "Life isn't all a matter of keeping score, look you," he growled, gently turning Glarsimber over.

"Oh? What else does it hold?" Craer asked innocently.

"Well, there's food," Hawkril replied, rowing hard. "And—" He glanced at Embra's shapely form, and then at Raulin. "Yes," he growled. "As I said, there's food."

Craer snorted—and then fell silent, his eyes narrowing in suspicion. A bat had come flying out from the shore near the docks, despite the full light of day. It circled them slowly, flapping low over the water, then flew away, turning once in a brief whirl, for all the world as if it was looking back.

Steel clanged, and then was gone, trailing a scream. Blackgult sent a snarl after it. Another Aglirtan he'd had to slay—another good man who should have drawn sword in the name of the Rightful King for years yet.

Men were dying and screaming all around him, and his warhorse had crashed to the ground seemingly hours ago, almost taking him with it into death. Now he stood hip deep in dead warriors, sending forth fire from the two Dwaer whirling serenely above his head—blasting down this band of warriors, and then that one.

They hadn't made it to the trees. Halvan was dead and the loyalty of his Swords with him, there seemed no end to the armsmen—and hedge-wizards, too—who'd rallied to Bloodblade, and the Royal Host of Aglirta was now no more than a handful of wounded or exhausted men.

He would not abandon them, these loyal few. They'd fought for him, standing when they knew it meant their doom, and he'd fight the Three alone and unaided before he'd call on the Dwaer to flee, and leave good men to be slaughtered behind him. To die knowing they'd been abandoned by the regent who'd led them into this.

And yet there were wizards here in the fray, however feeble their magics—*could* he escape? If he fought on to the bitter end, no magic could snatch him away if he was struck senseless, or overwhelmed by pain or an arrow in the eye or throat . . . and what of the Dwaer then?

How could Embra escape—or Aglirta withstand the lurking Serpent-clergy—with the Dwaer-Stones in the wrong hands?

Embra! Yes! That was it!

Through the Dwaer he called to her, shouting with his mind: *Embra, daughter mine! Farewell! Blackgult must fall, that Aglirta live—but lass, use your Dwaer to call mine to you, or they'll be lost with me! Embra, swiftly! Call my Dwaer, and take them from here!*

His cry echoed away into nothingness. No familiar mind brushed his, no warmth of regard or even fury . . . nothing.

Three Above, was his Embra dead?

"Gods," he whispered despairingly, swinging his sword almost out of habit to turn aside the blade of a snarling armaragor, and sidestep the lunge of another. Almost absentmindedly he spun to slice the throat of one man, and called on the Dwaer to blind the other, hacking the man down ruthlessly an instant later.

Waves of knights were advancing towards him, now—stalking menacingly forward, and then drawing aside. Through the gap they were creating, the Regent of Aglirta saw more armaragors striding proudly forward—and, glaring at him over their drawn swords, Sendrith Duthjack. Bloodblade was coming for him.

Embra, hear me!

Bloodblade was pressing forward now, and the knights crossing swords with Blackgult were falling back, bringing up their blades to ring him with glittering steel, where he stood alone among the fallen.

Alone with—his heart leaped—a sudden burst of magical radiance, in the air before him. Armaragors shouted, some snatched out daggers to throw—and out of the spell-glow stepped a tall, slender, darkly handsome man, in dark garb. A small vertical dagger was emblazoned on his left cheek.

He reached up for Blackgult's Dwaer, orbiting out of reach, and the regent saw that his long, slender fingers bore rings—rings that flashed and made Blackgult's blade sear his hands ere he could swing it, and bring this stranger-wizard down.

"I am Jhavarr Bowdragon!" the man snapped, as if that name would make men tremble, or bow down.

Blackgult glared at him, reaching for his dagger. "Aye. So?"

"*Give* me those," the wizard snarled, stabbing a pointing hand up at the two Dwaerindim, his eyes alight with excitement. "Such power! I *must* have them! Yield them to me, Blackgult, or die!"

10

Confounded Wizards Everywhere

The scrying whorl turned serenely—but the Koglaur from Sarinda suddenly extended an impossibly long finger down at its brightness, to point at the scene therein, and more specifically at a bat flapping low across the Silverflow in broad daylight. "I've seen that before! That's a wizard, or a spy of his!"

"The latter," the whorl-caster agreed calmly. "The Master of Bats, scrying in his way as I do in mine."

The taller Koglaur sighed. "Wizards," he muttered. "They seem to be *everywhere* in Aglirta!"

"You're not the first of us to make such an observation," the whorl-caster said wryly. "Magic lures them—and baronial gold. Steady employment, that is, as walking weapons for one baron to threaten another with . . . and barons of Aglirta, it seems, are always threatening other barons of Aglirta."

"This much war is usual?" The Koglaur from Sarinda spread his hands. "I must confess a certain bewilderment: given such bloodshed, how is it that any crops get harvested, and the land survives, king or no king, down the centuries? It should all have become beast-roamed waste by now!"

The whorl-caster smiled. "Tension and intrigue are constant, yes, but such open battle—no. The people whelm behind Bloodblade, their new hope, all of the barons seek the Throne—and behind it all are the Serpent-clergy. They've finally risen in earnest, to make a concerted bid for the Throne."

"And if they succeed?"

"If they take Aglirta, Sirlptar will in turn fall. Then, city by city—unless some as-yet-unknown foe arises from nowhere to foil them—they'll take all Darsar. A bard sang of it, once: 'a cloak of death and tyranny flung across the land.' Fear will then drive some to flight before them, and freeze others into helplessness, to be mastered where they cower."

"You soothe me," the taller Koglaur said bitterly. "So why have we wasted our time down the years meddling with lesser foes and matters, when alongside us, the Snake-lovers have grown into something much greater?"

The Koglaur bent over the whorl did something with his hand, and the whorl sank, slowed, and began to go dark and fade away. "We've struck at the clergy of the Great Serpent again and again," he said grimly, "but have often been slain or foiled . . . as if our foe knew just how, when, and in what shape we'd be acting."

The Sarindan Koglaur made a restless movement. "Well, it can't have been the Serpent, asleep. Is it these confounded wizards again?"

The whorl-caster looked even grimmer. "No."

"Who, then?"

"Who better to fight us than one of our own?"

The tall, spar-headed creature raced through dry, dead underbranches in a loud chorus of snappings, fragments tumbling in its wake. As it ran, leaping fallen and rotten tree trunks and vine tangles, it murmured, "Swifter, Thuulor, swifter! This Flaeros will be halfway to the ends of Darsar before you catch him, at this rate!"

There came a place in the green and shaded gloom where the forest fell away in tumbled rocks beneath its pounding feet, and the hurrying figure plunged into space. There was a twisting and blurring, and then a frantic flapping of huge wings, ere the crash of crushed bushes came. A leathery, winged thing sprang up from that hard landing and flew on—and with each wingbeat its wings grew smaller, and its body longer and more slender, until a gigantic many-winged eel or snake was darting between the trees.

Every breath burned like fire, his legs felt weak and wobbly, and Flaeros Delcamper had no idea where he was running to—or where he was. In this confounded forest, yes, utterly lost and blundering along where bears and worse dwell, yes, but he must go on running—or die.

Something was crashing along after him, something that could change its shape, something large and fast that was hunting *him*.

Twice he'd deliberately made a sharp turn and headed in a new direction—and twice it had followed, sometimes running, sometimes flying . . . and always drawing a little closer.

Flaeros gasped for breath, stumbling and almost falling for the hundredth time, staggering on he knew not where, through dark, old, moss-covered trees and wet leaves underfoot, roots like gnarled boulders wandering under his boots like rope strewn across a barge deck, and oh, Three Above save me, when would this *end*?

There—again! The human fool was holding the scepter openly in his hand, now, as he ran on, shirt torn away from one shoulder by branches, panting in deep, exhausted groans, stumbling like a drunken man in his weariness. Perhaps it'd be better to draw back a bit, and lurk unseen,

before this Flaeros broke something in his fleeing. Let the
lad catch his breath, rest, and then—

The winged serpent swooped around a tree that was as
large around as a small cottage, over one gigantic bough,
and then under the nex—

The two boughs clapped together like slashing blades,
and then drew apart a little. The snake writhed in shuddering agony, half-crushed and transfixed between them on
many thorny spikes that hadn't been there moments before.
Branches that had sharp cutting edges like swordblades
whipped out and back, and severed sections of snake
plopped down onto a moss-cloaked stone. A humanlike
hand was protruding from the tree there—and from a ring
on one of its fingers fire erupted. The sections of snake siz-
zled in that cone of snarling flames, seared, and then crumbled into ash—as the two branches slowly bent down to
thrust the rest of the winged serpent into the stream of fire.

In a matter of moments the snake was all blackened,
shapeless ash. Abruptly the flames were gone, and the
branches silently melted back into something slate-gray
and headless that boasted two stumpy legs. Those legs
stamped on the ashes, and then took a stride—and half the
tree quietly walked away.

Flaeros Delcamper was several tree-cloaked hills away
by then, blundering into trees in his terror and exhaustion,
and so missed seeing these makings of a very fine terror
ballad. He would have been fervently thankful to know
that the walking thing wasn't headed in his direction at all.
Yet he might well have been almost as alarmed if apprised
of other lurking beasts of the forest, that he was now much
closer to. For bards as for others, life remains a process of
stumbling blindly between perils.

"Yes, there are windows behind all of those shutters," Tonthan "Goldcloak" said solemnly. "Rest assured: there are
no other rooms here save the taproom and jakes below us.

No passages, secret or otherwise. We've chosen a good place for our shared purposes. You may speak freely."

He waved a hand that glittered and gleamed with fat gold rings crowned by thumb-sized gems at the empty chairs drawn up around the table. "By all means examine the underside of the table, the floor, and the ceiling; we'll not be offended. Sit where you like, and on the chairs of your choosing."

The representatives from the Isles of Ieirembor regarded him expressionlessly, and then did all of those things, lingering for some time at their examination of the seats and backs of all the chairs. Tonthan and the other wealthy Sirl merchants waited patiently, goblets in hand—and when the Ieiremborans were seated, brought decanters and empty glasses to the table, silently offering them.

Just as silently the Ieiremborans refused that offering. Their heads then turned to regard one of their number, a large, dark-haired man with fierce and full eyebrows, who put the knuckles of one of his hands under his chin, stared at all of the Sirl merchants across from him, one at a time, and with a total lack of expression on his face said, "We are met this day because we of the Isles seek revenge on Ezendor Blackgult, who dared to try to conquer us, and did much harm in failing at that. We seek your sponsorship in working that revenge."

Tonthan nodded over the rim of his glass. "And the intended form of this revenge?"

"The death of Blackgult—dealt openly, by red war, not by poison or a night-hurled dagger. All Aglirta must know why he falls—and know also that we can at will strike to the very heart of their land."

Tonthan steepled his fingers wordlessly and looked at one of his fellow merchants—a man in yellow silks with large, dark eyes and a curving, short-spike beard on the end of his chin. "Sathbrar?"

Sathbrar leaned forward. "It was our assumption that your revenge would not end with Blackgult's death, but extend to something of lasting benefit to us all: the ascension to the River Throne of a man all of us here in this room could have some measure of control over."

The Ieiremborans sat like stone statues for the space of a very long breath before their spokesman said in carefully neutral tones, "You are in favor of installing a figurehead king?"

"Indeed," Sathbrar replied.

"You might even say our financial support depends on it," Tonthan added, leaning forward. "A man we approve of, moreover."

The eyes across the table from him narrowed. "A king of your choosing?"

"I did not say that. Say rather: a king of *your* choosing, whom we find agreeable."

The spokesman for the Isles sat back and exchanged glances with his fellow Ieiremborans. It took but a few moments of looks traded with that same careful lack of expression before they reached some sort of consensus, and the spokesman leaned forward again. "We find this acceptable," he said, "so long as all magic used upon this king, and counsel given him, is also a matter of mutual agreement—beforehand, and with full knowledge of what is being attempted, on both sides. That is, all of us here at this table are informed fully, equally, and—as much as is possible—at the same time."

He lifted his brows in query, and Tonthan and Sathbrar both nodded without bothering to confer with each other.

"Have we agreement?" the spokesman for the Isles asked.

"We do," the Sirl merchants said in unison, before Sathbrar held up one finger, and said, "There is one caution we must place before you at this time—before we speak of how many hireswords, under whose command, and where and when whelmed. Although we appreciate both the patience you've shown thus far and the fire of your cause, we are loath to proceed in haste just now. Aglirta is erupting into wizards' wars again."

Ieiremboran faces acquired slight frowns. "Explain. We heard talk here in the streets of 'confounded wizards everywhere' upvale, but were given to understand that this is by no means an unusual occurrence in Aglirta. Yet Blackgult brought no strong force of mages against us."

"Wizards are numerous in Aglirta, yes—though none remain who could seriously challenge the greatest mages of this city, we believe. But as to the warfare we spoke of: the Serpent-followers have been tossing coins to hungry warriors all over Darsar for some time now, and bringing their hireswords to Aglirta. Many of the barons of the realm are riding to war as we speak. Moreover, one mercenary captain by the name of Duthjack—probably better known to you as 'Bloodblade'—marches on Flowfoam Isle itself, with the stated aim of becoming King of All Aglirta. Many Vale folk flock to his banner, seeking an end to strife among barons, lax justice, no peace—and no king they can look to, to set such things right."

"Blackgult remains regent?"

"If he yet lives. He whelmed a paltry force in arms to meet Bloodblade, but we've heard nothing yet of how either fared."

"It matters not," an Ieiremboran who'd been silent all this time said suddenly. "Both of them drew sword on our Isles and shed the blood of our people. Both must die. Yet it would feel better were we to wield the blade that slew Blackgult ourselves—so we can be certain he is dead, and so that he dies by our hands and knowing it."

"Better but less prudent," the Isles spokesman put in. "I've no taste for wading into a realm at war, with unfamiliar foes riding at us from all sides—and even less eagerness for making enemies of the Serpent-priests until a time and occasion of our choosing."

Tonthan nodded. "We of Sirl share your tastes in this matter. We would prefer to bide our time in this matter of your revenge until a victor emerges in Aglirta. That one will have to be the puppet of the Snake-priests, or acceptable to them—or they'll move against him soon enough. We wait, then, until *their* king is on the Throne—and then we strike, slaying king and priests, and so win all."

The spokesman traded looks up and down his side of the table again, then said heavily, "We agree with and accept your counsel in this matter. We wait, then, with but one query more: is there some wizards' way of keeping watch over Blackgult, so that we *know* if he dies?"

"I will try to arrange what you desire," Tonthan replied carefully. "It is not a matter of cost, or of any shortfall in skills of the more discreet and, ah, biddable mages available to us here in Sirlptar, but rather that Blackgult bears some magic of his own—granted to him as regent, we believe—that often foils the spells of others."

He leaned forward until his nose was almost among the decanters. "We, too, see a value in what you propose. If all the tales of the regent being able to summon the Sleeping King are true—and many respected men of Sirl were present when Snowsar named your foe regent, and swear this is so—and further, that Snowsar's awakening will also unbind the Serpent, as the king insisted upon that occasion, then we of Sirl feel we must all know what happens to the regent, and when."

The spokesman for the Isles nodded slowly. "Thus far agreement has been both surprisingly plentiful and easily reached between us. If I may propose one additional matter for us to agree upon, admittedly more trivial: let this tavern be our meeting place henceforth, upon signals between us being exchanged as before. Have we—?"

Tonthan smiled. "We do. Is our mutual business concluded at this time, then?"

"It is." They rose in a scraping of chairs and extended their hands towards each other across the table, empty palms up but not quite touching each other, in the usual parting of merchants.

To Tonthan's astonishment, the Ieiremboran suddenly smiled. So they *could* smile, after all.

* * *

All who'd met departed at intervals, and took various routes away from the tavern through the Sirl alleys. So it was that Sathbrar took his leave of Tonthan moments after descending into the taproom, and was quite alone when he turned onto Sandraea Street, and paused at a spot where many folk do, where the street looks out over the trees of gardens below.

There he gazed out and down whilst pulling his cloak over his yellow silks. "A last glass of thraevin," he murmured, voice slurring as the length of his jaw changed and the nose above it also shifted shape, "and then it's high time I went to whisper in a certain regent's ear."

Without wasting breath on a reply, the Regent of Aglirta hurled the full power of the Dwaer at the young wizard. The very air around him shuddered with the force of his strike—but Jhavarr's howl was louder.

Blackgult watched as his foe was hurled away across the battlefield, lightnings spitting from fingertips as the rings thereon exploded, and shook his head. "Jhavarr Bowdragon?" he asked the dead warriors all around him heatedly. "Graul and bebolt, who is Jhavarr Bowdragon? Just one more young fool of an overambitious wizard? And why must he challenge me now?"

His sword was cool enough to take up into his hand again, but as he hefted it, he saw armored men hastening towards him. Blackgult sighed and took up a stance ere he recognized a face or two—these were not Bloodblade's men coming to slay, but battered men of Aglirta who greeted him with smiles and his battle cry: "For the Risen King!"

Blackgult gave them a grim but smiling greeting. "Well, at least I'll fall in the company of friends—and these fields are as good a place to die as any!"

"What?" one bristle-bearded armaragor growled in

mock horror. "Not lying in a pool of wine with a dozen lovely lasses? I thought the Three and I had a solemn agreement on that!"

There was a chorus of rueful laughter—but it ended abruptly when the bearded armaragor pointed across the strewn bodies, and said warningly, "Lord Blackgult, 'ware!"

Jhavarr Bowdragon was flying low over the field towards them. His hands were blackened claws, his eyes were two flames of fury, and a Dwaer-Stone was circling in the air above his head.

Blackgult's face tightened. "Get back!" he said warningly to the men around him. "Well away, and lie low among the fallen—there'll be wizard-fire all over this hill in a moment! *Go!*"

Jhavarr's first bolt turned the bearded knight into a screaming torch, and the others needed no further prompting. The regent stood alone when the young wizard came to a halt, standing on air not far off, and snarled, "Regent of Aglirta, for what you allowed to happen to my sister, you shall die! For what you just tried to do to me, know this: your passing shall be slow and painful!"

"I know your sister not," Blackgult replied quietly, "though I recall hearing of a Bowdragon among the archwizard Tharlorn's apprentices—but I fear I know the Stone you bear all too well. How came you by it?"

"I took it from one who deserved it not, nor had power enough to keep it from me," the young wizard sneered, "and now I'll—"

Blackgult was not in a mood to waste time or breath this day. He called on his two Dwaer to slash with blades of unseen air at the man facing him, seeking to break limbs and the man's neck and jaw, too, ere this Jhavarr finished spouting doom.

Flashes of light heralded his attacks—or rather, their strivings against an unseen shielding spell. Somewhere behind those raging radiances the young mage shouted derisive laughter at him, and struck back.

Ezendor Blackgult was no accomplished wizard who might make Dwaerindim dance, empowering webs of intricate and many-layered enchantments and conjurations—but he'd dabbled in sorcery for years as best a cunning warrior could, and knew a few magics very well.

Wherefore the dark bolt that hurled him into the air, flinging many dead men aloft to whirl limply around him, slew him not.

Blackgult used the Dwaer to twist it, so the fire that should have ravaged his innards gave him scales instead, and from the midst of his tumbling smashed back at Bowdragon—two fists of force, one behind the other.

The first shattered the wizard's shielding spell, and the second drove him to the ground with brutal force. Blackgult heard the dull snapping of ribs ere Jhavarr's Dwaer flamed bright and forced his onslaught away.

"*Graul* you, old bastard!" Bowdragon shouted, a thread of pain in his furious voice, "I'll *kill* you!" Wincing, he clambered to his feet, not waiting to snatch his balance ere he hurled bursts of flame at Blackgult.

"You already have," the regent told him grimly, striding forward with the fires of his own Dwaer whirling around him, sucking in Bowdragon's flames to make themselves stronger.

Jhavarr found his footing, strode forward to face the regent—and then met the eyes of the grim warrior stalking forward in blood-spattered armor, and involuntarily took a step back. Then another.

Blackgult raised his sword as he came. "If you've slain my daughter in seizing her Stone," he explained almost gently, "and keep me now from fighting alongside my men as Bloodblade reaches for the Throne, you slay me as surely as if your blade pierces my heart."

Jhavarr sneered and threw up a shield, calling on the Dwaer to make it strong and abristle with many whirling swordblades. Blackgult strode towards it, never slowing, and the young wizard's face grew pale as the regent's two whirling Dwaer winked and flared, forcing the shield of many blades back, step by step, towards its caster.

"So you storm through Aglirta striking folk down in the name of your sister," Blackgult continued, eyes dark and angry, "and slay or do harm to folk who never knew her. I think you're just one more greedy young mage who wants a cloak of righteousness to cover your butcherings and thefts. Tell me: how many farms have you burned? How many commoners have you casually struck down?"

The sword was reaching for him. Jhavarr cast a swift and desperate spell to make it burn again, but this time his flames spiralled off it in wisps as they formed, plucked away to join the tunnel of racing fire around Blackgult.

Jhavarr's shield was almost touching him now—and in sudden alarm he saw that its blades were receding into it—no—*reversing* through it, so that their glittering points menaced *him* now, and not his foe! They reached for him, growing longer, sliding out at him with Blackgult's own sword at their heart . . . the regent was bending his own magic back on him, bearing him back, breaking his—

With a snarl of rage that was almost a shriek of fear the wizard sprang into the air, his Dwaer-Stone spiralling around him, and let his shield fall away into nothingness. Let the regent try to reach him now! He'd bide his time, and return to—

Another figure was in the sky with him, rising from the field of armored men and shouts of "For the Risen King!" and "Down the regent! Bloodblade for king!"

Blackgult, trailing flames of red and black, his Stones whirling around him!

Jhavarr snarled again, fear overmounting his fury. The Dwaer were just too strong! He needed two Stones, too, for his spells to have any good chance of reaching Blackgult, to slay . . .

And for the first time that day, the young wizard began to wonder if the man with no escape from this battle might be—Jhavarr Bowdragon.

"That's the last of them?" Bloodblade snapped, his eyes on the sky above.

"Yes, Lord," the swordcaptain panted, reining in. "We don't think any reached the woods. Those who took their stand yonder are all dead—I've set men to walking among the fallen to slay the wounded and any who feign death."

"Good. Scour me this field," Bloodblade said slowly, all his thought on what befell overhead. He waved a vague and bloody-gauntleted hand at a hilltop. "Keep back from those shimmerings, there—that's some evil Blackgult worked, some slaying magic that can do nothing if we go not near. Search everywhere else."

He frowned, and waved his hand again, back and forth. "All others: scatter, that no great whelming of men be in any one place—at least until *that* is done."

The swordcaptain knew very well what "that" was. Two tiny figures stood on empty air above, flashes of magic streaking betimes between them—and one of the two had begun to blaze with light, like unto a star in the night sky. He turned his horse towards the nearest armsmen, to relay the Lord's command to spread out, glanced up at the blazing star overhead, and swallowed. Against whatever might stab down out of the sky, a soldier had no good shield.

Hmmph. No wonder so many priests insisted their god was up in the sky, always watching.

You'd think some of them might stir themselves to help, from time to time.

Or wait; would that be the worst doom of all?

* * *

"What are you *doing*?" Jhavarr screamed, as his Dwaer slowed around him and he started to fall—so had Blackgult's; he was falling, too!

Frantically Jhavarr clawed at his Stone with his mind, abandoning the spell he'd been going to cast. *Move, be-bolt you! Move, and give of your power again, unto me . . .*

There! Hah! Torn from Blackgult's clutches, whatever his crazed plan!

"Were you trying to kill us both?" he shouted. "Tired of life at long last, Regent of Aglirta?"

"It will be some years," Blackgult said, his voice sounding calmly right beside Jhavarr's ear despite the goodly span of empty air between them, "before you gain wits enough to battle me with words, Bowdragon. Didn't your sister ever get tired of your endless shouting?"

Fury flamed in Jhavarr once more, white-hot and so bright that for a moment—just a moment—the air around him blazed like fire, too. It had been some time since he'd been able to see Blackgult, but the starry radiance cloaking him could only be another Dwaer-trick, after all . . .

When his throat loosened enough that he could form words again, he spat, "You *dare* to mention Cathaleira? To taunt me with what was done to her?"

"Young mage," Blackgult reminded him coolly, "you've dared rather a lot of things, since arriving unheralded in fair Aglirta. As regent, I'm sworn to defend this land—and if I have to dare things and taunt you to best do that, be assured that I will."

Jhavarr's Dwaer slowed again, his radiance winked out, and he fell again—not so far, this time, but enough to choke him once more. "W-what are you *doing*?" he screamed in bewildered rage, when he could speak.

"Taking control of your Dwaer, if I can," Ezendor Blackgult said in a voice of iron. "I've no more time to spare for yapping young puppies who think sorcery is all

lording over others and blasting whatever's handy without
thinking or seeing what flows from their deeds—even if
their name *is* Jhavarr Bowdragon."

And then the young wizard found himself swept around
in a helpless spiral in the air, high above the warrior-roamed
battlefield, his maimed hands clawing at the whistling wind
and finding no aid or hold to cling to. A singing sound was
erupting from his Dwaer, rising, rising . . .

Bright blue flame suddenly burst into being in front of
him, a huge sphere of fire that completely hid the glimmering star that was his foe—along with that half of the sky.
The roaring of wind in Jhavarr's ears died, and his Dwaer's
song fell into a confused, discordant chiming.

"Blackgult!" a woman's voice cried from out of those
flames, high with rage and exultation. "At last!"

"*Strike*, sisters!" another female called. "Strike now!"

Fire and lightning and bright and deadly spell-arrows of
a sort Jhavarr had never seen before leaped up from the
flames, arcing high over Blackgult's suddenly bright
Dwaer, then stabbing down like claws coming in at the regent from all sides.

"Die, Blackgult!" A third woman shrieked, rage and
grief making her voice tremble on the edge of tears. "In the
name of Raevur Talasorn, *die!*"

Jhavarr Bowdragon opened his mouth to shout in delight
and triumph, raising a fist to beat at the air—and then the
air before him shattered in blinding brightness, and bolts
were lancing every—

Horses screamed and bolted, tumbling more than a few
men from their saddles. Men shouted and ran in like fear,
wildly, running to nowhere, fleeing the great smiting in the
sky. A few fell, or cowered under their shields, awaiting the
next great blow—as their ears rang and the echoes of that
great blast rolled around the woods and across the fields,
from Sarth to the mountains and back.

No other blast followed—nothing but a hissing in the darkened sky, and here and there wet thuds. They heard those same thuddings in Sarth and in Helm Hollow beyond—and even along the backlands road, where men came out of their steadings to stare at what was raining down into their hog troughs and orchards alike, all around: small pieces of Bowdragon and torn-armored Aglirtan warrior.

11

Going to Flowfoam to Die

The way ahead was dark. Yet he knew it all too well, every painful stone step that he was crawling down, headfirst, resting his chin on cold and dusty stone as his crushed and broken fingers shrieked protests. His gaspings echoed loudly around him, in the chill, deserted underways of Flowfoam. None came here but the rats—and Ingryl Ambelter.

He smiled into the darkness. Aye. None came here but the rats, indeed.

The stair ended—good, 'twas the last one. Now across this little unseen room—to the right, here, where there was a tilted flagstone . . . the doorway waited, somewhere beyond . . .

His probing hand struck the edge of the frame a little too hard, and the pain-wracked Spellmaster sobbed and curled up to shudder away the pain, until he could master himself enough to crawl on again. Not for the first time he wished he'd left Gadaster a little closer to the ways above, just a few bebolten rooms nearer—

Surge, all afire *gasp* such *power* gone, rolling away . . .

What was *THAT*?

"Something mighty has happened," Ingryl gasped, to the empty air around. His own hoarse whisper echoed . . . and then faded. No other sounds followed. Nothing had been awakened, nothing scurried or crumbled and fell, and that was good.

He let his forehead sink down onto the cold stone, and lay still. His mind was still atingle, but he knew very well what he'd felt—a great surge of sorcery, racing up from the south and west, invisible but as *alive* as a hundred shouting men. Farmers and armsmen might not even feel it, but it would serve every wizard as it had him: crashing into their heads, roaring—and then, having washed over them in its flood, race on, leaving them dazed.

Some great act or shattering cataclysm of sorcery had just befallen, somewhere nearby in Darsar, possibly in Aglirta itself . . . and here he was, crawling like a sick child across a cold stone floor, on his way to embrace a dead wizard's skeleton.

Gadaster Mulkyn no doubt lay waiting just as grinningly patient as always, his tutor and tormentor no more. Ingryl had laid him low and made him the Spellmaster's best little secret: Ambelter's own personal bones of healing. Bones that said Ambelter sorely needed once more. Until he'd undone what Blackgult had done to him, he was little better than a crawling worm.

Perhaps Blackgult had died in that spasm of sorcery, doing something to Bloodblade—or trying to. Dabblers in magic seldom succeeded in what they tried, after all . . .

Or succeeded all too well, to richly rue their deed.

That meant, Ingryl supposed, that the gods had very cruel senses of humor. But enough of wizardly wit and hazarding; he was growing cold and stiff, and no hint of what the cause of the great wave of spell-force might have been came to him—or would come. His dazed mind was as dark as the Silvertree cellars around him.

"Something mighty has happened," Ingryl Ambelter repeated to himself, a little angrily, "and I've missed it." Feebly and painfully he wormed his way through the doorway, and dragged himself onward into the cold and waiting darkness.

Light flashed like the lashing lightnings of a wild storm, racing across the splendid high ceiling of a certain chamber in Arlund, where a sphere of spell-radiance floated. Thrice it burst from the sphere to snarl around the room. The five robed Bowdragons in the chamber trembled uncontrollably as it clawed through them.

Even when smoke curled up from their robes, pain lashed their eyes to tears, and blood filled their mouths and streamed from their noses, they ignored the stabbing lances of wizard-fire—to stare intently into the sphere.

Abruptly one of them made a halfhearted grab at the glowing orb, choking back what might have been a sob.

The other four recoiled from the sphere in horror. "No!" one of them shouted. "Not again! Not Jhavarr!"

"That's *it*!" another snarled, drawing himself up to his full height and shaking a fist in the air—a fist that suddenly crackled with tiny fires and lightnings of its own, spitting from between clenched fingers. "Aglirta and all of its cruel, grasping mages must be *destroyed*!"

Bloodblade seemed not to notice the gentle sighings of his own shielding spells dying away around him. He peered through the fine rain of blood at smoke and ruin, seeking a particular hilltop—where—yes!—shimmerings he'd warned the swordcaptain against were winking out.

"And so passes Blackgult!" he chuckled, watching the last one flicker and die. "The swaggering Shield of the Risen King is shattered!"

Snatching the rally horn from his belt, he blew it and spurred his snorting, fearful mount to the nearest hilltop, beckoning his warcaptains with great sweeps of his arm.

* * *

Soon enough he was ringed by eager faces, staring at him hungrily out of helms adew with blood. Everything had that iron tang—and everything was covered in a dripping wash of red. Gods, but sorcery bought impressive deaths, if naught else!

"Get you to Flowfoam as fast as you can," he told his men grimly. "Seize me the Throne! Once Kelgrael is good and dead and I'm king, the rest of the barons will come to me—on their knees, or waving vain swords, or as corpses. Barons always come to Flowfoam, as surely as water flows downward. There I'll be victorious!"

They still stared at him in eager, expectant silence.

He looked around at them all, struck the flat of his sword against his thigh with a ringing clang, and shouted, "What're you waiting for? *Ride!*"

"For Bloodblade!" one of them roared. "Ride!"

"Ride!" they took up the cry, and were off, galloping like madmen, blowing their own rallying horns wildly as they went. Bloodblade waved his sword on high to his troops, and allowed himself a grim smile. With a sound like reluctant thunder, his whole army started to move. East, to the docks—and thence to Flowfoam!

"Embra," Sarasper muttered, as their boat grated against the Flowfoam dock. "Embra, awaken! I need your wits, quickly!"

"You're not the only one," Lady Silvertree murmured drowsily. "In fact, if I gave a piece of mind to all in Aglirta who needed it . . ."

"Not now!" the old healer hissed, as both Craer and Hawkril, busily mooring the boat, snorted their mirth. "Leave the feeble jokes to Craer, and tell me this: where on Flowfoam is some magic I can get my hands on, quickly?

You're hurt, and Brightpennant's worse—he'll die on us if I don't get magic I can drain, *quickly*!"

Embra opened swimming eyes, and tried to stare at him. "Top of the dock stair—little door in the topmost torch lantern: a glowstone, for when there's wind or rain or over-much snow . . ."

"Raulin!" Sarasper snapped, and the young bard launched himself up the steps like an arrow shot from a bow.

"Uh, Raulin—?" Craer asked, on the stair, as the young bard stormed past. "Hadn't you better wait for us, in case whichever wizard raised that barrier is lording it up there? And might be struck by the urge to turn you into a rotten gourd? Or, say, a pillar of ale, with no flask or handy tankard to hold you together?"

The hurrying youth paid him no heed, slowing not a step in his rush.

"Our 'whichever wizard' is going to be Ambelter, I'll be bound," Hawkril growled darkly, striding up the stairs three at a time with warsword in hand.

Raulin came back down the stairs even more quickly. He bore the glowstone in his hand, but looked sick.

"What ails, lad?" Hawk snapped.

"B-bodies," the young bard called back. "Blood, and flies crawling on their *eyes*—"

He was suddenly, noisily sick just to one side of the stone steps, and ran on, almost sobbing, to where Sarasper waited in the boat, with Embra and Glarsimber slumped on either side of him.

"Spew some more right now if you can, lad," the old man told him with a sour smile. "I'm going to need your help pulling the sword out of our bold baron, here!"

Raulin stared at him, face white—and then, abruptly, did as Sarasper suggested. The healer threw a hand under the nearest Castlecloaks elbow and spun him around just in time to avoid being drenched.

"Such obedience is rare in the young," he commented, as Raulin's shoulders stopped shaking.

The bard hissed a bad word at him, then threw back his head, breathed deeply, and followed it with an apology. "There's been a battle up there," he told the healer. "Bodies everywhere."

"Flowfoam court guards? Courtiers? Strangers?"

The bard shrugged. "I don't—all of them, I guess. Just blood, blood—"

Sarasper clapped a hand on Raulin's shoulder, and said, "The glowstone? Thankee. Now into the boat—we've got a lady sorceress to get on her feet."

"But isn't Glarsimber—?"

"Yes, and I'd be seeing to him first save that we *all* might need Em's spells in a hurry; us for healing Brightpennant, here, or Hawkril and Craer if they run into the Spellmaster or some *other* crazed wizard, Aglirta's got plenty to spare—a step or two inside the palace! Now get down here! I need you to hold her still, in case she thrashes if there's pain and loses us this glowstone into the water, see?"

Raulin saw, and got down there in as much haste as he could. He was only sick once more, and that was safely into the water.

"The lad was right," Hawkril muttered. "Looks like a hog-slaughtering!"

Craer nodded, but put a finger to his lips for quiet as he glided forward into the next chamber. Bodies were slumped everywhere, and all was dark and silent, as if not a man yet lived—

There! Something had moved over there!

In a crouch, the procurer crept forward, darting along beside a grandly gilded lounge that half a dozen armaragors could hide behind. At its far end he halted, low to the floor, and peered around the corner, head swaying out like a snake's.

The man at the far end of the chamber was stumbling

along blindly, blundering into walls and doorframes, and—yes, his face drooped sickeningly, eyes great pits and flesh hanging like melted wax. Another lurched into view, shuffling mindlessly through another doorway, a sword dangling from its hand. It did not even seem to see the first stumbling man—or the procurer peering at it.

Craer ducked back the way he'd come. "Melted! The place is full of Melted!" he hissed.

"So which wizard commands them now?" Hawkril growled. "The one we're going to find and slay, yes?"

Craer gave him a wry grin. "You have a knack for reducing things to simple, clear tasks, Tall Post!"

"It's a better life than some lead," Hawkril replied meaningfully, watching a Melted shamble along a passage towards them. It did not appear to see them, even when Hawkril waved his warsword in front of it, and stumbled past as they exchanged wary glances.

"Perhaps someone already took care of the wizard for us," Craer murmured.

"I don't like this," Hawkril growled. "Back to the boat—Em will know best."

"Doesn't she always?"

Hawkril gave his friend a dark look, but made no reply.

Raulin turned his head away, wincing, his hand so tight around the hilt of the blade in the baron's guts that it was going numb already.

"Just pull it straight out, lad," Sarasper said. "Whatever you do, don't twist—just pluck it *straight* out, hmm?"

Raulin clenched his teeth. "I'm going to . . . be . . . sick again . . ."

"Here, let me," said a crisp voice at his shoulder. Raulin blinked at the Lady Embra, and she gave him a small, quick smile, ran a finger along the line of his jaw that did anything but soothe him as she'd intended, and firmly removed his fingers from the hilt of the sword.

"*Now,* Em," Sarasper said, looking up from the glow of magic between his hands. The Lady Silvertree leaned over Raulin, bosom brushing against him so that he blushed and swallowed again—and tugged the blade forth, straight and swift.

Her hand stabbed in at where it had been almost as swiftly. Blood was spurting everywhere, and Raulin cringed away until he saw with shame that lines of gore had splashed across Embra's face and breast, and left Sarasper's intent face a dripping mask of blood, and neither of them had so much as flinched.

"A bad one," Sarasper murmured, the glow flickering between his fingers. "Yes . . . a bad one."

Embra reached out her other hand and laid it on one of the old healer's hairy forearms. For an instant, something flashed between them, something Raulin almost saw . . . and the air tingled. Magic, strong magic . . .

Glarsimber jerked, under them, snarling and clawing blindly at the air . . . and then fell limp again, and groaned.

"Oh, gods," he cursed. "Three Above, that was almost my doomsword . . . or was it? Am I—?"

"Alive, I'm afraid," Sarasper chuckled. "With flagons still to drain, and ladies still to . . . ah . . ."

"Still to kiss," Embra said gleefully, bending to Glarsimber's astonished lips.

The baron's eyes flashed, under her—and he gave Raulin a wink, an instant later, ere the Lady of Jewels released him to gasp for breath delightedly.

"My," he purred, "that was almost worth carrying a cold sword through my guts for most of an eternity . . ."

"Almost," Sarasper agreed dryly. "Almost."

"Either he's dead or he's delighted," Craer said, as they pounded back down the steps to the dock. "She's kissing him."

"Stop your *teasing*," Hawkril snarled. "It's like the little lasses giggling and teasing, when I was a brat—except that your tongue never stops, but them at least I could make howl!"

"Oh, you could *probably* make me howl if you handed me gems enough," Craer replied.

"Aye, a heap of sparkling stones higher than a wagon," the armaragor snorted. "Forgive me if better uses for such a hoard—assuming I could ever *find* so many gems in all Darsar—spring to mind."

"Making Embra howl? I think if we burned all her gowns, we'd find she has that many stones already."

"That many and more," Embra replied, looking up from the boat. "I'd trade them all, right now, for my Dwaer back!"

"So would I," Hawkril growled. "There's got to be a wizard up there—the place is crawling with Melted, stumbling around unseeing."

Embra's eyes narrowed: "As if something has happened to whoever was commanding them." She sighed, tried to wipe blood off her face and rearranged it into a big smear instead, and said grimly, "Let's to work, then. Glar, can you stand?"

"I'd rather go right on lying here with you on top of me, actually," the baron told her in tones of mock innocence.

"*Up*, Baron of the Realm," she told him crisply. "We'll be needing you to die far more spectacularly than in the situation you describe."

Craer raised his eyebrows. "There are more spectacular situations?"

"You can belt up and go forth to die, too," the Lady Overduke told him fondly. "All of you—get!"

They got. Craer took the lead, the rest of the Band of Four followed, and Raulin found himself assisting the baron—who by the top of the steps knew just how weak and easily winded he still was.

Flowfoam was dark and empty, save for the flies, the

dead, and the eerie, silently wandering Melted. "Hurry," Embra hissed, looking around. "I don't like this at all."

"Hurry *where*?" Craer asked. "I know you grew up here and might remember this on your own, but this castle *does* cover the entire perimeter of the island, you know."

"The throne chamber, you dolt," the Lady Overduke told him witheringly. "I can call on the Living Castle linkages anywhere, but if I do so when someone else is sitting on the throne, he can see right where we are—and strike at will. Once I'm on the throne, I can search all Flowfoam without shifting my shapely behind an inch."

Hawkril raised his eyes to the ceiling. "I'm glad you said that, my Lady," he growled. "I'll be even more thankful if Craer resists the urge to comment cleverly, about now."

Craer smiled, winked, and said nothing at all.

"Should I shift shape?" Sarasper asked reluctantly, as they headed for the throne chamber, and the messily sprawled bodies of guards and courtiers grew more numerous.

"Not unless you'd be much happier as a beast," Embra told him. "Personally, I find it hard to converse with a longfangs."

"That fails to surprise me," the old healer told her wryly, stepping smoothly to one side to let a Melted blunder past without touching him.

"Quiet now," Craer warned. "One more passage, and we'll be looking into the throne chamber."

The doors stood open where the procurer was pointing, huddled bodies in plenty to keep them that way. Embra sniffed at the air, frowning, and shook her head. "I don't like this," she whispered again, and led the way onward. Craer and Hawkril quickly moved to flank her, while Sarasper looked behind them—and found Glarsimber already grimly doing the same thing.

Embra paused at the last door and crouched slightly to peer ever-so-cautiously ahead. Without a word Craer put a hand on her arm to make her stop, and slid past her into the gloom like a fast-drifting shadow. The first place he looked was up at the ceiling, the others saw, ere he glided from view.

Hawkril took a quick step forward to keep his friend in view, warsword raised at the ready. Craer was peering behind the throne, and then at the doors to either side of it. Embra joined Hawk, and they both saw the procurer shake his head and turn and beckon them to join him.

The throne chamber was crowded with Melted, wandering everywhere. The Lady Overduke was relieved to see that when they collided, they didn't start hacking at each other, but merely staggered back and turned to wander elsewhere. Still, she twisted and darted like a procurer to avoid even brushing into any of them, as she made her way across the wide expanse of marble.

Guards and courtiers lay dead everywhere; she tried not to look at them. When she was standing before the River Throne at last, Embra gazed down at its emptiness, drew in a deep, shuddering breath, and said to Hawk, "Stand guard before me. Please."

He nodded, swung around, and drew his dagger, spreading his arms so that edged steel barred all ways to the front of the throne. Craer raised an eyebrow in a question, and she murmured, "See if you can guide one of those—things—out of a doorway, without getting attacked. If it works, get rid of a few more. Then bar all of these doors."

Craer nodded and glided away, heading for Sarasper, Brightpennant, and Raulin to relay her orders.

"Hawk," Embra whispered, as she turned around to sit down on the High Seat of the Kings of Aglirta, "if my voice seems . . . not my own, or I speak harshly to you or say things I wouldn't, strike me senseless and get me off here as fast as you can—but throw down your steel before you do it!"

The armaragor merely nodded, over his shoulder. Embra bit her lip, put out her hands to grasp the arms of the throne—and sat down.

* * *

The seat was cold and hard under her, and there was the strange tingling she always felt, as the familiar, waiting Living Castle enchantments stirred, recognizing her. Yet the Melted did not turn to charge at her, no crawling magic clutched or stabbed at her, and . . . nothing untoward happened. Yet.

Swiftly, she let her awareness flow out, and then reached *down* into webs of laced and intertwined magic—spells laid by Ingryl and Gadaster before him and half a hundred other mages, all mighty . . . and all treacherous and sly, laying traps and secret linkages of their own.

Yet this felt like home. She had always known these powers, these bindings. Here, present herself *thus*, endure the flood of fearsome images laid to scare away the timid, and call upon this thread of power. Follow it, deeper now, until—yes! There!

She came to a place deep within the palace and deeper within herself where she could call on the old, deep-seated enchantments of Flowfoam. In a trice she sourced them to scry the state chambers.

Nothing. No magic, strewn or fallen or even hidden, and nothing alive but a few rats scurrying in the walls. 'Twould take hours to search all of the interlinked keeps and underways across the Isle, and somehow she already knew the regent was either dead or not on Flowfoam.

She could not feel him.

Not near, not anywhere. Even with Flowfoam's magic. She had no Dwaer now, to call to his—and she had precious little time to search for anyone or anything.

Something had happened here on Flowfoam. No regent, no court—no one left alive. Who had done this?

The enchantments had not been tampered with, or damaged. If there'd been a spell-battle, it had been elsewhere— or all of the combatants had either refrained from using the ancient magics of the Isle, or been so familiar with them that they could wield them so skillfully that no trace was left, and no damage done.

Where was her father?

Her father, the man she'd been reared to hate, the hereditary enemy of all Silvertrees, the nemesis of the cruel tyrant who'd called himself her father.

Baron Blackgult, the darkly handsome, laughing Golden Griffon. Scourge of the high ladies of the Vale, striding confident in his black and gold from bedchamber to bedchamber. She still could not quite believe what she knew to be true: he had sired her—and he was far less the monster many Vale folk thought him to be than any Silvertree. Perhaps including herself.

The Lady of Jewels, folk still called her, fear and envy in their voices more often now than the pity or veiled hatred she'd heard when she was younger. All Aglirta had trembled when Faerod Silvertree had looked their way, then, and some saw her as his pawn, and others as one talon of his claws.

So much had happened since then. The tyrant was dead, his outlawed enemy had returned to Aglirta and been named regent by the king she and her swordbrothers had awakened—and now he was nowhere to be found, and the throne stood unguarded, and she needed answers.

King Kelgrael named us overdukes, we Band of Four, we lawbreaking adventurers. He bade us protect his realm. Oh, how we've failed in that . . .

Ezendor Blackgult—Father—where are you?

Silence. Emptiness. Far-questing thought, feeling for that dark, rich mind, that humor, that fierceness . . . like unto his griffon namesake, something of the gold-eyed hawk in the man . . .

Flash of blue mind-flame . . . awareness . . . four watchers, magic fierce in all, regarding me . . . not friendly—

*   *   *

Embra screamed.

Hawkril whirled around.

Her head was thrown back, blue-white lightnings were arcing from her eyes—and more bolts were crackling across her, from arm to arm of the throne, holding her down like chains as she writhed and arched, struggling under their fury.

Stone smoked where those bolts spat sparks, but Hawk flung away sword and dagger and snatched at his lady without hesitation. Em was hurting! He had to—

Roar out his pain, helpless in the grip of magics that howled through him, stabbing, searing spells he had no defense against. He was dimly aware of his hair standing on end, his armor creaking and giving off smoke, his body trembling in the flow of fell magic like a spiderweb in a gale . . .

And then Embra did something that hurt her very much, and hurled him away, freeing him from that slaying storm of fire. Hawkril crashed to the floor through many mindless Melted, gasping, too weak to even make his arms obey him as he flopped and panted.

Embra sobbed, and he struggled to rise. He couldn't even lift his head—and above him, around him, the entire *room*—vaulted ceiling, great broad battlefield of polished marble floor, and all—was shuddering! Craer skittered towards him, waving his arms crazily in a wild scramble to keep his balance and not fall headlong into the crackling spell-lightnings.

He couldn't even see Embra, somewhere beyond his feet where he couldn't look! "Three aid me!" he roared. "Any of you! *Help!*"

Four of them—kin to each other, and all "shes" . . . sisters?

Embra winced as they hurled fresh bolts into her. She didn't even *know* them, had never seen them in her life before! They couldn't be of Aglirta, they couldn't be some-one she'd angered even unwittingly . . .

The pain! Oh, Three, the PAIN!

Yet she was alive, thanks to the old magics of Flowfoam running through her, and the River Throne to empower her own castings.

Oh, Hawk, what you must be feeling now, with none of those things!

Embra bit her lip again, not caring if she had any face left at all. If she could but raise a shield . . .

Thrice she tried—and thrice they smote her, just as it was about to form. They knew quite well what she was at-tempting, they must do, and so she could only fail: each time the shield started to form, they could overwhelm it with a fresh attack, and . . .

The palace had seen so many spell-battles, down the years, wild storms of magics, spitting and thrusting and ex-ploding . . . and yet it endured. And she was linked to it—*it* could be her shield. Sink down through those Living Castle linkages, take on the cloak of stone, settle deep and dark and cool . . .

Yes . . . battered she was still, her body torn and wracked by their spells, but now the pain was but a dull, roaring ache, and she could think again. Weave spells again. Scry and probe and perceive again . . .

Fierce they were, these four. Young, and yes, sisters . . . strangers to her, yes, though there was a proud name wo-ven into some of their incantations.

Embra frowned, and bent her will to listen. It was hard to sit still while bolts were spun that would be hurled to hurt her, to do nothing but wait for the twisting, sickening instant when the magic struck deep into her, clawed, and then receded amid spell-echoes . . .

Tala . . . *Talasorn!* That was it: Talasorn. There'd been a Talasorn in Sirlptar, a private man, of good reputation among mages. Were these his daughters?

And if so, or if not so, why were they savaging her?

Or did they slay everyone whose minds they met, while riding their sorcery?

"Lady forfend, what's that?" Baron Tarlagar gasped, as a man whose flesh was gray and hung from his face in grotesque wattles and flaps, for all the world as if it was wax frozen in middrip from a candle, lurched out of an archway and walked stiffly down the terrace steps, almost falling twice. The Melted strode unseeing right past the armaragors of the three barons, who watched it with open mouths and pale faces, and vanished into the trees of the southern-side Flowfoam gardens.

"Three Above," Loushoond said. "The Melted walk again!"

Ornentar nodded grimly. "That means a wizard awaits us. Let us go slowly, and skulk about this palace. A charge to the throne chamber may be a race to our deaths."

Tarlagar nodded grimly. "Better alive and barons, than dead with crowns on our heads."

Loushoond winced. "No grand bardic phrases, please! Say rather: the most attractive tactic is to carefully search this palace, avoiding the rooms of state until last—in hopes that only one surviving foe will face us there, when at last we do venture therein. A weakened foe."

"Not another wizard like Silvertree's Spellmaster," Tarlagar said fervently.

"Agreed," Ornentar said tersely, and pointed with his sword down a garden path he knew. "That way—and keep together."

"That way" led to Griffonguard Door, a side way much mutilated by Faerod Silvertree because of its resemblance to the badge of his hated foe Blackgult, and hence little used. Loushoond and Tarlagar nodded. For once in this armed rush to seize the Throne, prudence was advisable.

When blue flame burst into being in the sky above the docks, the armaragors did not wait for orders to duck down and begin running through the gardens—and the three barons did not tarry to discuss tactics further.

"Embra!" Sarasper called, hurrying through the maze of moving Melted with a grim Glarsimber and a frightened Raulin in his wake. "Are you well? Need you healing?"

Craer turned a pale, trembling face towards them—and Sarasper saw the procurer's eyes suddenly blaze with blue fire.

Then that same radiance came into the faces of the Melted, too, and they ceased their stumblings and turned in smooth unison to face the south wall of the throne chamber. Sarasper cast a quick look in that direction, but could see nothing but the wall that had always been there, unchanged.

He could hear something, though. Something hissing or roaring, distant but drawing swiftly nearer . . . more than one something, of the same sort. Three or four identical snarling, crackling noises, like wind-driven fire racing through dry trees . . .

And then blue fire was flaming behind the doors on the south side of the throne chamber, and those doors burst open, booming back against the walls in an instant where usually three men had to strain to slowly shift them.

Blue fires raced along the passages beyond those doors, drawing nearer. Spells, leaping blue lightnings of magic, and riding them—as if those crackling bolts of magical fire were steeds—four women.

Dark-gowned, furious, and similar in looks. Sorceresses all, sweeping the room with their frowns and dismissing all as unimportant except the throne—where their blue lightnings clawed and snarled around one weeping, writhing woman.

One Talasorn sorceress smiled unpleasantly—and all four of them roared towards the River Throne on plumes of angry blue fire, raising their hands like claws to slay.

12

To Spit upon a King

$\mathcal{P}$ale fire flowed in the darkness. The Spellmaster gasped in relief as the pain started to ebb, flowing away from him into the glow. Ahhh . . .

Lying in the open casket, sprawled awkwardly atop Gadaster Mulkyn's grinning skeleton, Ingryl Ambelter growled softly as the tension that had governed him, keeping his limbs obeying him through stabbing agony, faded at last.

He'd been a fool to try spells against someone with two Dwaerindim. Gods, but the Worldstones were strong! Blackgult, too, had been a surprise. Oh, the smiling cunning any could see, and all of those intrigues and back-bedchamber doings take swift wits and boldness as well as low guile—but the man could work magic, too. His mind was as sharp as a sword, even before he seized on the power of the Dwaer. It would be wise not to strive spell to spell with him again . . .

The glow around Ambelter was growing dim, and his pain was almost gone. Old Gadaster was losing strength even faster than he was; 'twould be best to rise now, before the bones of his onetime mentor crumbled away entirely.

Abruptly the glow brightened, and the solid stone walls *rippled*. Three Above, what sort of magic could do *that*?

The palace around him seemed to gasp, too, and he could *feel* magics surging through it, storming through ancient bindings. Somewhere stones fell with a clatter, and ages-old dust swirled in the air around him.

Gods forfend, this had happened the *last* time he'd had to crawl here, too, and—

In gasping haste Ingryl clambered down off the casket, staggering as he found his own feet and his weakened legs groaned their own complaint. Great magics were surging overhead, now, contesting and grappling in the palace above.

He had to get gone from this place! At any moment the ceiling might smash down, or bolts of ravaging magic flood through this forgotten chamber and sear him in their passing. Crossing the chamber was like walking against a gale, slow and struggling work in air that seemed as thick as river water, while the tinglings that betokened titanic magics came and went as swiftly as flames leap from a campfire.

"Serpent and Dragon!" the Spellmaster swore, as frightened now as he'd ever been—before his fingers found the shelves of scrolls and small coffers of rings and talismans and spell-gems, and began to snatch and gather in feverish haste.

Something fell from his grasp as he snarled the spell that would take him away, but he cared not. Flight was more important now. Ingryl Ambelter finished the spell, drew in a deep, shuddering breath of the swirling dust as more stones crashed down, somewhere closer—and vanished from Flowfoam.

Four plumes of flame crackled to a halt, hanging like balconies in the lofty vaults of the throne chamber—and on each of them a sorceress stood, more blue flames raging around their hands.

Sarasper started to curse softly, knowing how powerless he was. On the River Throne Embra gasped and twisted under stabbing lightnings, still trapped in torment. The sorceresses looked down at her coldly.

"Slay her?" Ariathe spat, looking to Olone. Craer's daggers were spinning through the air towards the Talasorn sisters, but they paid no heed—and one by one, those spinning blades melted into blue flame ere striking, and fell away into nothing but brief sparks.

Olone shrugged. "If she dies, she dies—but the throne, sisters, strike at the *throne*! If we shatter it, surely the Sleeping King will be destroyed—and the royal line of Aglirta swept away forever! In the name of our father, *strike*!"

"Raevur Talasorn!" three voices shrieked in answer, as balls of blue fire were hurled.

Hawkril struggled to his feet, empty-handed, and stood swaying. Aglirta endangered—but how could he charge someone standing high above, on air?

His blade . . . he needed his blade. He—*gods*!

Slender Talasorn arms weren't much practiced at throwing things, it seemed—or the four were too enraged to spell-guide their hurled infernos. A whirling sphere of flame spun right at Hawkril; desperately he flung himself to one side, bowling over two Melted, and crashed to the marble floor, skidding a long way—and thankful for it, as blue fire burst on the marble and sprayed hissing streamers in all directions. Melted caught fire and staggered, here and there around the room, and as Hawkril rolled over, new bruises shrieking, he saw Craer snatch up a fallen dagger, and fling it hard at the closest sorceress.

Her head turned, blue fire flashed in her eyes—and the procurer grunted as unseen magic plucked him off his feet and smashed him against the back wall, limbs bouncing wildly.

"Craer!" Hawkril roared, but there was no reply. Aglirta beset . . . what to do now? He needed sorcery to fight sor—Embra! He had to get Embra off that throne . . .

The armaragor struggled up again, ignoring the raging blue fires—wherever Talasorn flame had struck, the marble seemed to be burning like dry fire-tinder—and launched himself towards the throne. It seemed to be the only thing these she-wizards feared, but it was massive; there was no way he'd be able to lift it as a shield against them, or hurl it, or . . .

Hawkril stopped trying to think about what he'd do when he reached the throne, and just ran. Off to one side, Sarasper, Glarsimber, and the lad were also trotting through the Melted and the fires, heading for the high seat where Embra writhed.

The Talasorn sorceresses were spinning other spells now, launching thin beams of silver and ruby-red radiance that stabbed at the dais and then clawed at the throne itself. These magics seemed to vanish into old, much-enchanted stone without effect—but when one of them strayed across Embra, her shriek smote Hawkril's eardrums like daggers driven into his ears, and she sat bolt upright, clawing at the air as if it was a wall she could climb, raking nothingness with her eyes wide and staring.

"Lady preserve her!" Hawkril swore, terror overmastering his rage. "Embra, I'm coming! *I'm coming*!" Empty-handed in his armor, the armaragor burst right through searing blue flames—an instant so hot that it seemed like the touch of ice, and a momentary smell like spices as they licked, seeming to do more harm to his armor than to him—and sprang onward.

Someone else was swearing, not far overhead. "Such *power*!" Dacele Talasorn cried, her hands trembling. "Sisters, are you sure—?"

"Strike at it with Sarandor's Seekings!" Olone shouted. "Waver not! This *is* the way!"

"The Sleeping King must die," Ariathe snarled, lips

drawn back from clenched teeth, spell-sparks swirling from her eyes, "and Aglirta with him! Strike, sisters—*strike!*"

Hawkril was still a few stumbling strides short of the River Throne and Embra's pleading eyes when the murmured chantings ceased, and the air above his right shoulder suddenly shone with a strange shifting light—first coppery and bright, and then green, deepening to dark emerald.

"Back!" Sarasper shouted from somewhere. "Hawkril, get back!"

The armaragor could not have stopped if he'd wanted to—and with the lady he loved struggling in pain right in front of him, Hawkril Anharu didn't want to. *Gods*, for a Vale free of all sorcery! If the Three were in no mood to grant that, what he wanted was somehow to have magic enough in his hands that he could turn and rend these Thrice-cursed sorceresses, and all others of their ilk, too, smashing them up into the sky and out of Aglirta forever!

What Hawkril did was lumber dizzily on as copper and emerald lances of light stabbed down around him, seeking the throne—and then, as the armaragor stretched out his hands to try to snatch Embra from the faltering, spitting lightnings once more—finding it.

The River Throne flashed as the beams of magic touched it, and suddenly blazed up as bright and orange as glossy-polished copper, with Embra frozen at its heart a handspan above the stone seat, fingers and every tress of her hair outflung in all directions like a bristling of straight, rigid arrows. Emerald lightnings snarled warningly at Hawkril's fingertips as he flung himself nearer, and then there was a sound like the shriek of a great bell riven in twain, and—

There was nothing in front of his eyes but white emptiness.

He was falling, flung off his feet by a great upleap of the unseen marble beneath him, and there was a strange, discordant singing in his ears. Other things were falling, too, and whirling past, felt more than seen, and—something hard and heavy struck him across the face and chest, and he was tumbling through the air, clutching at nothing . . . nothing . . .

Raulin Castlecloaks sobbed, clutching Baron Brightpennant's arm so tightly that Glarsimber roared in startled pain—a roar unheard amidst the ear-shattering cacophony of the River Throne exploding.

Magic erupted in sprays and bolts and struggling helices of light so bright that it hurt the eyes, and Embra Silvertree was hurled screaming across the room, carrying Hawkril with her. They cartwheeled through Melted who'd all suddenly ignited into a walking forest of greasy flames, and in their wake—as Craer Delnbone was flung along the back wall like a torn corner of parchment caught in a gale—the ceiling began to fall.

Sarasper Codelmer stared up at spreading cracks and tumbling slabs of stone, and found the only possible shield: he got himself right under one of those floating whorls of blue flame where sorceresses stood shrieking their triumph.

As tons of stone began to fall, shattering marble in a deafening, never-slowing thunder, he only hoped that Raulin and Glarsimber would have time to do the same.

The ground trembled under racing hooves, and more than one man fell from his saddle. Lord Bloodblade of Aglirta clutched at his reins as the armaragors around him, riding hard, shouted their alarm and amazement.

The rumbling went on, the leaves of the swaying trees hissing loudly, and they all knew where it was coming from, even when it spread to the mountains and echoed back, until it seemed all Aglirta was atremble.

The thunder was coming from Flowfoam Isle.

Men cried out in fear. "The Risen King!" an armsman shouted, not far away. "The king returns!"

Others took up that cry. With a snarl of rage Sendrith Duthjack stood up in his stirrups, snatched up his rally horn, and blew a blast that cut across the shouts, overriding even the rumbles of the land shuddering around them.

"*Ride on!*" Bloodblade bellowed. The cowled man riding on his right made a tiny gesture, and the warlord's words rang out like a trumpet into every man's ear, across his entire army. "If perchance the king does dare to stand against us, he *will* fall before our blades, and Aglirta shall be cleansed at last! Ride on! To Flowfoam, and victory!"

"*To Flowfoam, and victory!*" a thousand throats echoed, and the thunder of hooves began again, drowning out the last echoes from the mountains.

Curved slabs of stone crashed down, shattered—spraying shards of marble in all directions as they broke what they landed on, too—bounced or rolled over ponderously, and came to a halt, trailing dust.

Crushed and mangled Melted lay half-buried everywhere, and Sarasper scrambled through the choking dust to get out from under descending blue flames. The coughing and retching sounds from overhead told him that the four sorceresses weren't going to be smiting anyone or anything for the next few breaths, at least.

Time enough to find Raulin and the baron, if they yet lived. In the next moment he was twisting desperately aside from a sword, and then hearing Glarsimber's muttered apology. Time enough, indeed!

"Where're Embra? And Hawk?" Raulin hissed, at the baron's elbow.

Sarasper gave them a shrug in the dust-gloom, and pointed in the general direction of where he'd seen them tumbling through the air—into the far reaches of the room, thankfully beyond where the ceiling had collapsed.

He glanced up, into the darkness of what had been the

gallery above the throne chamber, and was now an even higher ceiling for it. Nothing but swirling dust. The blue flames were dying away now, at floor level, flickering feebly around the booted ankles of the four tall, dark-gowned women.

They looked slender, agile, discomfited by all the dust—and furious. If they hadn't been so angry and so dangerous, they might have seemed beautiful.

Gods, even cloaked in dust, they *were* beautiful. Like so many of the perils the Three sent to torment other mortals: alluring but deadly. Sarasper waved at Raulin and the baron to crouch low behind a heap of broken stone slabs, and took himself to his knees, a hand over his nose against the dust.

One of the Talasorn sorceresses glanced right at him, but seemed uninterested. Her gaze, like those of her sisters, strayed again and again—when they weren't looking at each other, glances that were clearly silent converse—at the riven throne.

A glow was growing there, an eerie blue darker than the flames of the Talasorn. Darker, yet growing slowly brighter and lighter in hue. Three broken shards, like reaching fingers, were all that was left of the River Throne, mere fragments of its back . . . and this radiance was growing brighter and stronger in front of them.

Ariathe Talasorn lifted a hand to hurl magic at it, but Olone said sharply, "No! Not yet! See what befalls, first!"

"I am so *sick* of waiting to see what befalls . . ." Ariathe said in a voice of low, angry warning—but although she kept her hand raised and ready, no blue fire kindled in it.

The light before the throne was white now, and the sorceresses gazed at nothing else; Sarasper rose and went softly to join Raulin and the baron, pointing again to where Embra and Hawkril had been thrown. Slowly they proceeded in that direction, carefully threading their ways around the smouldering, half-buried bodies of the fallen

Melted and much broken stone, pausing often to glance back at the throne.

The radiance in front of the throne seemed shot through with whirling stars, now. Olone Talasorn took a cautious step closer to it, and then another, and her sisters did the same. As they watched, that light grew brighter, more slender, and taller.

Abruptly the whirling motes within it rushed together, into a shape—and Kelgrael Snowsar stood looking at them, drawn sword in hand. The King of All Aglirta was wearing a sad smile as he gazed upon the ruin of his throne room and the four furious women standing in it.

The white light was fading around him, now—and a sudden, angry sob or snarl erupted from Ariathe Talasorn, a moment before she hissed an incantation—and a ruby-red beam of fell magic stabbed out from her fingers to smite the king.

Kelgrael turned a little to face her, but did no more. Her spell raced at him, seemed to be sucked aside into his sword—which glowed briefly, as if white starlight had raced down it, from tip to pommel and back—and then sent her own ruby radiance back at her.

"*Die*, murderer!" she shrieked, her cry echoing strangely in the ragged vault overhead. Its echoes were still shouting back at the room below when the red fire reached her, washed over her with horrible speed, and left only crumbling ashes in its wake. In so fleeting an instant, Ariathe Talasorn was no more.

"No!" Dacele cried, and swung her head around to glare at Olone. "Sister, aid me! Together—thornarrows!"

"*Yes*," Olone snarled, her hands already shaping intricate gestures. The last sister—it was the one who'd slipped him the healing potion, Raulin saw—stood silent, her hands raised but unmoving, as she watched her sisters. She took a step back and shook her head slightly, looking uncertain.

Sarasper and Brightpennant exchanged grim glances.

There was nothing they could do against spells—even if they hurled something right now and by some miracle struck down a sorceress, it would be too late.

Olone was a skilled spellweaver; she brought her magic to readiness and held it there, risen force keening in the air around her, until Dacele's thornarrow spell was ready. They nodded to each other, took a few strides farther apart—and hurled their spells in unison at the king, striking at him from both flanks at once.

Kelgrael lifted his sword and held it out before him, shaking his head slightly. Long, slender dark needles of force—maroon thorns two feet or more long—raced at it, swirled somehow *into* and then out and *around* that sword, despite their length—and sped back at the sorceresses who'd cast them.

The deaths were bloodier this time. Raulin choked after one glimpse of Olone swaying and spitting blood, transfixed by a dozen dark needles, one sprouting from an eye—but before the young bard could look away, the thornarrows erupted in angry maroon fire. In an instant of raging flame the sagging, arrow-bristling women became forms of ash amid dying purple flickerings . . . dark things that sank, crumbled, and were gone.

The only light left in the throne chamber now came from the king's sword. He held it up like a lantern so that Sarasper, Raulin, and the baron could clearly see him raise his other hand in salute to them, and then wave at them to stay back and keep clear of what he was about to do now. Thrice he gravely waved them away, ere turning with sudden speed to stride across the broken, littered marble to where the last Talasorn sorceress knelt by the ashes that had been her sisters, sobbing.

She looked up when the glowing blade came down, eyes streaming—and the king put the sharp point of his sword to her trembling throat.

Despite the king's gestures, Sarasper took a step or two nearer, to see clearly what befell. The Talasorn sorceress was staring fearlessly up at Kelgrael, fury shining bright through her tears.

"Who are you," the king asked quietly, "and why did you four do"—his free hand waved at the wreckage around, but his eyes never left her face—"all this?"

"Tshamarra Talasorn am I," she spat, "and we came here, we sisters, to *slay* you, King of Aglirta! Our father's dead because of you, and—and if you gave me a blade right now, I'd use it on you! So kill me now, King Snowsar! I've sworn to be your bane, and by the blood of my sisters and of my father, I *will be* your death. I'll never rest until one of us is dead!"

The swordtip moved ever so slightly at her throat, like an icy finger stroking her skin. "I've grown so very tired of slaying," the man above it said wearily, and his eyes looked as old and tired as the seaswept mountains of the Isles. "And the death Aglirta's seen thus far is nothing to the slaughter that's soon to come."

Tshamarra's eyes blazed up the king's steel. "How can that be?" she snarled at him. "Or have you forgotten the fallen, these past few years? Armaragors and armsmen and farm folk beyond number! Raevur Talasorn, my father! The Baron Esculph Adeln, whom he served! Baron Cardassa, and Eldagh Ornentar, who was baron before the sly fool who holds that castle now! The former Baron Loushoond, too! The wizards Corloun and Oen Darlassitur! Faerod Silvertree and his Dark Three! Ilisker Baerund, Tersept of Tarlagar, and half a dozen tersepts more! The archwizards Tharlorn of the Thunders and Bodemmon Sar, gods spit on you! Are you *blind*, King of Aglirta? Or are so many lives nothing to you?"

"They are everything to me, daughter of Raevur," he said grimly, "but they are a list that a trained bard could remember, and recite entire during, say, a single meal. *You* have doomed countless more, you and your sisters."

She laughed incredulously. "*We*? How have we doomed anyone?"

King Kelgrael shook his head slightly, those old, old eyes on hers, and under that sad gaze she fell silent. "You awakened me, you four, and destroyed the only swift means of my returning to Slumber, all in the same stroke."

He waved at the ruined throne behind him, and asked gently, as if patiently schooling a child, "Now, Tshamarra, you are the sorceress of us two, so you tell me: what does that mean?"

The woman on her knees looked up at him with something strange kindling in her dark eyes and moved her lips twice without saying anything, ere she murmured, "I-I, Lord, I know not. Tell me, please."

The king nodded, as if satisfied, and said in the same gentle voice, "It means that, at long last, the Serpent is stirring. Awakening as I have done, with no way—short of almost every wizard in all Darsar whelming to work together, or all the Dwaer-Stones being found and properly used—to drive Aglirta's ancient foe back down, in time."

"And so?" Tshamarra whispered, foreboding in her eyes.

"And so it has come down to this," the king said slowly, and threw back his head to draw in a deep breath. "All I can do now," he added, more briskly, "is use the binding 'twixt the Serpent and myself to buy Aglirta a little more time."

He turned his head, then, and raised his voice. "Overdukes, hear my royal command: get to the Serpent swiftly, with force enough to slay—and do what must be done. This is imperative, if Aglirta is to survive."

A frown crossed the king's brow, and he asked, "Lady Embra—any of you—where is my regent? I can't feel either Blackgult or the Dwaer—why?"

Glarsimber and Sarasper traded long glances, and said nothing. Then they both turned to the young bard standing with them.

So it was left to Raulin to spread helpless hands and gulp, "Gone . . . all of them."

"Aglirta has always been thus," Kelgrael growled,

swinging his sword aloft and glaring at it. "What must I do, to win peace at last?"

He shook his head sadly—then looked down, as keen as a striking hawk, at Tshamarra Talasorn. Her hands were moving in stealthy spellcasting, and her eyes, fixed on him, held open hatred once more.

With a speed she'd never seen in any man before he bent and caught both her wrists in his free hand, snatching them together with astonishing strength. He shook the sorceress slightly, as the ruined spell curled away in little twinkling motes and sparks from her fingers, and bent the rest of his body to stare into her eyes from only inches away.

"Do you truly want me dead, Lady of the Talasorn?" he murmured.

Her eyes blazed up into full fire again. "Yes!" she snarled, and spat in his face.

King Kelgrael smiled slightly, then lifted his head, and called, "Overdukes, keep back!"

Sarasper took another stealthy step to one side, bending to peer and hear every word.

The king put his face back nose to nose with Tshamarra again, her spittle dripping unregarded from his chin, and muttered, "There is one way—and only one way—you can make sure of that. Turn from me, and use your spells to hold off my overdukes, and the others with them, *without* doing them harm."

Her eyes narrowed. "While *you* do *what*?"

"Slay myself with this sword whilst calling up a certain magic—and so drive the Serpent down for a time."

She gaped at him in disbelief.

"Choose, daughter of the Talasorn," Kelgrael Snowsar told her gently. "Or I'll sharpen this sword in your innards before I use it on myself."

Trembling, she stared into his eyes for a long time ere she whispered, "I—I'll do it, Lord of Aglirta."

The king smiled at her and released his grip on her wrists.

She stared at him in mute astonishment for another long moment before slowly stretching out one hand and carefully, delicately wiping his chin. Then she rose, stepped around the king, raised her hands—and cast a shielding spell.

It rose in a whirling of sparks, to wall off that end of the chamber.

She cast a quick glance back over her shoulder at King Snowsar, and he smiled at her, nodded approvingly, and then lifted his eyes to stare straight at Sarasper.

Hear me, faithful Overdukes.

Aglirta is yours now. Watch it well, as I know you have done. Have my thanks—and in time, I hope, all Aglirtans of good wits will join me in that gratitude. Watch over our land, no matter who sits the River Throne. My hope is that one of you will take the Crown—my only sadness is that it can't be this crown I wear. It dies with me, unless my hand places it on the brow of my direct descendant. I had my own hopes in this regard, and regret your choice, Lady Embra, while at the same time praising it. We must all do as our hearts bid. So I have lived for Aglirta—and so I will die for Aglirta.

Raulin, Glarsimber, and Sarasper all stared at the king, too dumbfounded to speak or move or even glance at each other.

Kelgrael was murmuring something that sounded like an incantation. Tshamarra Talasorn whirled around to watch and listen with her own astonishment plain on her face. She knew a few of those phrases, and what it cost to guide one's will through them; the Risen King was mightier in magic than any archwizard!

Kelgrael gave her a little smile as he went on, raising his sword upright, point high, at arm's length. A glow was gathering around it, rose-red and white, slowly growing brighter. A thin mist seemed to curl up and down the blade, and a singing sound stole softly out of the blade to chase that mist, growing higher and louder—not a keening or a high horncall, but a wordless singing, as if from the throat of a maiden.

Kelgrael let go of the blade, and gestured to the Talasorn

sorceress that she touch it. Gently, with one fingertip and fresh foreboding in her eyes, she stretched forth a finger—and then drew back, shaking her head.

Sarasper took another step nearer the shielding, and so was close enough to hear Kelgrael murmur, "'Tis no trap. Touch the blade, and take what magic it pours into you, that it not be forgotten. Expect no usable spell, mind, but words of power and snatches of incantations and instruction that may find their uses in years to come."

Tshamarra looked at him doubtfully, and he smiled, and said, "Please, daughter of Raevur. Your father sought spell-lore all his life; will not you?"

The Talasorn sorceress drew in a deep breath—and touched the sword.

Sarasper saw her shudder, and snatch her hand back. Her other hand lifted, as if she wanted to take the blade from where it hung in the air and wield it herself, but Kelgrael smiled, and said, "Nay. For this to work, the hand must be my own."

And as Tshamarra watched with a strange look in her eyes, he took hold of his sword in both hands and murmured something even she did not catch.

His arms trembled, then, and slowly grew longer . . . impossibly longer—until it was a simple matter for him to turn the glowing, singing blade around—and drive it, hard, into his own breast.

The sword flashed, Tshamarra's barrier fell away into bouncing sparks, and the Risen King threw back his head and cried out in pain. Magical fires flooded from his mouth—and the Throne Chamber of Aglirta went dark.

Light flashed and flared in that darkness: the royal sword, shattering into many shining, flaming shards. By their fading, descending light, they saw Kelgrael Snowsar melt away into dust. Dust that fell away into drifting nothing—as the world rocked.

13

Godly Favor and Handy Graves

There was a sudden rumbling in the distance.

The snake-headed man looked up sharply, shrugged off his cloak of scales, and strode naked to the nearest rocks. There were scales on his back and thighs, and a stump at the base of his spine that looked like the stubby beginnings of a snake's tail.

The Serpent-priest embraced a sloping rock taller than he was, flattening himself against it to feel what was causing that rock thunder. Here in these rocky, barren uplands, few tumults disturbed the endless sighing of the wind—and no eruption of a smoking mountain, such as sprouted in Sarinda and Harthlathan beyond, must be allowed to disturb the Sacred One!

The Serpent-priest threw back his head and tasted the air with a long, darting tongue—but it seemed almost needless, now, as the rumbling grew to an echoing roar, the ground started to shake under him, and the rock he was embracing thrummed under the goad of—something deep and titanic beneath Aglirta that was racing towards this place!

The priest sprang away from the rock, whirling to rouse the other holy guardians of the Great Serpent—but they were already darting out of the caves and watch posts and running aimlessly about, looking and shouting.

The rumbling grew even louder, and small stones came rolling down the rock slopes from above. The shaking was now strong enough to numb the feet and make teeth chatter, and the Serpent-priest saw with alarm that cracks were forming in the dirt and rocks beneath him—spreading with wild speed there, and there, and everywhere!

Then there were shouts—almost screams—of joy, and the Serpent-priest's head snapped around to see the cause. A moment later he was on his knees, throwing up his hands and shouting, too—using all his ready magic to make his voice trumpet-loud.

His words crashed across the dell, to roll back their own echoes to him, as he cried, "Rejoice, Blessed Brethren of the Serpent! The time we have waited so long for, striven so hard for, is at last at hand! The cursed Risen King must be dead at last, his bindings broken! It is the moment of the Awakening of the Serpent! All Aglirta, all Asmarand, all *Darsar* shall soon tremble before the holy might of the Serpent, his Awful Wrath that only we faithful shall be spared! Aglirtans cower before wizards and regents and an iron-headed brute called Bloodblade, but soon they shall know what it is like to *truly* cower!"

Breath failed him at last, but the Serpent-priest seared his way on, empty lungs carried by magic into one final shout. "The Awesome One is freed at last! On your knees to make reverence! On your knees, and cry him forth fittingly! The Awakening comes—NOW!"

As the thunder of his voice died away, exultant shouts filled the dell, cries that soon settled into a ragged chant, "Arise Eroeha! Arise Eroeha! *Arise* EROEHA!"

Though the shaking of the ground had lessened—racing on, it seemed, to the mountains, leaving the cracks in its wake just as they were—the grassy earth in the center of the rocky dell, in the midst of the kneeling priests, was bulging upward. It was already higher than a man, and surging towards the sky more and more swiftly, shedding great clods of earth to tumble and roll aside from gigantic black coils beneath . . . coils that slithered but slowly, yet . . .

Yes! At long last! 'Twas true!

"The Serpent Awakens!" the naked Serpent-priest roared, springing to his feet as his fangs grew longer and his scales brighter. "The time has come at last! Eroeha, command us!"

As the scaled men and women danced in heartfelt exultation, a single red-gold eye opened amid those inky coils. A slitted pupil as tall as the roaring priest regarded the world with savage fury and glee, more earth fell away as the black coils bunched and heaved—

And then a mist of shadows stole across that blazing eye. The Rising Serpent came to a halt, frozen in midrise— as the scaled priests all stared in dismay, and silence fell.

Silence that was broken only by weeping, here and there, across the Place of the Serpent.

Of all the birds that wing the Vale, the waterswift is perhaps the most beautiful. Deep blue of back and wing, gray of head and tail, with rainbow iridescence of breast and glossy black eyes set in a black eye-mask stripe, it darts here, there, and everywhere. It may chitter softly, or make deep liquid bubblings, or mew loudly if angry or alarmed. Ever-curious, cocking its head to look at things, it often befriends fisherfolk, drovers watering their beasts, and bargemasters, and will flit in to visit, day after day, ere swooping away in pursuit of the insects that dance above the Silverflow. It has a sense of humor, but none of the thieving ways of the stormjack or the drale, and is also known to sit still as a statue on strange perches for hours—human heads among them—just watching its surroundings.

The waterswift now whirling above the river was older than most, and no stranger to Flowfoam. It swooped and darted above the Silverflow, dining on shimmerwings and stinging mierye, and did no more than peer curiously, once or twice, at the cloud of shadow that seemed to cling to the Royal Isle.

When the shimmerwings were all gone, it turned to cross Flowfoam, and dine on whatever droneflies might be found above the rushing waters on its far side. Chittering to itself, it darted into the dimness—and froze.

Had another waterswift happened by and turned a curious eye on the gloom upon seeing the motionless tail of a fellow swift, it would have observed a bird hanging motionless in the air, stopped in midwingbeat, beak parted to chitter, eyes staring ahead, and claws drawn back in its haste.

Alive and unaware—frozen by magic. On Flowfoam, in the wake of Kelgrael's sacrifice, all that moved was air and dust.

Frozen in grief, frozen in darkness with great magic roaring through and past him, Sarasper Codelmer had the dream again. It had haunted him before this, in his sleeping hours, at first rarely but in recent days almost every night. Always it left him wide-awake and as cold as winter ice, drenched with sweat.

Always, 'twas the same vivid thing: *a dragon, red-gold and large and terrible*—no beast of bardic legend, but very much alive!

Alive and staring right at him, *gaze golden and knowing as it challenged him*. He hung frozen, every time, as it turned with lazy, ponderous grace and began its dive towards him, jaws and claws opening . . .

Which is when he always came awake—silent but bolt upright and trembling in terror. To gasp for a long time and stare wide-eyed into the darkness, before sinking back down into dreams that never held the dragon again, the same night.

Why Sarasper so feared it he did not know. Perhaps every man fears what comes plunging towards him unbidden out of the night, long-taloned claws outstretched to clutch . . .

Empty air shimmered above the grave of Maeraunden Silvertree, dead some eight hundred years—and its cracked and crumbling slab suddenly grew a dark-eyed, rather slender man in robes whose face was far less forgotten in the Barony of Silvertree than Lord Maeraunden's. The Spellmaster cast a quick glance around at the overgrown graveyard, smiled in satisfaction—free of watchful eyes, and wildly surging magic, too—and strode around several cracked and leaning memorial columns, up through the tall grass and creeping vines towards the Silent House.

Whatever mighty magic had rocked Flowfoam—right behind him, out in midriver—did not seem to have reached here. Ingryl Ambelter smiled again as he peered around at familiar overgrown Silvertree crypts and tombstones and found no lurking children at play or farm folk tending snares.

Let the game begin again, then.

He headed for one of the doors of the Silent House that he'd spellsealed on the orders of Faerod Silvertree years before. There were safe chambers within, and one hideaway is as good as another—this one, with its view of Flowfoam, would be the best hide-hold of all in Aglirta just now, for watching various armored brutes arrive to slay one another. When scrying showed the situation best suitable, he could return to the Royal Isle to parley with—or simply destroy—the last survivor.

"Barons, barons everywhere," the Spellmaster purred, "and not a one of them worth a tankard of his favorite ale."

Idiot sword-swingers, the lot of them. Betimes more

biddable and less dangerous than wizards, and useful for fetching and carrying—but to think that such as these warmed thrones all over Darsar, while many mages were hunted and hated!

Why, if ever wizards got together and founded a realm of their own, then th—

There came a sudden crashing in grass and snapping of branches from the far end of the graveyard, and Ingryl whirled around, gliding two swift steps into the shadows of a particularly tasteless, two-wizards-tall Silvertree grave marker.

Someone or something large had entered the shunned Silvertree graveyard and was hurrying onward heedless of the sounds they made, the track they left—or their own comfort, as they burst through thornbushes and pounded through whipping tree branches.

Whatever or whoever it was turned towards the Silent House and started crashing uphill, breathing hard—nay, panting.

In a few moments they'd round that row of crypts and be but a few running paces away from a particular tall grave marker. Ingryl Ambelter's mouth tightened in irritation, and he muttered something brief, made a stabbing gesture with one hand—and was gone.

Meanwhile

Flaeros Delcamper could run no more.

Every breath was shuddering fire in his chest, the world swam crazily around him, and he was stumbling and tripping almost constantly, now, his feet heavy and yet numb. He knew no other place to hide from whatever was after him, the *thing* that could change shape at will. The Silent House was a deadly labyrinth of traps, yes, but perhaps he could find a crypt outside that he could scramble to the top of, and there lie hidden . . .

It was hide or fall on his face and be taken if he tried to go on. The gruff words of one disapproving uncle came into his head suddenly: "Phaugh! We're not breeding Delcampers like we used to!"

Well, *that* was certainly true. And if the gods weren't with him now, this particular Delcamper wouldn't live long enough to breed at all. Smiling grimly, Flaeros clutched the dragon scepter in a hand that was slippery with sweat and wobbled up to an archway that he could cling to, and look back, and if the Three were smiling, choose his crypt—or, if they were not, perhaps see just how close on his heels the thing pursuing him was, and what horrible shape of many fangs and claws it now wore. *Something* unfriendly was watching him right now—he could feel its cold, malevolent regard heavy on his shoulders as he struggled on, trying not to think that he might just be choosing the particular span of Aglirtan turf that would soon be his grave.

Useful enchantments, jump spells. Ingryl Ambelter now stood on a high balcony of the Silent House, from which he'd once watched Silvertree serving wenches chasing his more disobedient apprentices with barbed whips. Ah, those had been the days. Long, sinister talks with Faerod Silvertree as they plotted Aglirta's future and Blackgult's doom together, no mage yet risen to challenge him in Faerod's service . . . yes, it had been fun, seeing the clumsy dolts who'd never master sorcery cringing as their blood flowed, just down there . . .

Ah, here was the blunderer in the graveyard! Panting and staggering, his finery sweat-soaked and torn—of course! Everyone's favorite naive buffoon, soon to be hailed the Bard of Bards, Flaeros Delcamper!

He'd wasted a jump spell on *that*. Well, then, 'twas only fitting that he waste another, more appropriate magic . . .

Gleefully Ingryl Ambelter threw back his sleeves with a flourish, made a lazy gesture to begin the casting, and opened his mouth to begin the short, familiar incantation. Halaezer's Scourge—a whip to flog the backside of a foolish bard with, to be sure, and—

The Spellmaster made a strange whuffing sound, and without uttering another word pitched forward over the ancient battlement, plunging headlong into an even older Silvertree tomb that—fortuitously both for his personal future and for the heart of the already fearful Flaeros Delcamper, who was too blinded with sweat to see the wizard's fall—had long since collapsed into a pit.

Someone on the battlements murmured a soft curse, and lowered what he'd used as a club. The Spellmaster still had a back side to his skull purely because too much haste had been necessary to deliver a proper, killing blow—a mistake that would be addressed next time.

The problem was that wizards not thoroughly dealt with always charged Darsar such a high price to arrange a "next time."

Something was happening, up ahead. Men were falling—no, their *horses* were falling, spilling riders in all directions, of course—and his hurrying host was riding over them. There were screams, and men cursing, and fights breaking out, as everything slowed into tight-packed confusion.

Furiously Bloodblade snatched out his horn again—but already swordcaptains were blowing theirs, calling a halt.

"Three Above!" the warlord snarled, standing in his stirrups in a vain attempt to see what was going on. Everyone was crammed together along the road, with the trees standing like dark walls close by—walls that could sprout arrows at any moment, or even a few enraged boars, for that matter!

He wanted to get to Flowfoam *now*, before anyone could

steal away with the crown or the Throne, or whelm a force
there against him!

"What befalls?" he shouted. "Why're we stopping?"
The nearest swordcaptain relayed his shout, and others
took it up, over the heads of the cursing, clanging, packed-
together armsmen.

With Blackgult gone, if he could but outrace word of the
regent's passing to the Isle, he might just be able to take the
Throne without bloodshed—and without any courtier having the chance to sneak off with royal riches or treaties . . .
or, graul it, with their own heads still on their shoulders!

The shouts were bringing word back, now. "The horses,
Lord Bloodblade!" a swordcaptain called. "That blast in
the sky—many of them now bleed from the head, and cannot keep balance, and so fall! And all are exhausted!"

Duthjack was too good a warlord not to see, now that
everyone was halted, that many of the horses near him—
and the men riding them, too—were weary. He saw no
mounts staggering or streaming blood, but for some under
his eye, the choices were rest or collapse. He was not so desperate, yet, that he need gain the cloak of cruelty in the eyes
of Aglirtans, before he even took the Throne over them.

Raging inwardly, he called to the nearest swordcaptain,
"Spread the word: we halt, and camp. The foreguard are to
walk their horses far enough ahead for us to have room to
dismount, tether, and lie down for sleep. All others, dismount and be easy."

The robed figure on the horse beside Bloodblade turned
his head, and a single soft word came out of his shadowed
cowl: "No."

Bloodblade scowled. "'Tis true: men and mounts *are*
spent. The best deed for us now is to make camp, right
here."

"And what if you all stood at the Flowfoam docks right
now?" the robed man murmured. "How weary would you
all be *then*?"

Bloodblade stared at his questioner, his face flaming and his temper rising to match it. He saw a cold smile in the depths of the cowl ere the robed man turned in his saddle to snake out a hand and close it on the neck of an armsman who rode nearby, helm in hand and his hair a tousled, sweat-stiff tangle.

The armsman stiffened, turned his head to see who'd touched him—and froze in that twisted position, his angry eyes acquiring a staring, wide-eyed gaze.

The cowled figure raised his other hand and cast a spell. Bloodblade watched, fury falling away to a faint feeling of sickness, as here and there throughout the host, he saw other robed, cowled figures grasping other warriors. Their other hands rose more or less in unison, to cast the same spell that had just been worked beside Bloodblade.

As Bloodblade watched numbly, he saw that there was nothing left in the eyes of the armsman he'd seen touched— no, nothing left *of* the eyes: they were empty, dark pits!

The armsman toppled from his saddle onto the saddle horn of his cowled slayer, and Bloodblade could see that all that was left of him was a bloodless husk, crumbling and weighing but little. Other such corpses toppled or were let sag to the ground as the cowled men withdrew their hands—and Bloodblade saw fangs protruding from the fingertips of some of those hands. They shrank back into flesh almost immediately, and were gone—but the warlord knew very well what he'd seen, and his hand was clenched white on his sword-hilt.

And then the world around him changed, trees and armored men and horses all sliding into liquid distortion as a great hissing arose, like a hundred snakes all crying menace at once. The hissing echoed all around Bloodblade as everything swam and swirled before his eyes, leaving him to stare only at vivid, racing colors . . . that suddenly whirled back to normal.

Sendrith Duthjack blinked, but he neither swore nor

shivered. The narrow road through the trees was gone; his host now stood, boots and hooves, on the south Silvertree shore, with shattered docks and splintered boats before them—and Flowfoam, crowned by its palace, standing oh-so-close across the water before them.

Bloodblade stood up in his saddle, and cried, "Behold the favor of the Three upon us, to bring us down upon our foes! Let us crush them and end this, *now*! Find us boats in yon wrack, or upriver yonder, at Treehallow—to Flow-foam, and *victory*!"

The cowled figure smiled again, and Bloodblade sat down hearing his words echo back from the walls of Tree-hallow itself; once again, a spell-trumpet had carried them to the ears of every man there.

There was a momentary silence as those echoes died—and then, with a roar, Bloodblade's warriors rushed down into the shallows, seizing drowned boats and oars, clawing aside ropes and shattered dock planks, and dragging vessels up out of the water to pour their small shares of the river out of them.

In the space of a few breaths seven were found that would float—and eager armaragors were setting out across the swift-flowing Silverflow under the shouted commands of swordcaptains, to bring death to the River Throne.

"Jhavarr was our brightest," the gray-bearded man said curtly. "Of *course* all our younglings are afire for Aglirtan blood—*and* half of you who should know better; oh, yes, I heard your shouted boasts and vows of vengeance. As for our offspring, so close that they call each other brother and sister and not cousin—how could they not be afire? They *are* Bowdragons."

He turned from the gem-adorned circular garden window to face them, and added with no little asperity, "Yet answer me this, Multhas and Araunder and Ithim: how swiftly do you want to lose your striding sons and raven-eyed daughters? Pride and grand words and fury are poor weapons against wizards the like of whom we see walking Aglirta or hiring themselves out to Aglirtans in Sirlptar— and if they chance on even a hedge-wizard who has hold of a Dwaer-Stone, well . . ."

Multhas Bowdragon ran his fingers along his long, thin moustache, and nodded slowly. "Your every word awakens rage in me, Dolmur—because, by the Three, as *always*— you are right."

"I do not think I can stop one of my sons, at least," Araunder Bowdragon said slowly, rubbing at his balding head as he started to slowly shake it.

"Then bid him your last farewell and consider him dead," the eldest Bowdragon said bluntly, "for he soon will be. Go you back to your hotheads and tell them again the tale of the Sword of Vengeance."

Three brothers frowned at him in puzzlement. "The Sword of—?" Multhas said slowly. "I do not know that tale."

Dolmur gave him a mirthless smile, and said, "Of course not. You haven't made it up yet. Yet it's a grand yarn, of the five-summers-old daughter of a swordsmith slain by a cruel baron. She grew to be a woman taking no husband, knowing no lover but the forge, teaching herself to make and temper mattocks and scythes and then swords, until at last long years of work gave her the skills to craft a magnificent blade. This she presented to the baron as a gift—right up his vitals, telling him its name was Vengeance, ere he gurgled his last. I'm sure you can embroider it enough to—forgive me—drive the point home."

"Dolmur," Ithim snarled, "your humor has always . . . grated."

"Better that you glower at me," his older brother said gently, "than weep over more fresh-carved tombstones. You doted on Jhavarr rightly, as your bright heir—but I loved him for the greatness in him, and had already decided to give unto him my staff of magics when he learned a shade more prudence."

All three brothers looked at him sharply again. There were sudden tears in Ithim's eyes, but Araunder looked troubled, and Multhas looked angry.

"Dolmur," Multhas said carefully, "what of Erith? He *is* your son."

The eldest Bowdragon waved his hand dismissively. "And only surviving offspring, yes. A dreamer, not a mage yet, if ever. When I lost my Cathaleira, I knew where my staff should go, one day."

He turned back to the window. "Now, my Lords Bowdragon, I know not where to bestow it. And if we fail to rein in our heirs, I doubt me that anyone, no matter how dunderheaded or craven, shall still walk Darsar bearing the name Bowdragon when the staff falls from my failing hand."

"I could take me a new wife, and make more Bowdragons," Multhas growled.

"And school them to prudence and cool temper as well as you did your first brood?" Dolmur asked calmly. "Multhas, how? How does fire craft ice?"

Multhas clenched and unclenched his hands, face dark in anger, and said nothing.

"My Lords," Dolmur added, "for all our sakes, and a few seasons, at least: keep our heirs out of Aglirta—and so keep them alive."

Meanwhile

Sobbing for breath, utterly winded, Flaeros Delcamper staggered another few paces through the graveyard and turned to see if the next crypt along looked climbable.

Exhausted, he overbalanced in turning, lurched back on his bootheels with arms waving wildly—and slammed down, to bounce on his back amid the long grass.

The world spun crazily, he groaned out a curse on all unhelpful gods and buried Silvertrees, and struggled over onto his side and thence to a sitting position, feeling weak and sick.

The door of the crypt he'd wanted to look at was ajar—and it took Flaeros a stunned moment or two to realize that it had suddenly swung completely open, swinging inward to show him darkness—and then, stepping out of the tomb with a strange, shuffling motion, a man in long robes, his face hidden beneath a lowered cowl.

A hand rose to throw back that cowl, and show him the smiling face of a man he'd never seen before. It was not a nice smile.

Flaeros struggled to rise, panting, slipped and fell, bruising and winding himself on the dragon scepter. The man undid a clasp at the throat of the rope, and then another, lower down.

The bard got himself up on one elbow again, tried to use the scepter as a prop to push himself up by—and slipped again, reeling in his weariness.

The robe fell away—revealing not a torso and legs, but the undulating coils of a snake. Flaeros stared down at it, and then back up at that terrible smile.

The man's eyes were fixed on him—and they were now vertical slits of gold in black, staring pupils. Scales sprouted along the man's arms, racing up towards his shoulders, as he threw back his head and hissed.

As Flaeros stared at what could only be a Serpent-priest, that hiss went on and on. The man's mouth was widening, his face flattening and growing broader along with it, and that maw gaped wide to display rows of fangs.

The bard whimpered, or tried to, and backed away—clumsily, scrambling on one hip. Almost lazily the snake-man slithered forward to loom over him, upright and swaying, now all snake except its human arms—arms that spread wide to grab hold of Flaeros no matter what dodge he might try.

Weakly the bard tried to rise again, but the snake was already above him, forked tongue flicking in that hideously wide smile. Its coils curled, its tail flicked—and like a cracking whip, lashed around to strike the bard's limbs out from under him, tumbling Flaeros once more onto his back.

Delicately the snake laid another coil over his chest, pinning him, and in breathless, helpless horror he watched it rear up against the sky, throwing back its head. Those white fangs grew visibly longer as he watched, and so did its neck, if that's what one called the part of a snake just behind its head. . . .

That longer neck arched, those black-and-gold eyes looked down, the jaws widened into a horrible maw, and— there was a sudden green-and-gold flash of light, a wild burst of gore and scales and tumbling fangs, and a beam of golden radiance was sizzling through empty air, above the headless trunk of a serpent.

A wild spasm seized that trunk, whipping it so wildly that Flaeros was flung into the air and rolled over there, thrice, while coils raced crazily through the air all around him, buffeting him even as the golden ray melted them away into little tendrils of smoke—and then the tiny bit of snake tail that was left struck the bard like a cruel drover's whip, and hurled him through the air to crash into tall grass and creepers, bouncing and rolling painfully and helplessly until he fetched up against something cold, and hard, and old.

That bright beam of magic had come lancing out of the Silent House, his mind told him brightly, and Flaeros considered that thought dazedly for a time, his face pressed against crumbling stone.

A Silvertree tomb, of course—what else could it be?

My, but his mind was full of useful observations this day . . .

And then Flaeros heard something that brought his thoughts to a quivering, chilled halt. Slow, shuffling footfalls were approaching him, thudding heavy and deliberate on the grass, from the Silent House.

Closer, and closer . . .

14

Serpents and Stormharp

Darkness hung like a heavy cloak over the stillness. Gently drifting dust was all that moved in the ruined Throne Chamber of Flowfoam. Amid the tumbled stones with no courtiers crowding forward to see them and the dead strewn all around them, a few folk stood like statues, unseeing and unhearing . . .

Tshamarra Talasorn stared at a spot near her where there was nothing now, not even dust. Her lips were parted slightly, her eyes wide, astonishment and wariness and triumph all warring on her face, with just a hint of sorrow in her eyes. Her hands were half-raised, to ward off what could never be warded—and the fingers of that hand were the first thing that moved.

Ever so slowly, drifting like the dust, her fingers rose and straightened.

Raulin Castlecloaks, face frozen in midshout, was the next to move, his jaw starting to close around a word that no one would ever hear. Let it be writ that this word was "No!" and that it was delivered with all the despair of a bard who sees what he holds dear shattered and swept away before him, taking some of the brightness of his childhood dreams with it.

Glarsimber Belklarravus, Baron of Brightpennant, was also shouting—as his head turned the other way, seeking the one whose name he was crying: "Embra!" His cry, too, would go unheard, as his wounded, pained whirl around resumed, slow inch by inch.

Sarasper Codelmer stood facing the king who was no longer there, a dragon fading before his eyes. The old healer's arms were still rising to sweep apart in the first surge of shapechanging that would give him wings, and diminish him into a bird that might, just might—though he knew it could not, even as he strove to do it—reach Kelgrael Snowsar in time to pluck that sword away, to snatch it and fly on with it, over river and farms and forest, to where it might be plunged into the head of a Rising Serpent and end Aglirta's doom forever. The stuff of fireside dreams—but a day's work for an overduke, it seemed, in all this tumult and treachery and time of great need.

All across the throne room, the living were moving, now, while yet the uncanny silence reigned—moving ever so slowly, as if their limbs were drifting in thick molasses . . . as the darkness seemed to lessen, ever so slightly.

Away above the endless foam of the river rushing past the rocks at the base of Flowfoam's southern battlements, a waterswift hung frozen, utterly unmoving. Even rough change takes time to touch all things.

The armaragors and armsmen peered warily ahead as the boats neared Flowfoam's docks. A cloud of shadow cloaked the entire island, a still and silent gloom that they feared. "Magic," one man spat, clutching the hilt of his sheathed sword more firmly. "Always, 'tis Three-cursed magic!"

The robed and cowled Serpent-priest sitting beside him laughed coldly, and the warrior shrank back from him. Other Snake-clergy joined in that exulting laughter—and stood up, one by one, to throw off their cloaks. Scales glinted in the sun, legs lost already in serpent coils, and as Bloodblade's warriors stared in horror, scales raced up shoulders and down forearms, those arms shrank away to spindly, child-sized limbs, hair gave way to scales on dozens of laughing heads—and they were sharing their boats with huge serpents, swaying upright taller than a man.

As the boats swung around and bumped the docks, warriors leaped ashore with even more alacrity than usual—as the serpents struck again, and again, gleefully biting everyone within reach. Armaragors who could not flee in time slumped down in heaps around the serpents, who were now hissing incantations that stabbed at the lifting darkness.

The foremost armsmen never knew they'd paused in midstep as they rushed up the stone steps to seize the palace. They never saw the serpents wriggling eagerly onto the island, or a lone waterswift flying on at last, or the swordcaptains plunging into the water to cling grimly to dock rings, hoping the snakes would slither past and leave them alive to clamber aboard the boats again and return for the next ferrying of warriors.

Then, priests standing there or no priests, those swordcaptains intended to tell Lord Bloodblade a thing or two about serpents and their fangs. At about that time it dawned on most of them, as the hissing continued above their heads and darkness receded, that all, or almost all, of the robed and cowled figures riding with them had crowded aboard for the first crossing. So eager to die? But then, Serpent-priests did not fear what fighting men might . . .

About then, as the first clang of arms rang out from above and the first shouts joined them, most of the silently raging swordcaptains returned to a dark thought every one of them had visited and often revisited already: why did the Hope of Aglirta welcome Snake-lovers at his side, and ride with them to war?

Serpent-priests who now surged up the steps towards

the River Throne as fast as their undulating coils could take them?

"Whatever spell it may have been," an aging armaragor growled to a swordbrother, as together they fought to catch breath after sprinting up the steps to Flowfoam's southern gardens, "'tis gone now, or seems almost so . . . making me a wagonload or two happier about rushing into yon palace with my steel drawn, let me tell you!"

The other armargor nodded, head down and fighting for air. "Let me . . . rest just a . . . moment more . . ."

"Of course, Landron! I could use a breath or two more mysel—*horns!*"

Frenzied hands seized Landron by the arms and more or less threw him across the terrace where they'd been standing.

"What?" Landron snarled, snatching for his sword. "Telez, what're you—?"

"Run, Lan! *Run*, graul you!"

"What?" Landron Stonetower cried, in a last, futile protest, ere Telezgrar Rethtarn burst past him, plucking at Landron's swordarm as he passed.

Spun around and staggering, Landron found himself looking at the reason for Telezgrar's sudden renewed enthusiasm for a breathless assault on Flowfoam.

Rearing up above the topmost step with black-and-gold gleaming eyes fixed on him and many-fanged jaws widening eagerly was a snake twice as tall as a man already—and its coils ran down out of a sight a good way, with another serpent-head just coming into view lower on the stair.

Landron choked in midcurse and spun himself around this time, sprinting to catch and then pass Telezgrar on an impromptu tour of the Flowfoam gardens. That stand of tall ultharnwoods at the far end of the Isle looked particularly attractive, all of a sudden . . .

* * *

"Look!" an armaragor snapped, pointing with his sword. Two knights were running frantically through the gardens, whooping for breath as they came.

"None of ours," the Baron Loushoond said shortly. "Nor, it seems to me, are they guards of Flowfoam."

Ornentar made his own frowning inspection—as the two running men slowed, looked fearfully back over their shoulders, and then slowed once more, panting wildly. "No," he said.

"Smite them down?"

The baron's smile was as brief as it was sour. "Best have them tell us what they're running from, first."

"That darkness," Tarlagar said slowly. "Magic, I *swear* it must have been—and lasting some time, too: look at the sun!"

"Will you still your tongue about your precious darkness?" Loushoond snarled. "So 'twas magic—so your eyes are green! What boots it? I—"

"My eyes," Tarlagar said stiffly, "happen to be gray."

"Cease this, both of you!" Ornentar snapped, loudly enough for the two fleeing armaragors to hear, even from a good distance past the watching men. They traded glances—and then started to flee again, with renewed vigor.

"Well," a swordcaptain by Loushoond's shoulder said heavily, "*I'm* not chasing them!"

"And why not?" that baron asked silkily, turning his head to give the man a cold and meaningful glare. "If I order you—"

"You need not," the man barked, pointing with the mace he bore in his hand. "Look there: *that's* what they were fleeing from!"

Serpents as long as two good-sized horses were gliding along through the gardens, heads raised to look about as they came.

"The regent was in league with the Snake-lovers?" Tarlagar swore. "Three Above, we should have slain him right there when Snowsar named him, Risen King and scores of guards or no!"

"Who's to say they're not just guardians of the Isle," Loushoond asked peevishly, "conjured by whatever pet mages Blackgult still has?"

"He *has* no 'pet mages,' to use your well-aimed words," Ornentar told him.

"Except for the Silvertree bitch," Tarlagar reminded them. "Lady Embra of the Many Jewels, foe of her father. She might obey Blackgult just because of that, whatever fancy title Kelgrael invented for her."

"Overdukes!" Loushoond snorted. "The king's lover and her three pack-dogs, more like!"

"I've heard that Blackgult is her father," Baron Ornentar said quietly.

"Ho-ho!" Tarlagar cried. "No wonder Silvertree hated him so! Why, the sly fox! I've been hearing for years how he tumbled every baroness and terseptress in the Vale, but you know how such tales grow in the tel—"

"We're all well shut of Faerod Silvertree," Loushoond said heavily. "His schemings and daggers in the dark make the regent look like a loving mistress to us all!"

"Ware!" the swordcaptain who'd spoken before said suddenly.

"*What*, man? You presume overmuch, to be giving us ord—"

The swordcaptain gave him a dark look, and barked, "I'll serve you no longer, Lord High Fool of Loushoond! You three idiots can stand here bickering the day long, for all I care—but mind you carve up yon serpents yourselves—ere *they* dine on *you*!" And with a defiant wave of his mace, he burst through the branches behind them, and was gone.

"What? By the Three, man, I—"

"After that bebolten whoreson, you l—"

"*Graul!* Swords out, all of you!" Ornentar cried, in sudden fear—as a great sleek scaled head slid into view around the tree in front of him, smiling a very wide smile.

"Ssssso," it hissed, eyeing all the men snatching at their swords and trembling, "we're all gathering to sssssee a new day for Aglirta together. That'sss good!"

And its jaws took off an armaragor's head, helm and all, with one lightning-swift bite.

Another serpent-head swung into view—and with a common cry of terror, three barons and their warriors whirled and ran, to crash headlong through the trees with hissing laughter loud at their heels.

"In!" Tarlagar cried frantically, beating at the rump of the armaragor in front of him with the flat of his sword. "Get *in,* graul you!"

"There's a man lying here burned to death," an armsman called back gloomily. "Not long ago, by the smell of him."

"Phaugh! He was rotten before he burned!" another warrior complained.

"Out of my way!" Baron Tarlagar shrieked, as serpents glided swiftly across a lawn and onto the terrace that led right to where he stood. He hammered and beat on the armored back of the man in the doorway until that armaragor cursed and shoved someone else hard enough to let the shouting, weeping baron claw his way into the palace.

"Close the door!" he shouted, the moment he was through. *"Close that door!"*

Three armaragors sprang to do just that, snarling in fear at the cold smiles of the snakes rising to eye them, just outside. The door boomed shut, and chains rattled as the doorbar was slammed down into place and its pins thrown to keep its stay chains in place.

"What now, Lord?" one of the knights asked as he turned away from the door, just a shade wearily.

"They're going along to that low window!" an armsman

shouted fearfully, watching dark shadows surge past the windows of the gloomy hall they stood in. "They'll get in!"

"Then we'll outrun them," a grizzled armaragor grunted. "At least they're slower than boar!"

"Where's Loushoond?" someone shouted. "And Ornen-tar?"

"They got in by another door," someone said curtly. "Loushoond lost most of his bodyguard doing it."

"Any orders, Lord Tarlagar?" the armaragor by the door asked again.

"I-I don't know," the baron replied in a quavering voice. When the knights turned to look at him sharply, he pointed ahead into the darkness.

Three passages led into the hall they were standing in—and down the right-hand way armaragors were advancing, with swords out and determined looks on their faces.

When Tarlagar's armsmen moved to get a good look at the oncoming warriors, those knights broke into a run. "For Bloodblade!" they shouted. "For Aglirta!"

The baron sobbed and ran wildly down one of the other passages. His knights and armsmen looked at each other, shrugged—and burst into their own clanking runs, after him.

Bloodblade's charging warriors howled and ran faster, seeking to catch up to Tarlagar's men before they vanished from sight in the cluttered, darkened palace.

From somewhere not far off in the many dark chambers, there came a sudden roar of shouts and screams and the clash of swords as another band of Bloodblade's swords met with the forces of the Barons Loushoond and Ornen-tar—and began to hack them down.

Meanwhile

"Up, Flower of the Delcampers. Aglirta has immediate need of your watchfulness and keen bardic memory—to say nothing of that scepter you're clutching, too."

He *knew* that deep voice.

Flaeros rolled over to stare up at the man who must have just saved his life.

The Regent of Aglirta stood as tall and darkly handsome as ever, though his clothes were torn and full of holes, locks of white now ran through his raven-hued hair, and deep lines of pain marked his face and had left dark hollows around his eyes. He wore a wan smile, and a lone Dwaer-Stone circled in the air just above his brow.

"L-Lord Blackgult!" Flaeros stammered. "What *happened* to you?"

"I rode into one battle too many, as we all do," the regent told him, unclipping a rather battered flagon of chased silver from his belt and handing it down to the bard.

Flaeros took it eagerly, unstoppered and sniffed, decided it was fiery amberglelt of the very finest sort, and took a cautious swallow.

Ahhhh. The finest, indeed. He shuddered, sighed, and reluctantly handed it back—or tried to; Blackgult waved at him to have another swig.

Flaeros smiled. "And at that battle?"

Blackgult's smile was broader. "I won, then lost, then got caught in magic."

Flaeros let his second sampling of amberglelt trickle slow fire down his throat ere he dared say, "Lord Blackgult—Great Regent—you *know* that answer was a clever tease no bard can let pass. You defeated whom? Then lost to whom? Were caught in magic how? What magic was it, and who cast it?"

Blackgult held up a hand in a "stay thy words" gesture. "The priests of the Serpent whelmed their own host of mercenaries—from every far corner of Darsar I know of—and them I defeated, with *my* mercenaries, whilst riding to fight the army of Bloodblade Duthjack, who fancies himself King of Aglirta. The Snake-swords were a complete surprise to me— and they cost my Royal Host dearly. I had barely enough blades left to give Bloodblade something to charge at."

"Which he did," Flaeros added with a rueful smile, handing back the flagon. He didn't have to have been on Sarth Fields to know what the gods had unfolded for the regent. This tale was something that had happened a time or eighty before.

The regent nodded. "There is no Royal Host any longer. Unfortunately, I was visited by a wizard just then—Jhavarr Bowdragon, seeking to avenge the death of his sister, who was one of the archwizard Tharlorn's best apprentices."

Flaeros nodded. "His lover, I heard."

"And victim, when he tired of her," Blackgult agreed. "Unfortunately, as her death possibly befell somewhere in Aglirta, and Tharlorn also seems to be dead, this Jhavarr blamed me—and King Kelgrael—and anyone else holding palace authority—for it. The overdukes, for instance; he had Embra's Dwaer with him. He tried to slay me."

Flaeros had got his breath back, but still felt like a weak and aching sack of bruises. "The Lady Embra? Dead?" he asked quietly, knowing that he was speaking of Blackgult's daughter—and that one Dwaer was orbiting uncomfortably close by.

The regent spread helpless hands. "I know not her fate— Jhavarr said only that he'd seized it, and his fate, too, is a mystery to me. I suspect he, at least, is dead."

"Ah . . . suspect?"

"With my two Dwaer, I struck at him," Blackgult said grimly. "There was an explosion. I snatched myself away from it, calling on my Dwaer, and . . . escaped, after a fashion."

"After a fashion?" Flaeros asked gravely, his eyes on the regent's face. Ezendor Blackgult's expression seemed to change often, as if different emotions were flowing across it and laying bare different flesh, each time. Flaeros had an uncle like that, whose moods showed bright and clear upon his face, but the Golden Griffon had always been so cool, so—utterly in control.

"The blast did not tear at my body," the regent said in a

low voice, "but through the Dwaer it touched my wits." He tapped his head, managed a flickering smile, and added, "You might say it 'mind-blasted' me. My memory comes and goes, and for some time—I think a long time, but you can count the passing days better than I, now—I was little better than a numb, shuffling shell. I lack the skill properly to call on a Dwaer for healing, but it seems to me that I am better than I was."

"You seem as formidable as ever to me, Lord," Flaeros said hastily, feeling the cold stone of the tomb against his arm and wondering if he dared move. He didn't want to stir the regent out of this mood of openness, nor goad Blackgult to slaying rage if he was truly so . . . unstable. Yet would he have hurled a spell to save a young bard, and revealed much to that same Flaeros Delcamper—speaking of Aglirta's need for him, too—if he intended to then harm said songster? Surely not . . . and yet, every man has but one life to lose, and it was all too true that the Bard of the Delcampers had already hazarded much with his. . . .

Blackgult smiled thinly. "It's good to know that bards, at least, I can still fool."

That sounded not so good. Flaeros decided there was no better way ahead than to continue doing what a good bard does. "What happened to your other Dwaer?" he asked. "And the one this Jhavarr was using, for that matter?"

The regent smiled and nodded approvingly, as if Flaeros had passed some sort of test. "Vanished in the blast, both of them," he said, spreading his hands in a gesture of helplessness. "Gone I know not where. I would have felt it—I would probably be mindless now—if they'd been destroyed. They were flung . . . well, elsewhere. Somehow it seems to me that they each went to a different place, but I've no way of knowing I am right in that."

Flaeros nodded, and their eyes met. "And what, Lord," he dared to ask, "will you do now?"

The regent shrugged and spread his empty hands. "I find it all matters less and less, friend Flaeros," he said sadly, "with my daughter dead. But I'll be blasted and broken by the Three before I'll let the damned Snake-kissers—and mincing wizards who lord it over everyone and never once in their lives chop wood or draw water—have Aglirta!"

He took two restless strides away, then spun around and snapped, "I'll take as many of them with me as I can, if I have to fill up all Silverflow Vale with blood doing it!"

As if in answer, the ground rocked, sending up birds from trees and bushes all over the graveyard in a squawking cloud of alarm.

A deep rumbling made the earth shudder beneath them, and Flaeros could have sworn that one of the tall old stone tomb markers, at least, swayed. That shuddering raced under the two men from the direction of the river, rippling under the Silent House—which groaned its own brief stony protest—and beyond.

They both looked towards the Silverflow. A dark cloud was curling up and away from Flowfoam Isle, high into the sky over the Vale.

It was a greasy brown-and-purple plume unlike anything Flaeros had ever seen before. As they watched, it seemed to be shaping itself with a life and sentience of its own, darkening swiftly into jet-black, but with none of the billowing that races up from a wood fire or the ruin of torched barns or castles. No, this smoke was *smooth*, as if—spell-shaped.

The two men saw the smoke become the dark image of a huge snake, rearing up to regard all Aglirta with its great dark eyes. A forked tongue licked out and vanished again, and then huge fanged jaws gaped, as if to swallow the Kingless Land entirely, splitting the sky with a vast maw of darkness.

And then, ere its jaws closed, the Serpent started to fade away—not scattering with the winds, but thinning out just where it hung.

The bard and the regent both looked at the Isle whence the apparition had come—and then Blackgult reached down a long and muscular arm to pluck Flaeros bodily onto his feet.

"Come and bear witness, Bard of the Delcampers," he growled, "and try to think of a really striking tune for your next ballad, *The Last Stand of Stormharp*, will you?"

15

Standing Too Close to a Throne

Darkness fell away as suddenly as a shroud snatched off a corpse, and the wisewoman sat back with a hiss of surprise and dismay. Had the impatient merchant known her better, he would have recognized dread in her face as she stared down at the tanthor cards, back up at him without seeing him, and then down at the cards again.

Them she saw, all right. Peering, and shaking her head as if she could not believe what she saw, and peering again, staring slowly at every last card, as though she'd never laid tanthor before!

Now, the blood she'd let drip from her fingers into the customary chalice had caught fire somehow in the dark and burned away in a trice, leaving behind only a thread of smoke, and he'd never seen *that* before, but there was nothing wrong with the array that he could see, nothing out of place and no fault in the tanthor magic.

Aye, the cards were good!

Kirlstar could see that as well as anyone; their vivid blue spell-glows were bright and strong on her black cloth now that the customary Shadow of the Gods she'd cast had passed. The heart of the array was crowded with gold— there, the Laden Ship, then a cluster of the Goldsack, the

Fall of Gems, and the Crown and Rubies. Over there, the Wagonwheel, the Bright Castle, and the Fortuitous Bridge. No Map of Fools, no Brigand Snatch—how could this be a cause for dismay? He was going to be rich! He was—*yes*. Three Above, but he'd never had cards this good before!

The Hill of Skulls was the only bad card in view, below the cluster—battle, that meant, and the death of someone in it. Well, Kirlstar of the Splendid Silks certainly wasn't going to be joining in any battles soon! Leave that to the fools in Aglirta, now busily tearing their land asunder one more time, when they could be making coins hand over fist!

But what was this? The wisewoman was pushing his coins back across the table at him, her face as white as beached bone. "Go," she whispered, in a voice as raw and hopeless as if she saw the Doom of All Darsar and no way to avoid it. "Keep your coins, Goodman Kirlstar. I cannot tell your fortune today."

"What?" Kirlstar roared, as dumbfounded as he was angry. "Cannot—? Woman, what foolery is this? Look at those cards—Goldsack, Fall of Gems, Crown and Rubies *all*, look you, and all gathered at the heart!" He was almost pleading, he knew, and rushed on nonetheless. "I've *never* had cards so good! What d'you *mean*, you can't tell my fortune? Why can't all those riches be mine?" His pointing finger stabbed angrily down at the cards—until a fat blue spark snapped back from one of them to sear and numb him, and leave him staggering back in fresh astonishment.

"Please," she whispered up at him, and the cards began to spark and smoke beneath her. She was crying, he saw, tears falling onto the tanthor array.

Suddenly afraid himself, but not knowing why, Kirlstar snatched up his coins, stared at her again with mounting alarm and the plaintive need to know why rising together in his gaze—and whirled out of the tiny shop on Graemere Street without another word, the heavy curtains swirling in his wake.

Orathlee the Wise stared down at the cards again and

then reached for the bell that would summon her daughters. Her hand trembled. They would have to pack and be gone this very night, if she read this right. The Dragon At Dawn here, and Morning Over Towers *here*—it was impossible to say if the Lady's clear warning meant that the danger was going to fall like lightning from the sky in a very short time, somewhere nearby but not actually in Sirlptar—or fall in the morning right here in the city.

"Dragonfire," she whispered, as the bell rang and she heard her daughters start up in alarm and come running. She stared down in disbelief at the cards again, shaking her head.

Dragonfire.

The cards did not lie.

It could be nothing else.

Centuries it had been since such a reading, the Seers of the Tanthor had been very clear about that—and on that last occasion, two dragons had torn each other apart above the fair realm of Loroncel, and laid waste to it in their death throes, so that it was but a wasteland to this day.

The time before that—oh, she remembered those lessons vividly, because the stories had been so good; they always were, weren't they, when it had all happened to someone else, somewhere far away and long ago—it hadn't been a real dragon at all, but a storm of spells that got out of hand. Fed by many angry hurled magics until it took on a crawling, wizard-seeking life of its own, a cloak of "dragonfire" that had drowned tall-towered Chalsymbryl, City of Enchanters, beneath the waves, battling mages and all—leaving behind the reefs and whirlpools that sailors called Lost Chalse, a region shunned for its hunger to devour ships.

Ships! They'd have to catch the next ship leaving the docks, no matter what it was or where it was bound. Even if its captain took slaves, they'd at least be alive. It would be hard for her daughters, but Orathlee had been a slave before.

She shook her head again as Meleira and Talace came thundering down the stairs, daggers in their hands and alarm in their wide eyes. "Dragonfire," she whispered again, helplessly. What had someone done, to anger the gods thus?

Darkness fell away as suddenly as a shroud snatched off a corpse, and the dim light of day coming in the windows of the galleries above lit the Throne Chamber of Aglirta again, casting faint shadows amid its dust and riven throne and tumbled stones.

Raulin blinked at the empty place beside Tshamarra Talasorn that had held a king. Sarasper stared at the same spot with despair growing in him, and froze in midsurge. Briefly the shapeshifting healer grew feathers and then lost them again, sinking back into man-shape: an old man who was shaking his head sadly.

Glarsimber whirled to a stop and took two quick paces forward, peering. There, behind those stones! Hardly daring to take the next few steps, the baron growled at himself—what price a barony, if the holder not do what is needful for Aglirta?—and scrambled forward, to where he could stare down.

Embra Silvertree and Hawkril Anharu were sprawled awkwardly together. The Lady Overduke's arms were flung wide and her hair made a great swirl on the stones around her. The armaragor was lying on his back, partly beneath her. His dazed face blinked up at the riven ceiling from beneath Embra's boots.

Hawkril's mouth twitched, several expressions raced rapidly across his face as the baron bent over him, and he made a faint sound that might have been a moan. Embra was utterly silent as she suddenly rose on hands and knees and crawled a little way forward, staring at the far wall of the room with her back to them all.

"Lady Embra?" Glarsimber asked roughly, taking a cautious step after her.

"I saw . . . a dragon," Embra murmured, and then turned her head sharply to look at him. "Here, in this room, towering up just there—but that cannot be!"

"Embra," the Baron of Brightpennant asked gravely, "are you . . . all right?"

The Lady of Jewels looked at him expressionlessly for a moment before her lips twisted into a thin little smile. "If I were Craer, I'd tell you I was considered much better than 'all right,'" she murmured, "but in truth—I think so, Glarsimber. I . . . hope so."

With more weariness than grace, she found her feet, turned away again, and took a few exploratory steps. "Nothing broken, at least," she announced, shaking her head so that her hair fell back around her.

Then she sighed, spun around with her hands on her hips, and asked, "Hawk? Are you—?"

"Alive, or I'd not be hearing you," the armaragor groaned from beneath the hands he'd flung up to his face, to rub at eyes and brow. "For more than that about my present hurts, best ask the gods!"

For some reason Embra found this very funny. She clapped a hand to her mouth and giggled as she went to her knees by Hawkril's head and added her gentle hands to his. He peered at her from between two fingers, and her mirth deepened into a chuckle—ere she bent to kiss him.

His hands reached up to her shoulders, and their embrace tightened, Embra's hair cascaded down to conceal their faces, and she made a delighted, wordless sound. Hawkril growled just as wordless a reply, almost as if he was purring.

"They're *fine*, I see," a familiar voice said in mocking tones, from close beside Glarsimber. "I couldn't help but fail to notice, mind you, that no one came running and calling after *me*."

The baron grinned.

"That, my Lord Overduke Craer," he said, turning to regard the longtime thief, "is because we all had every confidence that you were fine—moreover, that your recent journey along yonder wall was no harmful and involuntary matter, but a skillful tactic of some sort on your part!"

"Three Above," Craer replied, rolling his eyes, "make them barons and they soon learn to talk like barons, do they not?"

"I learned," Brightpennant told him, drawing himself up in mock dignity, "from the best. I listened to thieves—ah, pray pardon: *procurers.*"

"No doubt," Craer agreed, showing his teeth in a mirthless grin. "No doubt. Too many barons have listened to procurers these last score of years, and brought Aglirta to"—he gestured around the ruined throne chamber—"this."

"The king," Raulin said abruptly from behind them both, the rich Castlecloaks voice trembling on the edge of tears, "is dead. I saw him—kill himself."

"Aye," Sarasper called grimly from a goodly distance down the room. "So did I—*we.*"

Glarsimber and Craer turned to see the reason for that last word. Sarasper and Tshamarra Talasorn stood mute, eyes locked. They'd suddenly found themselves staring at each other, both in awe of what they'd seen.

"That was," the Talasorn sorceress started to say, a quaver in her voice. She stopped, swallowed, and started again. "That was the greatest—"

"The Serpent-priests have struck down Kelgrael's bindings!" Embra said sharply, her voice snapping across the room like the crack of a drover's lash as she scrambled up from Hawkril, her hands rising in alarm. "They'll be here soon—I'll need all the magic I can get, to have any hopes of standing against them!"

Six faces stared at her—Hawkril's from right beneath her—and the Lady Overduke said crisply, "If the king has fallen, Aglirta has not, and he left us all—save *you*, Lady—with sworn duties. I need your service, my lords!"

Embra's tone made it clear that she was a little puzzled as to why none of the others were battling the last Talasorn sorceress—and why she in turn wasn't trying to spellslay them—but there was not time for explanations now, however grand the tale, and the Lady Overduke accepted things as they were, without comment.

"When Baron Faerod Silvertree ruled this house, and I was being bound to it by fell enchantments by the wizards who served him," she added, "I learned where certain items of magic were stored. Those that were hidden may still be found by us now, if the Three smile down—and you hasten!"

"Command us!" Craer snapped. "We look where?"

"On the back of yon door, behind the throne," she replied without hesitation, pointing across the ruined chamber. "Filigreework there holds a wand—bring it."

She spun, and pointed again. "Down that passage, the third shield on the wall bears an enchantment. A bracelet hangs from the same hook, hidden behind the shield—'twill seem like but a loop of hempen rope, but that's part of its magic. Bring both."

She turned again.

"Craer, know you the gallery that overlooks the ferns, along that passage? The arch window: its sill can be made to lift out by pressing on the two darkest stones of the running border, beneath. Bring everything you find in the storage hollow there."

She paused, her mouth open to say more, and then sighed and made a dismissive wave of her hand. "The rest are probably too far off to fetch in time."

Craer limped away on his errand, plucking at Raulin's sleeve and pointing at the door that led to the shield and bracelet. Glarsimber set off for the door behind the throne, seeing at once why Embra hadn't sent Raulin on that shortest of fetchings: the way was blocked by fallen stones almost certainly too heavy for the young bard to lift.

"Hurt, Longfingers?" Hawkril rumbled, seeing the pain on Craer's face.

"I'll live until I die," the procurer flung back, without slowing. Craer had heard that crisp tone of voice from Embra only a few times before—when she was desperate, and danger was close.

When he flung open the door, Craer saw just how close. Perhaps forty paces down the passage, armored men were backing slowly towards him. They were fencing with other men, beyond, and being forced back, blade to blade. As he watched, a man gurgled, clawed vainly at the sword that had slid into his throat and back out again, and fell, to be trampled underfoot. The man's bright blood ran across the stone floor—to join more than one ribbon of gore already lacing their ways across the flagstones.

Craer peered, eyes narrowing. He could see shoulder badges of Loushoond, Tarlagar, and—Ornentar, was it? Aye.

"Trouble come already," the procurer reported to his companions, unnecessarily. They could all hear the clash and skirl of arms before he slammed the door, shrugged at its lack of a bar or surviving lock, and added, "Three barons come calling—or their blades, at least. Someone else is out there, too, fighting with them." Craer waggled his eyebrows, and added in mock consternation, "How unusual for Flowfoam, these days." Then he sighed, and murmured so softly and bitterly that none of his companions heard, "How unusual indeed. Some great overdukes we've turned out to be. Everyone snarls about what they'd do if they could command armies and set realms in order . . . but when the chance comes, things never work out as one intends . . ."

"Shield and bracelet!" Raulin called, holding them up triumphantly as he came trotting towards Embra.

"Hawkril," Glarsimber grunted, from the door behind the throne. "I need a hand here—"

"Done," the armaragor growled, staggering across the room in obvious discomfort. Sarasper frowned at Hawkril's obvious pain, sighed—and then shuddered and *flowed*, becoming a longfangs.

As spidery legs lengthened and the wolflike head arose, the Talasorn sorceress gasped and flung up her hands to cast a spell at him—only to freeze at Embra's warning look and sharply raised hand.

Swallowing, Tshamarra watched the wolf-spider climb the nearest wall and proceed onto the ceiling, swarming swiftly along its cracked and crumbling edges until it—no, *he*; she had to remember that this monster was Sarasper— hung above the door Craer had slammed, awaiting the arrival of the warriors.

For his part, Overduke Craer Delnbone had taken a step or two back, and was feeling in his boots and along his forearms, to be sure daggers were loose and ready in their sheaths. Seeing a Melted lying nearby half-crushed under a fall of stone, he plucked up the dead man's sword and hefted it calmly.

Tshamarra Talasorn had stood very still since Embra's glare, only her eyes moving to watch all the preparations for battle. "Is there anything I can get, Lady, to help?" she asked now, hesitantly.

Embra's eyes narrowed, but she paused for only a moment before pointing at a door in the far corner of the throne chamber—where, down the years, Ilibar Quelver had stood guard, deciding who would be allowed passage to the River Throne, and who would not—and said, "The forehall beyond that door opens into three rooms. The one on your right has three suits of armor posed along the wall like guards, holding banners. Bring back the helm of the farthest one from us here."

Tshamarra bowed her head. "Lady, I will," she replied, and hastened across the littered floor.

Embra watched her go, thoughtfully, and then asked, "Raulin?"

"Yes, Lady Silvertree?" the bard answered eagerly, from beside her.

Embra took the bracelet from him and slid it up her arm to the shoulder, and then took hold of the shield in both hands, standing it protectively in front of her legs ere leaning on it. "Tell me—briefly, mind—what happened to the king. Who did what, and—"

She saw the Talasorn sorceress cautiously open Quelver's door, peer out, then slip through it, out of sight.

"—what part the lady sorceress who just left us played in it all."

"Uh, well, Lady," Raulin began, with as much smooth eloquence as most flustered young bards can muster when battle is about to break over them and they know it, "the four Talasorn ladies—uh, that one and her three sisters, who are all dead now—they—uh—"

The bard's next stumbling words were lost in the crash of the door guarded by Craer and Sarasper booming open, and the clank and clangor of armed armaragors reeling into the room.

"Craer! Sarasper!" Embra cried quickly. "Not yet! Hold back for now!"

Craer nodded, giving way to stand back among the piles of fallen stone with borrowed sword in hand. "You've been right thus far, Em," he called, as cursing, panting armored men killed each other by the door. "Just let's not change that now, hmm?"

"Lady Embra!" the Baron Brightpennant called from behind the ruined throne. The Lady of Jewels turned her head—and Glarsimber tossed the wand smooth and straight towards her, underhanded, as Hawkril struggled to get the door closed again.

"My thanks!" she said, snatching the wand out of the air. Just as she remembered: a coppery dapple-sheen metal tube, capped at one end with a stylized flower. The rest of the matching filigree had been even more hideous. "Hawk, leave it! We may need a way to flee!"

"Or at least a narrow place to stand in, and defend," Glarsimber agreed, as beside him the armaragor straightened up with a nod, letting a huge chunk of stone thud back onto the shattered floor again.

Other doors were banging open now, all over the throne chamber, as armsmen and armaragors in the livery of Loushoond, Ornentar, and Tarlagar backed into the room, hacking desperately at ever-advancing warriors who were shouting, "Bloodblade! Bloodblade! *Victory!*"

With a purring growl the longfangs sprang down from the wall, slamming a handful of warriors to the floor and breaking the necks of others by the slaps and curling clingings of his long legs as he swept down. Ere blades could find him, he sprang up to promptly smash down another harvest of armsmen, biting throats and necks savagely before springing again.

Bloodblade's warriors were shouting in alarm now. "A longfangs! Wolf-spider!" and "With evil magic they summon monsters to fight for them! Slay them! Slay the longfangs! Flee Aglirta!"

Blades were hewing the wolf-spider's limbs, now, and men were hurling themselves on those legs, seeking to drag it down and hold it to be butchered. The legs of a longfangs, however, are stronger than many a charging warhorse. Sarasper pulled them back in, dragging each clinging man within reach of his powerful jaws—and many warriors' heads were soon lolling, throatless, leaving those long legs free to lash out and break bones beneath armor or necks— ere the wolf-spider sprang again, and more men died.

Where Sarasper was fighting, the rushing ranks of Bloodblade's armaragors looked more like a battlefield of the fallen—yet still the warriors flooded in through the throne chamber doors, more and more of them, bright-armored and eager.

"Bloodblade! Bloodblade! *Victory!*" the shouts rang out.

Hawkril's warsword flashed as he drew it and shot glances in all directions, deciding whom to charge at first. His mouth tightened as he saw figures in splendid, fluted armor stumbling along in the midst of ragged rings of baronial warriors. The three barons themselves were here—no doubt strolling hence on an idle day, to see if perchance any fallen crown might be lying around for them to pluck up.

Well, there were worse ways to enliven a dull afternoon . . . but most of them involved floods, forest fires, earthquakes, mountains erupting in fires from below, or several reckless archwizards hungry for battle.

Sarasper growled and sprang away from a forest of reaching blades to the wall once more, out of reach—for just an instant. His blood-slick legs could not hold, he slipped, and a roar of hope arose in the warriors below him.

A roar that lasted until the wolf-spider kicked out against that wall as he slid, to twist in the air and pounce, slamming two tall armaragors broken to the marble beneath with screams and a horrible bouncing splintering of shattered bones. Sarasper came up biting and tearing, slashing faces and throats with his teeth and slapping out with his legs with such swift savagery that men were thrown into their fellows, falling outward from the raging wolf-spider by the dozens.

Still Bloodblade's warriors came swarming into the room, slaying men of the three barons with eager, vigorous speed, and Craer had to scramble to avoid being cornered and hewn down. "They're coming up every passage, converging on us," he puffed, coming to a halt beside Embra. "This bids fair to be entertaining."

"As the gravediggers say," Glarsimber agreed in a dry voice, as he and Hawk joined them.

Then swords were ringing all around them as Bloodblade's foremost knights came seeking the blood of overdukes, and there was no time for converse in the brief, frantic skirling of steel.

Sarasper sprang up to the wall again as warriors with

spears came striding over the dead, to slay this deadly longfangs—and his limbs caught and clung this time.

There he hung, just out of reach of their seeking pole-steel, with two legs raised to bat aside any hurled spears, and panted visibly. Longfangs or not, Sarasper Codelmer was old—and, as the bards said solemnly, growing older by the day.

The last man of Bloodblade gurgled to the floor, and the Baron Brightpennant tugged back his bloody blade, peered at the longfangs clinging to the wall above the door, and asked, "That *is* Sarasper, isn't it?" Upon Craer's nod, he added, "What's he doing there, just hanging from the wall and watching?"

"Oh," Craer replied airily, "it's his way. Healers like to watch damage done, you know; the thought of all that business to come excites them."

Embra sighed and shook her head. "Craer," she murmured, "don't ever change. I'd miss all the inane comments."

Whatever biting riposte the procurer might have intended was lost in the sudden crash of Quelver's door, as it was flung open to boom against the wall and rebound, shuddering. The screaming figure racing through it was safely past it by then, and well across the throne chamber towards them, as Craer raised an approving eyebrow at her speed.

Tshamarra Talasorn was sprinting in wild-eyed terror, sobbing between shrieks as she slapped busily at things that kept curling towards her face, out of her own hair. The helm Embra had sent her for danced from the crook of her elbow as she came.

"Snakes!" Hawkril swore. "Horns of the Lady, her hair is full of snakes!"

Embra frowned, held up the wand, and murmured something. The wand seemed to glow for a moment, and then darken a little. Its tip crumbled away as she pointed her other hand at the fast-approaching sorceress.

There were suddenly plumes of sizzling flame in the air

behind Tshamarra, curling and writhing things that crackled, smoked, and fell to the floor to twist and burn. Embra kept her hand leveled and will intent until every last snake had been purged from Talasorn tresses.

As the sobbing sorceress plunged into their midst, and Craer flung soothing arms around her to wrestle her to a swaying stop, Embra bent her gaze on the doorway Tshamarra had returned through, and murmured another phrase that made the wand in her hand darken from end to end, and lose a lot of its length in crumblings.

The Talasorn sorceress wept uncontrollably into Craer's shoulder, and the procurer rocked her and muttered soothing words with a strange expression on his face. When Glarsimber grinned at him, Craer calmly raised one hand in the corkscrewlike twisting gesture whose rude meaning is known from one end of Aglirta to the other.

A moment later, an expected sight met Embra's watchful eyes: three Serpent-priests appeared in that doorway, smiling coldly as they surveyed the room. Embra sent their flaming serpents back at them in a fiery hail that made them draw back in alarm and embark on hasty spellweavings.

Tshamarra fell silent, and then moved in Craer's arms, seeking freedom. When he gave it to her she patted his shoulder in silent thanks, gave him a red-eyed smile, sniffed loudly, and turned to face her tormentors—in time to see one of them gasp and reel back out of sight, as Embra turned the flames he was battling into something else. The Lady Overduke smiled tightly as the wand she was holding crumbled entirely to ash and trickled away between her fingers.

The stricken Snake-cleric was still falling when a second Serpent-priest received the crowning surprise of his life—literally. The longfangs none of the priests had noticed scuttling across the ceiling and down the wall above their doorway chose that moment to swing down into view with a jagged piece of rock as large as a man's head held delicately between two of its legs. The speed of its swing gave the released stone more than enough force to crush the top of the priest's skull.

Spitting blood from several places, the man crumpled, knocking over the third priest—and that was when it became apparent that there were other Serpent-clergy behind, who were growing impatient at not being a part of all this reeling and dying. They pushed forward into the room, hurling gouts of magical fire from their palms—and the longfangs came scurrying back across the ceiling, skirting the great gap, to hang upside down about Hawkril, who gave him a grim smile, and said, "Swords out, all. 'Tis time to take a stand—'twon't be long before Bloodblade himself gets here, all blood and thunder, and we'll be fighting for all Aglirta. Again."

He glanced up, and added, "No swords for you, old man. Stay a beast for now—'tis safer."

"Old man?" Sarasper growled, the maw of the wolf head blurring briefly into a human mouth. "*Who's* an old man?"

Hawkril snorted, but said with a grin, "My apologies. I mistook you for some *other* lurking longfangs."

"Gods, but this throne room's seen more than its share of blood spilled," Craer said wryly. "Now, unless I'm mistaken, it's our turn to wash the tiles red."

"Raulin, to me," Embra said quietly. "I need someone to ward off hurled things coming my way, and to hand me all this gathered magic as I need it."

Tshamarra held out the helm to her, and then to Raulin, and then back at Embra with a grin, and the Lady Overduke wrinkled her nose at the Talasorn sorceress and jerked her head at the young bard to indicate where the armor should be bestowed.

"If you ladies are finished with pleasantries," the Baron Brightpennant said grimly from beside them, "we'd best be backing towards that door we left open, I'm thinking. There might even be a chance that what's left of the throne might have some magic left in it that you could use, Embra."

"Well said," Hawkril agreed, but they'd barely begun to

move, staying carefully together in a ring as fighting armaragors whirled closer, when the last of the closed throne chamber doors burst open—and a wedge of Bloodblade's knights charged into the throne room with a roar. There were baronial banners in their midst—and one man strode along under them in plate armor that gleamed as bright as a new-burnished blade.

"Bloodblade! Victory! Bloodblade! Victory!" the armaragors chanted, as they hacked down all who stood in their way, and strode across the ruined chamber towards the ruined throne.

"Death to all barons!" Bloodblade cried. "Let Aglirta have a new king and a new way!" He waved the sword he held—and with a wordless howl, his warriors put down their heads and charged.

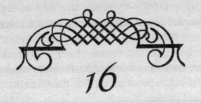

16

Barons, Battle, and Bloodblade

The fading but ornately lettered sign above the foul-smelling, slippery steps read:

> Dolstan Drearihead
> Scribe For Hire

—but that inscription had been improved upon by the starkly scrawled amendment:

> Found Dead.
> Burned All
> But Still Many Rats.

An inspiring text, to be sure—and coupled with the complete darkness the steps curved down into, and the litter of bones to be found on those steps, few wanderers in this poor neighborhood of Sirlptar felt welcomed enough to proceed down into the deep, water-dripping cellar, slosh through the ankle-deep, filthy water to the door at its far, unlit end, and give the correct knock. Those who failed to do so, but tarried in the cellar, often heard slight grating sounds, coming at once from either side of them.

One was made by a sliding shutter that revealed a window in the wall, into a room where a bright lantern hung, flooding that side of the cellar with light—but the other shutter, across from it, opened in the locked door just enough that a crossbow could poke out—and give swift death to whoever was outlined against the light.

The bodies of such overly inquisitive visitors, huddled in the water at the corners of the room, added to the welcoming reek of the cellar. One addition was too recent to have been cleared aside yet: a drunken carter who'd mistaken the cellar for the entrance to his own damp hold, and attacked the door with ever-increasing rage. Now stiffened in death, he lay with one reaching hand rising like a claw into the cellar darkness.

Its unfeeling fingers tugged at the cloak of someone else, arriving in some haste. With a growl of revulsion the owner of the cloak tugged free, strode straight to the door with long, sloshing steps, and knocked in a careful rhythm.

There came the muffled sound of two heavy bolts being thrown back, and then the door opened inward, without a sound.

The man strode through it in matching silence, not slowing for pleasantries or to help close the door, but straight on towards a distant arch, and even more distant lantern-light, glimmering beyond it. Not for the first time, the man in the cloak wondered sourly why, in all of intrigue-ridden Sirl town, it was necessary for this particular cabal to meet in such a filthy place. Deep cellars were fine for hiding contraband and bodies best forgotten, but a warm fire and some good wine would not come amiss, just once . . .

He came out into the light, ignoring the sullen stares of the grim guards lounging against the wall with weapons at the ready, and made for the only empty seat at the table.

"Ah, my Lord of Haeltree," Baron Cardassa said with a joviality that fooled no one, "you're late!"

"I was followed," the Tersept of Haeltree said shortly, doffing his cloak with a contemptuous disregard for the

sudden, threatening movements his action provoked in
several of the guards, and seating himself with a sigh.
"Wizards again, seeking to pry. Every titled Aglirtan is a
marked man in Sirl town right now, I tell you."

"I'm not surprised," Maevur of Cardassa said with a
smile. "Even Sirl mages and merchants are eager to find
friends at Flowfoam—or should I say, eager to greet the
coins that might flow their ways if they help someone new
to be seated on the River Throne."

There were sour mutters of agreement from the others
around the table—tersepts all, and most of them as new in
their offices as this smooth-tongued new Baron of Cardassa. Haeltree knew for a fact that some of them didn't
even know the difference between an armaragor and an
armsman. Not that knowing who was a knight sworn personally to you and who was a warrior of the barony would
matter much if you were a tersept ignorant even of your
own obligations of office, and never intended to keep the
peace or draw sword in battle against anyone.

This moon-faced, oiled-haired Maevur, for one,
wouldn't soil his hands in battle if he could possibly avoid
it. A distant cousin of the Old Crow, this new Baron Cardassa had spent all his wastrel, formative days in
Elmerna—which city, popular Cardassan belief held, was
far enough downwind of Aglirta for the Old Crow not to
gag at the stench of his perfumed, always-idle relation.

Maevur gave Haeltree a condescending smile and said,
"*If* I may continue—?"

Haeltree became aware that the baron was actually expecting a response. From him. "But of course," he said, leaning forward to better feign apologetic, hearty eagerness.

Maevur beamed like the brightest sun of a hot day,
reached behind him to receive the bundle a guard stepped
forward to place in his open palm, and swept this mystery
around in front of him with a flourish, unrolling the tube of
bright new parchment grandly.

Ah, yes, of course. The map. Fledgling conspirators

were nothing without a map. Every man here knew each bend and twist of the Silverflow, and every way inn and horse pond on the overland roads, too—but they all crowded forward to look, as if the map held new revelations. A barony they'd never noticed, perhaps, or town or two someone had flung up overnight, or when they last took time to bathe—whatever decade ago that might have been. Some even reached out to put their fingers on their home castles, as if reassuring themselves that all of this was real, and they really did hold titles.

Well, they'd lose both titles and their heads if any slips were made on the road ahead—and possibly even if not, when this Maevur decided to be rid of the most capable of his fellow conspirators and replace them with underlings just as falsely loyal but incompetent enough ever to rise as rivals. He'd be on that "have accidents happen soonest" list, Haeltree knew. Maevur knew he was too clever to be left alone—and had already clearly judged him disobedient, to boot.

Ah, but obedience was always the problem, wasn't it? Whether you ruled a sty full of hogs or a barony full of people . . .

"Behold Aglirta," Maevur announced, as proudly as if he'd created the whole realm himself, this very morning. "A realm that can be ours, once this upstart Bloodblade and the justly feared and hated regent have slaughtered each other. They butcher each other even as we speak, and even if one is left standing at the end of their bloodbath, he'll be too weak to do more than sneeze without the permission of a wizard."

The Baron of Cardassa turned away from the map he'd been so grandly waving at and commenced to strut across the cellar, hands clasped behind his back. Gods, but you could *see* how his belly had grown since their last moot! The man must be a veritable boar at the trough . . .

"Now, *wizards*," Maevur of Cardassa said with supercilious authority, "have been the bane of Aglirta all my life—

and these last three centuries at least, if half the tales I've heard and read can be credited with truth. Hired in by this baron and that tersept, they worm their ways to the best wine, the most gold—and true power, using spells and fear to rule in fact even if someone else holds the local title. Many of them hail from Sirlptar or even farther afield from Aglirta, and none of them love the land as we honest men do, or care for it, except as a source of food to gorge on, wine to guzzle, servants to fawn over them or fear them, oddments to use in their conjurations—and women for them to mistreat."

Growing growls of agreement up and down the table gave answer to this rising peroration, and the satisfied baron wheeled around and headed back towards the map.

"So any wizards we welcome into the new Aglirta, *our* Aglirta, will be men we can control by some leash or other, or"—his bubbling, gloating chuckle was pure, slithering evil—"or women *we* can mistreat."

There were answering roars of approval, up and down the table. Haeltree moved his shoulders and murmured in time with the rest, knowing that the cold eyes of the guards were marking who betrayed what, all the time.

As it happened, time was the theme of Cardassa's next weighty speech. "And so, my friends, our long-awaited moment has come at last. Yes, now is our best time!"

He paused, waiting for the roar of approval that was supposed to erupt, but he was moving too fast for the dullards he'd chosen to ride with him, and they gave him only silence. It was left to Haeltree and one of the guards to begin the expected cry of eagerness; the tersept only hoped no one detected the lacing of mockery he'd been unable to keep entirely out of his cry of, "Brilliant!"

Maevur smiled like a great cat as the hubbub of approval erupted at last, and let it run its course. Then he leaned forward over the map with a soft smile, and said, "My reasons for asking us all to meet armed and ready for travel at our every moot should now be clear. We leave forthwith, straight from this place, all together—down tunnels that link this cellar to others that have barge docks leading right out to the river. My men have already roused yours, and taken them by other ways to those same docks. We load our warriors aboard the trade barges I've purchased these past few months, and start upriver slowly, with no show of arms. Let the wizards rage and storm, and wear themselves out. We shall dock at Flowfoam, bring our archers ashore, and go mage-hunting. I think all of us here know which wizards will look better with their eyes growing arrows. Almost every last one of them, yes?"

There was laughter—nervous laughter, in some cases; Haeltree wondered what plans some of these tersepts would be leaving in tangles behind them, outfoxed in any schemes to inform others or tarry by Maevur's boldness—and sounds of agreement, or the show of same.

And then the map was rolled up, Maevur drew on black gauntlets—his men promptly slipping glittering rings onto his armored fingers, leaving him looking like some actor playing the Buffoon King rather than the formidable leader of a rebel conspiracy—and the new Baron of Cardassa started snapping orders.

Chairs scraped back, cloaks swirled, and men hurried to where guards with lit torches were now beckoning. Haeltree hurried with them. Well, that was one thing, out of all this foolishness: naive idiots these other tersepts might be, but they wouldn't all end up as fat and lazy as Cardassa obviously hoped to be. None of them were men who liked waiting, when there was swordwork to be done.

Bared bodies writhed as the two tall, attractive women danced together once more, the piping and chiming music rising to a frenzied crescendo. The one who wore only much blood, and a red silk cord that made her long, raven-hued hair into a mare's tail, thrust her breasts forward as if offering them to the wench whose hair was bound in blue.

That taller, darker dancer responded by thrusting her last flaming skewer crosswise through both of the Red Dream's breasts. Sizzling flesh and spurting blood doused the flames along the needlelike blade as it slid in and through.

Red Dream gasped and writhed, the music falling silent so every sob of pain could be heard. She was still trembling when Blue Passion bent forward to kiss her, and they embraced hungrily—despite the gentle clashing, as they pressed together, of the skewers that transfixed them both striking against each other. Men all over the room sat like gargoyles, frozen leaning forward over their tankards and goblets to see and hear everything. No one called for more drink or even stirred in his seat as the chiming continued and two entwined dancers slowly twirled around, displaying slender, shapely backs and behinds to everyone. It had been a long dance, and a good one.

Then one of the minstrels of the House ran his hands down the strings of his maraun in a plunging, liquid fall of notes—and everyone moved again.

Tray wenches strode out of the pantries, folk started talking, and men around the tables sat back and murmured their wincing approval as the bleeding women broke apart and knelt hand in hand to receive applause, tears of pain streaming down their faces.

Amid a chorus of lewdly encouraging comments, a man who'd paid a tableful of gold for the privilege was brought forward to pull the skewers slowly out—while ringed with the swordpoints of other wenches in scanty armor, who were there to prevent him excitedly driving home a skewer or two himself.

Red Dream and Blue Passion pressed themselves against him for more kisses, but could not stifle their screams when the traditional dousing of wine was done to wash their blood off the pleased—and visibly aroused—guest. As the stinging lessened and they could control their spasms once more, they caressed him skillfully but regretfully, for he'd not paid the proprietor of Dragonrose House that extra small fortune that would entitle him to kiss away their hurts in private for a night.

He, too, looked forlorn as the two dancers took the waiting handfuls of skewers from the armored wenches who'd just collected them from his eager hands. Red Dream and Blue Passion looked at each other, and then swiftly undid the cords that held their hair and laid them in his trembling grasp.

There was a fresh roar of approval, and they smiled back at the tables of watching men, spun around once so their unbound hair swirled about their shoulders—tresses long enough to brush the upper swell of their behinds—and left the stage, to a small fanfare that sounded somehow mocking, and a last smattering of applause.

The armored wenches quickly barred the way behind them. With weary smiles the two dancers proceeded along a dim passage to where a portcullis slammed down behind them, leaving them facing a row of nine identical heavy ironbound doors. They went to the unmarked one that was theirs, slipped through it and shot the bolts, and mounted a short flight of steps to where they could relax at last.

Shuddering amid the warmth of many candles, they padded barefoot to the full and waiting bath and slipped into it with grateful sighs, letting the warm, petal-scented waters carry away ribbons of blood as they let their voluptuous forms slide into quite different shapes, and shared a chilled decanter of waiting saransor.

"Dragonrose dancers certainly lead luxurious lives," the younger Koglaur commented, holding his goblet up to gaze through its amber-hued depths.

"Short ones, mind, even with ready healing magic—if they don't happen to be of our kind," the older Koglaur replied.

"*Humans* did this, before—?"

"Of course. Who do you think I learned the dance of the skewers from, all those years ago?"

"You've done this before now? I thought no one stayed

at this long, except as punishment or when they had long-running Sirl business!"

"Raegrel," the older Koglaur said feelingly, "only gravediggers and poisoners have long-running Sirl business. When you're sent to make me wiser, you'll often find yourself here. Now let's have your report."

Raegrel put his glass down with a sigh. "So *my* punishment begins, eh?"

"This won't hurt as much as the skewers did. Just answer my questions, sit through my occasional boring musings, drink as much saransor as you like, and we'll be done. Then you, too, can pay overmuch gold to plunge into the fleshpots of Sirlptar."

The younger Koglaur made a face. "And how will I know any lusty wench I take to bed won't be you or one of the other elders, keeping watch over me?"

"We'll wink, to warn you," was the dry response. "Now: the Serpent actually rose?"

"As high as a well-built cottage," Raegrel said without hesitation, "though earth still crowned it and was thrown up around its coils like the walls of an oven. It was aware, too, looking about with at least one eye, before everything simply"—he shrugged—"stopped."

"The binding held, though those who believed that the slaying of Kelgrael would also bring death to the Serpent were proven wrong."

"I believe so. The Great Snake's eye filmed over, and it became as a statue—but it lives. I'd swear to that, Thaebred."

"As Serpent-priests all over Darsar are their usual bold, cruel selves and not foaming, shrieking madfolk running through the streets, I'd say you're right. So the Serpent again sleeps—which is a good thing for Bloodblade and all the other ambitious barons, wizards, brigands, and the Three alone know who else now hurrying to snatch at the Throne of Aglirta. They'd soon learn what *real* tyranny is if the Serpent ever sat the Throne of Flowfoam."

"What, the epitome of tyrants isn't the sly, cruel, duplic-itous old regent? You disappoint me!" Raegrel replied, rolling his eyes. "To hear these Aglirtans squawk and scheme, you'd think he was emptying their coffers and barns, seizing their wives and beasts, and flogging their backsides to boot, every morning!"

"When he grows tired of such onerous ruling duties, I sometimes step in for him," Thaebred replied wryly. "Now tell me of Bloodblade, and the Bold Barons Three, in whichever order best describes what's befallen."

"Loushoond, Ornentar, and Tarlagar are as foolish a trio of ambitious, ungrateful *dolts* as I've ever seen. Barely mantled long enough to know where their own castles are, they reward Kelgrael's trust by seeking to seize his throne, figuring he'll never awaken to smite them because he's so dedicated to keeping the Serpent out of Darsar. They scheme with enthusiasm but no secrecy whatsoever, and gallop back and forth along the shore roads—with ever-larger groups of bodyguards who practice for battle by ca-sually swording a handy peddler or herder or two, per trip—visiting each other. They wear bright new armor day and night and wave drawn swords at table and in bedcham-ber, ordering their maids to fetch that goblet or to strip. The moment they hear the regent has taken horse against Bloodblade, they storm the docks to seize Flowfoam, not sparing a single thought for what will happen to them the moment whoever wins the great battle between regent and Bloodblade comes looking for the throne. It's almost as if they believe the Three Above reach down to bestow prizes upon anyone who sits on the throne for a moment!"

"And so, Master of Vitriol? What's befallen said trio of fools thus far?"

"A wizard riding with them did his best to destroy the Silvertree docks, and in the resulting wreckage they fought the four overdukes, apparently for possession of a few sur-viving boats. In this manner they lost much of their battle strength ere the Band of Four embarked for Flowfoam, but followed shortly thereafter—not all that far ahead of Bloodblade, who evidently prevailed at Sarth Fields. Did the regent die?"

"We think not. Dwaer were used in the air above the battle, and there's some confusion as to Blackgult's fate and . . . other things. Continue."

"We rapidly approach the limits of my knowledge," Raegrel replied. "All three forces in turn voyaged to Flowfoam, Bloodblade's requiring many ferryings, and none have departed that isle yet—nor have we seen bodies floating downriver."

"That'll come," the older Koglaur said with a grim smile. "Believe me."

"Oh, I do. They must be hacking at each other already—and there was some sort of Serpent-shaped apparition raised by magic above Flowfoam Palace, not long ago. I've no idea as to what it meant to the real Serpent, because I was hastening here."

"So as to shed blood so prettily in the early show," Thaebred agreed, his smile broader this time. "Well, there are worse destinies."

"For me, or for Aglirta?"

The older Koglaur only smiled, and refilled both their goblets.

"Noisy, aren't they?" Craer commented, raising his borrowed sword in a swift parry—and then driving home the dagger in his other hand, and ducking his face away from the spray of blood that followed.

"They'll learn," Hawkril grunted, shaking a gurgling, dying armsman off his sword. "Those few who live to heed the lesson, that is."

"You're going to leave some alive?" the procurer gasped, in mock horror, springing aside from an armaragor's snarling lunge.

"Some always flee," the tall, burly armaragor said regretfully, leaning over to chop the lunging knight's sword-wrist into bloody ruin.

And then they were too busy to try to do anything but keep themselves alive.

The room was aswarm with enthusiastically hacking men, crowded together until their armored shoulders clashed, and still they poured in through the doors, in a flood of bright blued steel that swept past the tumbled stones and sprawled Melted and frightened men of the three barons, to thrust and hack and stab at the small band of overdukes and their allies gathered by the throne.

Glarsimber and even Hawkril grunted and staggered back under the sheer force of that charge, jostling Raulin up against something soft that he realized with a shock was the Lady Embra's bosom. "Ss-sorry, Lady!" he shouted desperately, struggling for balance.

"For what? 'Tis a battle!" she shouted teasingly into his ear. "Now make up for it by slipping between Lady Tala-sorn and me, here, and holding this helm above your head. Straight up, but not so high we can't both touch it!"

Tshamarra was already weaving a swift spell of thornar-rows, but she eyed the young bard with interest rather than hostility as he carefully ducked between them. The clang-ing and singing of steel was almost deafening as men hacked and hacked with frenzied fury, as if they could thresh their ways through armor to reach the blood and bone beneath.

Cringing as one long blade burst in over Craer's shoul-der and almost touched his nose, Raulin feared that maybe, just maybe, the threshers might prevail.

"Hah!" Tshamarra cried then, in satisfaction, as her thorns sprayed into the faces of armsmen several ranks back—men who were busily shoving at their fellow war-riors in their eagerness to get at the overdukes. Some of them screamed as they were blinded, some gurgled as they choked on their own blood and died—and more than a few just threw back their heads and perished in shuddering silence, to sag limply and bleed as they were held up in the press of bodies.

"*Now*, Lady Talasorn," Embra called, tiny white arcs of lightning coursing between her fingertips and the helmet as she raised her hand towards it. "Touch the helm!"

Two slender-fingered hands put fingers to the curving metal in unison, one from either side. Embra knew what to expect, and had braced herself, but the surge of magical power rushing down Tshamarra's arm almost made the last Talasorn sorceress reel and fall.

Raulin caught awkwardly at her hip to keep her upright—and then shouted in fear as the tingling he'd been feeling in his hand grasping the helm became a full-fledged hammering of power through him, leaping through crackling air to his fingers from Tshamarra's flank even as he snatched his hand away.

"*Don't* let go!" Embra shouted. "Stand, Raulin!"

Stand he did, teeth chattering in fear and from the sheer force of the mighty flow of magic racing through him, but Raulin Castlecloaks could not hold back a gasp of awe when bolts of lightning burst out of the helm, died in a spitting of sparks about an arm's length in front of him—and then burst forth again from the outstretched hands of the two sorceresses.

Armsmen and armaragors roared in pain and reeled, too tightly packed together in their armor to fall, even when the stink of their cooked flesh grew strong, and their armored heads lolled loosely in the shouting, convulsing press of bodies.

Again and again the women lashed out with those bolts of leaping death, slaying at will and reaping many lives, until it seemed like half the throne room was full of swaying, head-lolling dead men, but there seemed to be no end to Bloodblade's warriors—and the helm over Raulin's head was growing blacker and smaller, dwindling as swiftly as parchment curling in a crackling fire.

As the humming and crackling of the bolts died away into occasional snappings, Raulin heard both Craer and Glarsimber sobbing with the effort of swinging blades in battle—the baron because of his wounds, and Craer because he was used to springing about and hurling daggers from afar, not standing blade to blade against armored brutes twice his size and playing "batter thy foe down" with swung steel.

Embra's lips tightened in determination, and she spent her last few feeble bolts carefully striking down men close to the Four and their three friends, to win them some respite. When Tshamarra saw what the Lady Overduke was doing, she did the same, raking the nearest foes with spitting lightnings that where they didn't slay, clawed at visors or ran up under gorgets, to leave men blinded or gasping to breathe through seared face.

Suddenly the helm, shrunk to scarcely the size of Raulin's gathered fingertips, fell away into ash, and the spell ended. Raulin looked rather dazedly at the two tall, grinning sorceresses as they leaned across him, brushing his face in a very distracting manner, and said, on Embra's part, "'Tis always nice to welcome a new friend! Lady, have my hand!" and on Tshamarra's part, "Lady Embra, we've not been properly introduced. I am Tshamarra Talasorn—and I am honored to fight at your side!"

The two women kissed—quick pecks on cheeks that nonetheless forced Raulin to lean back sharply or be smothered—then broke apart, Embra smoothly plucking the shield from Raulin's grasp as she did so.

"I don't want to use this yet," she murmured, as Craer and Glarsimber shuddered, stamped, and blew great gulps of air like winded horses right in front of them, and Hawkril clapped steadying arms around both men, "but if I have to . . ."

"Onward! In at them, you fools!" Bloodblade roared, from the rear of the throne chamber. "Their magic must be near spent! Can you not sword down three men, a boy, and two maids? Strike *now!* Strike for Aglirta!"

A few armaragors struggled to obey, but found themselves shoving against the dead, their ways forward choked with bodies. With a grin Hawkril turned his warsword crosswise like a staff, and fended off corpses that might otherwise have toppled, holding the slain upright and packed together. The men around Bloodblade put down their shoulders and heaved, and here and there about the room bodies clattered and clanged as they fell between stones or over their fellows into heaps—but for the nonce the jam held, and the three weary nobles of Aglirta could lean on their swords or each other, and snatch more breaths.

Embra kept the shield up to just below her eyes and peered over it, keeping careful watch. Any moment now one of these iron-heads would remember that maces, daggers, and even swords can be hurled, and they'd be facing a hail of spinning steel.

Wordlessly Raulin reached out and took hold of the shield for her, holding it up as he had the helm, and with grateful glances the two women pressed in against him to shelter behind it.

"*Move,* Three curse you!" Bloodblade shouted across the room at warriors he didn't know were all dead, and then turned to the swordcaptain at his side. "*Where* are the Serpent-priests?"

The man spread helpless hands. "There were some here when we came in, Lord, but—"

Bloodblade threw back his head and roared with anger. "Right!" he bellowed as he brought his chin back down. "Where are those wizards?"

"A-all dead, Lord, save one left witless by that blast in the sky. I saw one in the boats, but he was dead on the stairs up from the dock, later. I . . . think he'd been stabbed in the back."

Bloodblade growled again, and then blew out his nostrils like an angry stallion, and snapped, "*Right*, then. Well

enough. Our swords have brought us this far, and our swords
will take us this last, little way to that throne yonder! Forward—throw aside bodies when you find them! Clear a way
to the regent's last few sycophants, and *sword* them *down*!"

His bellow was answered by a sudden flash of light and
a deafening crackle of spell-lightnings that sent even Duthjack staggering, heralding a surge of force that tumbled
warriors away like armored dolls. Others ducked down
against the momentary gale and shouted in alarm, raising
their blades to somehow ward off—

Two men who'd appeared in midair, standing on emptiness with their boots a little above the helms of the tallest
warriors, above the center of the throne chamber. One was
the Regent of Aglirta, Baron Blackgult, with a lone Dwaer-
Stone orbiting his head—and in one hand he held the
shoulder of a frightened-looking, much younger man: the
Bard Flaeros Delcamper.

The regent hurled sharp glances in all directions, taking
in the scene—and his eyes widened.

"My daughter *lives*!" he shouted exultantly, his Dwaer
flaring overhead like a star. "Embra, lass! I'm here!"

"The regent!" Bloodblade howled, flailing at the armored backs of the armaragors before him with the flat of
his blade. "*Slay him!* Kill him before he can use his dark
magic on us all!"

That danger goaded them as no other words could have,
and Bloodblade's warriors charged forward into the ranks
of the dead, plying their blades with frantic fear, wrenching aside corpses and forcing their ways on.

They threw daggers at the men standing on air—and then
axes, and swords, too, whirling end over end to—clang
aside from nothingness that suddenly glowed to match
Blackgult's Dwaer, as the regent muttered hasty incantations
and crouched, dragging Flaeros around almost behind him.

That barrier shone brighter as a quickening hail of
weapons were flung against it, falling away amid flashes of
tortured magic. Then Bloodblade's armaragors reached the

floor beneath the two men and stabbed upward, springing up with grunts of effort to hack and thrust—and fall back with startled cries of pain, as blue fire surged down their blades to wash over them, leaving them staggering or falling.

"*There* they are," Embra murmured. "Farewell to our shield." Raulin and Tshamarra followed her gaze, to where men with scaled heads and forked tongues had appeared around the edges of the riven ceiling, to gaze down on the battle from the galleries above.

"Raulin," the Lady Overduke added with some urgency, "take this back." She boosted him under one elbow to raise the shield as swiftly as possible as he fumbled it aloft, over their heads.

A moment later, green fire crashed down on them, and Tshamarra snarled between clenched teeth as she stumbled bruisingly back into the bard, fighting off the Serpent-spell with a hasty magic of her own.

"Uhh," she groaned, panting for breath as the green fire faded, "I—haven't much magic left, Lady . . . if you can source more lightnings for us both . . . that might be a . . . good idea about now . . ."

"But of course," Embra said with a grin. "Let there be lightnings once more!"

"Are you always," Raulin said in disbelief, "so crazily *cheerful* in battle?"

Embra winked at him without halting her fast-muttered incantation, but Tshamarra said with a smile, "I begin to believe it's expected of heroes, friend Raulin. Gods, what a slaughter!"

A moment later, three faces tightened in unison as Embra's magic tugged at the enchantment on the shield, started to drain it—and power surged through them, snarling forth as lightnings. The Lady Overduke spread her fingers and sent her bolts up at the Serpent-priests—more than a dozen of them now, their own hands moving in spellcastings as they stood glaring down at her.

Tshamarra lashed them with lightnings, too, as Raulin stood holding the swiftly shrinking shield. Bolt after bolt flashed out, to crack and hum and sear its way across scaled flesh, and more than one snake-man stiffened or convulsed ere falling with smoke rising from their scales.

The clang of swords meeting in anger off to the right heralded the breaching of Blackgult's barrier, perhaps simply overwhelmed by so much vigorously plied steel, but neither sorceress dared spare time to look. They could hear Hawkril growling as he swung his warsword in great slashing strokes, and that was reassurance enough that nothing had gone horribly wrong—yet.

The Serpent-priests were fending off the shield-spawned lightnings now, warding spells of their own glowing as each bolt bit into those unseen barriers, flared out in a spreading flood, and faded. Embra's eyes narrowed—yes, the snake-men's shieldings must be *drinking* the power of the bolts, growing stronger with each lightning that struck!

Frowning, the Lady Silvertree sent her next bolt lower, striking not at grinning Serpent-priests, but at the broken edges of the throne chamber ceiling beneath their boots. For a breath or two nothing happened but lightning clawing and snarling its way along jagged stone—but then a large chunk of vaulted ceiling broke free, and fell.

That huge stone plunged through the throne room, spilling dust and rubble—and then the floor tiles of the gallery above—all down onto the heads of shouting warriors below. They were men of the three barons, and what few shields they raised did no good against stones as large as men, that simply smashed everything standing against them down to the floor.

Screaming Serpent-priests joined that cascade, and Tshamarra Talasorn grinned and fed them bolts as they fell, suspecting that some of the shieldings would hang in the air where they'd been cast, in the gallery above, and not cling to their creators. She was right—and more than one scaled man burned on the way down, or landed gouting smoke from various places, and lay still.

Embra kept her gaze on that upper gallery, expecting spell attacks from the snake-men who'd been wise enough to hastily back away from the edge, but their attention— and their hurled magics—were aimed elsewhere.

Even as Tshamarra merrily raked the broken edges of rock again with her lightnings and sent fresh showers of stone down onto the trapped armsmen below, varicolored fires snarled down from scaled hands at Ezendor Blackgult's barrier.

At the heart of their fiery onslaught, as tongues of flame splashed and raged outward, the air around the regent began to flicker with dark, flamelike shadows interspersed with lightninglike flashes. In its midst, Blackgult and the bard sank towards the floor, the Dwaer winking and sputtering fitfully above them—and eager blades were waiting for them, thrusting in ruthless unison.

Ezendor Blackgult had been a giant among warriors long before he'd ever seen a Dwaer-Stone, and he swung his sword in one hand and his dagger in the other in great roundhouse sweeps, striking aside enemy blade after enemy blade in a shower of sparks. All the while he was muttering something that made his Dwaer flash and pulse with redoubled vigor—and when he let go of his dagger it did not fall to the floor, but whirled up into the air around him and became a dozen shining fangs of metal, racing back and forth in a bright barrier of steel that rose around the regent and the bard, keeping Bloodblade's warriors at bay.

Blackgult gave them a savage grin, and then reached up and plucked the Dwaer out of midair with his freed hand. Looking over at Embra, he cried, "Lass—*catch*!" and threw it.

End over end the mottled tan stone flew, as Serpent-priests hissed in eager unison and spun snake-swift magics,

Bloodblade's warriors stared in horror—and a Lady Over-duke's long, slender arm reached up to just the right place.

And caught hold of the Stone.

The shield in Raulin's hands burst into tiny shards with a scream of tortured metal, Blackgult's barrier of whirling daggers flashed into silver flames and was gone, and Embra clutched the Dwaer to her breast with a moan of what could only be described as—rapture.

White flames suddenly wreathed her about in a soaring white column, and she was snatched up in them, spiralling upright off the floor. Raulin and Tshamarra cried out and shrank away in pain from that whirling, blinding fire, a few last lightning bolts stabbed out across the throne chamber at random, and an overeager Serpent-priest overbalanced on the edge of the riven ceiling and fell, wailing, onto the head of the Baron Tarlagar below. This time the baron's warriors were ready—and four blades met in the scaly form ere it reached the floor, but not before it smashed the baron into a moaning heap beneath it.

Craer and Hawkril sprang forward to try to reach Black-gult's side, but they were met by a dozen men or more, and held back in a ringing contest of blades. Another dozen armaragors stepped warily forward to slay the regent and the pale-faced, trembling bard.

Ezendor Blackgult drew himself up, his blade ready in his hand, and gave them a soft smile and a question: "Who wants to die first?"

The usurper's men came to an uneasy halt, and he asked them another. "How much of your blood is the price of a Regent of Aglirta?"

"Hah!" Bloodblade snarled, as his men faltered. "One man, alone?" he shouted. "And with his magic gone?"

"*Not* alone," the Baron Brightpennant growled, as the armaragor he'd been fighting sank to the floor with a dying groan, and he strode to Blackgult's side. "For Aglirta!"

"Oh, so it's *two* old men, is it? *Now* we're trembling! *Die*, fools!" Bloodblade sneered, and blew his rally horn. With a startled roar, his armaragors and armsmen charged forward.

Hawkril roared right back, and by main strength heaved the warriors he and Craer were battling back on their heels, into their charging fellows in a tangle of shouts and curses and skirling weapons, so the two overdukes could burst past and reach the regent, too.

Tshamarra plucked at Raulin and dragged him firmly away from the door that might take them to safety, around the whirling column of flame that held Embra, to stand between it and Craer. "Pick up a sword and hold it out in front of you," she growled, "and I'll do the rest!"

Raulin blinked at her.

Not far away—unless you had to hew your way there at this moment, through so many roused and full-armored men—another bard was also striving for battle valor. "Uh," Flaeros stammered, plucking at Blackgult's arm, "perhaps this isn't the best time, but—" He thrust the dragon scepter under the regent's nose.

"What's this?" Blackgult snapped, taking hold of the scepter above the bard's grip on it, and dragging it—and Flaeros—a foot or two closer. He peered at the dragon head in snatched glances, whilst parrying the blade of a howling armaragor.

"W-what you were looking for, Lord Regent."

Blackgult stared down at the scepter, as power suddenly flooded out of it to thrum through him, causing his sword to glow brightly. The armaragor he was battling drew back with a gasp.

"I never . . . *wait*. Yes!" The scepter flashed in Blackgult's grasp—and he and Flaeros suddenly vanished.

The scepter clattered to the blood-smeared floor where they'd stood—an instant before the swords of four armaragors ran Baron Brightpennant through.

17

Serpent Rising

Glarsimber Belklarravus had never felt such pain in his life before. Four ice-cold and yet afire lengths of steel were deep in him, sliding—nay, *twisting* as the armaragors wielding them grinned savagely into his face, and turned their blades in their hands.

The Baron Brightpennant slashed at them with his own sword, reaching out despite the sickening agony, and they all drew out their blades hastily to avoid being cut across their throats or faces.

That left him free, as wet, awful fire bubbled up inside him, to defiantly spit out the blood already coursing into his mouth, and gasp, "For Aglirta!" at them.

Staggering a step sideways, he plucked up the dragon scepter, and then threw it as hard as he could, back and to his left, where the Four were fighting. He did not have time to turn his head to see it go, or say the things he wanted to say, because everything was going dark, and the bloody tide behind his eyes and choking up through his throat could be fought back no longer . . .

He fell, or thought he did, but the Smiling Wolf could suddenly hear nothing. Everything was going dim, and a mail-shod boot swung past close by his head, the marble suddenly looming up very near . . .

Out of fire, back into bloodbath. Embra Silvertree blinked away the last white haze of the roaring exultation that had whirled her up, and now set her back down, so gently that her boots struck cracked marble with nary a jar.

A moment later, something struck her ankle gently and skirled away—to where a longfangs dropped from the ceiling and stood guard over it, causing two hurrying armaragors to shrink back in horror. They were the first two knights Embra killed, ere she turned and saw that Glarsimber was dead.

He'd been an unexpected friend—and now the baron was sprawled in his blood, with another pair of armaragors making sure of his passing by driving their swords between the sagging plates of his hacked and battered armor, right through him. They were the next knights she slew.

Behind her, the longfangs dwindled into Sarasper, a man who seemed truly old now. The hand that reached for the dragon scepter trembled, and its skin was mottled and wrinkled. The healer grasped the scepter slowly, almost reluctantly, and there was a strange look in his eyes. Sarasper glanced over at Brightpennant's body, shook his head, and stared at the scepter again.

Embra Silvertree saw none of this. She was aloft again, whirling up into the air with a wordless snarl of fury bubbling from her lips, the Dwaer a bright star in front of her brow and her eyes blazing tears of white fire.

"You *rogues*!" she shouted. "You slaying bastards! *Die*, all of you! *Die!*"

And she stretched forth her hands and called on the Dwaer in earnest. Deadly lances of white light lashed out from her hands, stabbing through dozens of Bloodblade's warriors as if they were made of parchment.

Raulin whimpered in fear as he saw scores of men die in

a heartbeat, heads seared off or bodies burned through. He shrank back, and turned to run—only to be grabbed and spun around by Craer, whose own face was wet with tears. "Prefer her when she's cheerful," he hissed into the bard's terrified face. "Prefer all of us that way. Always."

And then the procurer spun around with a wild cry and hurled himself at the nearest armaragors, springing so high that his codpiece slammed into a helm. Craer promptly wrapped his legs around the head of that knight—a foe who was dead before crashing to the ground, as Overduke Delnbone rode the enemy armaragor down to the marble, sinking daggers into throat and back of neck and eyeslits in a snarling fury.

"Halduth!" Bloodblade roared. "Strike down that sorceress!"

Hawkril Anharu looked wildly for whoever Halduth might be—and behind the press of armaragors in front of his blade he saw an armored arm rise up, holding a spear as large as a horse-lance. With a roar he gave ground, planted himself on the shifting bodies of the dead before the men he'd been fighting could rush forward, and sprang into the air, chopping—and the spear shrieked as the overduke's blade struck it aside, hurling Hawkril back to crash down on more of the dead—crash and roll and find his feet, in time to sword a rushing man and sidestep another, slashing backhanded at the man's neck.

Hawkril's blade caught in armor plate as that man died with a splintering of bone and a frantic choking sound, and he tugged, kicked, and staggered free of his foe—in time to face the next charge.

Embra struck again, more deadly lances of searing magic striking down dozens of armsmen. Men were shouting in fear, now, and trying to flee, everywhere—everywhere, that is, save above, through the hole in the ceiling, where angry-eyed scaled priests were murmuring incantations, their eyes on Embra.

Armaragors melted away in terror before Hawkril, leaving him standing face-to-face with the spearman—an armored giant who was dragging a huge mace out of a baldric-sling and hefting it in his hands. Hawkril charged forward, found his blade parried by the mace about where he'd expected, found the arm behind that mace was every bit as strong as he'd feared—and also found that his free hand had a clear path to the man's eyes. He punched and rode with his blow, scraping the sharp knuckles of his gauntlet back and forth across the man's brow, trying to blind the giant with his own blood.

They fell together, and rolled, the giant underneath—and grunting in pain as they went over the points of dead men's weapons. Hawkril let go his sword, plucked his belt-dagger, and made sure the giant had no throat left ere their rolling was done. Then he snatched up his sword and glared around, seeking foes. Everywhere, now, men were running . . .

After her first awed, hard-swallowing glance at what a Dwaer could do when its wielder was lost in slaying fury, Tshamarra Talasorn had been glancing swiftly around the room, seeking perils directed at Embra, and ways to thwart them before they could do the Lady Overduke harm or interrupt her in cooking Bloodblade's army. Upward was the first place Tshamarra looked, and the moment she was sure that none of Bloodblade's warriors had brought bows to this battle, she glanced up at the Serpent-priests again, and murmured a spell of her own. It was almost her last—but then, if a sorceress worried about such things and allowed such prudence to guide her, every spell she cast might prove to be her very last, forever.

With careful swiftness Tshamarra worked her casting, her eyes never leaving the hissing Serpent-priests—and none of them had finished their spellweavings when her green fire struck and raged among them, swift and painful. It was nothing beside the searing oblivion that Embra was dealing, but it was enough to leave the scaled men reeling

or on their knees, their spells ruined. One of them oblig-
ingly fell into the throne room—and Baron Ornentar raised
his blade in desperate haste and spitted the Snake-priest
while the scaled man still lay twisting on the floor, winded
and shuddering.

The surviving Serpent-priests retreated from the edge of
the hole in the ceiling, weaving hasty shielding spells, and
Tshamarra raised her hands, feigning the casting of another spell, but did nothing. She had too little fire left in her
to waste anything.

Armed with her Dwaer, Embra had no such cares. As the
Worldstone flamed above her, the Lady Overduke slaughtered on—and, in moments, an army was slain.

The three barons saw their handful of armsmen ducking
behind stones and among corpses, and hastily did the
same. Here and there around the room armaragors of the
usurper did likewise—particularly after Embra took special care to burn down anyone who tried to flee out a door.

Crouching behind one of the largest piles of fallen stone,
Bloodblade watched in disbelief as these last few of his men
died. The room before him was a charnel house, and only a
bare handful of his swordcaptains remained, clustered
grimly around him. Wondering what door he dared try to
flee to, the warlord glanced up at the riven ceiling—and saw
the Serpent-priests looking down at him coldly, from within
the spark-shot flickerings of many overlapping shielding
spells. Thus protected, they had returned to the very edge of
the hole, and now stood watching—doing nothing.

Something in dusty leather burst over the heap of stones,
and an armaragor who had sword up and ready died with a
dagger in one eye before he could even cry an alarm. A
second gurgled, throat cut, ere the other three got their
blades up to force back the procurer.

Delnbone, the little rat of the overdukes! Well, his
swordcaptains could deal with—

An armored form loomed up over the stones and smashed aside Bloodblade's swift thrust with one swing of a long, well-used warsword. The Lord of All Aglirta sprang back, stumbling on rubble, and Hawkril Anharu stalked after him.

Bloodblade looked up at the snake-men. As before, they stared dispassionately down, arms folded and shields strong.

"Aid!" Bloodblade called to them desperately, as Hawkril hewed through Duthjack's parry and drove the warlord back.

Bloodblade caught the overduke's next titanic swordcut on his blade, but the blow left his arm burning and without strength. He couldn't feel his fingers—fingers that his sword was already slipping from! Frantically, Bloodblade snatched it in his other hand and backed desperately away from Hawkril's slow, grim advance. His swordarm, the warlord knew, was broken.

"Aid!" Bloodblade cried, looking up at the Serpent-priests. "You promised!"

At the far end of the room, a woman was weeping bitterly.

Scaled faces smiled coldly down at Sendrith Duthjack. "As a certain bold mercenary said before another throne, not so long ago," one of them sneered, " 'No, I think not.' You need us—but *we* don't need *you*. You've served your purpose, Bloodblade. The Serpent thanks you; die comforted by his approval. Die *now*."

The priest smiled coldly, and added, "There are *so* many fat, decadent, arrogant fools of barons, aren't there? Better to be rid of them all, and their king with them—whichever idiot of a sword-swinger that may happen to be. The Serpent should rule from the River Throne, bringing true glory to all Aglirta."

"No!" Bloodblade cried despairingly, trying to parry that great warsword and failing. *"No!"*

"Serpent-priests, behind all! I might have known," Hawkril said grimly—and drove his blade home, stabbing right at Sendrith Duthjack's chest. His warsword struck sparks off the thick breastplate of Bloodblade's grand armor and ran up that shaped steel, shrieking along in a shower of sparks, to catch the edge of the would-be usurper's gorget, and go up—and in.

The man called Bloodblade staggered back, eyes wide with pain, gargling on his own blood, and stared despairingly into Hawkril's flinty stare. The armaragor took a step to the side, to where the side seam of Duthjack's armor could be reached—and then Hawkril Anharu lunged with all his strength, piercing the lighter plate and running the dying Bloodblade through.

"*I* should have known!" Craer added darkly, hurling a dagger. "Who else so hates Aglirta as to unhesitatingly *ruin* it in their strivings to conquer it?"

The Serpent-priest who'd told Bloodblade his doom waved a hand, and its fingers were suddenly a writhing forest of hissing snakes. The procurer's razor-sharp blade sliced off more than a few of their heads as it flashed towards its target—but it was snared and brought down before it could find the holy scaled throat, beyond.

Embra Silvertree knelt in all the blood and cradled Glarsimber's head in her hands. Sightless eyes stared past her, and more blood drooled from the baron's slack mouth.

Blackgult and now Brightpennant . . . Two brave barons dead, in the space of a few breaths. Her father was gone, and Flaeros with him, blasted by some magic because he'd given her his Dwaer, and left himself defenseless . . . oh, Lady Above, there was no laughing deliverance from this sorrow . . .

Hawkril shook Bloodblade half off his warsword, and then twisted it and drove it home again. Dripping blood, the would-be usurper staggered and threw up feeble hands in a beseeching gesture.

"'Tis just a little late for mercy," Hawkril told him softly, in a voice that trembled on the edge of tears, "when Aglirta lies scarred by your hand, all law broken and the king gone forever and so many dead because of your deeds. I would slay you once for each death you've caused, if I somehow had the magic to bring you back to feel each and every slaying!"

Bloodblade reeled off the dark, slick end of Hawkril's blade, eyes glazing over—and the hulking overduke sprang forward with the roar of an angry lion and swung one gauntleted fist as hard as he could. Duthjack's neck broke with a horrible splintering sound, as the warlord's feet left the floor for one last time.

"For Aglirta!" Hawkril Anharu shouted. "And for us all!"

Overhead, another Serpent-priest finished hissing a long and intricate spell, and lifted one scaled hand.

In answer, something black—like smoke that somehow *glistened*—boiled up from the floor of the throne chamber, sprouting wherever no bodies lay or blood was smeared, and roaring up into . . . serpents! In moments there was a black, rising wall of snakes, hissing and biting the air and curling out to snap their jaws hungrily at anyone nearby.

"Embra!" Tshamarra Talasorn screamed, shaking with revulsion. "Embra, help!" Snakes were hanging down from the ceiling and boiling up from the floor, between her *very legs* within her gown! Shrieking, she sprang away, kicking and slapping, and landed hard on tumbled stone, scrambling up in horror as she saw the black, hissing wall of snakes drifting closer, upright but moving, closing in . . .

Tshamarra stared around wildly. On all sides, in a tightening ring. *"Embra!"*

Hawkril slashed furiously at the nearest snakes, slicing hissing heads in all directions—but wherever they landed, they sprang up like leaping trees—and the severed stumps grew new heads with just as frightening speed.

Craer was hurling dagger after dagger up through the hole in the ceiling, but the snake-men were laughing at him and transforming them into wriggling snakes in midair.

The Lady of Jewels looked up through tangled hair at that cold laughter—and stared around in sudden fury, her Dwaer flaming into fresh brilliance. White fire slashed out from her hands as she rose, melting away black snakes at a touch—but the ring of snakes gave way only sullenly, and regrew a pace behind her ravening fire.

"And so the famous Band of Four feels the fangs of our little trap at last," a mocking voice floated down to them from the gallery above. It was the Serpent-priest who'd taunted Bloodblade.

He smiled into Embra's fierce glare, crooked a green-scaled little finger—and the Crown of Aglirta was suddenly gleaming upon his brow. The Serpent-priest promptly sketched an elegant court bow, smiled even more widely as Embra's Dwaer blazed brighter in her fury, and mockingly held out his hand to her, as if inviting her onto a dance floor.

There was a Dwaer-Stone glowing in his open palm.

"Lady Silvertree," the priest commanded in a voice suddenly deep and powerful, as Dwaer-fire rose around him like white lightning and his eyes glowed with sudden fire, *"give me your Dwaer."*

"No," Embra spat at him, *"I think not."* And power rushed out of her with a roar that echoed back from every corner of Flowfoam Palace like an agonized shout.

In a deep and dusty room, a glowing skeleton sat up in its casket, just for a moment, and two tiny flames kindled in its empty eyesockets. Its jaw swung open, stiffly, and worked, struggling to say something with lips, throat, and lungs that were no longer there—and then, with one arm half-raised, it fell back into the casket, to lie in silent stillness once more.

* * *

Her Dwaer-Stone danced in the air like a small star afire, so bright that it hurt the eyes—and where Embra's cone of ravening white fire struck the smiling Serpent-priest, it parted, touching him not—and snuffed out the lives and bodies of half a dozen other scaled clergy, leaving nothing behind but wisps of lazily curling smoke.

Other Snake-priests went to their knees dazedly, holding their heads, and many reeled briefly in pain.

The Serpent-priest who had a Dwaer of his own gave the Lady of Jewels a brittle smile, then began to chant a simple incantation—a few words in the hissing, fluid tongue of the Believers of the Great Serpent, repeated over and over again.

His Dwaer flamed red, then black, and then red again, raging above him—and as the priest's chant went on, and the other surviving Snake-clergy began to join in, his Worldstone grew slowly brighter.

Embra knew what that chant was—and it did not take long for Tshamarra or Craer to correctly guess what was befalling.

It was Raulin who asked, raw-voiced, "What is he—it—doing, Lady?"

"He's summoning the Serpent," Embra told him grimly, her face as white as bone, "and there's nothing I can do to stop him."

Her white fires wrestled with the black wall of snakes, and beat it back a pace or two, but could gain no further ground.

The invocation went on, louder and louder, its insistent rhythm quickening. Other voices joined in, from far down the passages that led to the throne chamber, and snakes larger than men came gliding in through some of the doors.

"Give me your Dwaer, Embra Silvertree," the Serpent-priest hissed triumphantly, as the chant rose to an echoing crescendo in the palace around them. "Give it to me on your knees—or I'll come down there and take it, adrip with your blood!"

As his last word hissed out, a deep, thrumming roar of triumph arose all around—and the roof of the gallery above burst off in a thousand flying fragments that were whirled away over the gardens and into the river.

The six heroes blinked up at the bright open sky, with ribbons of white cloud scudding past serenely high above—and then lost sight of those clouds as the Serpent surged up into the sky, huge and dark and terrible, towering higher than the mountains.

Eyes glittering like black flame, it roared its exultation to all Darsar—and then turned its great head and looked right down at them.

No, down at the ruined throne, seat of the king who'd bound it for so long. With a thunderous hiss of rage that seemed almost a sob, it spread huge jaws—and its vast head came hurtling down, fangs agleam.

Hawkril Anharu swallowed twice as he took a stance, his face white—and stood ready to meet the Great Serpent, warsword upraised. "For Aglirta," he whispered. "I have only one life to give, creature . . . take it, if you can." He bared his teeth and added in a snarl, *"If . . . you . . . can."*

Fangs descended, long and deadly, maw so large and dark between . . .

"So you see," Tonthan "Goldcloak" said smoothly, raising his goblet to the Elmeran as the wizard accepted a goblet of his own from a servant's tray, "this could be a great opportunity for us all. The richest realm of all—if restored to peace, of course, and held free of burnt and trampled crops and barns, slaughter, and spending on hireswords and battle-steel for, say, three growing seasons—and a whole barony of it to be yours, to rule as you see fit."

A ring flashed momentarily on Mranrax Arandor's hand. Ah, seeking for spell-taints on the wine, no doubt, though

Sirl poisoners preferred more subtle—and inexpensive—
herbal ways, as the wizard raised his glass and his bushy
white eyebrows together.

His dark eyes were suddenly very direct and penetrat-
ing. "And how would the good folk of Aglirta view a wizard as baron? Would I have to worry about every
bed-servant coming in to greet me with my late-night wine
in one hand and a dagger ready in the other?"

Tonthan shrugged. "Mages have not been well regarded
in the past, for two reasons: they have 'experimented' on
unwilling, captive folk—pretty local lasses in particular, if
you take my meaning—and most of them have come to
Aglirta as the hired scourges of this or that baron, and have
served in such capacities all too well. If you show promise
of gentle character rather than cruel arrogance, and show
no signs of the warlike whims of recent barons, you'll escape such opinion."

Arandor of Elmerna smiled so blandly that his expression betrayed nothing of his mood or thoughts, and asked,
"And what of the Ieiremborans? How will they feel if a fell
and mighty archwizard suddenly joins their conspiracy?"

Tonthan shrugged again. He was getting quite good at it.
"They want Kelgrael and Blackgult dead, and a king of
their choosing on the throne. They need our coins to fund
armies enough for the bid, and are in no position to dictate
who holds every last barony and terseptry. If they think to
do so, or come ashore to occupy such positions themselves, you will serve as a—salutary surprise."

Arandor raised his eyebrows again. "What? A tight rein
on ambition? What a strange role for a wizard."

The Elmernan's voice was wry, but Tonthan had not
made more coins in Sirlptar than many wealthy trading
families amass in three generations by being a fool or less
than keenly perceptive. "A capable wizard might well
come to dominate two or even three baronies," he said
carefully, "or, even better, rise to advise a figurehead

king—but a wizard who conquered barony after barony, even through others, or who sought to warm the River Throne personally, would remind Aglirtans of the tyrant-mages of their past, and . . ."

"Steps would be taken?"

"Indeed—steps involving the Lady of Jewels and Dwaerindim, I fear."

Mranrax Arandor could not keep his features as expressionless as stone after all. "Ah, yes, the Dwaer. I must adm—"

Deafening sound smote their ears, and the room rocked. Darkness flashed outside the windows, tinkling glass fell, and someone screamed.

A thunderclap greater than any storm Sirl had ever tasted, in Tonthan's recall, and this was no storm.

He and the wizard spun around together, to gaze out through the frame where glass had been, moments ago. From this highest ridge in Sirlptar, they could look right up the Vale—miles upon miles of green trees, glimmering curves of river, and verdant shoulders of farm, as far as the eye could see. The keen-eyed claimed to be able to see Flowfoam Isle, amid the trees cloaking the horizon, but Tonthan—whose eyes were quite keen enough—doubted such claims. He'd never been quite able to decide if *that* smudge of trees was the Royal Isle of Aglirta, or that one, a little way to the right.

Now he thought he knew. What was towering up into the sky almost had to be on Flowfoam. As high as a cloud it loomed, black and terrible, coiling up clearly: a serpent—no, *The* Serpent, no fancy-beast of bards' tales after all—whose every movement was gloating. It spread jaws that must be wider than the length of most of the ships down at Sirl's sea docks, right now—and plunged its head down, striking at something below.

"Well, now," Mranrax Arandor said softly, in a voice that was not quite steady. "Well, now."

Tonthan glanced over at him. The room was still frozen in gasps of awe, with the cursing, screaming, and fleeing still to erupt, but the archwizard was trembling.

"And then, of course," he added smoothly, "any wizard sitting on the Throne of Aglirta right now would have to deal with *that*. Before it bit him into small, bloody gobbets."

His calmness was both surprising and pleasing. Tonthan waited for the wizard's response, but someone else answered, and that was another surprise.

"Very calm, very swift-witted, Tonthan Runthalan. We'll remember that." The voice spoke from very close behind him, and it was one he'd never heard before. And no one—*no one*—knew Tonthan's true surname. Or so he'd thought.

By then, Tonthan had whirled around. No one was there, of course. Sathbrar blinked at him in mild surprise from half a dozen paces away, from over a plate heaped with grapes and splundroons. The glass the silk-clad merchant was holding was as rock-steady as Tonthan's own.

Or as steady as Tonthan's had been. He whirled around again, and saw fear stark and clear on Mranrax Arandor's face, his eyes still fixed on the distant, titanic bulk of the Serpent.

Thirst for baronies had melted away before a sudden longing to be home in Elmerna, it seemed. Perhaps some small part of Aglirta could be conquered another day . . . at another time, say, than Serpent season . . .

The screaming and running had begun now. "It turns this way!" someone shouted. "The Serpent comes!"

Sathbrar joined him. "Splundroon?"

"Thank you," Tonthan said. "I believe I will." Selecting one, he gestured gently in the direction of Flowfoam with his glass. "How can we make some coins off that, do you think?"

Sathbrar shrugged, chewing. There was a sudden movement on Tonthan's other side, a whirling of robes. He turned.

The wizard Arandor was backing away from *him*, his face pale. "How can you—just—don't you know what that *is*, out there?"

Tonthan shrugged. Yes, he was getting the hang of these shoulder shiftings; one can convey a surprising amount of information with just the right . . .

"Of course," he said, mild reproof in his tone. "The Serpent, awake at last. Greatest mage ever; one of the crafters of the Dwaerindim; completely mad; cruel and ruthless beyond peer; driven by the need to rule everyone, everywhere, and everything; able to force men forever into beast-shape with a glance—have I missed anything?"

Mranrax Arandor made a wordless quailing sound, eyes wide—then whirled away from the two Sirl merchants and ran, robes streaming out behind him. His screams followed many others, down the stairs.

Tonthan and Sathbrar turned back to the ruined window, drinks and fruit in hand, to watch the show.

Tonthan shook his head. A good revel, but all wasted. No spells from Arandor to save on hiring—and burying—hireswords, after all. Aglirta was going to have to fall the old, tried, and expensive way.

Ah, well. They don't make archwizards like they used to.

Mulgor was used to restless sheep, here in the uplands with so many wolves and foxes and stalking bears.

That was why he liked Ul's Hollow so much: a grassy bowl with nary a tree or thornshrub for a hunting beast to hide behind, two bare hills on either side of it that a shepherd could keep watch from, plenty of bustard and dunfeather to fill his cookpot with and keep his bowwork sharp . . . and he could get clear shots at predators, too.

He could still see that wolf, two summers back, tumbling over with his bolt in its eye. Right down yonder, it had been. Yes, this was a good place, and almost his own, these days, with so many gone to wars and not come back. It'd be a hard winter for some, and he'd get better coin for his mutton.

Then he could buy old Throrkan's fields, at last. Overgrown and neglected, these five years, now—but his sheep would make short work of that. The hills, behind, too—Throrkan took just enough grapes for his own use, to slump about in drunken grumbling day after day, but there was enough there for proper vinting, and wine to sell downriver. Estlevan Mulgor, Fine Wines and Fleece. Three smile down, but that had a fine ring to it! Why, h—

What the bebolten *sty* was *that*?

All of his sheep were on the move, flooding forward in the same direction—not stampeded, but trotting purposefully towards the lip of the dell. He sprang to his feet, bow in hand, and launched himself down the slope as fast as he could, heedless of a possible fall. Gods, they could all be over the edge in a moment, and—

The world rocked under him, hurling his thudding feet skyward, and the sky seemed to explode with a dark roar.

The ground slapped Estlevan Mulgor, hard. He was lying on the side of his face, dazed, his bow gone. The sheep! This storm would send them scattering, for sure! He scrambled up, gulping. From wine merchant to nothing, in a single thunderclap!

He'd best—Mulgor stopped, jaw dropping, and just stared. The sheep had all crowded to the front of the dell in a long line, their heads turned to watch one thing—and there they stood frozen, as still as so many dirty white statues. There was no storm in the sky above them, only high white clouds like finger ribbons.

They were staring downriver, at Flowfoam Isle. Or at what was rising in the sky above it. As high as a mountain it loomed, huge and black and coiled—a snake! Taller than the Old Claw, taller than the Mornbeacon—taller than all the Windfangs!

It must be the Serpent bards spoke of, that was bound

into Slumber by the king. And that meant . . . that meant King Kelgrael must be—

"No," Estlevan Mulgor whispered. "Oh, no." If the Serpent was loose in the world, there'd soon be no Aglirta, but a dead waste . . . or a dark realm of hissing, wriggling Serpent-priests and slaves.

He stared at it, towering above the distant palace. It reared up—he could see one black, gold-rimmed eye clearly, and for one heart-freezing moment thought it had noticed him, and was glaring right at him—and shook its coils out, gloating in its power. Throwing back its head, it opened jaws that must be wider than two Ul's Hollows— and with its fangs bared, struck, plunging its head down into the palace.

Kelgrael must be dead already—and someone else down there must be dying, right now. A snake that size would take a lot of feeding. . . .

And there he was, with his sheep a white, welcoming beacon on the green hillside. Mulgor started to shake, and then looked around wildly. His bow . . . if it came hunting this way, he'd need his bow. . . .

Stones fell like rain amid snarling dust, and cracks raced across the floor and walls and ceiling. Up and down the dark, forgotten halls and rooms of these Flowfoam cellars, the stones groaned loudly, threatening collapse . . . and then it all died away, and the glowing bones of Gadaster Mulkyn settled back into their proper places, reassembling themselves into a skeleton—or what was left of a skeleton, after Ingryl Ambelter's ravagings.

Careless and reckless Gadaster's onetime apprentice had certainly been. Not content to steal his master's life and title, this new Spellmaster had contrived to get himself hurt unto death time and time again, struggling down here to clamber into the casket and embrace all that was left of Gadaster often. All too often.

Not for Gadaster—what use are whole and handsome bones to a man who has passed beyond death and sanity, into the enduring dark madness beyond?—but for Ingryl Ambelter himself. With every healing he partook of, a little of Gadaster's will seeped into him, stealing within silently to join a whelming of what was already there.

He seemed oblivious, too, smilingly confident as he went blithely on calling himself Spellmaster . . . and could not even see or feel Gadaster's regard when he lay drinking Gadaster's power.

There would come a day, if this went on, when Ingryl would taste the other edge of the sword of spells he'd used on Gadaster—and his sentience would be torn apart in torment for a suitable time . . . a year or three, perhaps . . . ere Gadaster quenched it forever and took Ingryl's body for his own, repaying his apprentice in kind for his treachery.

Yes, there was no greater danger for a mage than dabbling in magics he did not really know. *All* must be understood, every last detail and consequence, not just the flash and the fire—or what difference would truly stretch, between a wizard and a small boy playing with a burning brand from the hearthfire, carelessly setting this tapestry and that chair alight, and so dooming himself and a grand house together?

Yet this magic that had so disturbed his bones was one Gadaster did not know. It had shaken the oldest enchantments of the palace, underlying spells that had been old and forgotten and many-layered when Gadaster had cast his first timid magics here, in the service of Silvertree.

Did he dare to send his awareness stealing forth, when he might be noticed by someone truly mighty? He must.

Curiosity is the bane of wizards, and the goad that drives them on. He *had* to know.

Something was gone, something missing. Destroyed, not taken . . . the throne! The River Throne stood shattered, amid much lesser destruction, and that meant all the binding enchantm . . . but what was this? A singing of shattered spells, a tangle of incantations about emptiness . . . Kelgrael was dead! The Sleeping King had awakened—and been slain!

So what of the Serpent? Th—Horns of the Lady! Gadaster became aware of a deep, dark, and fell sentience very close by above him, pervading all of the palace above, and now seeking down, down into these cellars. . . .

He must sleep as Kelgrael had, must spin himself away from this place, or be discovered!

Gadaster did something hasty in his mind, drawing a glyph with mental fire in the gloom with frenzied haste, racing along it in mounting fear . . .

Just in time. The glow faded from old bones lying in a casket, and darkness reclaimed the room Ingryl had so carefully prepared.

A bare breath later, minor magics on its shelves—and one small, fallen thing, on the floor—flashed briefly blue as the mind that had been called Irtle Eroeha, and other names besides, became aware of them . . . and drank their power, leaving crumbling dust behind.

The bones lay still and silent as the dust of Flowfoam Palace started to settle once more.

And when the next great crash came from above, a few moments later, nothing in the casket was aware of anything.

At the top of a tower far from Aglirta was a round, high-ceilinged room dominated by a tall arched window that was always open.

Bats flew in and out of that window almost ceaselessly, whatever the hour, and the rafters above, as they reached up to meet in a central downspire of carved and turned wood that was far grander—if shorter—than the matching spire above it, outside the tower, were encrusted with thick clusters of hanging bats.

A dark-robed man sat at a desk in that room, reading. He seemed scarcely to notice the dozens of bats that perched and then flapped away from his shoulders and head, or clung there with the passing hours. He was reading a spell-book that many a mage would have cheerfully given many lives for but their own, and his name was Arkle Huldaerus.

Though that seemed a suitably grand and arcane name for a wizard, he'd acquired a better one—a calling that had so eclipsed the name he'd been born with that few now remembered it. To all Darsar, when they thought about him at all, he was the Master of Bats.

He turned a page, his eyes seeming to glow for a moment, and nodded thoughtfully. This was how he spent much of his time, not being the sort of mage who loved bubbling and burning experiments, and crafting new magics that might—rarely—delight or do just what was desired, but that more often destroyed days of work or cottages or unfortunate apprentices—or all three. This was how most wizards spent their time: reading, and so learning new spells or magics to replace what they'd cast, and slowly losing their eyesight in the doing.

Huldaerus rubbed at his eyes now, as he set down the book, looking thoughtful. Hadn't Orstal done the same spell as this Waereuvin, but with a better incantation? Saving live frogs was always a good thing, considering the time one spent getting wet gathering them . . .

All around him, without any fuss, fluttering bats froze in midair.

The glow he'd conjured to read by sank away to nothing, and the Master of Bats stiffened in alarm, peering about, his eyes glistening palely in the darkness.

He'd felt no disturbance of his ward spells, no presence of any intruder . . . so what?

The bats were simply motionless. Not dead, not even enspelled that he could see, but—

The world rocked, and there came a thunderclap out of the north like a leaping fist, darkness flashing across the sky. From down below there came the sounds of glass breaking and falling from all his windows.

Aglirta. Oh, there were other places north of here, almost half Asmarand—but somehow Huldaerus knew that whatever had befallen to so shake the world, it had come from Aglirta.

Well, things always did, didn't they?

He smiled thinly at that, and murmured the word that summoned up out of the floor his scrying eyes. Gleaming spheres of nothingness melted up out of the solid stones, rising silently to become upright, glowing ovals of radiance, gently drifting as they arranged themselves in response to his will, almost filling the room.

Gently, slowly, the bats started to move again.

The Master of Bats peered into the nearest seeing sphere, bending his will to look upon . . . the Throne Chamber in Flowfoam. Always a good place to start.

His bats were fluttering around him as usual by the time the sphere showed him shaking stones—no, stones being flung everywhere—and something large and dark. *Very* large, by the gods! Huldaerus frowned at it for a moment, and then commanded his sphere to show him the outside of Flowfoam.

He was in time to see the head of the Great Serpent rise into view, men's bodies trailing from its jaws, turn to coldly regard something below—and then, as muscles rippled beneath its blue-black scales, plunge back down into . . . yes, by the Dark One, into a great gaping hole in the roof of Flowfoam Palace.

Well, well. The Great Serpent, free at last. That meant the bindings were broken, Snowsar was dead, and soon all Asmarand—all Darsar—would have a large, dark, and hissing problem to deal with. If they could.

If we can, rather. Archwizards and court mages and hedge-wizards all working together—hah, the Three alone knew when *that* would happen!—just might have power enough . . .

Was there anything here he truly dared not lose? If so, where to hide it?

The Master of Bats looked around at his tower, smiling slightly, and shook his head. He went back to his desk, put his feet up, and sent some bats to fetch a bottle of iyrilith from his cellars. The seeing sphere obediently drifted to hang right in front of him, and grew as he merged other spheres into it—until he could see every last glance and glare and shifting scale moving in the throne chamber.

The iyrilith was cold and black and wonderful, with an aftertaste of cherries. Huldaerus sipped and watched other people dying.

Yes, it was still a good time to play vulture.

18

Scepter, Dragon, and Serpent

*L*uckily, not all of his spells had failed him. One had brought him here, out of the dark rubble and scurrying spiders of a Silvertree tomb. His head still ached abominably, and from time to time red fire surged behind his eyes, leaving him dizzy and half-blinded, but Ingryl Ambelter knew he was fortunate to be alive.

He wished no such good fortune on whoever had smitten him with magic on the Silent House battlements. He did not even know who it was—might never know.

He didn't even know how long he'd lain there, crumpled on the stones—and, thankfully, on a thick web of vines that had grown over them. There'd been no sign that anyone had tried to rob him or do him more harm as he'd lain senseless in the tomb.

He'd stumbled around that pit, after coming to. Some long-lost Silvertree had been foolish enough, or perhaps had an heir miserly enough, to build a room-sized crypt out of *wood*. Inevitably it had rotted away and collapsed. If there'd been any magic or anything else useful entombed there, it had been carried off long ago, or buried so well that he'd not been able to find it.

Perhaps it was best if his unknown foe thought him

dead, as Blackgult probably did after their mind-wrestling. Gods, but he *had* to get a Dwaer!

Hah. Easily said.

Well, get one somehow, and keep hidden until then. Ingryl shook his head and shuffled across the little dell to Tharlorn's old refuge—his little hide-hold, now.

He could have the spells of lost Tharlorn and Bodemmon Sarr both, and fabled Eroeha, too—and still not prevail against a Worldstone, wielded by someone who knew how to use it.

Ingryl looked around the familiar bowl of shrubs and stormgrass, to make sure no shepherd or woodcutter was watching, and then stepped around the first trap, to begin worming his way into his refuge. Yes, he was done with Aglirta for a while; best go to ground and wait to see who survived—and where the Dwaerindim ended up.

"Farewell for a time, idiots of the Vale," he murmured, looking out over the Silverflow. "I'm sure the realm will be glad to be rid of me—but will yet fail to find peace. Forget me, fools . . . but I'll be back when you least expect me. It's fitting that *I* rule Aglirta, someday—for I love this land so much that I want to hold every last inch of it in my hands, and let no one else have it. When a Dwaer is mine, I can bind taproots and deep streams and land spirits to me like I bound the wench Embra to her father's castle, and *make* Aglirta mine."

He grinned. "Until then, let us be absent and fond friends," he added lightly, and waved a jaunty farewell to the Vale.

Aglirta nearly threw him into the trap anyway.

The sky went dark for a moment, with a clap of thunder so loud it made him cry out in pain and clutch at his ringing ears—and then the ground threw him off his feet, so that he sprawled painfully on rocks on the very lip of Tharlorn's nasty pit trap, and had to cling there through the rumbling that followed, to keep himself from being hurled in.

As the Spellmaster snarled curses into the weeds now

tangled in his mouth and nose, there was a flickering of movement, off to his left.

He looked that way swiftly, out over the Vale, to be sure no doom was headed this way—and froze, gaping in astonishment, at what he saw.

The great stone heart of Flowfoam Palace was shattered, the southern rooms gone and a great gaping hole in the roof of—the throne chamber, or at least the gallery above it. Where those rooms to the south should have been were the great black coils of—the Great Serpent Eroeha! It had to be!

It was real, no spell-spun illusion. As he watched, stones fell from a broken wall, dislodged by the great black-scaled bulk as the Serpent straightened, towering up into the sky. So high it went that Ingryl found himself rolling over to look at—no! Oh, *no*! He clawed at the stones until his fingers bled to keep out of Tharlorn's damned pit, dragged himself back from that danger, then looked again at the Great Serpent and shook his head in awe. It had to be higher than the tallest of the Windfangs behind him, almost brushing the clouds!

The gigantic snake looked around the Vale with a gloating, knowing eye. That orb was black ringed with gold, and seemed to see *everything*. Ingryl cowered down as its gaze swept past, hoping for the first time in his life that he looked small and insignificant. Then it spread fanged jaws far wider than his dell—far wider than *four* such dells, by the looks of them—and plunged that great head down, into the rent in the palace roof, striking at someone below. Someone in the throne chamber, judging by how far the head went in.

Ingryl shivered, and scrambled hurriedly into the little cave that led to the second trap. So Kelgrael Snowsar was dead, the Serpent was loose, and Aglirta was doomed.

Worse than that: he'd have to get to the Dwaerindim fast, and find all of them, before the Serpent did. For if Eroeha—who'd helped to enchant the Worldstones—ever got hold of them all, it wouldn't just be Aglirta facing doom.

It would be all of Darsar.

* * *

"But you were Red Dream *last* time," the spectacularly beautiful woman said poutingly, one long-nailed hand posed on a bare hip, and the other holding a red cord still swaying from just being caught.

The taller, darker woman on the far side of the room shrugged and threw her the blue cord, holding out her hand to receive the red one back. "Suit yourself, Raegrel, but mind you match my looks exactly. Darker, see? Longer legs, just here."

The procurer hanging head downward outside the window swallowed. He couldn't quite hear what they were saying, but the one farther away from him seemed to be critical of the nearer one's breasts, and—yes, she'd grasped her own nipples now and was tugging on them, laughing! Gods above, you do know how to torment a man!

He'd never seen any women so *beautiful*, and—

The world exploded in a clap of thunder, there was a flash of darkness, and suddenly shards of glass were tinkling all around him and he was *in* the room, by the Three, and falling helplessly towards that bath-pool! He was going to—

Raegrel snaked out one feminine arm until it was over twenty feet long. Quite long enough, in other words, to slap the ragged little man's back in midair, driving him down headfirst under the water. "Shall I drown him?"

"Stop playing and look out the window!" Thaebred snapped, extending his neck in a grotesque, rubbery thrust of flesh that took his head clear across the room. Frowning, the younger Koglaur did the same, and together they peered out.

And stared at distant, dark coils, the frantic bubbling sounds behind them forgotten.

"W-what is it?" Raegrel asked. "Illusion magic?"

"No," Thaebred whispered. "No, it's not. It's the Great Serpent, come at last."

Silence stretched for a long time before the younger Koglaur asked, in a small and frightened voice, "So what do we do now?"

"Run, hide, and pray."

"What? To the Three Who Heed Not?"

"To every god you've ever heard of," the older Koglaur replied, and did something with a jerk of muscles that freed the procurer from Raegrel's drowning grasp and sent him sailing out through the window.

A moment later, as the far-off snake opened its fangs and struck at something beneath it that they could not see, there came a wet splat from the cobbled street far below.

"He would have been just as dead in here," Raegrel said, a little reproachfully.

"He's still alive," Thaebred said slowly, his eyes on the distant Serpent. "I dropped him onto Jarambur's latest delivery of full wineskins."

Raegrel stared at him. "You mean the street's full of wine?"

"For now. It'll be full of blood when yon Serpent gets here."

Raegrel frowned at the older Koglaur, went a little pale, and swallowed. "You're serious, aren't you?"

Thaebred nodded. "I'm one of the few beings yet alive," he said softly, "who can remember what it was like the last time the Serpent was loose."

Raegrel looked at the older Koglaur. Thaebred was trembling slightly.

He'd never seen Thaebred frightened before. After a moment, he whispered, "So what do we do?"

"I don't know," the older Koglaur replied simply, and turned his head away from the window.

Raegrel watched him retract that long neck, and then, quite suddenly, started to cry.

Thaebred's head turned to look at him. "Come on, Red Dream," he growled. "Pull yourself together—hmmph, literally. We've got a show to do."

* * *

"Dolmur! What was that?" Multhas called, from outside the locked door. He sounded more bewildered than angry, for once.

The oldest surviving Bowdragon smiled thinly and called back, "Multhas, bring everyone. Every living Bowdragon. Here, at once."

"What? Dolmur, what're you playing at? Just *tell* me! Did one of your spells get away from you?"

"No," Dolmur said. "Get the others, and you shall have your answer."

"*Dolmur*, you're . . . you're . . ."

" 'Eccentric but to be indulged' is the appropriate phrase, Multhas. *Go*—this is important!"

Carefully he cast the necessary spells. He was barely done, and the door unlocked, before Multhas was striding into the chamber, with Araunder and Ithim—and, by gods, all of the children, even his own Erith, who was looking as bewildered as usual.

"What you're about to see—" Dolmur said to the younglings, making sure he met the gaze of each and every one of them. Three Above, but his brothers had sired beautiful daughters! As sullen and preening just now as any their age would be, yes, but still . . .

"—is the reason why none of you must go storming off to Aglirta to avenge Jhavarr, or Cathaleira, or the honor of the Bowdragons, or anything else."

Without waiting for any queries or replies he turned his back on them and released the chain of spells he'd just finished crafting.

A window appeared in midair, well off the floor of his spellcasting chamber. It was a window all of them knew: the gem-adorned, circular garden window in his study, or rather, a spell-spun duplicate—and it grew swiftly until it was a huge disc twice as tall as a man, glimmering bright before them.

Through it, then, he showed them what he'd seen. Every detail, just as he'd remembered it, from the flash of darkness accompanying the thunderclap to the serpent lifting its head with bodies dripping from its jaws, only to plunge it down again.

Some of the lasses gasped, and Erith went white and trembled visibly. Dolmur's three brothers, too, grew pale.

"That's the Great Serpent, isn't it?" Araunder asked quietly.

Dolmur nodded. "It is. No illusion, no trickery—and it's not just a huge beast. It's the most powerful archwizard Darsar has ever known, and he may well still be able to use all of his spells. All of us Bowdragons—yes, even if we embraced the Klethlars and the Yarltowers as friends, and cast spells side by side with them—"

He waited for the younglings to make their sounds of anger and disgust at the mere thought of cooperating with their worst rivals, and then continued. "—lack the collective sorcery to harm him more than enough to, say, get his attention. He can destroy us in the space of a few breaths."

"So just like that, Aglirta is off-limits to us? Sirlptar, too, I suppose?" Ithim's oldest daughter—Maelra, yes, *that* was her name—asked angrily, her dark eyes snapping. "Honored Uncle, are you going to use this—this *beast*—to keep us imprisoned, safely locked up here where all of you elders can keep watch over us? And tell us a hundred *more* times the tales of what happened to our mothers because they disobeyed, and strayed?"

"No, Maelra," the oldest living Bowdragon told her sadly, banishing the image of his window with one wave of his hand. "No, I'm not."

"Maelra," Ithim murmured soothingly, "this is not a time for—"

"No, Father, I'm not going to be silent! As Uncle Multhas said when he came in to snatch us away from a very nice spell-show, this is *important*." She whirled back to Dolmur, long hair flying about her shoulders, and asked,

"Then, Honored Uncle"—her tone did not quite make that title a mocking insult, but she came close—"what exactly are you asking us to do?"

"I'm asking all of you younglings not to be fools, not to throw your lives away—and when you must die, to do so to some purpose and with dignity," Dolmur said, his eyes locked on hers.

"Die with dignity?" she asked, bewildered. "You speak as if we'll all be slain on the morrow!"

Dolmur shrugged. "It may be months farther away than that."

"When, then?"

"Whenever the Serpent decides to come here."

The Master of the *Fair Wind* gave her another frowning, questioning look. In a moment, Orathlee knew, he'd ask her again why she'd been so eager to pay the deliberately high price he'd charged, and be away from Sirlptar in such haste.

Yes, here he came, along the rail. This time Orathlee did not turn away. There were only so many places one could go on a sea rel like the *Fair Wind*—particularly when you needed the master of such a ship to keep the more hot-eyed men of his crew away from you and two far-too-beautiful daughters.

The winds were strong and the sea under them a rhythmic series of large but gentle swells. Perfect sailing weather, even to the high cloud and complete lack of storm smell. They were making good time, south to Teln, and had already left Coelortar astern and sighted the long green coast of Elgarth, ahead.

"Goodwoman Orathlee," Master Telgaert said carefully, "'tis good to see you on deck. Most of the few passengers I get huddle below, with buckets to hand, if you know what I mean."

Orathlee gave him a pleasant smile. "Master, I do. Yet

this is fair passage thus far"—she let him see the warding gesture that all make when saying such things at sea, to keep fortune from turning—"and I and my daughters are very grateful to you for taking us aboard in such haste, and with no warning."

Telgaert looked out to sea and shrugged. "The cabin was empty." Carefully not looking at her, he observed, "You seemed to be in some need—and in great hurry."

The words hung between them, and Orathlee smiled ruefully to herself, sighed as soundlessly as she could, and squared her shoulders. This seemed the right time, and it had to be said sooner or later.

"Master Telgaert," she said firmly, putting a hand on his arm so that he turned to look at her, and then stepping smoothly back, "you seem in some need of reassurance. Let me speak plainly: I and my daughters are not running from a brutal husband, I am not guilty of or suspected of a murder, a theft, or an abduction—and you can probably tell, if you look into their faces and mine, that Meleira and Talace *are* my daughters. I am not fleeing a feud or debts, no one in Sirlptar knows or cares that I am gone, and I am not secretly a princess, a shapeshifting monster, or a sorceress. I am not even a young, bored noblewoman out to see the world on a lark. I'm looking for no husband nor lost treasure, and lack all intention of piracy. I'm not even going to rape you."

His embarrassed chuckles had begun way back in her list; her last sentence made his eyes widen, left him in surprised silence for a moment—and then plunged him into a guffaw. A guffaw that built into a full-throated roar of delight.

Telgaert slapped his thigh as crewmen here and there turned their heads to see what was afoot—and knowing they'd be looking, he took a careful pace away from Orathlee, recovered himself, and said, "Well, that's a relief. By the Three, but I like you, Goodwoman!" His grin flashed. "Take that not the wrong way, mind."

"Master, I will not," she said with a smile, "and assure you of one thing more: every word I have told you is true. Plain, on-any-altar truth. You have nothing to fear from me."

Telgaert bowed his head as if they were two master merchants sealing a bargain, and said, "That is always good to hear. Please understand that I'm not trying to pry, but only curious, and perhaps desirous of offering aid if it's something within my power. Orathlee, forgive me, but 'twas clear to me then, as it is now: you left Sirl town in haste, unwillingly, and upset, fleeing something. Is the 'something' a matter you wish to share?"

"Master Telgaert, it is not. Please understand me: not becau—"

Out of a clear sky, a clap of thunder that smote the ears like a fist broke over the ship, and darkness flashed across the blue vault—flashed and was gone again, as sailors shouted their alarm and Telgaert gaped up at the sky.

"What by all the Claws of the Dar—"

"*There*, Master—look there!" Orathlee snapped, pointing north and east across the decks, at the horizon.

Telgaert stared at her, and then along her pointing arm, and saw. Tiny, it was, and yet clear, through the Coelortar Gap: the head of a serpent, rising to brush the clouds, spreading fearsome fangs, and then plunging down out of sight, striking as he'd seen many a fang-viper take a rat in sagging warehouses in the southern ports. As he peered, the ship riding up a swell, it rose into view again; its jaws clamped on prey—and plunged down to strike again.

And then the sea carried them on past the Gap and mountains hid the snake from view. Telgaert turned to regard his passenger with a face that had gone very pale.

"Suppose," he said, in a voice that was not quite steady, "you tell me what that was."

"The Great Serpent," Orathlee told him bluntly. "Not a bardic whimsy or scare-tale for the fireside, after all. *It* is what I'm fleeing—and no, I'm neither a priestess nor a worshipper of the Serpent."

"For the Serpent to be free, the Risen King of Aglirta must be dead," Telgaert murmured, and then his eyes narrowed. "How did you know—?"

"Master," Orathlee said, pulling open her bodice to show him the brands put there on both of her breasts by priests of the Three when she was but a girl, "I am of the Wise. I was doing a tanthor reading for a client, and foresaw this without knowing which great peril of Darsar would befall. I just knew that I did not want to greet that danger, whatever it was, in Sirlptar, city of grasping merchants and cruel wizards."

The Master of the *Fair Wind* was staring at her brands not with horror or lust, but in pity, shaking his head a little. She did not reach to pluck her bodice closed again and tighten the laces, but held her chest calmly out to his gaze, until he dragged his eyes back up to meet hers. "You were but a lass when they did that?" he asked roughly, waving one hand gently to indicate that she should cover herself.

When she nodded, he said, "Lady, my granddam was of the Wise. They flogged her to the bone when she was young, so her shoulders were a ruin and she walked bent over all the rest of her days. All because she could foresee, as you do, and the priests found out." His hand closed into a fist—a fist that shook. "You and your daughters shall have every coin back that you paid me for your passage."

He took a step closer. "Say nothing if you'd rather not, but—where will you go from Teln?"

Orathlee took a step towards him, until they were almost touching, and replied, "Master, I know not. From the Serpent, there is no escape."

"But on the wave," he murmured.

"Telgaert, I can cook," she said brightly, and when he looked down at her sharply, she added, "and heal with herbs, and sew. I've been a slave, and often sewn sails and spliced cables and scrubbed decks and worse. Oh, yes, I have other brands—and probably more impressive scars than any of your crew. Moreover, I'm quite willing to sleep with every man on this ship, often—so long as my Meleira and Talace are left alone until *they* choose to take one of you to bed."

The Master of the *Fair Wind* swallowed and gripped the rail so tightly that his hands went white. "Are—do you know how sailors dream of . . . women?"

"Of course," Orathlee said. "I am of the Wise; dreams are my business."

Telgaert smiled, and held out his hand to her. "Then, Lady, it is my pleasure to accept your offer. I trust our business together will be long and happy."

"Serpent willing," Orathlee murmured, making a warding sign of the Wise. Telgaert matched it with his own fingers, precisely.

When her eyes widened, he smiled, and said, "I am of the Wise, too—but I know little. My granddam died before she could teach me properly, you see." He hesitated. "If you'll join me after eveningfry in my cabin, I'd like to tell you of her. I'll show you my best wine."

Orathlee winked again. "And I'll show you my other scars."

She giggled then, at his shocked look, and took his hand. Arm and arm they went to the way down to her cabin. "You will want to tell your daughters of . . . your decision," Telgaert said, handing her down the ladder.

"And of the Serpent," she added, "if they don't know already."

The Master raised an incredulous eyebrow, and she said, "Oh, yes, they're of the Wise, too—and carry knives. Your men had best be careful."

She left him grinning and shaking his head at the waves, and went down to where Meleira and Talace would no doubt be rolling their eyes and waiting for her, if they'd been mindriding her—or sitting frozen in terror, if they'd been practicing tanthor at the Rising of the Serpent.

She would let them do whatever they wanted, from this

moment forth. Their lives might be all too short, now that the Serpent was loose.

Fangs shrieked on stone as the Serpent bit down—striking not at Hawkril or anyone living, but at the throne itself, biting it right up out of the floor with a violence that hurled the armaragor headlong and shook several Serpent-priests off the gallery.

Their screams went unheeded as that great dark head rose, trailing stones and bodies of the Melted, and lofted once more into the sky.

Craer looked at Embra, and whispered, "Lady of Jewels, what shall we do now?"

She gazed at him incredulously through her tears. "You think I have the barest idea?"

The procurer smiled, as severed arms and legs of Melted tumbled down out of the sky, shrugged, and said, "You're the true nobility among us. Weren't you trained to act just as if everything was unfolding as it should, and you always knew what to do? Well?"

"Craer," she murmured at him, "you are such a mocking little *weasel*—and I love you so much."

"Well," the procurer said brightly, as the great dark head of the Serpent swept down again, jaws agape, "*that's* a comfort. I'll have need of such comforts in my old age."

The next cellar stank of the river—or rather, of the filth Sirl folk sluiced into the river. They must be at the barge docks at last.

Just ahead of him, someone ran into someone else, stumbled, and cursed. The swift reply was a more vicious curse.

The Tersept of Haeltree smiled to himself. Hail, bright conspiracy!

"Lord Baron?" a voice came out of the darkness ahead.

"Report, Suldun," Maevur Cardassa snapped, by way of

a reply. If his manner was intended to impress his fellow conspirators, it failed.

"All is ready, Lord," Suldun murmured. "The wizard says one of the men with you has a shielding spell around him."

"What? Torches, *at once*!" The Baron Cardassa sounded alarmed, and many of the men halted and fired questions; there was some shoving in the gloom.

Torches were brought, and a hired Sirl wizard with them; the baron looked less than happy, after his tirade against wizards, that his staffing secrets had been so soon revealed. "That one," the wizard said, pointing to the Tersept of Shaeltor. The other tersepts hastily drew back from Shaeltor, as if fearing the Sirl mage would hurl a lightning bolt—or Shaeltor would do something just as deadly.

"Why, Shaeltor, you astonish me," Maevur Cardassa said airily—though the sweat beading his face in the torchlight was so copious that his manner fooled no one. "To reach such heights of sorcerous accomplishment, and not tell us? I confess myself wounded!"

Not yet, Haeltree thought to himself, keeping his face a careful mask. *Not quite yet*.

Moving slowly and carefully and keeping his hands in the torchlight, the stout and sweating Tersept of Shaeltor removed a ring from his finger, put it down on the stones underfoot, and stepped back from it. "There's your shielding, I believe," he said. "Please touch it not. My grandsire gave it to me. 'Twas his lucky ring, but now 'tis all I have left of him."

"Not lucky enough, hmm?" Maevur said with a little laugh.

The wizard bent over the ring and straightened, walked towards Shaeltor and waved at him to keep moving away, and then stopped and nodded. "He speaks truth."

"I'm no wizard," the Tersept of Shaeltor said hastily. "I couldn't cast a spell if my life depended upon it."

Haeltree winced. *Oh, don't say such things around this Maevur. You'll but give him ideas.*

"Well, then," the baron said jovially, "it seems our little misunderst—"

A rolling boom that was almost a roar rang through the cellar, like a thunderclap—and the very stones beneath their feet trembled. For just a moment, all the torches went dim, though there was no rush of air—and they blazed brightly again.

Men shouted in alarm, even some of the guards, and the unseen water ahead was suddenly very loud; waves crashed against stone as if an angry sea was clawing at tall cliffs. A moment later, boats began to boom against rock, plunging and rocking wildly, as waves slapped back and forth savagely.

"I'm glad I can't see any of this properly," Haeltree muttered, and one of the guards gave him a heartfelt "aye" before he remembered that Cardassa had given him orders to be menacing to all of these useless tersepts.

"What was *that*?" Maevur Cardassa snapped, his voice more than a little wild.

"Careless and mighty magic," the Tersept of Shaeltor replied darkly, slipping his ring back onto his finger. "What else?"

"Aye, welcome to Aglirta," Tersept Haeltree added in a dry voice, reaching for his belt-flask.

The time for partings had come.

"Remember me," Sarasper Codelmer whispered, white to the lips. "Oh, friends, remember me!"

Craer was bounding out of the way of those gigantic jaws, and Embra had just hurled a beam of ravening Dwaer-fire into the gullet beyond, which made the Serpent roar and hesitate, even draw back for a moment.

Everyone turned to stare at him save the shuddering Serpent above them all, and the old healer managed a crooked

smile for them as he held up the scepter . . . and shifted
shape.

He let the scepter's magic guide him—a sudden surging
of power that warmed him within, even made him uncomfortably hot for a moment, ere he soared, growing larger,
stronger, and more sinuous, scales coming as he loomed still
larger, until the roof scraped his shoulders and back, and the
scepter tumbled from his talons—talons?—to the ground,
crumbling into fragments that trailed smoke. He was billowing up just like smoke, he was . . . a dragon at last!

"Tshamarra!" Embra cried, as she saw the scepter in
Sarasper's hands. "*Now!* At the Serpent, no matter what it
is! Hurl all you have!"

The Talasorn sorceress nodded through the wild tangle
of her hair, murmured something, and a feeble flare of
flame spat from her fingertips.

Gods, I am spent. Embra closed her eyes for a moment
in despair, but kept the Dwaer-fire going. They had to give
Sarasper the few moments he needed . . . or he'd be throwing his life away for nothing—and Aglirta's last hope
would die with him.

It befell with awesome swiftness. Suddenly he was surging upward, the scepter tumbling into smoking ruin, and
then Sarasper billowed up into massive, wide-wingéd solidity above them, red and gold and mighty: a dragon, such
as had not been seen in Aglirta in living memory!

Vast and terrible it loomed, opening its jaws with a terrible roar. Flame spurted from them—a tiny, feeble flame, as
paltry as Tshamarra's spell.

The Serpent swallowed Embra's fire, spasmed in pain,
and then arched itself, drawing its head back. Tshamarra's
flames fell away harmlessly from shimmering black scales
as the Serpent reared—and then struck with the speed of
leaping lightning, sinking its fangs deep into the dragon's
throat.

* * *

Embra choked back tears, white-faced and trembling. There was nothing she dared do now, with those two gigantic bodies locked together. This was their battle now, these titans . . . and one of them had once been the grumbling old man who'd healed her so often and so tenderly. The one with the Serpent's fangs locked on his throat . . .

Sarasper struggled, spasming and clawing at the air, his lashing tail bringing down more of the palace. He tried to twist away from the Serpent—but that great black serpentine body stretched and stayed with him, its fangs sunk deep.

Foaming at the mouth, the Dragon roared, or tried to—but what came out was a strangled croak. Clawing the air, Sarasper tried to straighten, but the Serpent was coiling around him now, its great weight bearing the dragon to the ground.

Sarasper fell on his back with a crash that hurled everyone in the throne chamber into the air—which was a good thing, given the thrashing fury of the Serpent's tail as it busily coiled itself around its foe.

Tshamarra Talasorn sobbed in fear and amazement. How long could the old shapeshifter survive? He was doomed, and all Darsar doomed with him . . .

The two wrestled like mongoose and snake.

Sarasper raked at the Serpent with his taloned feet, shredding its scales and leaving deep, smoking furrows in the scarlet flesh beneath. Smoking gore spilled from those wounds as the Serpent and the Dragon rolled over together, tearing the western rooms of the palace asunder. Shrieking in pain, the Serpent reared back to strike again.

Those great fangs came down, inescapable . . . and

Sarasper darted his snout right into its gullet, wedging those jaws apart. Cruel fangs bit at him, and bit again, trying to close and savage and crush, but failing.

Then the Serpent tried to draw back, but it was coiled around Sarasper, much of its bulk pinned under him, and his neck was long enough to keep his head wedged into the Serpent's maw. Angrily, desperately, he breathed fire.

Again it was feeble, a ragged spitting of flame that flared white for but a moment—but it went in deep, and there were squallings and rumblings somewhere in that vast body. Around his head, the Serpent's jaws opened as it shuddered uncontrollably.

With a growl that shook all Flowfoam, Sarasper Codelmer breathed fire once more—and the world exploded into purple, white, and red-gold flame, forever . . .

The Serpent exploded, and Sarasper with him, in a wet and roaring maelstrom of spattering flesh and searing gore—and as it rained down on everything and Raulin sobbed in terror, the air was riven by the hoarse, raw scream of every last Serpent-priest.

Staggering to his feet and blinking through gobbets of Serpent-flesh, Hawkril saw priests capering up in the shattered, roofless gallery. Some were barking and drooling aimlessly, and others were running in circles. Some stood as still as statues, except for their tremblings and whimperings—and others leaped down into the throne chamber, howling, to their deaths—or ran at jagged spars of broken rock in the galleries, trying to impale themselves. The rest clawed and bit at each other in a bloody, reckless frenzy, literally tearing each other apart as he stared.

The Dwaer-wielding high priest reeled among them, but those watching numbly from below saw his Stone flash—and a shielding sparkle into life around him.

Another priest's body flowed and shifted as they watched, taking on the likeness of an armsman—and just for a moment, but clearly, Embra saw the glimmer of an awakened Dwaer cradled in one of his hands. Feverishly she called on her own Stone to weave a swift tracer, hoping the shapeshifter—a Koglaur?—hadn't laid a trap for anyone trying such a thing . . .

Craer ran up the tallest heap of stone, a sloping slab left behind by Sarasper's struggles, and sprang into the gallery. A dagger flashed from his hands at the shapeshifter as he landed, and he sprinted in its wake, bounding forward to pounce—

—as a Dwaer flashed, and the false armsman vanished. Craer struck empty floor, hard, and skidded along on his elbows until he met with a wall.

Then Embra shrieked as the counterspell she'd feared flared up from her Dwaer and slashed at her with whirling flames. Reeling, she moaned in pain as her garments began to smoulder—and desperately hurled the counterspell on, at the only other Dwaer nearby. Her tracer was broken, and oh, *the pain* . . .

As she crumpled to the shattered, bloody marble, trailing smoke, it was the Serpent-priest's turn to shriek. His Dwaer erupted into flames with such force that he was plucked off his feet and hurled against the nearest wall, the Crown of Aglirta clanging to the tiles.

His Dwaer spun in midair, the shreds of his shattered shielding spinning from it, tantalizingly close. In the shattered throne chamber below, Tshamarra reached up a hand—and then drew it back, shaking her head in disgust. She had not a wisp of magic left to snare anything or harm anyone.

Craer struggled to his feet, wincing, and had not yet seen the unattended Dwaer. Much closer to it, the Serpent-priest stretched forth his hand, fear and determination mingled on a face that scales were fading away from. His snout and wide jaws slowly became more human as he frowned at his Dwaer, willing it to him . . .

. . . and the tendrils of shattered magic faded from the Stone as it drifted to his hand.

Craer was still two desperate running steps away when the priest's hand closed around the Stone—and he vanished, leaving the procurer pouncing on nothing and sliding along the floor again.

Cursing, he glanced down into the throne chamber—and sprang to his feet with a snarl and leaped into space, aiming himself for the largest heap of bodies below. . . .

His landing was a bruising crash that left him limping, but Hawkril was already charging towards the same danger.

Tshamarra had snatched up Embra's Dwaer with a smile. She held it up as they ran towards her, and it began to sing, softly.

Holding it, she knelt over Embra, and did something.

"*Back*, Lady!" Hawkril roared, "or—!"

Without waiting for a reply, he hurled his warsword.

It struck home, deep and true, and Tshamarra Talasorn reeled on her knees, threw back her head and sobbed, and then moaned, "Pluck it out! Pluck it *out*! I can't use this to heal us both!"

"Oh, gods!" Hawkril gasped. "What've I done?"

He reached her a stumbling moment before Craer. "Hold me up," she gasped at them both. "If we break apart, we'll both die, she and I . . ."

With as much tenderness as they could muster, Hawkril and Craer held the sorceress just as she was.

For a long, trembling time the Dwaer-glow pulsed from sorceress to sorceress, ere Tshamarra sat back with a sigh, and said, "She's well. Now, *please*, take your sword out of me. Three, but it hurts!"

"Lady," Hawkril said, his face agonized, "I'm so sorry . . ."

"You couldn't know," she said softly, and then gasped and bit her lip as the warsword came out. "Hold me, as before!" she snapped, almost crumpling in the armaragor's arms.

Hawkril and Craer held her, as Raulin danced anxiously

around them and the Dwaer pulsed, until Tshamarra drew in a deep breath, smiled, and said. "Done. I, too, am whole."

She looked up. "Whither now? Run and hide, to heal and whelm and then fight again as every ambitious fool comes Throne-seeking, or shall we go gathering barons and force them to accept a new king?"

"Why do you care for Aglirta's kings, Lady?" Craer asked softly.

She met his eyes and shrugged. "I'm of Aglirta, too."

"You're Sirl," Hawkril growled slowly.

She whirled around in his arms, to face him. "I was born in Glarond and grew up in the woods and hills there, not in Sirl town." Her tone was fierce, but her words barely louder than a whisper as she stared into his eyes, and added, "I am Aglirtan, and—and I stand with you. For the first time in my life, I'm doing something of worth, something that *matters*."

"Be welcome," Embra said faintly, from beneath her. "And . . . thanks."

"Hey!" Raulin cried suddenly. "Help!"

They looked over at him. He stood pointing down at something amid the tumbled stones, something blackened and smouldering.

"I-it was the tip of the Serpent's tail," the bard said, his face white. "And then it turned into *this*."

By then Hawkril was beside him, warsword in hand. Amid the stones lay the tattered, blackened body of a man, its face little more than a sheet of bubbled flesh with two eyesockets and a mouth. That mouth moved, trembling, trying to speak, and one stump of an arm—the only arm it had, the overduke realized—reached up towards him.

With a snarl of rage and revulsion Hawkril hacked at it, shearing through that arm and then cleaving the head, again and again, until—

His warsword exploded in ringing, riven shards that spun past his face and sent him staggering back.

"*Hawk*!" Craer shouted. "Here!"

Hawkril turned, blinking—and a dagger spun towards him, turning lazily, tossed by the procurer. Hawkril plucked it out of the air and raised it to stab down—but the body of the mage who'd become the Serpent so long ago was burning as he stood over it . . . dwindling, as he watched, to nothing. Dead and gone.

Just like Sarasper and Brightpennant.

19

Entertaining the Gods

The light of the scrying spell faded, and the man staring into it snarled in irritation. It flared back brightly
once, showing him an enraged armaragor hacking at the
charred, feebly moving remnants of a man, but then died
completely, falling away into a scattering of sparks that
winked out, one by one.

"By the Three," Ingryl Ambelter said thoughtfully to the
warm darkness of his refuge, "but I did the right thing for
once. If I'd stood against them—"

"Spellmaster?" a voice called, from behind him. Gods, it
must be coming from near the entrance to his refuge—but
on the *inside*.

Ingryl whirled around, snatched up two wands, and took
two swift steps to fire them down the entrance tunnel.
Streams of fire roared, and he let them rage for a long time
before he called back sweetly, "Yes? Which fool is it?"

"This one," the Baron Phelinndar replied crisply, stepping through the doorway with Ingryl's flames still curling
vainly around his strong shielding. He held what had spun
that shield in his hand: a glowing Dwaer-Stone.

"I'm enough of a fool," he announced calmly, "to know
that I don't know how to use this properly—but I've bound

myself to it, so any treachery you do to me will also be visited on *you*." He strode forward. "I need you to conquer Aglirta, and you need me. Have we the beginnings of a deal here?"

Ingryl swallowed, set down his wands, and waved the baron towards a vacant chair. "I suppose we do," he said faintly. "Claws of the Dark One, but I used to think I knew who was whom in Aglirta, and what spell would defeat which. Now . . ."

"It's never too late to learn new tactics, I believe," the baron observed calmly. "Have you any wine to share that isn't poisoned?"

After a moment of startled silence, Ingryl threw back his head and laughed.

Meanwhile

Somewhere, in darkness, Ezendor Blackgult and Flaeros Delcamper fell forever.

There were no stars, no sounds, and—nothing. Nothing but endless tumbling. They were falling slowly through nothingness to the accompaniment of the regent's ceaseless flood of oaths. Blackgult cursed softly, on and on, spewing forth a great splendor of words that left the young bard marvelling.

When at last the regent grew tired, or ran out of fearsome phrases, and fell silent, Flaeros asked timidly, "Did I do something wrong, Lord?"

"No," Blackgult said shortly, "I did. The scepter has a 'take refuge' power of some sort, and I aroused it when I meant to do something else. That's what comes of snatching up in battle something one has only read about, and trying to use it."

He glanced about, all around them, and spread his hands in a flourish to better indicate—nothing. "We're in a place that only magic can reach—an endless void, if the books tell true . . . and they seem to." Fixing Flaeros with a sour gaze, he asked, "So, young Delcamper, do you have any *other* little surprises for me?"

"I . . . no . . . well, what d'you mean?"

"Magic, and suchlike—are you carrying any?"

"N-no . . . well, wait. Just this," the bard said slowly, extending the hand where he always wore the Vodal.

Blackgult seized hold of his fingers, peered at the ring with a frown, and nodded slowly. "I believe this'll do. It'll cost us both blood and the ring—but it will return us to Aglirta. The alternative is to be trapped here forever, I believe—though we'll probably lose interest in 'forever' when we starve." He glanced up. "Shall I?"

Flaeros stared at the Vodal. Familiar, comforting, the family treasure he'd always worn . . . he ran his fingers over its familiar curves one last time, then looked at the regent. "Yes. Serpent and all, we must go back."

Blackgult nodded grimly, and drew his dagger.

Flaeros looked at him warily, but the regent grinned. "Just a little blood, lad—I'm not looking to cut your throat."

"Everyone *else* in Aglirta seems to be trying to," Flaeros complained, and the regent laughed as he nicked the back of the young bard's arm and murmured something. Then he cut himself, made the same murmur, and held out his hand for the Vodal.

Reluctantly Flaeros gave it to him. Baron Blackgult touched it to his own blood and then to the bard's, said the last incantation of his spell, looked up with a grin, and said, "Just wait until you're a baron, lad. *Then* ask your throat how hunted it feels."

A moment later, with a sudden whirl of blinding lights and a roar of sound, Aglirta came back to them.

"Quick—*run*! Serpent-priests!" Narneth hissed, shoving his sister's shoulder. She shrieked and plunged away through the rindolberry vines, leaving generous amounts of hair and her dress behind on various thorns as she crashed along—and Narneth pounded after her, just as uncaring of his hide.

Berries spilled out of the basket on Briona's arm, but she cared not. To be caught here nigh the altar would be their deaths.

Not for the first time, Narneth wondered angrily *why*, in all the Vale, the Snake-lovers had to choose the very best rindolberry patch for their altar. Not that he minded watching ladies bare themselves and dance about it, mind—but seeing them grow scales and snake-heads and fang each other brought on the shivers.

Worse than that—they'd stopped using the drum. Its slow beat chilled the heart, to be sure, but gave clear warning the Snake-lovers were coming. Now they were just suddenly—*there*, some of them slithering along like gigantic snakes with human arms. Most of them were still people—people with slit eyes and a few scales and fangs and forked tongues, yes, but *people*. There were a few, though . . . well, more than a few, who had snake-heads all the time, or tails, or both. They gave Narneth nightmares— and just seeing them from afar set Briona to screaming.

"Quiet," he hissed, catching up to her. "Y'want them to come after us?"

Together he and Briona crawled on to where they could crouch under a tangle of thorny vines, where the rindol lay looped and draped thickly over dead trees. Narneth chose the best gap to peer out of, and Briona just laid herself down, panting like a forge bellows.

They were coming. Snake-heads suddenly slid into view, regarding the world expressionlessly with forked tongues flicking. Six—no, seven full serpents, with half serpents walking behind. A dozen, or more.

Two of the lightly scaled ones carried a terrified village lass—one of the Alhand girls, the one who worked at the mill—tied to a pole slung between them. They'd torn away most of her clothes, and her wrists and ankles were bound over the pole with—curling, angry snakes! Other snakes lashed her throat to the pole, and another was jammed into her mouth, tail first, so she couldn't do more than moan. Her eyes were wide with terror—and Narneth shivered and sank down as low as he could as the Snake-lovers carried her past.

They were going to make her into one of them—or more likely, sacrifice her!

Yes. The ones to be made priestesses did their own walking, while priests whipped them with living snakes; this one must be a sacrifice.

She'd be laid on the altar while they hissed prayers and set one poisonous snake after another on her. She'd be bitten until she went mad and died, foaming at the mouth and with her skin gone purple—and then they'd roast her over their spit, and feast.

Narneth had watched such deaths before, though he never stayed long. Afterward, the Serpent-priests always spread out through the forest, to hunt.

"What's happening?" Briona whispered, trembling. Narneth put a stern finger to his lips and crawled a little way along under the vines, to where he could see the altar.

Serpent-priests were busy around the fire, lighting kindling above the cold coals of their last feast. Narneth watched them with fear and hatred coiling together in his belly, feeling increasingly sick . . . and then it happened.

One moment the priests were strutting or slithering about with their usual cold arrogance—and the next moment they went mad. The two carrying the girl dropped her and went for each other, biting and clawing at each other bare-handed, while one of the almost-snakes ahead of them drew itself up and started hammering itself against the ground, its head thudding down repeatedly before another snarling priest slammed into it, dashing its brains out against the stone altar. He was promptly bent over the altar himself by another priest armed with a knife made of snakes' fangs and stabbed repeatedly until his kickings and

screams grew feeble. Other serpents bit at each other in a
frenzy, or threw their coils around everything in sight, trying to crush and throttle. One tried to devour its own tail,
biting repeatedly, up and up the thickening scales, until it
choked.

Narneth shivered and backed away. He was almost back
to Briona before he remembered the Alhand girl, hesitated,
and slowly crawled back again.

By then, though some coils and tails still twitched and
thrashed, the Serpent-lovers were all dead. When Narneth
took his belt-knife to the snakes that bound the mill lass—
Jalebra, he remembered her name, now—and freed her,
there was no sound for a long time but her weeping as she
clung to him, and the occasional snap and crackle from the
neglected fire.

The hissings he hated so much were silenced forever.

The meal had been splendid, and so was the wine, though
Orathlee had been somewhat startled to receive it in a
tankard—a tankard that comfortably held the contents of
an entire bottle, at that.

"No needless glass aboard ship that might break with
the seas," Telgaert explained, "and I got tired of goblets
toppling, too. Was the fare—?"

"Wonderful," Orathlee told him, as she stretched con-
tentedly and lay back on his bed in the narrow cabin—and
meant it. "I don't know that I can match it."

"You don't have to. Three of us can cook: gruel, fish-
head stew, fried fish with sauces, and—after we've stopped
in at a good port, a roast fowl fry-up like this. That's the
entire span of our fare."

"Oh," Orathlee replied, nodding as she sipped from her
tankard. "I can see how that would be . . . less than ideal,
as the months pass."

"Salt fish by the barrel in winter, and sometimes eels

snagged over the rail, too," Telgaert added brightly. "I almost forgot."

She giggled, and he left off caressing her bare feet to take a generous swig from his tankard (even larger than hers, and adorned with an ornate coiling-dragon handle) and reached higher.

"If I may be so bold—?" he asked softly, his eyes suddenly serious, as his hand went to the lacings of her bodice.

"You may," she purred, reaching for his codpiece, "if *I* may be allowed to unfasten *this*."

Telgaert's eyes widened, and a wide grin flashed across his face. Shaking his head in mirth, he said grandly, "But of course, my Lady. How can I refuse?"

"Well, cursing and rolling away is the usual way," she replied, as gentle fingers peeled back fabric and her breasts were bared to the gentle breeze blowing in through the porthole. "But if you'd rather . . ." She gestured down at herself.

"I would," he murmured, and bent forward to lightly kiss her skin. Again, and again, like the brush of a moth.

"I'm not ticklish," she murmured. "You needn't be . . . tender."

His response was the lick of his tongue, slowly and teasingly over the twisted flesh of a brand to her left nipple. Orathlee sighed and arched to meet him, murmuring something wordless as she reached her tankard over onto the bedside shelf, to free both her hands to get to work properly on the laces of his codpiece.

He took hold of her nipple in his teeth and bit down, very gently.

"Yes," she encouraged him. "Harder."

He obeyed, tugging gently, and she twisted under him, moaning slightly—and then she shuddered, jerked back from him until her nipple tore free of his teeth, trailing blood, and shoved him away, sitting up frantically, and drumming one frustrated fist on the bed linens.

"Lady?" Telgaert asked, in hurt astonishment. "What befalls? Have I—done something amiss? I—ah—"

"No," she gasped, wide-eyed, seizing one of his hands in both of her own and pulling it to her breast. "Something just happened. The Serpent is—*gone*."

As if her words had been a signal, there was a sudden, heavy pounding on the cabin door. Telgaert spun around to stare at it, and then back at her. Then he choked back a curse, pulled his hand away, and bounded to his feet.

"Yes?" he snapped, bending his ear close to the door, between the heavy bolts he'd thrown into place earlier. "What befalls?"

There was no reply—but after a moment, the pounding resumed, mixed with sharp knuckle rappings. From several small hands, it sounded like.

Telgaert threw a sharp glance at Orathlee. She hastily laced herself up and swung herself from the bed to his desk chair, reclaiming her tankard on the way.

The moment she was settled, Telgaert threw the bolts and pulled the door open.

Meleira was standing in the dark passage outside, with Talace peering over her shoulder.

"Well, they didn't *get* very far," Talace said, sounding disappointed. "Perhaps they *were* just talking about his grandda—"

Meleira elbowed her. "*Hush*," she snapped. "This is serious." Shooting a glance at Telgaert, she added crisply, "My apologies, Master. We've no intention of making a habit of disturbing you two—but this once, there's something my mother must know." She looked straight at Orathlee without waiting for his reply.

"Yes?" Orathlee asked softly, setting aside her tankard again—and already suspecting what was to come.

"I laid out tanthor," Meleira said, her eyes very large and dark, "and Doomdeath came up, over the Great Serpent. Twice I cast the cards—and twice, the same. One thing more, both times: Dragonfire."

"The Dragon has slain the Serpent," Orathlee whispered, and her face was suddenly awash with tears.

A silent flood of streaming tears, out of nowhere. "The last thing my mother ever said to me . . ." Orathlee managed to choke out through them, before real weeping took her. Her daughters stared—and then ran to her.

Telgaert awkwardly reached out an arm to comfort her, and then drew it back to let Meleira and Talace embrace her instead.

"Mother, what is it?" Meleira asked anxiously, holding her tightly.

"I thought it was a curse, or a way of telling me 'never,'" Orathlee struggled to tell her, and then threw back her head to draw in a shuddering breath. Her daughters saw that hers were happy tears, and some of the fierceness went out of their embrace—enough to let their mother reach out over Talace's shoulder for Telgaert.

"Mother told me I'd find my true man, my soul mate," she told him with a watery smile, "when the Dragon slew the Serpent."

Blackgult and Flaeros stared around the Throne Chamber of Flowfoam, at ruin everywhere.

It was now entirely open to the sky above them—and from what could be seen through the doors to the south, most of the palace in that direction was now rubble. Hawkril was grimly swording the last few Serpent-priests, and many more scaled men with forked tongues drooping from slack mouths were already draped dead over tumbled rocks in every direction. Flies were swarming thickly above the rest of the shattered room, where armsmen and armaragors lay heaped head high, and the stink of cooked flesh was strong. Raulin was wandering rather dazedly among the dead, silently mouthing names of those he recognized, trying to see and remember who had fallen here—as a good bard should.

Nearer at hand, Craer stood watchfully, with a dagger ready to throw, and beside him the Talasorn sorceress was kneeling over Embra Silvertree, one of her hands on the Dwaer glowing on Embra's breast—and the other pointing right at the new arrivals, in case it would prove swiftly necessary to blast them with magic.

A smile quirked the edge of Blackgult's mouth. "You didn't take very good care of the place," he commented, waving a hand at all the devastation.

"Father!" Embra cried, rolling over hastily. "Father, Sarasper's dead, and Brightpennant, too! I know not how to use the Dwaer to bring them back! Help us!"

She held out the Dwaer towards him, a tendril of glowing mist swirling up from it, but Blackgult shook his head sadly as he went to her and knelt to caress her cheek, and then gently wipe away the tears that started to trickle down it.

"From this sort of death," he said gently, lifting a hand to indicate the ruined room around them, "with magic surging through everything, there's no coming back."

Someone sobbed above him, and the Regent of Aglirta glanced up. Tshamarra Talasorn stood with her fists clenched at her sides, trembling. There were tears streaming down her face, too—but her glare down at Blackgult was like a lance of fire. There was a needle-bladed black dagger in one of her fists, but Craer had hold of that wrist, and his own dagger now menaced her.

Weeping in earnest, now, she turned her head away, and let go of her dagger, kicking it away before Craer could. "I—I . . ."

She whirled back to glare at him again, jerking Craer with her as if he was a child's puppet, and snarled, "I've s-sworn to slay you. And now, I—*damn* you!"

She bent over, lost in sobs and shaking. Blackgult put a hand on Craer's shoulder and jerked his head in a silent "get hence" command. The procurer nodded, let go of the sorceress, and quietly stepped back.

Blackgult reached down, heaved—and suddenly a star-

tled Tshamarra Talasorn was being carried in his arms like
a little girl, cradled against his torn and dusty black as the
Regent of Aglirta strode carefully along through broken
marble and fallen rubble, heading for the most empty corner of the room.

She stared up at him, face contorting as she fought to
control her tears and her rage. Ezendor Blackgult set her
down on a slab of fallen stone so large that it could serve as
a seat, reached to his belt, and then put a worn and heavy
dagger in her hand.

She stared at it, and up at him in bewilderment, sniveling.

Blackgult stooped until he was facing her, with their
heads level—and his face and throat were within easy
reach of the dagger. "Lady Talasorn," he asked gravely,
"how much blood is an oath worth?"

She set her teeth, jaw trembling, and said, "I don't
know." It was more a sob than a firm utterance.

"Nor do I," he told her, "and I've shed a lot of blood
and broken a lot of oaths. I've kept more, but I don't
know if the Three look down on me any more kindly for
that."

He looked over her shoulder and years into the past,
sighed, and said, "I've made two bad mistakes—two very
evil deeds. Seducing Embra's mother without slaying her
husband first, and invading the Isles. Both of those, I deserve to die for."

He looked straight into her eyes, and added firmly, "As
for the rest of my deeds or misdeeds, I ask no forgiveness
nor feel any need for it. I did what I had to do. I *am* sorry
your family has paid so much, in lives and grief. I've felt
such pain, too, but I suppose such words seem empty comfort to you."

Tshamarra looked back at him, and then down at the
dagger in her palm. She'd still not closed her fingers around
it. "Why," she whispered, "have you given me this?"

Blackgult shrugged. "If you slay me, it will be . . . a re-
lease. I've nothing to hide from the Three; they know me

all too well." He smiled faintly. "Yet they never seem to want to see me."

"It's a failing we share, I think," Hawkril said softly, from behind him. For all his size, the armaragor had come up to them out of all the drifting smoke and death in uncanny quiet, a borrowed blade ready in his hand.

"Or perhaps," Craer said slowly from behind Tshamarra, over the keen edge of yet another ready dagger, "they judge us to be a source of peerless entertainment."

White waves curled up from the bows of four barges as they raced up the Silverflow, thrust knifelike against the current by magic.

The tersepts on the second boat glanced often at the two hired Sirl wizards in their midst. Those mages were white-faced and sweating already from the strain of holding their spells together, but the barges were racing along, faster than the Tersept of Haeltree had once sailed downriver—and that had been in a small boat whose sails were filled with a strong wind.

Baron Cardassa smiled and drew his sword. It gleamed mirror-bright, and when he flourished it, the blade gave off a faint green glow. "While we were in Sirlptar," he announced, "I bought this blade. It's enchanted—to cleave armor like a kitchen maid guts an eel, I'm told!—and I don't think I'll tell you just how much I had to pay for it!"

"Either he stole it, or he can't count without servants holding out their fingers," Haeltree murmured to Shaeltor—who snorted in agreement.

"With this goodly steel," Maevur Cardassa boasted, waving it above his head as if to hack invisible river gulls into diced fowl and drifting feathers, "we cannot fail! The River Throne shall be ours forthwith!"

They *were* moving very fast, but Ibryn had just fallen astern and the towers of Ool were in sight; it was still a long way to Flowfoam. One tersept glanced at the sky, as farmers do when judging how much day is left to them, and the baron saw it.

Scowling, he swung around—almost gutting a guard in the process. "Faster," he snapped at the two sweating wizards, waving his magic blade. Emboldened by the flash it made then, he thrust it aloft, his belly wobbling in the wake of that grand movement, and laughed aloud. "Aye, we *cannot* fail!"

"I want to see—just once, and from a safe distance—the shop where he bought yon tunic . . . or anything else that size!" the Tersept of Shaeltor muttered.

"The shop where he stole it, more like," Haeltree muttered back.

Maevur looked down from being entranced by his blade and grinned around the boat—a grin that slid off his face into sickly, crestfallen quivering when he saw that no one was looking.

Sweeping his sword down to point straight at the Sirl mages, he snarled, "Faster, or whoever was hurling those spells earlier will be fathering heirs and feasting ere we get to the throne he's sitting on!"

One of the wizards reeled, and then fell over sideways in his seat, his eyes going dark. The boats slowed suddenly, wash dying away around their bows, and tersepts sprang to their feet, looked at the stricken mage and the terrified one who hadn't yet collapsed—and started to swear, horribly.

"Lord Regent," Tshamarra Talasorn said faintly, "please take your dagger back. I'm going to break the first oath of my life." She turned her head to peer at the procurer standing ready to slay behind her, and added wryly, "Even if it does leave Overduke Delnbone deeply disappointed."

Craer spread his hands in an exaggerated feint of utter innocence that fooled not a single watching eye.

Blackgult smiled down at the sorceress—who managed a shaky smile back at him—collected his dagger, and raised her to her feet like a courtier.

"And now, I suppose, the hard and slow work begins," he said to her with a sigh. "Rebuilding. These overdukes of mine always seem to have the fun of destroying things in wild battle, and never—"

"Father," Embra said softly. "*Please*. Sarasper died for us all, and . . . and . . ."

Blackgult whirled to take her in his arms, "Three Above, but I'm sorry, lass," he said quickly. "I—forgive a fool."

"Aye," Embra told him shakily, "of course." A crooked smile touched her lips then, and she added meaningfully, "I've been doing a lot of that."

A loud, triumphant hiss from above overrode her last word—and everyone tensed and looked up.

In the roofless gallery above, on the very crumbling edge of the riven throne chamber ceiling, stood a Serpent-priest, and the Crown of Aglirta shone in his scaled hand.

With a flourish he crowned himself, hissing, "Sssso! Aglirta hasss a fitting ruler at lassst!"

Then he flung himself aside with snake-swift speed, and Craer's hurled dagger flashed over his shoulder to tinkle and clang harmlessly down a wall.

With a high, wordlessly gibbering cackle of laughter, the Serpent-priest pranced across the gallery, avoiding another dagger by apparent luck, and clambered up a sagging ultharnwood great-arch wardrobe to the onetime ceiling of the gallery, heading for the roof.

Hawkril growled, hefted the sword he'd salvaged from Bloodblade—and threw it, hard.

End over end it whipped, large and heavy enough to howl a little as it sliced air.

"Pulls to the left," Craer commented.

"Aye, Cleverfingers," Hawkril agreed, "but 'tis to the left he'll have to go, to climb around that jutting bit of vaulting, and—*yes*."

To the armaragor's satisfaction, the drooling, gibbering Snake-priest stopped capering long enough to swing himself up towards the sky—and straight into the path of the hurled sword. He stiffened as it took him through one shoulder, overbalanced backwards, and they saw its bloodred tip standing out of his chest as he began a swift and tumbling return to the gallery that ended with a wet, bouncing crash.

The Crown of Aglirta rang once on floor tiles, above, and arced down into the throne chamber. Hawkril did not even have to take a stride to put out his hand and catch it.

"Hawkril!" someone cried, from a ruined doorway. It was a bedraggled, smudge-faced Flowfoam gardener, with his fellows behind him—and, by the looks of once-grand finery, one or two courtiers who'd been hiding wherever the gardeners had taken refuge, too. "King Hawkril! Long live King Hawkril, and Aglirta with him!"

A few servants peered hesitantly into the ruined throne chamber through other doors, now—and took up the cry.

Hawkril shook his head and turned to Blackgult, holding out the crown.

The regent shook his head, too. "None of the barons will agree to me ruling them longer—or, unless I read them but poorly, accept any from among their ranks, either. Someone new is needed." He looked right back at the huge armaragor. "A man such as Hawkril Anharu."

The warrior overduke shook his head again—and then, suddenly, turned to Embra. "Lady," he said gently, holding out the crown to her. "This is more your calling than mine."

The Crown of Aglirta glittered in his hand, before her.

Embra looked down at it, and then back up at him. "The people have named you," she said softly. "Take up your throne, Hawkril. Let the good folk of Aglirta be heard and heeded, for once. Rule well, Hawk."

Hawkril backed away from her, his eyes almost pleading. "What, sit on a throne and grow old, waiting for the day when someone decides to ride in and hew me down? Nay, let us have something different for Aglirta! The Serpent's dead,

and the Risen King, too. Blackgult sired you, of Silvertree—
Embra, take the Crown and rule as Queen of Aglirta!"

Embra shook her head, and there were tears in her eyes
again. "It's not that simple," she said in a rough voice, and
then cleared her throat and said steadily, "As Sarasper said
to me: it's never that simple."

The points of drawn swords ringed the last wizard, who
was gasping and shuddering, his face growing more lined
and cavernous by the minute. The barges seemed almost to
fly along, though, and the tersepts raised a cheer as they
rounded one last bend and caught sight of Flowfoam in the
distance.

"Can't . . . go on," the mage gasped then, his face a dripping mask of sweat. Ribbons of blood were running from
his nose and mouth now.

A hard-faced tersept put his sword to the wizard's
throat. "Do it," he snapped, "or die. In the new Aglirta,
wizards will know their place at last, and do our bidding—
or pay with their lives."

"Knowing wizards," the old man gasped, "I cannot help
but conclude that you'll soon have an acute shortage of
persons who can work magic." And with those words, his
eyes rolled up in his head, and he toppled forward to the
deck planks, landing with a heavy crash.

The barges slowed to a stop very swiftly, turned a little
in the water . . . and then started to drift backwards in the
tug of the Silverflow.

"We're almost there! Start rowing!" Baron Cardassa
shouted, dancing with rage—then, with a little scream of
fury, he swung his magic blade, slashing at the tersept
who'd threatened the wizard. As promised, it sliced armor
like eel flesh on a cutting board—and blood sprayed from
the tersept's opened throat.

Gurgling, the man reeled and fell out of the barge, the
Silverflow swallowing him with the smallest of splashes.

"Any other fools?" the baron roared, looking murderously around the boat. No one met his eyes or replied—but when he strode to the prow, growling, his back prickled under the weight of all the murderous glances that were directed back at him.

"Whoever reigns," the Regent of Aglirta growled, "his—or her—rule must begin with the fealty of the barons. Let's have them here." He stretched out his hand to the Dwaer Embra held, and it flashed.

Flashed, and flashed again. With each burst of light, someone new stood in the room, blinking around in bewilderment—and then, with awe, at the devastation. Baron Maevur Cardassa was one of the first. The Tersept of Bladelock appeared beside him, and they exchanged sharp looks—what of the barges? And all their armsmen? What *now*?—ere the Tersepts of Ironstone, Varaedur, and Starntree appeared, in swift succession.

"Hmm," Blackgult murmured, after some dozen tersepts stood facing him, "'twould appear that Phelinndar has a Dwaer. Or someone with him, who knows how to ward with it as swift as—sorry—a snake."

Craer sighed and turned towards the door. "Right," he said, "I haven't forgotten our mission. Where's his castle, again?"

Tshamarra Talasorn surprised herself, then, by bursting out laughing.

Cardassa's armsmen exchanged startled looks with his bodyguards as the fat baron was suddenly no longer on the barge with them—and then, before their eyes, one tersept after another vanished, too, leaving their oars unmanned and dragging.

"What, by the *Dark One*—?" Suldun snarled, half drawing his sword, but seeing no foe to bury it in.

"The wizards!" one of the armsmen snapped, pointing at the men of Sirlptar sprawled senseless on the deck boards. His sword flashed out of its sheath, and then stabbed—nowhere, as Suldun's blade met it in an iron-strong parry.

"Don't be a *fool*," he rasped. "Do these old men look like they can harm a *mouse* with spells, right now? No, there's something worse afoot, som—"

"*Enough* shouting!" Maevur Cardassa snarled from behind him. "Do you want all Flowfoam to hear us! Put those swords away—do you see *me* prancing around, waving *my* swor—oh."

Suldun swung around, his jaw dropping. His whirling was enough to shield the dozen or so armsmen who couldn't stifle sputters of mirth at the fat baron's rueful expression and hasty sheathing of his so-splendid magic sword.

The armsman he'd parried, however, was not smiling. His eyes were narrowing, and he was shouting, "He—you—the baron! He just appeared, out of the air! I *saw* him! And his face was all twisted, looking like someone else! Magic! Foul magic!"

"Don't be a fool," said a tersept who'd just reappeared at the baron's elbow—doing just what the armsman had described, in full view of all the staring armsmen on the barge. "Have you never sailed under arms to Flowfoam before? There's a spell-barrier, that snatches each one of us away and makes sure we're not ensorcelled, to keep the—well, to keep the Throne safe." He smirked. "Luckily, it does nothing to peer at our thoughts."

More tersepts vanished—and reappeared—as he spoke. One of them was the Tersept of Ruldor, an old and humorless man, and he strode straight to the baron and muttered something in his ear.

The baron looked devastated, and then at a loss. Then with sudden energy he drew his sword, pointed at the nearest dock—a ramshackle fisherfolk-shared affair of leaning pilings and rotting boards—and said, "Turn in and make fast! We've been detected, and twenty wizards wait at Flowfoam to slay us!"

"So we'll wait for them to come and slay us here?" one of the armsmen snapped.

The baron looked at him in wide-eyed rage, wattles quivering—and grew a sly look that descended rapidly into glee. "No, that's the lovely part of it," he hissed conspiratorially. "If we but wait, they'll very soon fall to fighting among themselves—there's a confrontation brewing in the throne chamber itself!—and on the morrow, we'll stroll in and take the Crown of Aglirta after all!"

There were grumbles of discontent from various of the armsmen, but the tersepts were all nodding vigorously. Moreover, the current was strong, and the dock was near at hand, whereas Flowfoam was a long, hard row against the fastest part of the river. The barges turned towards shore.

"Isn't Thaebred going a little heavy on the overacting?" one tersept muttered to the next, so low-voiced that no one else could hear.

"For playing Maevur Cardassa? I don't know that it's *possible* to overact, doing that," the tersept who usually answered to the name of Raegrel—or, these last few days, to Red Dream—answered.

The other Koglaur snorted. "I've never seen so many of us gathered in a single whelming before," he murmured, leaning even closer, "and I'm not sure many of these armsmen believed my little spell-barrier tale. Nor do they look like they believe in ghosts. They'll have us pegged as evil wizards, and will be watching for the slightest little spellwork."

"You're probably right," Raegrel muttered back, "but why shouldn't they believe in ghosts? There *are* ghosts. I've seen them."

The other Koglaur smiled. "Of course you have. They're

not as plentiful as we need to them to be, though. I've spent a lot of time being a ghost, to a lot of Aglirtans."

Raegrel stared at him, decided he was being truthful, and shuddered. Suddenly, the minor humiliations of being Red Dream in front of a lot of lust-ridden men thrice a night didn't seem like such a hard punishment.

The Tersepts of Haeltree and Shaeltor exchanged wary, fearful looks. A glance down the line of newly arrived nobility in the throne chamber told them they were among the calmest of Blackgult's sudden summonings.

There was a smell of fear in the room. Not a man among the nobles lacked guilty secrets—and some of them had been positively frenzied in their race to do treason, since swearing fealty to King Snowsar.

And Regent Blackgult, standing tall in his tattered garb amid all this ruin, did not look like a happy man.

"Welcome," he said at last, when they'd begun to stir and murmur among themselves, "traitors."

That brought icy, quivering silence down upon the room. Blackgult smiled, and added, "But no more of such unpleasant words now—it's all too late, and for Aglirta, everything's changed. I could spin you a long and clever tale of intrigues and treacheries and would-be usurpers, but most of you know more of it than you'll want to admit, and it really comes down to this: the River Throne and much of Flowfoam Palace have been destroyed in sorcerous battle, many folk have lost their lives, and among the dead are these individuals who should be important to us all: King Kelgrael Snowsar, who took his own life trying to bind or slay the Awakened Serpent; the warlord Bloodblade, who sought to seize rule of this land by force; the dread Serpent itself; and Overduke Sarasper Codelmer, who was a healer, and took the shape of a dragon to die slaying the Serpent— that we all may live. He joins King Snowsar among the greatest heroes of Aglirta."

There was silence as Blackgult turned away, but a murmur quickly arose behind him—and he whirled around to still it again with the words, "But there'll be time to honor such great men later. We are gathered here to rescue what they saved for us: the realm of Aglirta. Someone must rule, and who 'tis we must choose now—and, for once, *also* choose to be loyal."

He looked again at Hawkril, but the armaragor backed away.

"No, no—no thrones for me," he growled. His eyes fell on Raulin, who was standing with Flaeros watching the proceedings with eagerness and awe—and he strode over and plucked the boy forward. "Here," the warrior overduke said fiercely. "Here be your king!"

"He's just a boy!" a tersept gasped.

"Aye, so? Fewer feuds and grudges and little debts than the rest of you," Craer Delnbone said lightly, his mocking tone almost a challenge. "And if he does ill, we'll set him straight or send him to his grave soon enough. We overdukes must watch over the realm, as we were bid."

Raulin stared around at all of the gazes suddenly bent on him, most of them openly incredulous or hostile, and went both bone-white and wild-eyed—before he suddenly spewed up his last meal, all over the well-trodden body of a Melted that lay sprawled under stones in front of him.

"Aye," Blackgult agreed in a dry voice, "he just might make a king, at that. He's wiser than most kings—and almost all lads. No bright excitement for a crown, just horror at what it means."

Baron Cardassa drew himself up. "Kneel to *that*? Some motherless *boy*? Do you insult us all deliberately? Do you seek to goad us all to war, and so doom Aglirta? Do—"

"Do you *shut up*!" the Tersept of Haeltree snapped, from not far down the line. When Maevur Cardassa trembled in whelming rage, the tersept added brightly, "O most masterful of conspirators!"

And then the nobles were all sneering and spitting scorn

at once, loudly ridiculing the very idea of choosing some random boy to be king over all Aglirta—only to be stilled by a thunderous roar from a most unexpected source.

"You will all *be still*!" Flaeros Delcamper shouted, his face as red as ruby wine. In startlement they fell silent, blinking at the young and slender buffoon who was now dancing on his toes with anger, that same rage making him bolder than he'd ever been in his life before. "*Listen to me*, Lords High and Mighty!" he snarled. "And heed—for once! I've heard quite enough preening and sitting in judgement from barons and tersepts in my life to fill a library of sneering words—but in my very few years of seeing Aglirta, I've also seen many brave folk fighting, with barons and tersepts either the very villains they must struggle against, or nowhere to be seen when the realm needs them! Where were you when Bloodblade came riding up the Vale, swording knights and armsmen alike for the crime of staying loyal to their sworn oaths of fealty? Where were you when the Serpent-priests made sacrifices of your own people whom you were sworn to protect, on land you were sworn to keep safe and peaceful? Where were you just now, when your king needed you and the Throne stood unguarded?"

A chorus of sneering shouts began, but Flaeros cut them off with a bitter, louder shout: "*No!* No, my Lords, your answers don't matter! If you choose to mock at the regent's choice, I choose to mock at your excuses and your intrigues and your own mockings—and, Lords, *I* am a *bard*! When I mock, the world hears! From Carraglas to Gloit, from the shops of Sirlptar to the taverns in your own towns and villages, folk will hear my mockeries of you! Yes, and they'll sing along, and whisper my words at your backs, and tell their sons and daughters, and long after I am dead and gone—and you are dead and gone, too, taken by the Three just as we all are, for all your fancy titles—your sons and daughters will hear my songs and gnash their teeth at the truth of what their fathers were! Oh, yes, mock away at the boy king—and *I'll* spread a ballad of the churls who wouldn't trust a *boy* to rule, in their greed to seize the Throne, each one for himself!"

"Not if you're dead before you leave Flowfoam, you won't," a tersept growled. Craer gave that man a brittle smile—in the wake of a hurled dagger that took his cap off and pinned it to the wall behind him.

"More than one can play that game, Tersept of Fallen-bridge," he said softly.

"Bah!" another tersept spat. "Bards! Dogs of the realm!"

"Perhaps," the Regent of Aglirta said mildly, "but this one's also a Tersept of Aglirta."

"I am?" Flaeros gulped, all his rage spent—and as astonished as the line of nobles were.

"Aye," Blackgult replied, "I just made you one."

He let the gathering storm of scorn gather volume, and then crooked a little finger. The Dwaer-Stone flashed as it rose out of Embra's grasp and flew through the air to his hand—and every noble in the long line facing him was suddenly shocked silent, with all their hair standing on end and the air in their lungs a chilling, searing thing. More than a few hands also jerked away from sword-hilts that were suddenly as hot as roaring fires, to be left trembling.

Blackgult gave them a smile of cold promise and said, "I *am* still regent, Lords of Aglirta—and I can have every last one of you beheaded, and your families stripped of their land and titles, at will. Or take lands and castle from any one of you, give them to your most hated baronial rival—and give his to you. Or simply blast you all to ashes, here among the honest dead of this day, and appoint your own kitchen maids barons and tersepts in your place."

He hefted the Dwaer meaningfully in his hand. "Remember that . . . and tell me again if you'll pledge allegiance to King Raulin Castlecloaks."

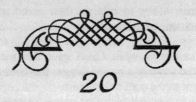

20

Four Once More

The Basket of Eels was not a well-favored tavern. No loud revels befell there, no high ladies nor young blades of Sirl desired to strut or be seen there, and its name did not feature prominently in daily discourse, social plans, or even juicy gossip.

Neither its owner nor its patrons desired it to offer competition to, say, the Dragonrose House. It enjoyed no endearing nickname, nor recommendations in polite Sirl society (if, foreign protestations to the contrary, there was such a thing as "polite Sirl society"). Yet it was not a place that neighbors feared, or that frequently hosted fires and stabbings and splinter-the-stools brawls—nor yet a shuttered, pinchcoin backwater whose master, tapsters, and wenches starved, or turned to darker work to keep themselves in daily gruel.

Rather, the Basket of Eels did very brisk trade among a select clientele that valued most its very anonymity. Situated a very short walk from busy Tharaeda Street, abustle with shops displaying many gleaming wares and fashionable "high houses" such as the Dragonrose, it was easily reached by persons ostensibly bound elsewhere. Persons who desired privacy and a place to meet other persons with similar needs—but not, for once, the needs catered to up half a hundred shuttered stairs in Sirlptar.

So popular was the tavern in this regard, in fact, that there were times when its most desirable meeting rooms were all in use by a variety of cabals, and conspirators belonging to others were forced to wait in the comparatively public taproom downstairs, murmuring less important business to each other in various of the discreetly separated, dimly lit groupings of chairs and tables.

So it was that a number of Ieiremborans sat in the deepest, darkest corner of the Basket of Eels on this day, with almost as many wealthy and prominent merchants of Sirlptar. Tonthan "Goldcloak" was in no particular hurry to ascend any of the well-hidden flights of stairs anyway, because Sathbrar was late, and he depended on the silk merchant's capable support to carry his will over the stubborn stances of men of Sirl who considered that their greater riches gave them the right to dictate everything—the vintner and wine importer Anglurthaul, for instance, whose barrels were widely believed to carry more than occasional slave cargoes. Anglurthaul was seated at the other end of the table right now, and as far as Tonthan was concerned, that wasn't far enough away. He had no doubt that the vintner entertained similar opinions.

None of the conspirators looked up when new arrivals stepped into the cool dimness of the taproom; one never did. Nonetheless, every one of them knew, by sidelong glance and use of certain cleverly placed mirrors on the tavern walls, that the newcomers were three in number, and that largest one—a fighting man, by the size of his arms and shoulders and the way he moved, with a long scabbard at his hip—was cloaked and cowled, and had gone straight to a small, empty corner table. He took a seat there facing the Ieiremborans, who as usual had taken the westernmost benches across from their Sirl backers, and would have been promptly dismissed by Tonthan but for the behavior of the cowled man's two companions.

These were a small, lithe man—a procurer, by the looks of him—and a beautiful young woman of the tallish, slender sort who might have been described by some as "all bones" were it not for the smooth grace of her movements. They strolled steadily across the taproom, neither signalling for wine nor pausing to look about, and went straight to Hardiman Anglurthaul, who was by far the fattest, most richly garbed merchant there.

The procurer stopped just out of blade reach of the vintner, tendered a pleasant smile, and said crisply, "News for you, Goodman: there's a new King in Aglirta. One anxious to make peace—and trade—with the Isles and with Sirlptar. Best save your coins and hides, and conquer in markets, not in castles."

The Ieiremborans froze, as one.

Anglurthaul looked up at him coldly. "And just who are *you*?"

The procurer displayed another airy smile, and bowed with a flourish. "Ah, I forget myself: Craer Delnbone, Overduke of Aglirta. You may place yourself at my service, Anglurthaul."

The vintner sneered without bothering to speak, and waved almost lazily over one of his shoulders.

A man lounging at a table across the room stood up, cloak falling away from leather harness, and threw a knife with deadly speed.

Craer plucked it casually out of the air and extended it to his female companion.

She smiled tightly, palmed it, and murmured a swift spell—and there were sudden, hastily stilled sounds of startlement all down the table.

In the hitherto empty air in front of every man a knife was suddenly floating: a duplicate of the one thrown by Anglurthaul's guard. The points of all of these menacing little deaths hung about a foot away from the throat of every conspirator.

"Consider this a warning," the sorceress announced

calmly. "We could instead simply kill you all, and be done with concern over your plans, forever." She gave them a gracious smile, and added as she turned to go, "I know you are sensible men, and will conduct yourselves accordingly."

Their seated companion stood up and threw back his cowl—and there were gasps of rage and dismay from the Ieiremboran side of the table as they recognized Ezendor Blackgult, smiling coldly at them from above a fist-sized glowing stone that hovered beneath his chin. It flashed with sudden white light, then, as his smile widened—and he, the procurer, and the sorceress vanished.

As one, the conspirators swore and started to scramble to their feet—only to fall suddenly silent and still again. None of the floating knives had vanished, and one man, at least—Hardiman Anglurthaul—could attest to their very real solidity . . . and sharpness. He dabbed at a goodly wound on one side of his throat, and had to bend to his boot-top with a grunt of discomfort to pluck out a brow-rag and staunch the bleeding. Thus he discovered that, solid or not, the floating knives could pass through tabletops to maintain their menacing positions.

For his part, Tonthan discovered the deep quality of the wine cellars beneath the Basket of Eels, as he sat sipping and pondering—with increasing suspicion—the where-abouts of Sathbrar.

The knives did fade away, hours later.

It would be a very long time before Flowfoam Palace was rebuilt, and the gardens to its west and south would be a scarred ruin for seasons to come. To the east, however, where Flowfoam Isle came to a sharp, high, prowlike point against the onrushing Silverflow, the tall stand of ultharn-woods stood undisturbed. They encircled a small green lawn of moss where Embra Silvertree had long ago buried all that she could find of her mother—a place that the sun touched and warmed at the height of day, above the unseen encircling fortress wall but below the palace towers and shielded from them by the trees.

There was a fresh grave in that splash of sun now, and a few grim folk standing around it. Three more came down from the higher, more floral gardens to join them: Craer, Tshamarra, and, walking a pace behind them, the Baron Ezendor Blackgult.

Embra looked up at their approach, all tears done now. Her hands were still bloodstained from the slow, painstaking hours she'd spent on her knees with spells and bare hands, gathering every last smear and droplet that had been Sarasper.

"Four no more," was all she said as Craer embraced her, and Tshamarra waited her turn to do the same. It was the procurer's face that was wet as they parted, and Overduke Delnbone went to the next waiting embrace—the arms of Hawkril Anharu, who stood grimly by the foot of the mound of fresh earth that Embra had so carefully armored in interlocked shards of marble.

The largest warsword that Flowfoam's palace walls could yield was planted in the earth beside Hawk, with his dagger-belt hung about its hilt. An armaragor set down his arms out of respect when laying to rest one of his betters.

Alone on the other side of the grave stood King Raulin Castlecloaks, unsure of what he should say or do, his own grief writ clear on his face. His hands still bore the dirt of his first royal act—digging this grave.

"Fare well, Lord Longfangs," Blackgult said simply, releasing Embra at last to turn and face the grave where the others stood with heads bowed. "Go now and heal the Three, old healer, and make all Darsar the happier." Then he looked to Raulin.

The king nodded, and said softly, "Tarry in a happier place, Lord Dragon. May it be many long years before we must dig another grave here."

There were murmurs of agreement, and then a few more

silent embraces—but no one needed to speak to reach agreement that they would part, to walk alone for a time.

"Are they done yet?"

"Patience, Lameira. I cannot *see*, I tell thee." The oldest Lady of Chambers peered again through the seeing glass that Alresse Delcamper had gifted her with these six summers ago to mark her fiftieth year of turning linens and dusting, sighed, and said severely, "Faerla, I won't be pleased to have to tell thee again: cease thy gasping and fluttering. Do you want all Flowfoam to think we of Varandaur have never seen fine things before? Or know how to comport ourselves before royalty?"

"Oh, Lady Orele, 'tis not this palace—though it does go on for *miles*, does it not? Nor yet these haughty courtiers that the river seems to spew up like the silver halake run, boat after boat of them! 'Tis that mighty magic that the Lord Flaeros commands, to snatch us all—in a trice—thither!"

"He did not command it, Faerla; he arranged it. Our Lord Flaeros is many things, but 'sorcerer' is thankfully not one of them." Orele raised herself a trifle and bent a little to one side, leaning on her silver-handled cane—another gift of the Delcampers, but Lameira knew quite well that she'd more than earned it, in the unwelcome embraces of at least three ardent uncles whose trust Orele had never, by so much as a glance, betrayed—to see the distant gardens better. "They have so allowed their trees to grow untrammeled," she said slowly, "that overlooking yon end garden is extremely difficult. They're moving apart, though . . . yes, I do believe they are done."

She straightened, whirled about, and clapped her hands. "Scamper, girls, scamper! The nightchambers won't prepare *themselves*, you know! I'm sure Lord Flaeros would not have gone to the truly fearsome expense of such a great spellweaving—and mind, Faerla, the *cost* is by far the

most frightening thing about that magic, not the hazy moment you spent being brought here, so *please* have done
about it—to bring, as you say, *all* of us all this way did he
not want us to show these Aglirtans how we of Varandaur
can set things to rights! Ignore the smoke and the blood
and the rubble; such things are no concern of ours—but if I
see the Lord Flaeros so much as frown when the king and
the other heroes of Aglirta come in to feasting and to retire
to bed, I shall be *most* displeased . . . and mark you this:
I've little doubt that my displeasure will be as nothing
compared to his!"

As if her words had been a warning from the gods, the
doors of the chamber burst open, and Flaeros Delcamper
strode in. "They're coming, Orele, they're coming! Is
everything ready?"

Orele leaned on her cane to make her deepest courtesy.
The youngest Lord Delcamper might be a wastrel and a
bard and always messing about with foreigners and their
wars—but he was the only Delcamper man she knew who
thanked servants, and thought of *their* trouble, or sprang to
help them when a carrychest was too heavy or a corner too
high for one's most perilous reach with a duster. "Not as
ready as I'd like it, Lord, but 'twill not disgrace us, no . . . I
hope."

Flaeros shot out an arm to help her to her feet, kissed her
hand as if she really was a highborn lady, and laughed.
"That tells me it's as ready as any outland place can ever be
that you haven't had years to flog into shape, Lady! I knew
you could do it!"

"B-but why?" Faerla blurted, too excited to be quelled
by Orele's furious look. The youngest chambermaid hadn't
scampered very far to do her last dusting, it seemed—certainly not far enough. "'Tis a pleasure to serve your will,
my Lord, and a delight to set anyplace to rights, still more
so a grand palace—but why all this trouble for folk half
Asmarand away from us? Aglirta has been here all our

lives—and at war all that time too, seemingly—why these few folk, now?"

Flaeros Delcamper turned to face her rather stiffly, but instead of the towering fury that Orele feared—and fully expected—to burst forth, the maids saw his eyes fill with tears. He smiled, and said, "I'm glad you asked that, Faerla. I'm sure many are thinking similar thoughts; always be bold enough to speak so, and save us all discomfort and unhappiness and time wasted."

He gestured to the windows as gracefully as any dancer, and said, "As a bard, I came here to Aglirta because I wanted to see and hear the greatest bard of all, Stormharp—who turned out to be one of the men you'll serve this night: Baron Ezendor Blackgult, the Golden Griffon. I stayed because I heard such grand tales, and saw folk fighting so valiantly, the Band of Four—one of whom was just buried, yonder—in particular. But we do them reverence now—*all Darsar* should bow before them now—because they have saved all our lives. The Serpent is dead, who would have conquered us all—yes, even in far Varandaur—and that fell beast was slain by their hands and valor. We should praise them forever, though I know that even with grand ballads folk all too soon forget.

"It was my honor to fight by their sides, and do what I could—in a small and fumbling way—and I would gladly be a slave to any one of them, for the rest of my life."

It was not just Faerla who stared back at him with wide, awed eyes as he bowed to them, smiled, and took his modest leave. Orele's gaze was as shocked as that of her youngest and least-well-behaved maid.

It was Lameira who grew indignant. "A-a Delcamper bowing to an *Aglirtan*? To be as a slave? To think that I should hear that!"

Lady Orele gave her a stern look. "Mind your tongue, girl. If a Lord Delcamper chooses to kneel before anyone, you can be sure that they are worth kneeling before! I shall

expect to see you doing so this night, when they come up
to chambers!"

Lameira looked at her. "Will *you* kneel?"

"Of course—and be happy to do anything else they ask
of me right smartly, Lameira—*anything*, mind."

Lameira looked scandalized. "If I ever thought that
a . . ."

Orele was staring serenely at her, and under that calm
gaze she ran out of fire and things to say all at once.

"That's better, girl," the senior Lady of Chambers said
quietly. "You'll be surprised, in life, at what befalls that
you've never thought of. And your memories will be the
richer for it, too, perhaps enough to keep you warm on
lonely nights."

She turned away, took a step that told the watching
maids just how much her reverence to Flaeros had cost her
old bones, and then turned around again, leaning on her
cane, and added, "If it comforts you, Lameira, I've heard
from no less than three folk—one of them this new king of
theirs, and the other two palace servants like us, and so to
be trusted—that our Lord Flaeros tongue-lashed every last
baron and tersept in this kingdom not long ago! The whole
glaring line of them, threatening them with his displeasure
if they misbehaved, when they stood battle-angry and over
thirty to his one! Told them off like children, laid down
their duty and their morals for them like old Galuster does
to us, when he shows how to lay a place at table—and they
took it, too! And these folk we're serving tonight stood
with him, and did not think it so strange that a Delcamper
should tell nobles of Aglirta their business!"

The awed look was back in their eyes again, and she
turned away in slow satisfaction and took another three
steps before turning again, and adding sharply, "Mind: this
does *not* give any of us license to hold ourselves above
these poor folk of Aglirta, and look down prideful noses or
speak slightingly. I've met courtiers here who do all those

things—just as I've met ill-taught servants in Ragalar who do the same . . . and it looks no more pretty from them as it would from you! Hold your certainty of your own peerless worth to yourself, as I do, and smile at all the world as you do it service!"

Her departure was real this time, and when Lameira made a face at where her back had been and muttered, "'As I do,'" with incredulity, Faerla struck her sharply with a duster, and snapped, "That's enough, Lameira! I won't have that woman mocked! Where would we be— Three heed me, where would the *Delcampers* be—without her?"

Lameira shot her a burning look, but then her gaze fell, and she said, "That's so. Flaeros—the *Lord* Flaeros—did say he was taking the best of Varandaur, because Aglirta needed us . . . and then he chose *us*, out of all the rest."

Faerla smiled. "Yes, he did—and—and, oh, Lameira, this is so *exciting*! Why, they tell me there're the bones of a wizard lying in a casket in the cellars, and traps everywhere down there, too—so we're not to go thither—and folk lying dead, and snakes as big as men lurking about that they haven't found yet, and the one they call the Lady of Jewels has chambers full of gowns all over with gems, enough to buy all Ragalar seventy times over, *and* she can walk right *into* the stones of this palace and then make its doors open and close and its lamps light and douse just as she sees fit, and—"

Lameira rolled her eyes. Ardent and demanding heroes or not, it was going to be a long evening.

"Now, now," Maevur Cardassa snapped, "there's no need to become *restless*. We'll just wait until the unpleasantness at Flowfoam is over, and then we'll make our move."

"Hmmph," an armsman said, staring around at the tilting tangle of half-rotten fishing huts for perhaps the hundredth time. "Couldn't we just invade as far as the Flowfoam kitchens tonight?"

There were chuckles and murmurs of agreement.

"No, we could not," the baron said severely. "I feel the pangs of hunger as deeply as any of you—"

"Deeper, by the look of you," someone at the far end of the boat commented, and there were more chuckles, which the baron loftily chose to ignore.

"—and yet I am disciplined enough to bide here in watchful patience until the time is right. We risk our very lives in this, I'll have you remember!"

"How will we know the time is right?"

"I—uh—well, when we see certain folk leaving Flowfoam," Cardassa said. "I'll tell you, you may be sure! And then we'll—"

"We're not going to be seeing many folk leaving Flowfoam, once it gets dark," another armsman observed loudly.

Which was about the same time as a familiar voice from high up on the bank cried angrily, "*There* you are! Three above, but we stood in the Throne Chamber in Flowfoam facing fell magic and Blackgult and all his bravos—and where were you? Alone we stood against them, and only through cool heads and fearlessness and—well, valor, though I say it myself—we prevailed! Aglirta has a new king—a motherless boy whom we can easily steer to our desires, or slaughter if he balks, and there'll be no need for swords right now, so—"

Maevur Cardassa had been puffing and staggering his way around a particularly ramshackle hut and down the bank all through these brave words, using his enchanted sword as a walking stick—but now he'd come to a disbelieving halt, with a straggling line of tersepts behind him.

Baron Cardassa stared at—Baron Cardassa.

Tersepts stared at their counterparts, and armsmen and Cardassan bodyguards aboard the barge looked from one to the other, eyes narrowing.

"Magic," an armsman growled. "I *thought* so!" He and

Suldun of the bodyguards drew their swords together, and advanced on—the tersepts and the baron who were sharing this barge with them.

"So," the armsman began, as his blade thrust out to menace the false Maevur Cardassa, "who are you, really? Sirl wizards trying to ruin our bid for the Throne, or—?"

"Wh-what treachery is this?" the fat man just beyond the point of his sword gabbled. "Do your sworn duty, and attack *yon* impostors! I, Maevur of Cardassa, *command* you!"

"What?" the baron on the shore howled. "What treachery is this? Those men aboard are the impostors! *Slay them!* Slay them with your swords now, before they can use their deadly magics on you!"

"It might be easier to slay them all," someone commented sourly—in the moment before the armsmen and bodyguards aboard the barge surged forward to hack at all the tersepts—some of whom promptly leaped into the river and sank like stones.

"Hold!" someone high on the bank roared, and there came the call of a battle horn. The baron and tersepts ashore and everyone on the barges swung around to look up, and found themselves gazing at a hundred or so armaragors and armsmen, some on horseback—and many with loaded crossbows leveled in their direction.

"Who," the Baron Cardassa ashore stammered, his fearful voice rising almost to a scream, "are *you?"*

"Men of Bloodblade, Rightful King of Aglirta," was the stern reply. "Who do you swing swords for?"

"A new king for Aglirta!" the baron on the bank said hastily.

"And you others?" the swordcaptain of Bloodblade snapped, looking at the barges.

There was a confusion of replies, as armsmen and bodyguards named their various lords, and the swordcaptain listened, looked disgusted, and brought his arm down in a curt signal.

Crossbows thrummed in deadly chorus, and the barges

were suddenly full of staggering, dying men, with quarrels standing out of them. Many leaped or fell into the water, but high on the bank windlasses were whirring away as the crossbowmen readied their weapons to fire again—and on the barges, there was no cover at all.

The barons and tersepts on the shore watched in horror, then took to their heels and fled. The swordcaptain waved his hand in another signal, and the horsemen around him spurred their mounts down the bank, drawing blades as they went.

The screams that followed were few and short. The crossbowmen took turns firing at the heads of the few who sprang into the river, until the waters were stained with blood and thick with drifting, unmoving bodies.

"Buldrim," one of the swordcaptain's men snapped, "a lot of those on the barges simply—vanished. Gone, with magic, while we were winching and choosing our next targets."

"How many?"

The warrior shrugged. "More than twenty."

Buldrim went pale. "That many wizards? Gods, we could be a thousand, and they'd still fell us in a breath or two! But whom do they serve? The regent?"

"We'd best begone, no matter what," the warrior replied, and Buldrim nodded. "Horsemen," he snapped, "upriver to Thuss Point, there! Seize those docks, and then put your horses in yon sheds and hide there with them. Forage for hay, but otherwise keep hidden. All others, seize those barges—we row to Flowfoam!"

"Shall we slay this one? Or roll him into the river, and let the water do the killing?"

Buldrim looked down, and a pain-wracked Suldun looked back up, bleeding profusely from the holes left by three crossbow quarrels being wrenched out of him.

"Well?" Buldrim asked. "D'you want to lie here and watch us conquer Flowfoam, or be free of your pain?"

"Beware," Suldun whispered hoarsely. "We were duped by wizards . . ."

Buldrim nodded. "So much we know." He glanced up at Flowfoam, rising above them now as the armsmen pulled strongly at the oars, opened his mouth to point ahead and turn and give the helmsman orders—then recoiled.

A man was standing on the deck facing him—where the bloodstained boards had been empty a moment before. It was Sendrith Duthjack, in full armor but helmless, and with a fresh swordcut on one cheek. His gaze was fierce as he looked at the swordcaptain with a nod of recognition—and approval.

"Lord Bloodblade!" Buldrim stammered, and went to one knee. "Lord, command me!"

"Turn about!" Bloodblade ordered sternly. "Turn about, all of you! Back to the docks whence you came!"

"At once," Buldrim agreed hastily, waving at the helmsman to turn the great rudder, "but Lord, why?"

"Pull in close, all four boats together so that all may hear, and I'll tell you," the warlord ordered.

When this was done, oars stretched and held at both ends to keep the boats rail to rail, Bloodblade strode to the very center of the joined decks, looked around, and said, "Loyal Aglirtans, hear me! You have been duped—horribly tricked! Misled into betraying your land!"

"We follow only you, Lord Bloodblade!" one of the armsmen called, and there was a chorus of agreement.

"Think you so?" The warlord smiled at them—and then his face changed, becoming green and scaled—a serpent's head, with forked tongue and all!

"What if I told you sssomething clossser to the truth?" the Serpent-priest asked them, looking around at the dumbfounded warriors on the gently rocking barges. "What if I told you the real Bloodblade wasss killed yearsss ago? I took hisss face and shape, to conquer Aglirta for the Ssserpent!"

An armsman yelled in horror and scrabbled for his

crossbow—and the snake-man's hand came up, with a slender wand in it that spat once. A beam of flame snarled forth, and they saw the warrior's face melt away into a skull mantled with ashes. As the man slumped over, the Serpent-priest asked calmly, "Anyone elssse?"

He spun around, to make sure no warrior behind him was readying a stealthy weapon, then told them, "Now, all isss over. You have won, becaussse the Ssserpent liesss ssslain. And you have losssst, becausssse I ssshall not leave you alive to gloat!"

And with a horrible laugh he slashed at the barges around him with more beams of flame, firing small snarling spheres of it into the faces of warriors who scrambled up to hurl daggers or their swords, until flames were licking up from the deck boards all around him.

And then, of course, he vanished into the same thin air he'd come from.

Men were screaming and shoving the rocking barges apart as fire snarled up around them; only Buldrim's barge had been spared the flames, and men tried to leap to it or to dive into the river—only to fall to a new slayer.

The helmsman had produced a wand of his own that spat long needles of dark force. His first took Buldrim through the belly, sliding through armor plate as if the swordcaptain wore none, and left the officer whimpering on his face on the deck. Then he dealt with men thrashing in the river or trying to board. When there were no more feebly swimming or desperately leaping men to be seen, the helmsman coolly raked the barge with slaying needles, putting them through heads until not a man still stood.

The barges drifted downstream, burning merrily, and the helmsman strolled his deck sending a thorn here and a thorn there—wherever he saw movement.

When there was no one left to slay, he booted Buldrim's sword into the water, bent over the stricken swordcaptain, and rolled him over.

Buldrim lay shoulder-to-shoulder with the sorely

wounded leader of the Cardassan bodyguard, blinking up at the familiar face above him. It was smiling.

"Wh-why did you do this, Ansyarde?" Buldrim gasped, through the deepening mists of pain.

The man grinned. "I'm not Ansyarde." His face wavered, flowed—and was suddenly Duthjack's, with swordcut—and then, the flesh melting into unmarked smoothness as Buldrim stared, without. "And I'm not Bloodblade, either."

The face changed again, becoming the scaled head of the Serpent-priest, and hissed, "Or a Sssnake-lover, either. That wasss all a trick, to turn you back from ssslaying *another* king. Thaebred'sss a good actor, isssn't he?"

"Who are you, really?" Buldrim gasped, urgently. Everything was going dim.

The scaled snake-head looked down at him for a moment, then the shoulders below it lifted in a shrug. "Very well— you'll die easssier, knowing, and we're not unmerciful."

His face changed again, becoming . . . utterly blank. A mouth slit opened in the smooth mask of flesh, and smiled down.

Buldrim and Suldun beside him gasped the same horrified name together: "Faceless!"

"Indeed. Koglaur, we call ourselves. The true guardians of Aglirta."

"You . . . you . . ." Buldrim struggled to speak against the blood and pain rising in him, and then blurted: "Bloodblade seeks a new glory for Aglirta, a new road to greatness. I and the others who ride with him can see that road . . . taste it . . . If you Faceless are truly the guardians of Aglirta, why d'you slay us?" He coughed, choked, and then managed to add, "As we try to hew that new road to glory? Why?"

The Koglaur smiled grimly. "Peace to you, Buldrim. You fought well, and made only one mistake: you chose the wrong road."

Buldrim moaned, then, as the pain and the rising blood he'd been wrestling with for so long rose to overwhelm him. He tried to sob, tried to lift his hand . . . and failed.

His head lolled to one side, and the last things he saw were the sky and the Silverflow, flowing endlessly . . .

When the last rattling breath died away, the Koglaur rolled the swordcaptain's body off the barge. Then he turned back to Suldun—who tried to shrink away, mewing in helpless fear, but came to a gasping halt as his wounded body failed him, and pain caught hold of him with fingers of fire.

The faceless head above him twisted again, flowing like porridge beneath a cook's paddle, and then suddenly spun into . . . the likeness of a beautiful brown-eyed lass. The most beautiful woman, Suldun realized dazedly, that he'd ever seen.

"There," the Koglaur asked, in a soft, husky, utterly feminine voice, "is that easier?"

She—it—the Koglaur looked down his body, then, as Suldun Greatsarn struggled to find words to reply, and murmured something he did not understand. It sounded like the tongue of another land, but not one he'd ever heard in all the markets of Sirlptar. Now she was laying long, rubbery-fingered hands on Suldun's wounds—right on the gaping holes left by the—*gods*!

Suldun convulsed with the pain, shuddering . . . then sank back onto the deck, sighing, as coolness flooded through him. It was slowly taking the pain with it, leaving him . . . whole. He knew it, somehow: he'd been healed completely.

And yet he was so weak he couldn't lift his shoulders an inch off the deck beneath him.

"Lie still," that husky voice said from above. "You've lost much blood."

There were surging sounds and splashes, the sounds of large bodies heaving themselves up out of the water—and so they were: water-dripping Faceless whose faces were smooth expanses of nothing, but who still seemed to *look* at him as they found their feet and padded off down the deckboards to take oar after oar, and end the drifting.

They were near the fishing dock they'd started from, and the faceless men rowed only a few strokes ere the barge grated gently against the pilings. Swift, rubbery hands moored it, tying its ropes securely.

"Fare thee well, Suldun Greatsarn," the Koglaur said to him, with a wink and a wave, as she—it was impossible to see that magnificent body move and think of it as anything but "she"—rose and stepped onto the dock.

"Wha . . . why did you heal me?" Suldun gasped. "What am I to you?"

"An Aglirtan," she said softly, looking down. "We like Aglirtans, and give our lives defending them, all too often." She bent closer, and added, "We always like to leave a few of you alive who've seen us, to keep the whispers alive about us, up and down Aglirta. Fear is like a second sword in one's hand."

"And if I tell folk you defend us, and are not to be feared?"

The Koglaur laughed. "They won't believe you. They never do." And she—he—it turned away, leaving Suldun believing until his dying day that those last three words had held more sadness than he'd ever heard in a human voice before.

They were human, weren't they? Well, what was "human"?

"You could have been king," Embra murmured, as they linked hands, walking slowly to nowhere through the gardens. A few courtiers were lighting hanging candle-lamps here and there, but they drew aside whenever the pair of overdukes approached, leaving them to walk alone.

"You could have been queen," Hawkril rumbled back at her. "Aglirta needs someone strong and loving and swift of wits. Why not a queen to rule the Vale? You'd have been better at it than any of us."

She lifted her shoulders in a shrug. "I don't know," she

said lightly. "Craer can look pretty good in a dress, when he has to."

Hawk snorted. A few paces farther on, he said, "We jest together all the time, we F—three. I like that. It warms me, makes me feel wanted and . . . welcome at table. And yet I want to speak plainly now, Lady."

"Lady mine," she corrected, and he came to a halt, holding her hand tightly.

"That's what I want to talk of," the armaragor said quietly, his eyes steady on hers. "I—I am too much lowborn Aglirtan not to want to bed a woman and feel she's either a friend, or bought for a night, or a warrior's wenching in passing—or someone he can stand with, lifelong, and should wed. You are the first of those choices, I will never let you be the second or third, and I—I very much want you to be the fourth."

Embra looked back at him. "Did you not hear me refuse Kelgrael before all the court, and cleave to you?"

"Aye. Aye, I did, and want the world to know. I want to shout it from the battlements," Hawkril growled with sudden fire. "I-I—can we be wed? I mean . . . you'll have me?"

Embra smiled. "Of course I will, you great dolt. All you had to do was ask."

His eyes glimmered in the lamplight. "And—and—you don't mind a 'great ox of an armaragor' beside you?"

"I don't even mind a great ox of an armaragor inside me," she told him gently, "so long as it's you. Marry me, my Lord Silvertree—please?"

"Ah—uh—that's what I was going to . . . ask you," Hawkril said in some confusion, flushing crimson.

"Yes, and I want to be your lady so much I want to beg you for it—here, on my knees."

She knelt before him, leaving the armaragor startled and looking around to see where the courtiers were. They stood nearer than he'd thought, but were carefully looking away.

"They'll think you—pleaded with me to—"

"I want them to," she told him, eyes bright. "As it happens, I do have to beg you for something else—and give you a promise."

"A—what?" Hawkril floundered, knowing his tongue wasn't forging ahead all that well, but powerless to free himself from this sudden confusion that seemed to have . . . overwhelmed him.

"Hawkril, please forgive me," Embra said in a voice that was suddenly small and on the verge of tears, "for using my magic to force you, compelling you against your will. I promise *never* to do it again. Ever."

"Force me? When did . . . ?"

"The night we first met, when we were fleeing my father, and I made you carry me into the Silent House."

"I hit you," Hawkril said slowly, remembering, and started to kneel. She thrust her hands up under his knees with unexpected strength to prevent his descent, and then with a grunt of effort stood, thrusting him upright again.

"Hawk," she said, looking into the armaragor's eyes as their noses almost touched, "don't do that. I don't need you to kneel to me like a servant. I need you to forgive me and tell me all is right between us."

"Oh." Hawkril blinked. "Well, 'tis, of course, my Lady."

She gave him a dirty look, and he amended hastily, "Embra, I forgive you. All is right between us."

She smiled and kissed him. "Good." She took Hawk's hand before his arms could tighten around her and stepped away, so they were walking together once more.

Embra promptly guided the armaragor onto another grassy path, to where it was darker. Then she turned her head to look into his eyes, grinned, and said, "You can hit me whenever you like, if it makes you feel better."

"Umm," Hawkril replied, his fingers tightening in hers. "You'll hit me back, won't you?"

"Of course."

* * *

They walked and talked a long time in the gardens, and when at last they came in, Lady Orele was waiting for them. She led them up into the east wing, showing the Lady Overduke first to her rooms—but hesitated not a moment when Embra said softly that she preferred to sleep with the Lord Hawkril, and in his chambers. Orele merely smiled and wordlessly led them on down the high hall to another door.

There the old lady plucked at Embra's sleeve, and when the Lady Overduke bent close, she whispered, "Three watch over you and keep you, Lady." Then she rapped on the door with her silver-handled cane, and added as the maids within started to draw it open, "May you be happy together—Darsar knows you deserve it."

And then the Lady of Chambers turned and was gone, without another look or word, walking very slowly and leaning on her cane.

"Had she a lover, ever?" a guard murmured to his fellow, as the Lady Orele stumped past, leaning more heavily on her cane.

"Vaevra will know," the other guard replied, "or be able to mind-pry and find out. You're too softhearted, Shalace."

"I don't know that there is such a thing as *too* soft-hearted for our kind, Mrivin," the first Koglaur said, with just a touch of sharpness. "When we know the likeness of her man, I'll shape it and go to her. Gods, but she's earned it."

"Careful with the hearts of the old," Mrivin cautioned. "Find out what became of him, if she knows, and how they parted, first. Unless you want to spend the rest of your days snapping at chambermaids and leaning on a cane."

Shalace shrugged. "There are worse ways to serve."

* * *

"See? The flowers themselves hide before your beauty," Craer said lightly.

"Those close up every night," the tall, slender sorceress told him calmly. "Is your courting usually this labored, Overduke Delnbone?"

"Lady, you wound me," the procurer protested, looking up into her eyes. "My intentions are honorable—entirely honorable."

Tshamarra gave him a rather wry smile. "I'm sure your lovemaking always is." She strolled on, and he had to hasten to return to her side.

Calmly, the Lady Talasorn put a hand across his back and clasped him against her, so they were walking hip to hip—or rather, hip to ribs.

"Your eyes are like those lamps they're lighting," Craer began again, smoothly.

"With little flames in them, and moths fluttering around them? I hope not," she replied.

"Lady, you're not making this easy," he protested.

Her teeth flashed in a soundless laugh. "You amuse me, Craer. I've never met such a master of madcap nonsense before, and—"

"Lady Talasorn, will you marry me?" Those words came out in a rush, almost snapped forth—and she felt him tense, and falter in his stride.

Tshamarra stopped, and his hand stole around her waist.

She reached down, took hold of that hand, and firmly slid it down to cup her behind.

"No, Lord Craer," she replied, "not for many years—or ever. I haven't the slightest desire to formally pair with any man—or woman or shapeshifting serpent either, before you ask."

"Oh," Craer replied, glibly.

"Nor will I join the ranks of the Four, as I heard you suggesting to Embra in a whisper that should have been just a bit softer."

"I . . ." He sighed. "I wanted you to overhear that."

"You surprise me not, Craer. Nothing you do is likely to surprise me in the future, either. I begin to know you too well."

"Too well?"

"As I said, it's something I'm beginning to do—and 'tis time to take another step on that journey." Tshamarra turned off the path, back onto the round lawn where Sarasper lay buried.

"I've never known a man's embraces before," the tall sorceress announced calmly, "and I would like to change that—this night, and with you, Lord Craer."

"Uh?" Craer commented, brightly.

"Remove your clothes," she said crisply, waving one hand at the ground before them and raising the other to the clasps of her gown. "There's no need to go inside when there's a perfectly good soft moss-bed here."

Epilogue

The servants seemed to know just when they reached that time of readiness for other things beyond awakening, stretching, and greeting one's bed partner. Wonderful smells heralded the discreet placing of the covered trays—and warm spiced cider, a treat that made Tshamarra open her eyes wide and declare that from this day forth, last surviving lady members of the family Talasorn would greet opening days with no other throatslake!

"Gods, but 'twas good!" she murmured to Craer, when servants guided them together in a high-vaulted hall. "Nothing like the great Craer, of course. . . ."

The procurer choked, thumped at the base of his throat, and hissed, "D'you *mind*, Lady? A man has a reputation—!"

Tshamarra rolled her eyes. "Aye, and I'm still hearing bits of yours. From the servants, the guards, some of the gardeners—you know the grounds here quite well, I believe—several handfuls of courtiers, and no doubt many more good folk of Aglirta, if I perchanced to meet with them."

"Oh, *gods*," Craer muttered.

"Oh, yes, Lord Delnbone, I'm going to lead you a merry dance," she whispered, taking his elbow and steering him through the door that two sword-saluting guards had just thrown open. "Depend on it."

"Ahem," Craer replied brightly, as his eyes met those of Embra, which twinkled knowingly; Hawkril, who looked briefly at the ceiling; Blackgult, who grinned openly; and King Raulin Castlecloaks, who merely looked pleased to see him and entirely unaware of the look Lady Talasorn had thrown the shortest, most handsome Overduke of Aglirta as they'd parted to seek the last two seats at the table.

"Behold the Garden Room," Embra murmured, gesturing at the windows. The view looked east, out over descending terraces, lawns, and woods, and Craer sighed, smiled, and said, "Could we perhaps stay here for once— just for a few days?"

"As it happens," King Raulin said a little hesitantly, "Lord Blackgult and I have been conferring about that. I'd like you to—it's my . . . it's our royal request that you—"

"Raulin," Craer told him, "just say: 'I'd like you to' and when I say no, then say: 'That was a royal command, dolt,' and we'll get along just fine."

Tshamarra snorted, clapped a swift hand over her mouth, and shook her head ere she looked away.

Raulin flushed, licked his lips—and then laughed helplessly and complained, "How'm I ever going to do this right, Crae—Lord Craer—if I have to talk one way to some and another way to others?"

"That's what being king is all about," Craer told him. "You lie foully to some, and lie sweetly to others. You keep your true thoughts to yourself, and—oh, Three Above, Raulin, be different than all the others, please? Just speak plainly. Always. That will give you the pure pleasure of interrupting any courtier who starts in with silver-tongued tra-la and bidding him speak plainly. Or else. It might even set a new royal fashion, and you'll actually get some work done, and perhaps even win the respect of the people."

There were grins all around the table, now, and Hawkril

rumbled, "I warned you. Shut him up or send him out to chase a maid or something—or you won't get anything said or done."

"Ooh," Tshamarra chimed in, rolling her eyes. "Chase *me*, Lord Delnbone, chase *me*!"

"Hmmph. Send her with him," Blackgult told the king. At her sudden, anxious look, he added hastily, "Nay, Lady Talasorn, I but jest. I'm *not* trying to exclude you from our councils, or our company."

"Lord Blackgult, my name is 'Tshamarra'—hard to say and spell, I know, but—"

"Oh, *gods*," Embra said, looking at the ceiling, "we're going to be here all morning! You recall Craer's urging to 'speak plainly,' Raulin? Try it—right now. You talked with my father, and the two of you deci—"

"The *king* decided," Blackgult chided her. Embra gave him a withering look, and he spread his hands, and said, "Leave the lad some dignity, Embra, will you? He *is* king, after all."

"*Hoy!*" Raulin shouted, bringing his hand down on the table with a slap that made the goblets dance. As they all turned to look at him in startled silence, he winced, shook his hand experimentally, and announced, "That hurts!"

"Yes," Craer agreed. "That's why it's customary to grasp the throat of a handy servant and bang his head on the table, instead. Choose one who lacks a long nose; they bleed less."

Raulin snorted, shook his head, and laughed helplessly. "Bla-Black—" he appealed, reaching out a hand to the baron, who rolled his eyes and leaned forward.

"After due consideration and conferral with his trusted advisor—"

Embra snorted, but not with mirth; Blackgult ignored her.

"—the king has reached a decision, and now wishes to make known to you his royal command: that the surviving Overdukes of Aglirta resume their previously assigned mission, with an amendment. To speak plainly, you are to find the baron who secretly has a Dwaer—Phelinndar, I believe, from his success at blocking my attempts to summon him—as well as searching for the other two Worldstones. Bring them all back. Now that the Serpent is gone, whoever holds them may well think there's no reason not to experiment with the Stones or use them to do—anything."

"We are three, not Four," Embra said slowly, "and lack a Dwaer to fight with. How shall we survive to do anything more, if we do meet Phelinndar—or any others who bear Dwaerindim?"

Blackgult reached under the table. When his hand came back up into view, he was holding her Dwaer. He handed it to her, then looked around the table with a crooked grin. "How do you feel about taking a former baron and ex-regent into your ranks? Can you lower yourselves that much?"

Craer looked at Hawkril, who blinked back at him and turned to Embra. She looked at Craer, then at Tshamarra, who with a forth-and-back crook of one silent finger indicated that she would accompany Craer, and he would bide with her.

The Lady of Jewels lifted her eyes and looked at her father across the table, then. "Well," she said with a smile, "we could try."

Dramatis Personae

ALHAND, JALEBRA: a buxom, not overly bright young lass of Saerith in upland Ornentar, where she works at Saerith Mill.

AMBELTER, INGRYL: Spellmaster of Silvertree and strongest wizard of the Dark Three (the unscrupulous, evil mages who served Baron Faerod Silvertree); ambitious, shrewd in the ways of life and politics in the Vale, he's a creative and very powerful spellweaver. Though slain in *The Kingless Land*, he seems to have found a way to live on, beyond death. His spells have won him control over the Melted, stumbling zombie creations of the dead wizard Corloun (so named because their flesh has sagged and flowed, as if partially melted), and grandly proclaims himself "Spellmaster of Flowfoam."

ANGLURTHAUL, HARDIMAN: a fat, sneering, coarsely aggressive vintner and wine importer of Sirlptar who drapes himself in riches and never goes anywhere without at least one bodyguard—which is a wise tactic, given his great wealth of enemies.

ANHARU, HAWKRIL: "the Boar of Blackgult," an armaragor (unranked battle knight) in the service of the Baron Blackgult, whom he was once personal bodyguard to; a man of unusually large build and strength; member of the Band of Four and longtime friend and sword-companion of Craer Delnbone, who often calls him "Tall Post."

ARANDOR, MRANRAX: archwizard of Elmerna, growing increasingly ambitious—and short of cash.

ARATHRO, BAERM: a rather clumsy brigand working the coast road of Asmarand, nigh Shaunsel Rise (a farm-cloaked ridge between Elmerna and Teln).

ARDURGAN, BELTH: a retired hiresword, now turned village woodcarver. Much scarred and calm in a fray, still a good hunter and battle bowman.

BAERM: see Arathro, Baerm

BAND OF FOUR, THE: our heroes, the King's Heroes, the Awakeners of the Risen King; an independent band of four adventurers first thrown together in *The Kingless Land* (see Anharu, Hawkril; Codelmer, Sarasper; Delnbone, Craer; and Silvertree, Embra), whose adventures yet bid fair to change the face of Aglirta.

BELKLARRAVUS, GLARSIMBER: Baron of Brightpennant, formerly the Tersept (non-noble ruler) of Sart but promoted by King Kelgrael Snowsar in *The Vacant Throne*; a stout, brawny warrior going to fat, but still infamous as from his days as a mercenary war captain, "The Smiling Wolf of Sart."

BELRASTOR, SAURN: oldest and most respected uplands farmer of the Tarlagar backcountry nigh the Windfangs foothills, who habitually drinks at the Glory of Aglirta tavern, says little, and owns much land and a part of many local businesses. A former courtier and sometime warrior, more given to dignified tolerance than dominance of the many folk who owe him coins.

BLACKCLOAK, THAEKER: wealthy uplands farmer of swift tongue and some pride, who dwells in the Tarlagar backcountry nigh the Windfangs foothills, and habitually drinks at the Glory of Aglirta tavern.

BLACKGULT, EZENDOR: Regent of Aglirta and Baron (Lord) of Blackgult, known as the Golden Griffon for his heraldic badge, longtime rival to Faerod Silvertree for rule of Aglirta and leader of a disastrous attack on (planned conquest of) the Isles of Ieirembor just prior to *The Kingless Land*, which resulted in the seizure of his lands by Silvertree and his warriors (including Craer and Hawkril of the Four) all being declared outlaw. A sophisticated, intelligent warrior and esthete, Blackgult has dabbled in spellcraft and collected many enchanted items, using their powers to wear another shape, wherein, as the seldom-seen bard Inderos Stormharp, Master Bard of Darsar, he's become famous as the greatest living bard of Asmarand, if not all Darsar. He is the true father of Embra Silvertree.

BLADELOCK, MAURYM: this darkly handsome, taciturn tersept has always been short of money and long on foes and feuds—and joined Baron Cardassa's conspiracy in hopes that its success would free him of both shortcomings, forever. Increasingly, he hopes that it won't do so in a very final wrong manner.

BLOODBLADE: see Duthjack, Sendrith "Bloodblade."

BLUE PASSION: a pleasure-dancer at the Dragonrose House dining club in Sirlptar, recognizable by the blue cord that binds her hair. She's also taller and darker than her partner Red Dream.

BOWDRAGON, ARAUNDOR: the balding, stolid third Bowdragon brother, father of three sons and four daughters, all of whom outstrip him in sorcery—though he's no weakling with spells, and is indeed an "archwizard" in the reckoning of most realms.

BOWDRAGON, DOLMUR: the eldest Bowdragon brother, patriarch of the family, and a mighty archwizard in his own right. Sensitive, even-tempered, and serious, the father of Cathaleira (now dead) and Erith.

BOWDRAGON, ERITH: the shy, physically and magically weak son of Dolmur.

BOWDRAGON, ITHIM: the fourth and youngest Bowdragon brother, father of Jhavarr and five daughters, the eldest of whom is Maerla.

BOWDRAGON, JHAVARR: powerful young sorcerer of a family known for its magical might, who seeks to avenge the death of his "sister" (actually cousin; all of the current Bowdragon younglings were raised together, and regard each other as siblings) Cathaleira Bowdragon, who was slain by her Aglirtan master, the archwizard Tharlorn of the Thunders.

BOWDRAGON, MAERLA: the raven-haired, beautiful, hot-tempered, and icy-tongued eldest daughter of Ithim, who lacks but one year to have been alive for a score of seasons.

BOWDRAGON, MULTHAS: the hot-tempered second Bowdragon brother. Bearded, darkly handsome, and the father of no less than seven daughters.

BULDRIM: see Kavalanter, Buldrim

CARDASSA, MAEVUR: Baron of Cardassa, a fat, lazy, moon-faced and oiled-haired wastrel of Elmerna who inherited the barony of Cardassa upon the death of his distant cousin, the much older and far different Ithclammert "the Old Crow" Cardassa (a demise which befell in *The Vacant Throne*). He promptly began to nurse plans to snatch the Throne of Aglirta for himself, gathering tersepts and hiring wizards to his cause.

CASTLECLOAKS, RAULIN TILBAR: young would-be bard and son of the respected bard Helgrym Castlecloaks; briefly a companion to the Band of Four.

CODELMER, SARASPER: a healer and former courtier long in hiding in one of three beast shapes he can take: bat, ground snake, or (his most favored) the man-eating "wolf-spider" or longfangs; old, gruff, and homely; member of the Band of Four and friend to Craer when the latter first entered the service of the Baron Blackgult.

DARK THREE, THE: a trio of evil, powerful, and treacherous wizards who served the Baron Faerod Silvertree; they all perished in *The Kingless Land*, and in descending order of rank, power, and age, were: Spellmaster Ingryl Ambelter; Klamantle Beirldoun; and Markoun Yarynd.

DELCAMPER, ALRESSE: ancient, bedridden matriarch of the Delcamper clan, a spirited beauty in her day but now little more than a wrinkled bag of bones clinging to life through her sharp wits and sharper tongue. Alresse has not left the Delcamper castle of Varandaur in thirty summers—and will probably never leave, now; when she dies, she'll simply be taken downstairs to its crypt.

DELCAMPER, FLAEROS: young bard, of the wealthy Delcamper merchant family of Ragalar, equipped when traveling with the Vodal, an enchanted ring that's an heirloom of the Delcampers and allows (among other things) its wearer to see through magical disguises and illusions. Still quite naive but acclaimed for his bardic skills by no less than Inderos Stormharp, he's known (sometimes mockingly) as "the Flower of the Delcampers."

DELCAMPER, HULGOR: one of the uncles of Flaeros Delcamper. A big, florid, hunt- and wine-loving man, swift with his sword and swifter with his temper.

DELCAMPER, SARTH: one of the oldest uncles of Flaeros Delcamper. A tall, suspicious (of everyone and everything), and sour retired warrior, now feeling his age in earnest.

DELNBONE, CRAER: procurer (scout and thief) in the service of the Baron Blackgult; small, agile, clever-tongued member of the Band of Four and longtime friend and sword-companion of Hawkril Anharu, who often calls him "Longfingers."

DOROS, JANTHLIN: Aged, well-loved Master of Chambers (manservant) of Varandaur, family castle of the Delcamper family nigh Ragalar. Thoughtful, kindly, attentive to detail without being fussy, and a pillar of courtly dignity.

DUTHJACK, SENDRITH "BLOODBLADE": capable, charismatic mercenary warrior who served the Baron Blackgult in the disastrous attack on the Isles of Ieirembor, and later became the leader of an outlaw fighting band ("Bloodblade's Band"), whom he led in a foray to slay the Risen King and put himself on the throne. That attempt failed and the Band was slaughtered in the doing, but Sendrith retains his ambitions to rule Aglirta—and some call him "the Hope of Aglirta."

ELVRITH, BRIONA: a timid, curly-haired young lass of Saerith in upland Ornentar, much given to rindolberry-picking.

ELVRITH, NARNETH: a practical, swift-witted young half-shift shepherd of Saerith in upland Ornentar; older brother to Briona.

ELVURND, SUSKAR: a large, capable brigand working the coast road of Asmarand, nigh Shaunsel Rise (a farm-cloaked ridge between Elmerna and Teln).

EROEHA: see Serpent, The

ESMERSUR, ADBERT: old retired warrior, now a painter and woodcarver, who dwells in the Tarlagar back-country nigh the Windfangs foothills, and spends much of every day (and most of his coins) drinking at the Glory of Aglirta tavern. Known to one and all as "Old Adbert," he lost most of his left leg in battle years ago, and is a sour but fair observer of events in the Vale.

Faceless, the/Faceless Ones, the: see Koglaur

FALLENBRIDGE, TOARSIM: an ambitious but not law-breaking Tersept of Aglirta—a tall, pockmarked man unsure of his future or his own confidence.

FAUROLK, TARSAM: a successful but pessimistic sheep farmer who dwells in the Tarlagar backcountry nigh the Windfangs foothills, and habitually drinks at the Glory of Aglirta tavern. Well liked and usually gentle and kindly.

GARZHAR, LORN: better known as "Old Garzhar," this aging, grizzled, limping, and much-wounded armaragor grew old in the service of Blackgult. When Baron Blackgult was made regent, he named Garzhar his Ranking Sword (commander, whenever the regent was absent) of the Palace Guard of Flowfoam—because of Old Garzhar's diligence, loyalty, and levelheadedness.

GESTEL, ANSYARDE: phlegmatic armaragor in the service of Bloodblade, a former barge helmsman who serves so again when his swordcaptain, Buldrim Kavalanter, seizes a Cardassan barge.

GLAROND, NESMOR: recently installed Baron of Glarond; a onetime courtier and successful investor who—like so many others—has ambitions that include the Throne of Aglirta.

Golden Griffon, the: see Blackgult, Ezendor

GREATSARN, SULDUN: grim, attentive veteran armaragor of Cardassa, serving as swordcaptain to Baron Maevur Cardassa.

HAELTREE, NITHAS: recently ascended Tersept of Haeltree, this capable former armsman joins the conspiracy headed by Maevur Cardassa fully intending to betray it to the regent.

HALVAN, HAELITH: burly, jovial, and very capable mercenary war captain, leader of the Sirl Swords hireswords. Halvan's band was hired by Regent Blackgult to be the backbone of the Royal Host of Aglirta (the regent's army).

HULDAERUS, ARKLE: "the Master of Bats," sometime Lord Wizard of Ornentar, an ambitious, cruel, grasping

mage known for using bat-related magic, commanding
bats, and taking bat-shape; the minstrel Vilcabras once said
at a moot that "Aglirta's worst nightmare would be Huldaerus and Silvertree, working together—a terror for Silverflow Vale one year, and all Darsar the next," and
Huldaerus soon killed him for that utterance.

INDLE: a senior Koglaur, habitually male, who usually
works in Sirlptar with the Koglaur Oblarma, but takes the
shape of the Serpent-worshipping steward Qurtil in the
Delcamper castle of Varandaur to practice a certain deception on Flaeros Delcamper. He has also taken many other
shapes, and is skilled at casting scrying whorls.

IRONSTONE, BLASKAR: a stern, scowling Tersept of
Aglirta who looks every inch the grim armaragor he once
was.

ISRINDAR, KULDIN: senior of the two Sart bridge
guards; a good-natured, experienced armsman.

JARAMBUR, MOROLD: a fat, successful importer of
wines in Sirlptar, who supplies many of the better taverns
and clubs with bulk vintages.

JORANTHAR, HALDUTH: armsman in the service of
Bloodblade; a giant of a man, slow tempered and amiable,
but ruthless when ordered to slay. An expert spearman, and
possessed of prodigious strength and courage.

KAVALANTER, BULDRIM: trusted, able swordcaptain
in the service of Bloodblade, possessed of dark hair, the remains of good looks, and a ruthless streak.

Keeper of the Holy Place, the: a senior Serpent-priest,
head of the nine holy guardians of the Place of the Serpent

(a mountain dell where the Serpent lies buried and magically bound).

KIRLSTAR, AMADUS: bearded, flame-haired, aggressive, and quick-tempered silk merchant of Sirlptar, superstitious and grasping; known professionally as "Kirlstar of the Splendid Silks."

Koglaur, the: the "Faceless" or "Faceless Ones," legendary lurking humanlike shapeshifting beings who watch over Aglirta and meddle in its affairs for mysterious reasons of their own.

LOUSHOOND, RILDRA: Baroness of Loushoond; a lush, passionate woman who loves entertaining, large and dangling earrings, collecting statuary, and what Craer Delnbone describes as "yipping, perfumed, and beribboned lapdogs." Craer dismisses Rildra (and her procurer-chasing antics) as "silly."

LOUSHOOND, YINTER: recently installed Baron of Loushoond; an ambitious, energetic, clever, well-spoken, and utterly treacherous man.

LUROAN, GURULD: a loudmouthed, boisterous farmer who dwells in the Tarlagar backcountry nigh the Windfangs foothills, and habitually drinks at the Glory of Aglirta tavern. One of several brothers known locally for their coarse ways, feuds, and large, healthy herds of livestock.

MELEIRA: elder daughter of Orathlee of the Wise, and herself gifted; dark-haired, serious, and wise beyond her ten-and-six years.

Melted, the: men burned by a special firespell of the mage Corloun; their flesh droops and disfigures, and they become conduits of his magic (he can cast spells from afar, through their touch, or cause them to explode in flames).

MRIVIN: a young, sharp-tongued, habitually male Koglaur.

MULGOR, ESTLEVAN: an amiable and ambitious shepherd of uplands Blackgult.

MULKYN, GADASTER: first and most infamous Spellmaster of Silvertree; an aging, ruthless evil archwizard who was tutor to Ingryl Ambelter—and whom Ingryl slew by a succession of life- and magic-stealing spells that forced Gadaster into a strange unlife. The "Old Beast of Silvertree" retains his sentience, but largely serves as a captive means of healing for Ambelter.

NESKER, LORNELTH: young armsman sworn to the service of Bloodblade, but possessed of little experience.

NUINAR, LAMEIRA: sharp-tongued, opinionated Maid of Chambers (servant) in the Delcamper castle of Varandaur.

OBALAR, MALAVER: wealthy owner of a fleet of large, swift merchant "wavesword" ships that carry spices and silks from far ports to Asmarand. He dwells in Teln, which is also the home port of his fleet. All Obalar boats have white hulls and maroon-and-gold sails.

OBLARMA: a senior Koglaur, habitually female, who often spies in Sirlptar with the Koglaur Indle, but also takes the shape of the dead bard Taercever Redcloak.

OLAURIM: King of Aglirta so long ago that the realm then had neither barons nor baronies.

ORATHLEE: a beautiful young woman of the Wise (those folk who can foresee in dreams or by divers means, or have other inner magical gifts that they can call on without casting spells—but are branded by priests of the Three, and outcast, as "spirit-touched") who guides merchants of Sirlptar in their investments—for fees. Orathlee bears disfiguring brands on both her breasts, was once a slave in Sarinda, and is a widow and the mother of daughters Meleira and Talace.

ORELE, NATHA: oldest Lady of Chambers in the Delcamper castle of Varandaur; addressed as "Lady" and considered almost noble in her own right (as a former consort of several Delcamper uncles). Clear-witted, imperious, and walks with the aid of a silver-handled cane.

ORNENTAR, ILVRIM: recently ascended Baron of Ornentar, this former weapons merchant turned warrior is capable, aggressive, quick-thinking—and possessed of grandiose schemes (including one to personally rule all Aglirta) that outstrip his judgement. Deemed a "sly fool" by Tshamarra Talasorn.

PHELINNDAR, ORLIN: recently ascended to the title of Baron of Phelinndar, this urbane, treacherous man keeps to himself as much as possible, avoiding the intrigues and risings-to-arms of most Barons of Aglirta. He has a good reason to do so: since sometime before King Kelgrael Snowsar named him to his barony, Orlin—who was then Tersept of Downdaggers—had been the secret owner of a Dwaer-Stone.

PRESTAL, TARTH: a court page of Flowfoam; one of two dozen such lads, but possessed of more loyalty and courage than most of his fellows. Always hastening to obey, but terribly curious (and becoming adroit at spying and overhearing).

QUELVER, ILIBAR: a gruff, gentle, and loyal old warrior, once of Silvertree and later senior doorguard of the Throne Chamber of Flowfoam Palace (palace guardsman of Flowfoam).

RAEGREL: young, rebellious, but capable Koglaur sent to Thaebred for punishment and tutelage and to give reports of his spyings. Part of his punishment is to play the role of Red Dream.

RED DREAM: a pleasure-dancer at the Dragonrose House dining club in Sirlptar, recognizable by the red cord that binds her hair. Her brown hair is lighter than that of her partner Blue Passion, her skin a lighter shade (though both tan brown in summer), and she's slightly shorter.

REDCLOAK, TAERCEVER: a handsome, witty wandering bard "of all Asmarand," who died alone in the wilderlands of fever and a winter storm. His passing is unknown in Aglirta, save to the Koglaur—who shapeshift to take on his likeness when it suits them.

RETHTARN, TELEZGRAR: aging armaragor in the service of Bloodblade. Friend to the less-energetic Landron Stonetower.

RULDOR, MAERIMMON: an old, humorless Tersept, who was once clerk-of-coin to three barons in succession—hired by each to ferret out corruption, theft, and wasteful spending. The lawlessness of Aglirta drove him to join Baron Cardassa's conspiracy.

RUNTHALAN, TONTHAN "GOLDCLOAK": an ambitious, urbane merchant of Sirlptar, most successful in his dealings in short-term investments in the affairs of other merchants. He neither uses his surname nor wants it known (thanks to scandals and debts of his father and grandsire), and is very cool and swift-witted in moments of personal peril, seeing everything in terms of possible profits—and losses.

SARAEDRIN, THELMERT: a blustering, supercilious, glib-tongued lord of the court (courtier) of Flowfoam— one of the many dandies who attach themselves to the court of the Risen King.

SARANDOR, ILTOS: a long-ago wizard of Carraglas, who of old crafted a popular battle spell, "Sarandor's Seekings," that generates copper- and emerald-hued beams of force at the caster's foes. Sarandor bound his own life force into the spell, so that he died—but perhaps lives on, his sentience being called to wherever the spell is cast.

SATHBRAR, SULVAN: a wealthy silk merchant of Sirlptar, who's tall, usually bearded, calm in crises, forceful and well-spoken, and a frequent trade ally and partner of Tonthan "Goldcloak" Runthalan. Sathbrar is also, and has always been, a "false person" created and maintained by many Koglaur, who take his shape in succession.

Serpent, the: "the Serpent in the Shadows," "the Sacred Serpent," "the Great Serpent," "the Fanged One," a great evil being, formerly a human wizard (name now forgotten; it's thought he worked to purge records of it) who helped enchant the Dwaerindim, but went mad or was mad, and murdered several rival mages to strengthen the Dwaer enchantments; when confronted by the other mages of the Shaping, he fled into serpent-form to fight his way free of their spells—and was imprisoned by them in serpent-shape; now a gigantic serpent bound into Slumber by a mighty magic worked by the King of Aglirta (fated as sleep when he does); worshipped by humans who revere him as divine—and to whom he grants spells. Present-day worshippers of him (who are wizards using his secret spell-lore, though they call themselves priests to further the false belief that the Serpent is a god) call him "Eroeha," but this is believed to be a corrupt form of the Serpent's human rank or title, not his name.

Serpents, the: worshippers of the Serpent (humans who often become snakelike); they refer formally to themselves as "the Faithful of the Serpent," but others call them "the Cowled Priests," "the Fanged Faithful," "the Scaly Ones," "the Serpent-spawn," and worse; those with snakelike heads and forked tongues are known (not to their faces) as "Hissing Ones."

SHAELTOR, UNDRUTH: the recently ascended Tersept of Shaeltor, this burly, now-going-to-fat former armaragor and armor trader joined Baron Cardassa's conspiracy—over ever-growing personal misgivings.

SHALACE: a softhearted, experienced, habitually female Koglaur.

SILVERTREE, EMBRA: the Lady of Jewels (so-called for her opulent, gem-studded gowns), Lady Baron of Silvertree; a young, beautiful sorceress and member of the Band of Four. She was raised as the daughter of the cruel Faerod Silvertree, who although unaware that Baron Ezendor Blackgult had fathered her, intended to magically enslave her as his "Living Castle."

SILVERTREE, MAERAUNDEN: Baron Silvertree in his day; one of Embra's ancestors, dead for over eight hundred years and buried in the graveyard in front of the Silent House—but still seen as a ghost that walks and talks when the time is right and the deeds of the living are wrong.

SNOWSAR, KELGRAEL: the Risen King, the Lost King, the Sleeping King, the Sleeper of Legend, the Last Snowsar; King of Aglirta, the Lion of Aglirta, the Crown of Aglirta, Lord of All Aglirta, Master of the River and Its Vale; rightful crowned ruler of Aglirta, a wise and perceptive warrior and wizard who for (centuries) too long slept in a spell-hidden "otherwhere," while warring barons tore his realm apart. While he sleeps, the Serpent is bound also into Slumber by his spells; when he awakens, so, too, does the Serpent.

STARNTREE, MAERANTH: longtime Tersept of average looks, wealth, and influence; calm and unflappable in almost every situation—and completely unambitious. He'd prefer a stronger, more peaceful and just Aglirta, because then he could devote more time to raising chickens and seeing to the needs of his folk, and less riding around chasing after brigands.

STONETOWER, LANDRON: aging armaragor in the service of Bloodblade. Friend to Telezgrar Rethtarn.

Summoner of the Serpent, the: a magically powerful— even before he came into possession of a Dwaer—Serpent-priest who magically calls the Risen Serpent to Flowfoam.

TALACE: younger daughter of Orathlee of the Wise; curly-blonde-haired, tart-tongued, curious, and stronger in her gift at her ten-and-four years than many Wise ever get.

TALASORN, ARIATHE: swiftest-tempered and physically largest of the four proud, beautiful sorceress daughters of the accomplished wizard Reavur Talasorn (who perished in *The Vacant Throne*) and his wife Iyrinda (who died some years previously). Ariathe is best known for her mighty battle spells and her eagerness to use them, having inherited none of her father's sensitivity, patience, or tact.

TALASORN, DACELE: second eldest and quietest of the four proud, beautiful sorceress daughters of the wizard Raevur Talasorn and his wife Iyrinda.

TALASORN, OLONE: eldest, wisest, and most magically powerful of the four proud, beautiful sorceress daughters of the wizard Raevur Talasorn and his wife Iyrinda—and since their deaths, young but imperious matriarch of the family.

TALASORN, TSHAMARRA: youngest and most kindhearted of the four proud, beautiful sorceress daughters of the wizard Raevur Talasorn and his wife Iyrinda. Like her sisters, Tshamarra wears black gowns, has seen little of the wider world, and is sworn to avenge Raevur's death.

TARLAGAR, ORTHIL: recently ascended to the title of Baron of Tarlagar from a terseptry, this deep-voiced, pompous, handsome warrior is dashing in appearance (and a hit with many, many ladies) but a craven coward in the fray—which makes his ambitions to rise to a grander title than baron seem self-deluding at best.

TELGAERT, TASLAR: owner and master of the ship *Fair Wind*, of no particular home port. The *Fair Wind* is a sea rel: a fast, narrow coastal-running vessel that delivers small cargoes swiftly, up and down the Asmaranta Coast. Telgaert is a kindly, swift-witted, handsome man—and secretly one of the Wise, though largely untrained.

THAEBRED: one of the eldest and wisest Koglaur, who often trains others. He dwells in Sirlptar, and often plays the role of Blue Passion.

THARIM, ELTHAN: aging senior "throne guardsman" in the service of Glarond. A loyal, no-nonsense warrior.

THRORKAN, URL: an aging, semiretired farmer and vintner of uplands Blackgult.

THUULOR: a young and relatively inexperienced Koglaur, but vigorous and fearless, with perhaps too great a love of adventure.

URNTARGH, DARAG: trusted swordcaptain in the army of Bloodblade; a scarred, close-mouthed veteran possessed of ugly looks and much patience—but a love of discipline.

VAELROS, SAMMARTHE: a close-mouthed, worn war widow turned herb farmer, who sells her herbs in Sart market with her two young daughters, pushing a cart into town from her farm.

VALATH, FAERLA: a scatterbrained, careless, but enthusiastic and romantic Maid of Chambers (servant) in the Delcamper castle of Varandaur. Youngest and least-well-behaved of the Maids of Chambers; the despair of Lady Orele.

VARAEDUR, WOLVYN: a recently named tersept who's frankly bewildered by the duties of office, the intrigues gripping Aglirta, and his discovery that many, many folk who are fair to look upon can lie and cheat as badly as, or worse than villainous-looking persons.

WULDER, LORTHKUL: trusted swordcaptain in the army of Bloodblade; a good-natured armaragor of easygoing manner but tireless diligence. Possessed of shrewd judgement of folk and an aptitude for battlefield ruses and "hard weather" tactics.

XAUVROS, KELDERT: a sharp-tongued but loyal old warrior, once of Silvertree and later a doorguard of the

Throne Chamber of Flowfoam Palace (palace guardsman of Flowfoam).

YARONDAL, NILVARR: a tall, florid, deep-voiced, and imperious lord of the court (courtier) of Flowfoam—one of many such dandies who attach themselves to the court of the Risen King.

ZAURYM, DAERUTH: a loyal warrior of Silvertree, named by Regent Blackgult to the Palace Guard of Flowfoam. Smiling and pleasant to pass time with, possessed of a swift sword but terrible archery skills.

The adventures of the Band of Four
continue in

The
DRAGON'S
DOOM

by

ED GREENWOOD

———◆———

Turn the page for a preview

Prologue

$\mathcal{A}$ hard, sudden rain was lashing the rooftops of Sirlptar as the evening came down, driven ashore by a home-harbor wind. The storm-rattle on the slates and tiles of roofs quite drowned out the customary chimney-sighs for which the Sighing Gargoyle was named. Flaeros delcamper could barely hear his own harp-notes, but— newly esteemed Bard to the Court of Flowfoam or not— this was his first paying engagement in the City of the River and Sea, and he sang on with determination.

Yet even he knew, as he lifted his voice in the refrain of his newest ballad about the Lady of Jewels and the Fall of the Serpent, that he might just as well have saved his breath.

Not a man-jack was listening.

Every patron of the Gargoyle was bent forward over the table that held the tankard, listening—or talking intently. The mutter of voices held no happiness.

"And so 'tis another year gonem and how's Aglirta the better for it?"

"Aye, harvests thinner than ever, half the good men in the land dead and rotting when they should be plowing or scything—and now we have a *boy for a king.*"

"Huh. No joy there, yet he can hardly be worse than what we've had, these twenty summers now—wizards and barons, wizards and barons: villains, all!"

"Aye, that's so. Wizards have always been bad and dangerous—'tis in the breed, by the Three!"

"So we thrust a pitchfork through every mage we spot, and what then? Who of our Great Lord Barons can be trusted not to lash out on a whim? They've all been little tyrants to put the most decadent kings of the old tales to shame!"

"And here we sit. thinner and fewer, every year, while their madness rages around us and Aglirta bleeds."

An empty tankard thunked down on the table, and its owner sighed gustily, clenched his hand into helpless fist, and added bitterly, "And the great hope of the common folk, Bloodblade, turned out to be no better than the rest."

An old scribe nodded. "All our drems fallen and trampled," he said sadly, "and no one cares." A drover shot Flaeros a look so venomous that the bard's fingers faltered on his harp-strings, and growled, Now we have some boy for a King, and his four tame Overdukes scour the countryside for barons and wizards who took arms against him—and who cares for us?"